The Everything, Including Nothing

A Mostly True Account of Lies, Miracles, and Extremely Questionable Decisions

© Troy Harwood-Jones

20250912

ISBN: 978-1-0696985-7-5

www.harwoodjones.com

Contents

Things Were Going Well Until the Chair

> *"Where the tongue leads, the bones must follow."*
>
> — *ancient Ruanne proverb.*

Here's me: Face-down, lip bloodied, tongue reacquainting itself (unhappily) with floorboards seasoned in piss and shoe-leather. My shirt hung in tatters, tastefully exposing an absence of muscle definition. And still—somehow—I imagined I might talk my way out of this latest, exquisitely self-inflicted disaster.

The boot to my ribs suggested otherwise.

You see, in my infinite charm and questionable wisdom, I had arranged a private rendezvous with Lady Elenya di Veir—her name alone sigh-worthy, ballad-worthy, divorce-worthy. A golden woman with a golden laugh, a golden brooch, and, regrettably, a husband forged of equal parts iron and sadism. Lord Caurin: wealthy, vengeful, and ugly in a way that felt personal. He also, inconveniently, suspected his wife of exactly the kind of mischief I was in the midst of attempting.

My plan—as ever—had been foolproof. I'd plied her ear with wit and whispers, invited her to The Royal Dawn Inn: a wheezing, half-forgotten ruin of a place still pretending it hadn't missed its golden age by several wars. It boasted two things: hourly rates and fading wallpaper. She called it romantic. I called it cheap.

She arrived late, naturally. She wore the scent of a woman unaccustomed to hearing the word *no*, and I had the mouth of a man allergic to saying it.

She paid, of course. Not for the room—I'm not *that* kind of story — but for the wine, the food, the thrill of being seen with someone entirely inappropriate. I played my role with flair, drawing scandal and slander from the air like a magician with a grudge. I pointed at a quiet couple and whispered, "They come here every week. He, to escape her cooking; she, to get him drunk enough not to notice her slipping upstairs with the barmaid."

Then I gestured toward two northern gentlemen by the hearth and conjured dialogue for their silent tête-à-tête.

"I quite like my buttocks. How do you feel about buttocks?"

"Most certainly! Cast them in bronze and hang them in a temple."

She howled. She laughed like the gods had tickled her ribs.

I agreed with everything she said — except where I subtly disagreed. Everything was dull. Everything was beneath her. Especially her husband, who didn't deserve her. I'd never met the man, but I gave him a lisp and a hunch and a fondness for cross-stitching war memoirs.

She slapped my arm in mock outrage. Her silken blouse trembled with laughter.

With a wink, I suggested we slip upstairs. Just for a moment. Just for the thrill.

She looked at me the way a starving woman might regard a particularly decadent chocolate fountain.

She was mine. The cheque, the stairs, the sigh — inevitable.

Which, of course, is when the door burst open like a thunderclap, and in stormed vengeance himself. He filled it like a landslide — Caurin di Veir, lord of nothing I wanted, flanked by a goon whose forehead arrived several minutes before the rest of him. Both of them steaming with purpose.

I stood. Smiled. Opened my mouth to charm.

She got there first.

Her shriek might have bought me time. Her accusations —
He threatened me! Blackmailed me! I'm so frightened! — bought
me the rest. Not freedom. No, not that. Just enough of a
delay for his honour to be salvaged and my face to be
introduced to every available wall.

Now. I've been stabbed twice, exiled once, and dumped
more times than I care to count, but nothing — nothing —
hits quite like a woman you were about to kiss pointing at
you like you've just pissed in the soup. And yet — I didn't
flinch. Not because I believed she'd save me, but because
somewhere, in the cavernous back of my idiot brain, I
thought: *If I don't deny it, maybe there's still a chance she'll
come upstairs after.*

(Yes. I know.)

Too late to deny. Caurin had already bought the lie —
hook, line, and dignity. You could see it in the way his
nostrils flared. A cuckold can smell pity, and it's poison.
He needed a villain. I was wearing the hat. And then he
said it: "These filthy Ruanne bastards. Always lying,
always sniffing round the rich like stray dogs."

Now that — that — was when I flinched.

Not because of the slur. I've heard worse. But because I
saw it — the way the goon's mouth curved into something
hungry.

"Enjoy yourself," Caurin told him. "Make sure there's
nothing left to wag that tongue of his."

And then the fist came down.

Hard.

Here's how he beat me, and what I did about it:

(Hint: very little.)

First came the chair. Not gently. Not pulled out and offered. No, he lifted it like a cudgel and drove it into my side with all the finesse of a cart accident. Something cracked — probably the chair. Hopefully the chair. I flew sideways into the bar. Bottles shattered. Someone screamed. The barkeep ducked. I tried to run — honestly I did — but my foot caught the leg of the now-deceased chair, and down I went in a flourish of elbows and oak splinters. I scrambled. He followed. The table I'd so gallantly chosen for its romantic positioning? Overturned. The hearth? Kicked a log loose. Fire spilled across the rug. The rug caught. The smell turned from piss to burning piss, which, I assure you, is not an improvement.

"I think we've all made our points!" I shouted, ducking behind an elderly patron whose only crime was consuming soup slowly. "Let's be civil. My lord? Sir? Perhaps a quiet word — "

The quiet word was crack, as his knuckles met my temple.

Down again.

I flailed. Rolled under the next table. Crawled between boots, tried to find my feet. Found a mop instead. Wielded it like a sword. He snapped it over his knee.

"I didn't blackmail her," I wheezed, dodging left. "She blackmailed me! Her company was unbearable! I suffered!"

A punch to the gut took the wind from my lies.

I staggered. Stumbled. Crashed into the bar again. Someone threw a cup. At me.

Rude.

"Look," I gasped, hands raised, blood in my mouth and

on the floor. "I think we got off on the wrong foot. You're clearly a man of culture. Taste. Huge fists. But if we could — "

He grabbed me by the collar and lifted. My feet left the floor. My dignity keeled over. Dead, at last.

Then he drew back his fist — and paused.

Because the room had gone quiet.

Because the air had changed.

Because my deliverance had arrived in the form of something large, calm, and terrible that had just taken hold of Forehead-With-Fists' arm.

I tried to murmur thanks to the gods, but all that came out was "Fwuh."

Brin. To the rescue. Again.

Who?

You'd think I'd know by now. That I'd learn. That the pain might leave a lasting impression. But pain fades.

Brin doesn't.

No roar. No war cry. No bar-brawl bravado.

"Put him down." Three words. Measured. Low. Delivered with the patience of someone who means them.

Forehead hesitated. Not because he was brave, but because he was stupid.

It's always the same, with Brin. They look at the size of him first — broad shoulders, scarred knuckles, the kind of stillness that belongs to stone. Then they think, *I can handle that.*

I'm not sure how stupidity like that works. Not that I don't understand stupid. Gods, I've got more than a lifetime's supply of *my* kind. But the kind of physical stupid that looks at a wall falling on you and says, *Here is a really good place to stop* — that, I'll never understand.

In any event, Idiot made a very ill considered, but predictable, decision.

I was unceremoniously deposited — a broken pile of limbs that used to fit properly.

Brin's first blow came from nowhere. Open palm, sideways, fast as thought. It caught the goon just beneath the ear. A perfect, punishing note struck on a meat instrument.

He staggered. Swung.

Brin took it. Moved in. Two strikes — one to the gut, one to the throat. Surgical. Intimate.

Forehead's lungs had suddenly realized they'd rather be anywhere else. His feet decided it was time to leave, with or without him. He hit the hearth. Slipped on the burning rug. Landed hard. Smoke kissed his boots.

Brin reached down. Hauled him up by the collar. Looked him in the eye.

And then put him through the wall.

Not metaphor.

Wood splintered. Plaster screamed. A piece of The Royal Dawn Inn gave up on existence entirely.

Someone clapped. Genuinely clapped.

I dragged the bloody mess of what remained of me over to rest against the comfort of the bar. Attempted to look nonchalant.

Brin just stood there, breathing slow. Watching the dust settle. Watching Forehead groan in the wreckage, limbs twitching like a puppet with cut strings.

"You done?"

My brain eventually caught up with the fact that the meat slab under the plaster was not about to answer. That the question was for me.

"Define done," I mumbled. "Still got all my limbs. Most of my charm."

Then he looked at me. His face didn't change. Brin's never does. But there was something in his eyes—equal parts exasperation and that terrible, relentless, loyalty of his.

He held out a hand.

I took it.

Because I always do.

And now for the friend who's never there for me:

We were halfway out of the city when he joined us. I say we, but really it was Brin carrying most of me—an awkward bundle of torn shirt, bruised ego, and theatrical groaning. I offered to walk, of course. Several times. Each time Brin responded with a grunt and an adjustment of his grip that said, *You weigh nothing and talk too much.*

We took the back lanes, the ones that smelled like boiled cabbage, camphor, and sun-baked stone—like bad decisions left out too long. A goat tried to follow us for a while. I think I made an impression.

"You know," I muttered, blood still trickling tastefully from my nose, "I was this close."

Brin didn't answer.

"To what, exactly?" came a voice from the rooftops. Light, amused, and infuriatingly clean of breathlessness. "Choking on a boot?"

We both stopped.

There he was — Mero Vato — perched on the low wall beside the tannery, swinging his legs like a schoolboy. Sunlight caught in his curls. There was soot on his cuffs, a ribbon of silk tucked into his belt, and something in his grin that made me itch.

I gestured with a limp hand. "Lovely of you to finally arrive. Were you busy taking a nap? Watching me get turned into soup?"

He tilted his head. "I was robbing her."

I blinked. "You what?"

"The lady. Elenya. While you were getting obliterated for love or vengeance or the sheer thrill of it — hard to tell, really — I slipped into her carriage. False-bottomed powder box. Predictable, but profitable." He held up a gleaming brooch. "Gold. Poorly set stones. Still, sentiment adds value."

Brin kept walking. Mero fell into step beside us, cheerfully ignoring my visible suffering.

"She lied, you know," I said. "Said I blackmailed her."

"She did pay for lunch," Mero offered. "That counts, doesn't it?"

I groaned. "I hate you."

"You don't. You're just in pain."

He wasn't wrong.

But gods, I did hate how easy he made it all look. No bruises, no limping. Just quick fingers, quicker wit, and the utter confidence of a man who'd never once been punched in the face because someone else's wife found him interesting.

Brin grunted again. I think it was a laugh. Possibly indigestion.

I wiped at my nose. "Next time," I muttered, "you can seduce the noble's wife."

Mero shrugged. "Next time, don't seduce a woman with a husband who collects skulls."

"Next time," Brin said, finally, "stay quiet."

We didn't. Obviously.

But it was a nice thought.

Home, then.

Through the scrub hills and back beneath the ridge where the dry grass bowed like it remembered the wind. Past the stone tooth we used as a marker and the thorn-twist tree with Mero's old boot still hanging from its branches. And there—just past the stream—our people.

The Ruanne.

The camp was a mess of canvas and colour, wheels and rope, smoke rising in lazy curls from a half dozen low fires. Women argued in three languages. A child darted past wearing someone's stolen hat, nothing else. An old man carved a flute from bone and argued with it when it squeaked.

Home. Loud, unwelcome, and utterly ours. For now.

Shevra waved at us from the firepit, ash on her cheek and a pot of something bubbling dangerously behind her. "You're late," she said. "And more ugly than usual."

Brin gave a nod. That was enough.

Elior played his fiddle badly near the goat pen, eyes closed, wine skin tucked to his chest like an infant. The song he played had no beginning and even less of an end, but the goats seemed to like it.

We passed half a dozen others on the way to our wagon — each one giving me a look somewhere between amusement and concern, like they were trying to decide if they should help me or just record my condition for posterity.

Mero whistled a jaunty tune.

Brin lowered me onto the steps of our wagon with all the tenderness of a man setting down a sack of potatoes he doesn't quite trust.

"You're welcome," he said.

"I was getting to that," I winced. "Eventually."

He left me there. Mero flopped down beside me and unwrapped a stolen pastry like he hadn't just watched me nearly die.

"You going to tell the story?" he asked around a mouthful of sugar and flake.

"Of course I'm going to tell it," I said, already hearing the rhythm of it in my head — the shape of the thing, how it might begin, how it might bend. "But the right way. Embellished. Improved. Beautified."

He smirked. "With what, exactly?"

"Details," I said. "And poetry. And truth, somewhere in there."

He shrugged. "That ever get confusing?"

I looked out at the camp. At the smoke, the shadows, the people I'd bled for, lied to, and would probably disappoint again by breakfast. At Brin leaning against a post, arms crossed, eyes scanning like the world owed him something and he meant to collect.

I touched the cut at my lip. Winced.

"Only when it matters."

He leaned back, eyes half-closed, sun slanting over the hills like it didn't care about any of us.

"Do they?"

"What?"

"Words," he said. "Do they matter?"

I smiled.

"Only always."

City of Nareth; Sparkling Discharge at the Heart of the World

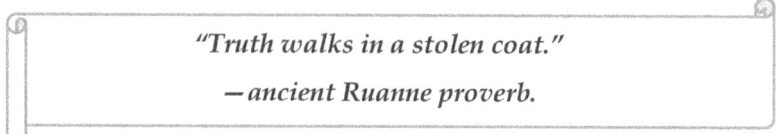

"Truth walks in a stolen coat."

— ancient Ruanne proverb.

People who say the Ruanne don't know the meaning of work have clearly never tried surviving Nareth with a bad haircut and a worse alibi.

Nareth squats at the mouth of the Sil'Arienne delta like a bloated bureaucrat guarding his lunch. The rivers Lise and Rocanta, after dragging half the Isarre desert in their teeth, finally meet here—muttering curses and dropping their silt like drunkards collapsing into a gutter. The city fans out between them like the skirts of an Ocharini dancer after three too many sweet wines: loud, uneven, dazzling, and dangerous if you stared too long.

There's no plan to Nareth. No mercy, either. It grew like mould on warm bread: sudden, ugly, and everywhere. Streets twisted at random. Temples mushroomed out of alleyways like toadstools after rain. Every building leaned slightly, either drunk or in mourning. Everything leaned against everything else, like if enough shoddy walls held hands, the whole mess might not fall over.

In Nareth, everything has a price. And I mean this both ways: you can buy anything if you pay enough—and *you will* pay, whether you know you're buying or not. Step on the wrong paving stone? Toll. Stand in the wrong patch of shade? Permit fee. Cough too loudly during a Holy Ordinance of Silence? Public apology and a fine.

There are at least twenty major religions here (more if you count the splinter sects, the rebel sects of the splinter sects, and whatever lunatic was preaching reincarnation by cheese fermentation outside the Fish Gate last week). *None* of them preach charity. At best, they sell hope at competitive rates. At worst, they rent guilt by the hour.

The Ruanne fit right in.

We know how to conjure gold from nothing — or at least coppers, polished until they pass for something better under a forgiving sun. Brin fights. Mero lightens pockets. And me? I perform miracles.

Today's miracle was selling nonsense for coin.

I was standing on an overturned crate outside the Temple of Lost Weevils (yes, that's its real name; no, don't ask), weaving a story like a drunk tailor stitches a wedding coat: colourful, crooked, and just convincing enough to distract you from the fraying seams. One boot planted heroically on a corner of the crate, arms thrown wide for maximum dramatics but kept just narrow enough to dodge the inevitable thrown shoe.

Before me, the temple steps spilled toward the main square — a boiling pot of pilgrims, pickpockets, petty scholars, petty priests, and petty gods. Brin leaned against a crooked post three paces away, pretending not to watch me. (Brin never watches. He *sees*. There's a difference.) His gaze flicked once to a merchant shortchanging a blind boy. Once to a priest adjusting the cudgel at his hip. Once to a baker slipping sand into his flour sacks.

Meanwhile, Mero drifted through the crowd like smoke through a sieve: impossible to catch, harder to trace. A jingle of missing coins here, a scarf lifted there. One moment he was admiring a pilgrim's belt buckle; the next, it was admiring him from the inside of his pocket.

And me? I was putting on the oldest show in the world:

The Sultan, the Goat, and the Stick.

Today, I played all three roles. The sultan fallen on hard times. The beautiful maiden who bought him for five coppers and a kiss. And the stick she used to beat sense back into both of them.

Three parts, one actor, no dignity whatsoever. And if I was lucky? A handful of coins for my trouble, and only one black eye.

Maybe two.

Depends on how the stick felt about the ending.

The Totally True History of the Sultan in the Skin of a Goat

"Listen well, friends! This tale is older than dust, older than priesthoods, older even than the invention of shame itself. A story of foolishness, fate, and grabbing more than your hands – or your pride – can carry. Some of the elder among you may recall the tale of the kingdom of Dur Taan, and its endowed sultan? A modest kingdom, it once boasted nothing more than the success of its children. That was, until Ur'tash the Pachydermatous rose in fortune."

My words carry across the square, drawing them in. That, or the turban. It's taller than my moral compass and has a mishmash of colour that screams *I'm lying, but enjoy the ride*. A child giggled. An old man with no teeth muttered "Ur'tash" like he'd heard the name in a dream or a debt.

"Ur'tash was a cruel ruler with a fondness for smashing pretty things, marrying anything with a title – and occasionally smashing those too. He was, as you may imagine, not beloved. Ur'tash had conquered precisely one neighbouring realm before declaring himself Emperor of the Softlands and commissioning a statue taller than his palace, wearing nothing but a smile and a grossly exaggerated up pointed appendage."

I paced as I spoke, letting the words curl through the crowd like smoke from a holy brazier that had never once seen a god. When I reached the statue line a butcher actually choked on his fig.

"This particular travesty of stonecraft was not only a towering lie, it offended the god Mercantes, who though showered in gold, had always considered himself somewhat shortchanged by father Onos in that particular capacity.

"Naturally, he could not stand the sight of Ur'tash's trumpet."

Gasps. Laughter. A woman in red fanned herself and leaned closer. A city guard nearby smirked and crossed his arms.

"Now Ur'tash was visited by the priestess of Mercantes, who ordered that he sever the offense, with precisely this warning: 'Should the member remain three days hence, you shall be remembered in the skin your soul deserves.'

"Ur'tash, being a reasonable man, had her flung from the walls."

Two street preachers debated loudly over whether my tongue warranted lashing or anointing.

"Three moons later, he awoke with his harem, craving hay and bleating.

"Goat. Not metaphor. Literal.

"Still possessing the mind of a man, Ur'tash did what any self-respecting goat-sultan would do: he skipped to his throne, began bleating imperiously, and hoped no one would notice.

"Alas.

"He was sold at market the next day. The asking price was a silver, but the merchant accepted five coppers and a kiss, once his wife wasn't looking.

"His purchaser? A girl from the provinces, nameless in the annals, but known in song as the Maiden Most Contrary. She

had wild hair, a sharper tongue than most men had swords, and a curious fondness for animals who deserved punishment.

"She named him Tulip.

"And she beat him, gently but frequently, with a stick carved from olivewood and poor decisions.

"The statue still stands today — crumbling, limbless, and as embarrassingly proud as ever.

"And that is why the descendants of Dur Tann snip their sons and offer the foreskin to Mercantes.

"Thus ends the entirely true history of Ur'tash, Sultan of Dur Taan, and Tulip the Goat."

A wave of laughter rippled through the crowd like a fish flipping belly-up. A woman dabbed tears from her eyes. One man laughed so hard he didn't notice Mero take the ring off his finger.

"Don't laugh, friend. It's five coppers for the story. Ten if you laughed out loud. I don't take curses, but I do accept kisses." Bow. Absurd turban magically transforms into a coin cup. Brin and Mero make sure no one's missed.

The temple priest across the square, pale and puritanical in his grey robes, clutches his prayer staff like a drowning man might cling to a floating door. His mouth works silently, scandal sizzling on his tongue. I wink.

"Good crowd," Mero said under his breath. "Mildly drunk. Generously distracted. I love religious districts."

I pocketed a few of the coins. "They'll be back tomorrow."

"Unless someone reports you to the Temple of Mercantes."

I nodded toward the scandalized priest. "That one? He's halfway to writing me into his sermons already."

Brin grunted. It might've been approval. Or indigestion. Hard to tell.

The square began to shift again—markets reopened, arguments resumed. I stepped down from the crate, a little bow, a final wave. No curtain call, no encore. Just me, stepping down from greatness like a slightly used jester, while the world returned to bickering about goat prices.

We moved on. Coins in our pockets, story behind us, city ahead.

A hard day's work done.

We lounged in the shadow of the Spicewall, bellies full, pockets heavier than usual, and free of obligation. We'd each learned that lazing about was best done in the city. The Ruanne don't condemn idle hands, but our propensity to get someone else to do the work rightfully assigned to us, cannot be overstated. If the three of us headed home, fair odds we'd be invited (with an express or strongly implied threat of violence) to help with basket-weaving, charm mending, or making potions that cured all ills that needed only time to heal.

Mero produced a bottle of something amber and questionably taxed. Brin leaned back against a crumbling fountain, arms crossed and eyes half-lidded in the posture of a man who never truly sleeps. I lay flat, hat over my face, letting the sun try to guilt me into motion.

"We should spend it," Mero said, flicking a coin into the air and catching it. "Tonight. All of it."

"We?" I murmured. "Is that a *generous we*, or a *Mero we* where you spend and I tell the story after?"

"Details," he replied, sipping. "You'll make twice as much from the retelling."

"Mm. And you'll be gone before the tab arrives."

He grinned. "Only a fool would stay."

Brin made a noise that might've been amusement, though it could've been the wine disagreeing with his principles.

Speaking of Brin, this would be a good time to tell you that he's not just a mobile pulveriser fittingly credited with being one of two main reasons why I'm still alive despite my best efforts (the other being my occasional ability to actually talk my way out of trouble). And he also fights for coin. He's got layers.

"Who you facing?" Mero asks. He doesn't care; he's just passing time.

Brin grunts, shrugs. "Don't matter."

Brin doesn't study his opponents. He doesn't practice. He doesn't train. He just has fists like hammers, hands like a vice, and doesn't feel pain. Seems to work for him. Not so much for the other guy.

"At camp?" I ask.

He nods. Of course, there are fighting dens in Nareth, and some fighters make really good coin working them. But those fights have rules. If you come fight where we live, there's no such thing as a dirty blow, so long as it stays this side of weapons.

And in that kind of fight, Brin's never lost. So, contenders keep coming, thinking they'll be the one to finally take down the "Beast of the Ruanne" (a name I coined, naturally). Brin keeps letting them.

They aren't.

Eventually, the sun's temper cools. It sags into the horizon, presumably to cook up new ways to try to burn the world to ash on the morrow. The city grows restless — shadows longer, tempers shorter. We gathered ourselves and began the long walk toward the outer gate.

The road out of Nareth passed under a stone arch flanked by two granite lions and watched over by two Wardens of the Oathbound — which, yes, sounds like something an insecure god might invent while compensating for a disappointing pantheon. They wore mirrored breastplates that caught the dying light, long sashes of indigo-and-bone, and helms crested with black glass feathers. Every part of their attire screamed *dignity*, by which I mean *pomposity* dipped in polish, and beaten with a rulebook. Now, I'm not saying they were *bad* at their jobs. Just that when your entire religion is based on the binding power of oaths and you've been taught to see lies as rot in the world's foundation, your bedside manner tends to suffer.

A line had formed at the gate. Not large. Just slow. At its front, a farmer stood huddled under a bundle of river reeds, his daughter struggling to manage two goats who appeared to only understand walking if it tangled their leads. The older Warden was inspecting their documents. The younger Warden, his face still soft from youth and sanctimony, held the girl's arm in a grip that made my stomach knot.

The father was pleading. Quietly. Respectfully. The girl was silent.

The young Warden smiled.

I hate that smile.

"No license to cross with animals," he said. "No exit tithe paid. No oath-mark for safe conduct."

"Old goats," the father said, in a thick Kantish accent. "Barely walk. We go—" He pointed, "My sister's. In

Arenne."

"No tithe," the Warden repeated, raising his voice to bridge the language barrier.

I felt Brin's hand on my arm before I realized I'd moved. His grip wasn't hard. Not yet.

I brushed it off.

"Gentlemen," I called, stepping forward with the confidence of a man who believes in the power of charm and deeply misunderstands *consequence*. "Surely, we aren't hassling hardworking citizens. That wouldn't be very *oathful*, would it?"

The older Warden didn't look up. The younger one did.

Slowly.

"Step back, vagrant," he said.

Which — rude.

"I prefer *freelance historian*," I said, sweeping a bow. "And while I respect your sacred duty to ensure goats do not flee the city unblessed, might I suggest — gently, humbly — that the power of your position could be better directed elsewhere? For example..."

The older Warden raised one hand.

A whisper in the air. A pressure.

And just like that, I *felt it*.

My tongue went dry and foreign in my mouth. I tried to speak and nothing came out. Tried again. Nothing. I stumbled back, panic rising. I opened my mouth to argue, to charm, to do *something*, and — Nothing. No voice. No sound. Just the thick, choking absence of words where words should have been. I clawed for language like a drowning man claws for air. And found only silence.

I stumbled back, throat raw, heart hammering.

Mero swore under his breath.

The older Warden approached. His eyes were pale. Almost milky.

"Oath broken," he said. "Meddling. False witness."

"Unregistered," added the younger, still holding the girl's arm.

And then Brin was there.

Not shouting. Not running. Just... *there*.

One step. One breath.

The older Warden blinked. A shimmer of whatever *held* wavered.

"I believe," Brin said, voice low, "you've made your point."

The old Warden studied him.

Then looked back at me.

And released the oath.

"Go," the old man said.

"To the camp," Brin growled.

So we did.

We walked. Silent. Fast.

Behind us, the Wardens resumed their holy tyranny.

And somewhere between the last stone of the gate and the first patch of dry grass, I stopped walking.

"Didn't work," I said, still catching my breath.

"What?" Mero asked.

"My charm."

Brin didn't look back.

"That's the thing with oaths," he said. "They don't care how good the story is."

The Authentic Ruanne Experience (Non-Refundable)

Six city boys stumbled into camp like they'd just invented walking. Pink from the sun, sticky with heat, and strutting with the blinding confidence of men who thought money counted as a second brain. You heard them before you saw them — laughing too loud, drinking too fast, already planning how to brag about their "authentic Ruanne adventure" before they even stained their boots.

Brin and I were parked near the centre fire, watching them stumble in like bored noble sons who'd run out of taverns to offend.

The camp around us stretched in a messy half-moon: twelve battered wagons, a couple lean-tos stitched from stubbornness and bad cloth, and Jorann's oversized kitchen tent belching out smells strong enough to stun goats. Which was impressive, since we had goats — about fifteen of them, wandering semi-loyal among the wagons alongside a scatter of chickens, two geese (Pickle and Plum, dignified as exiled royalty), and at least two dozen cats who mostly governed themselves.

People milled everywhere. Children — thirty or more — darted underfoot in a chaos of bare feet, shouts, and slingshots of dubious aim. Teenagers loitered like coiled springs, pretending to be unimpressed by everything. Adults fixed, cooked, argued, and told lies about what the weather was going to do. Elders squatted by the fires, shaking their heads at all of it, as if they hadn't invented three-fourths of our bad ideas.

We slept wherever there was space: wagons if you were lucky, tents if you were smaller, or the hard ground if you'd lost at dice or drank too much to care. Life was noisy, cramped, a little smelly — and ours.

And none of us forgot we weren't welcome here.

It wasn't the first time city folk had come sniffing around. They wanted colour. Mystery. Culture you could step into for an afternoon, then wash off before supper.

"Fresh meat," I muttered. "And it's still twitching."

Brin didn't look up from his carving. Just grunted. The appreciative kind. Brin's grunts are a whole language. That one meant they're dumb enough to pay too much for cheap wine and leave their boots behind.

I stepped up, arms wide. "Welcome, gentlemen! I am Aen, your unofficial ambassador to all things wild and questionable. Please keep your hands visible and your judgments to a dull murmur."

The ringleader — a thick-necked boy wearing five rings and an expression that said he'd never lost anything that couldn't be replaced with money — looked me over like I was a novelty hat. "We're fine," he said, already bored. "It's just wagons."

Behind him, his friends smirked. One adjusted his too-fancy boots like they were afraid of the dirt. Another was already eyeing the food stalls.

I stuck close.

Their first stop was the Tanviros' fire. Elior on the flute, Sada singing slow and low, like smoke curling into the sky. Mira and Teyra Callix were dancing — not for an audience, but for themselves. Barefoot, fluid, all hips and heat and history. They moved like they were made of silk and rhythm, the air between them charged with something private.

"That's what I came for," one of the boys muttered.

"Reckon they take coin?" said another, louder.

Mira stopped. Turned.

Her expression said: You absolute plank.

"I'd say you can't afford us," she said, "but we're not for sale."

The boys laughed, uncomfortable. So Mira twirled once and kissed Teyra full on the mouth. Long. Deliberate.

Silence.

One boy blinked rapidly. One whistled. The one with nice boots looked like he wanted to evaporate.

I grinned.

Next, they tried Jorann's cooktent.

"Three meat pies," one said, dropping silver like he was tipping a god.

Jorann handed them over without comment.

First bite. Pause. Grimace.

"What is this?" the ringleader spat.

"Flavour," I offered. "From the dangerous outer regions of Not Bland."

The leader coughed and spat into the dust. "Tastes like someone cursed my tongue."

Jorann appeared behind him, knife in hand, apron stained, eyes full of violent generosity. "If you want boiled gruel, go back to the city and ask your mother to chew it first."

One of the boys—freckled, nervy—picked his pie back up and began eating again, determined not to die first.

Then came the Strongman Haul.

An old wagon axle in the dirt. A length of rope. One end tied to a wooden sled stacked with sandbags. The challenge: drag it three paces. The reward: bragging rights. The cost: three copper and your dignity.

Brin ran it shirtless, arms crossed, eyes full of ancient disappointment.

I did the shouting. Naturally.

"Three copper to try! Beat the house and win your coin back—if your spine survives!"

A Ruanne girl tried first. Made it half a pace. Collapsed into giggles. A boy fared worse and blamed the sandbags for being "too sandy."

Then the city boys stepped up.

"I'll go," one said, stripping off his overshirt to reveal a torso with more polish than practice. He flexed, grabbed the rope, and pulled.

Nothing.

A second pull. The rope creaked. The sled sulked.

On the third, it trembled. Slightly. He let go.

"Rigged."

Brin yawned.

That set the rest off. One after another. Coins clinked. Rope was pulled. Sandbags remained unmoved. Even the ringed leader had a go. He made it almost two steps, red-faced and shaking, before collapsing to polite applause.

Then, of course, he made a mistake.

"How far can you pull it?" he asked Brin.

Brin raised one eyebrow.

The boy grinned. "What about a real fight? One gold. Unless you're scared."

Brin looked at me.

I smiled sweetly. "Make it five."

The boy, whose name turned out to be Tallo, produced five gold like it was lint. Tossed it to me. Brin nodded once. We cleared a circle.

Tallo stripped off his overshirt with a flourish, tossing it to one of his friends like a general handing off his battle standard. He hopped from foot to foot, cracking his neck, flashing a grin wide enough to drown in.

Brin just stood there. Arms loose. Shoulders easy. Face unreadable.

I stepped forward to announce. "Ladies, gentlemen, and anyone still making poor life choices: one round, open rules—no biting, no fire. Everything else negotiable."

The crowd whooped. A few coins changed hands. I caught Mero winking at a small knot of Ruanne kids already betting wildly against the city boy.

Tallo lunged first. Fast. I'll give him that.

He ducked low, feinted left, jabbed right—all flashy tavern tricks meant to impress drunks, not win fights.

Brin didn't bother to move. He just leaned slightly, and Tallo's punch whipped past his ear like a misguided love letter.

Another swing. Miss. Another. Miss. Sweat already slicked Tallo's forehead.

The crowd started to chuckle.

Frustrated, Tallo feinted a stumble — then grabbed a fistful of dirt and flung it straight into Brin's face.

The laughter stopped cold.

For a heartbeat, Brin blinked through the dust. Another man might've roared. Swung wild. Broken bones until he felt better.

Brin just... sighed. Like a man disappointed with the world's general decline.

Tallo charged, fists flailing.

Brin caught the first punch mid-air. Twisted. Dropped Tallo onto his knees like a puppet whose strings had snapped.

Tallo gasped, face tilted up, eyes wide.

Brin met his gaze for one long, heavy second. Then drove his open palm into Tallo's chest — hard enough to knock the air out of him in one ugly, helpless wheeze.

Tallo crumpled backward, coughing and cursing. The crowd hooted.

But Brin wasn't done. He stooped, caught Tallo's wrist again, and popped the boy's shoulder out with a sharp, efficient wrench.

Tallo shrieked.

The laughter faltered. A few Ruanne murmured low and uneasy. We might fight, but we didn't maim. Not unless we had to.

Brin paused. Studied him. And, almost gently, he set the

joint back into place with a sick wet pop.

Tallo whimpered.

Brin stood. Dusted his hands. Tossed the boy's overshirt onto his chest.

"Go home," he said.

Then he turned and walked away, five gold heavier and no more impressed than when he started.

As the city boys gathered what was left of their pride and their teeth, Mero drifted up beside them like a breeze nobody invited.

He wasn't obvious about it. Just casual — straightening one boy's collar, brushing dust from another's sleeve, a quick, friendly pat on the back. By the time they limped past the last wagon, Mero had helped himself to a silver brooch, two decent belts, and one fairly spectacular pair of boots — their original owner still too dizzy to notice he was leaving barefoot.

I leaned closer. "Thought today's special was spicy meat pies, not pocket-picking."

Mero shrugged, slipping the loot into his coat. "They came for the Ruanne experience. I'm just making sure they get an authentic one."

The city boys limped out, pride leaking behind them like spilled wine.

The quiet one lingered.

"Hell of a fight," he said to me. "Sorry about my friend."

I nodded.

"Next time," I said, "bring fewer friends. And more

humility."

He smiled, half-apology, half-understanding. Then followed the others.

Brin returned to the fire. I handed him a meat pie.

"You alright?" I asked.

He shrugged. "Got paid."

We sat, chewing in companionable silence.

Another day. Another performance.

But I wondered—briefly—how many more fights we'd have to win just to be allowed to stay. And even if we won them all, would they then hate us for it?

Probably.

How to Lose Salvation and Influence (with Cheese)

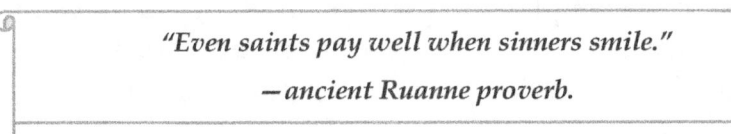

"Even saints pay well when sinners smile."
— ancient Ruanne proverb.

The city of Nareth births temples the way Mero expels gas: constantly, noisily, and with no appreciation for how others might not want them. But towering above them all — gleaming like a jewel carved from self-congratulation — stood the Sanctified Temple of Absolute Ascendance.

Its doctrine was simple: salvation scaled with silver, holiness was weighed in coin, and all devotion must be displayed in public.

The temple was a marvel. Domes like goblets. Spires clawing the sky — if not heaven, at least higher than the competition. Angels everywhere: mid-ascent, smug, gold-leafed. Literal halos.

Inside, a reverse pilgrimage. At the back: plain stone and incense that smelled faintly of regret. Near the altar: marble floors, velvet cushions, stained-glass saints weeping sapphires.

The altar? A slab of polished bribe — gemstone-encrusted marble flanked by velvet-lined Donation Podiums, ranked by the piety of the giver:

- Deserving — gold-tier contributions, where the coins barely touched the velvet before being whisked away.

- Aspiring — silver-tier, accompanied by the cleric's tolerant nod.

- Erring — bronze-tier. For those who'd sinned and

had bad taste in metals.

Outside the temple? The poor sat cross-legged in the dust, catching echoes of sermons through the open doors — until a Holy Usher repelled them with a sanctified broom.

But my favourite feature? The Punishment Pews. Splintered, warped, and so narrow that sitting was a form of repentance. One collapsed backward if you leaned wrong — helpfully labelled *The Seat of Wavering Faith.*

We arrived on a holy day. The temple was packed. The faithful glittered on every blessed bench. Up front, the blessed of the blessed lounged on Thrones of Divine Appreciation — some with footrests and alabaster cupholders.

Donations were announced by a cleric with lungs like temple bells. Worshippers gasped or clapped based on the amount — especially when a generous offering required the entire congregation to shift downward one seat. The poor soul on the Seat of Wavering Faith? Broomed.

High Cleric Glabryn the Magnificent stood at the peak, robed in layers of embroidered self-worth.

"Blessed are the prosperous," he boomed, "for they timed the market wisely. And woe to the undercapitalized!"

I found it...inspiring.

If the Ruanne had built this faith, maybe we'd be the ones reclining in sanctified comfort instead of roasting barefoot outside the city walls.

Still, I had a plan. Simple. Classic. Effective.

We would accept the kindness of strangers. Solicit generous acts of moral restitution. In short: we'd beg.

But not like amateurs. This was performance. Poverty as

theatre.

Brin stood at the main exit—silent, bruised, bowl in hand, radiating tragic masculinity. His size said *dangerous*. His eyes said *regretful about it*.

Beside him, Rinni and Tommo—two borrowed children—committed hard to the role. Rinni wore a coin-purse eyepatch. Tommo limped with such melodrama I feared dislocation.

Mero had dusted them in ash and river muck until they looked like a parable. About poverty. Or hygiene.

And me? Arms wide, smile wider. Among the blessed.

"Madame," I said to a woman dripping pearls, "might I interest you in sponsoring the spiritual trajectory of a tragically neglected soul—namely, mine?"

She sniffed. "Why aren't you at temple?"

"I was. The broom and I disagreed on doctrine."

"Sir!" I called to a man in furs. "Surely a silver for the Guild of Aspiring Redemption-Adjacent Youth?"

He handed me a pamphlet on moral hygiene.

A child gave me half a boiled plum. I took it.

Then the tithe parade began.

The copper givers trickled out the sides. The silver down the middle. But the gold-tier? They descended the grand stairs like angels in slow-motion freefall.

I nudged Brin. "Ready."

He shifted. Rinni and Tommo deployed. Mero vanished. I adjusted my shirt for dramatic clavicle.

First donor: hands chimed with rings.

"Blessed are the hungry," I intoned, "for lo, they would appreciate a fish wrap."

He dropped a grain of rice in Brin's bowl. "Let this nourish your soul."

"It's gluten-free," I said. "But my soul prefers jewellery."

Next: a perfumed baron with a gold-orphan walking stick. I leaned in. "Sir, might a silver coin redeem a sinner's ledger?"

He broke into uncontrollable laughter. The others caught it. He staggered off, wheezing.

Another donor in sunrise robes paused. I gestured to Rinni.

"My sister prays for silver to cure her eye. And fashion sense. But we're taking it one miracle at a time."

Rinni dropped to her knees, praying — possibly in tongues.

Tommo got a coin from an old woman. Then, calmly, she took it back.

"A lesson in resilience," she said.

He wailed like a funeral choir. Someone tossed him a button sewn to another button.

Brin's nose twitched. He sneezed — an exorcism by sinuses. Spiritual composure shattered.

A peacock-feathered pilgrim shrieked. A woman fainted.

Rinni doubled over. Tommo twitched operatically — until a sandal caught his ankle. A hat flew. A bracelet tumbled.

"Tell my story," he gasped. "To the angels."

I climbed the Holy Pulpit of the Bucket.

"Brothers! Sisters! Beneficiaries of mutual funds! Hear the

prophet's words!"

"A copper unspent is a blessing unmet!"

"That's not—" began the tithe clerk.

"And did he not cast the moneylenders *into* the temple to offer better rates?"

"That is—"

I gestured to Brin. "Behold the mournful mountain! A man who has *suffered upholstery!*"

Brin shifted. A child offered him a raisin.

"Give not to the gilded temple!" I cried. "It won't make us vanish. But give to us, and we'll sin quietly!"

That was the one. The broom line.

A dozen ushers descended like bureaucrats late for tea. One blew a whistle. Another unrolled a scroll titled *A Final Solution for Vermin*. By the stains, I assume their final solution involved bludgeoning.

Brin moved. Mero scattered pamphlets. Rinni grabbed Tommo. Brin picked them both up like luggage.

I brought up the rear. "Remember me kindly! Or inaccurately!"

By sundown, we limped into camp.

Cookfire smoke curled. Laughter floated—just enough to hide exhaustion. We slumped around a rug.

Brin sat like a man filing a bodily grievance.

Mero arrived late, smug, holding a wheel of cheese.

"You stole that," I said.

"Liberated."

"From where?"

"A cart."

"A *locked* cart?"

"Not when I liberated the cheese."

Tommo was asleep on Rinni's shoulder. She was still in character, braiding ash into her hair like a mourning widow.

Our righteous bounty:

- Seven copper coins (two bent, one sticky;
- One silver button (pig-shaped;
- Half a pamphlet on *Spiritual Modesty in the Age of Decadence*:
- A boiled plum pit:
- The grain of rice;
- Button sewn to button:
- One clean tooth (origin unclear);
- One fascinator;
- A flower (detachable); and
- Mero's cheese

"We are rich," I said.

Brin grunted: the sound of bruised realism.

"In disappointment," I clarified. "But it accumulates well."

Rinni pointed. "Can I keep the pig button?"

"Use it wisely," I said. "For trade. Or bribery. Or to confuse future archaeologists."

We broke cheese into pieces and passed them around.

And as temple bells rang somewhere out of reach, I

considered Glabryn's only true wisdom: *Be charitable to yourselves.*

So I smiled, took the plum pit, and made a wish — for something that couldn't be bought. And maybe, if the saints were generous, a handful of silver to go with it.

The Great Pilgrim Pass Hustle

> *"Every lock teaches the hand that picks it."*
> — *ancient Ruanne proverb.*

Did I forget to mention there's magic in the world?

There is.

And — naturally — it hates me.

Oaths. The spine of Nareth. Some cruel bastard, long ago, figured out that if you swore something just right — hand on heart, head bowed, maybe rubbing your left nipple (don't ask me) — it stuck. Not just metaphorically. Magically. Binding.

How? No idea. Probably blood. Or grief. Or a spleen.

All I know is: oaths have power.

Anyone can get snagged in one. Say the wrong thing with too much sincerity and — boom — you're magically contract-bound to the man who was only useful for one thing, one night. Explains a lot of marriages, really.

But there are those who don't just stumble into oaths. They shape them. Breathe them. Break people with them. As you saw, at the gate of Nareth, when my tongue stopped obeying me thanks to one particularly pedantic guard with oath magic — and the charisma of a moldy boot.

They call themselves the Oathbound. I call them the Breakers of Wind. (Hasn't caught on yet. I remain hopeful.)

Imagine a walking rulebook wearing a frown and you've got the Oathbound. Sanctimonious. Arrogant. Righteous as saints and twice as irritating. Gussied up with the notable personality of a lead brick—That's also your landlord.

They keep "order" in Nareth. And by order, I mean a cake baked from equal parts boredom, fear, and bureaucratic sadism.

You've got your bureaucrats, inventing new forms of torture involving triplicate scrolls and requirements to queue for hours only to be told this is the wrong line for that. Gate guards (such as the one my tongue unhappily met), who control who walks where, ensuring that wherever folks need to get, they will be compelled to proceed in the opposite direction, because, well, Rules.

And worst of all: the black-robed magi of Nareth's courts. They don't shout. They don't draw swords. They just glide by and speak your name—and somehow make it sound like your own funeral.

An oath is a door. Open it the right way, and maybe you get power. Open it wrong, and the Oathbound kick it off its hinges, drag you through backwards, and cite three precedents while they're doing it.

You'll be lucky if they only hit you with *Chapter Nineteen, Verse Seven* of the *Compendium Manifestium* (that's the one about "falsehearted intent and transverbal corruption" — I think). More likely, they'll escalate it to *Appendix B, Subsection 12(c)* of the *Codex of Binding Intentions*—a charming little passage that authorizes the "immediate suspension of liberties pending review of oathemetic integrity."

Swear something drunk, in jest, or—gods forbid—during carnal enthusiasm? Congratulations, you've triggered Clause Forty-Two of the Charter of Civic Sanctity: "oral contracts made in states of compromised virtue." A clause so vague it can mean whatever they want it to mean.

And don't even get me started on the *Scroll of Exceptionalist Enforcement*—a dusty relic with more red wax seals than actual content. But it's the one they invoke when they want to do something particularly self-righteous. Like trial by stone-memorandum. That's not a metaphor. It's a slab with your name on it and a bunch of carved misdeeds, paraded through the plaza so the pigeons can crap on your reputation.

They've got scrolls, cubes, citation discs, whispering tablets—one Oathwarden even consulted a spinning cube that muttered infractions in Old Tahlic, which no one speaks except the cube.

And if none of those apply, they'll fall back on the *Principle of Recursiveness*—which I'm fairly sure just means "we make up the rules as we go."

So yes. Make a careless vow in Nareth and there's a good chance some ancient, sanctified footnote will be located, dusted off, and used to sanctimoniously ruin your afternoon. Or your life.

But I digress.

Enough boring. You want the story.

Come with me then, if you will, into a chasm of my mind, where Brilliance lurks. In Brilliance—self proclaimed, of course—is rarely content. As he wanders around idly touching things clearly marked, in all caps, DO NOT TOUCH, he is generally inclined to ruminate. And such mental pathways tend down wonderful paths such as, *This is fine, but awfully cramped*, or *What would happen if*, or (his personal favourite), *What's the worst that could happen?*

And from just such an enlightened stroll, my latest cunning plan was born.

Here we go.

See that table just past the east road dust? That's me. Breastplate gleaming, hat feathered, flanked by my sanctified enforcer. Handsome as sin and about as trustworthy. It's late morning.

"Good morning!"

A small group of dusty folks are crowding around my table. Devotees of Saint Vash from distant Geth-Harram, seeking to end their 90-day self-denial from bathing and be purified in the black waters in the Great Cathedral of Sacred Ablution. I'm attempting to ply my craft while staying upwind.

"As I said, a mile or so east from here you'll reach the eastern gate of Nareth. I'm sorry to tell you, but it's stacked with queues of all varieties: livestock line, merchant line, wagon line, and pilgrim line – the longest, sadly – but such is the state of affairs when one puts together a city of drunken bureaucrats and the holiest month of the year in a half a dozen faiths."

Groans from my friends of the road.

I shake my head conciliatorily.

"Nareth is a mess of taxes, tariffs, and temple dues. Pilgrims have come in droves to kiss relics, be touched by the divine, and take souvenirs. More this year than last. It's a crush."

Albright, the leader—proclaimed with sanctified vapours most pungent—asks me again for the information needed to seamlessly enter the city.

"Certainly," I answer, obliging to a fault, "It's easy. Just continue on your way, but make sure you take the queue third to the *right*. Not the one that says, 'visitors check in here first,' but just to the right of that, between the carts and the wagons, where you get the wooden tablet that marks your place in line."

I wave my hand to Brin, who's standing in the shade mimicking a stone monolith remarkably well.

"My friend, Jannok, here, checked who they were serving about an hour ago, and they were on XXIV. Wasn't it XXIV, Jannok?"

Brin almost nods.

"Which means that they've likely already reached XXX, and have started again at I. So — if someone tells you they can sell you XXV, XXVI, XXVII, XXVIII, or XXIX, *don't buy* it – That's the next cycle. Buy those, you're waiting 'til tomorrow."

One of the young pilgrims worries out loud that they won't be let into the city.

"Oh, don't worry about that, sister. Everyone gets into Nareth. Eventually. And the fields outside the city are fairly safe at night. Unless it's a full moon..." I trail off, looking at the sky. A frown. It might be a full moon tonight.

At last — thank gods! — someone asks about the enormous stack of old, water-damaged travel permits placed at the centre of the table. Covered in holy seals, decorated with consecrated ribbons, and with enough ink flourishes to impress a half-drunk friar. Every single one, genuinely signed by an assistant to a lesser Magi.

The pilgrim lifts one upside down. Literacy's rare.

"These? Well, bless you for asking. These are limited-edition Pilgrim Priority Passes — fast-track queue skipping, blessing access, and front row seating in several approved place of worship. You know, I should check if Sacred Ablution has enrolled in our program..."

My finger runs down the list I made for myself of Nareth's various religious orders, their saints and martyrs, and what they espouse. Most had the notation, "hell if I know."

A dozen delivered. In trade, 12 Geth-Harramian silver crowns, 4 copper coins, and a chicken. The bread was dry, but it held a delicious bouquet of satisfaction.

Brin scowled. "Child needed that chicken."

I shook my head. "Child needs better parents. It's a terrible chicken anyway."

Brin remained unimpressed.

I refuse to have a conscience.

"Didn't you see them? We filled them with holy fervour, and anticipation. And if they use the passes at multiple temples, they'll get exposed to new faiths. Maybe find one that doesn't require nose-plugs. And technically, the passes do give fast-tracked access to something—a lesson learned: feed your children, don't take them on pilgrimages. Plus, they have a souvenir."

Mero whistles. More customers. I straighten the table and prepare.

Brilliant, Right? Alright. Work done, let's go home.

Dusk bled slow across the sands, trailing gold across the sky. Fires sparked in shallow pits, throwing lean shadows of canvas and smoke onto the slopes beyond the riverbank. Children squealed somewhere near the cookfire. Brin stood sharpening something that needed no sharpening. Mero was halfway up a fig tree, peeling fruit and thieving glances at the neighbouring tents.

Me? I was counting silver and trying not to gloat audibly.

Then the wind shifted. Which was odd, because there wasn't any.

Three figures crested the ridge where the east path met the upper road, their horses kicking up little puffs of dust that hung too long in the still air. The beasts — tall, proud, and gleaming with the kind of pampered sheen you only get when a stableboy fears for his job — tossed their heads impatiently as their riders reined them in.

Not pilgrims. Not merchants. Not any sort you'd want to meet on neutral ground, much less in the comfort of your own criminal enterprise.

First was the cleric — a man robed in iridescent linen, sweating despite the cool, who looked as though the mere act of existing beside our fire offended him deeply. He wore the sigil of the Sacred Ablution upon his breast: three interlocking drops of water on black — cleanliness enforced by threat. A badge of holy soap, sanctimony, and just a hint of mildew.

I was vibrating with enthusiasm at the drama to come, and already inventing ways to transmute rage into something operatic and absurd, until the shadows beside him resolved into two Oathbound.

You could tell them by the way the camp stilled around them — that quiet that descends when everyone suddenly remembers they had pressing business elsewhere. Cloaked in unrelenting black, hoods drawn, expressions carved from divine bureaucracy. No weapons. None needed. The magic hummed around them — low and inevitable, like a sentence preparing to be passed.

The cleric stepped his horse forward. His voice carried like a sermon written in vinegar.

"Where are they?"

Nema rose and slid forward, all grace, danger, and the kind of smile that makes kings reconsider their kingdoms. Matriarch of the Ruanne, leader of our little traveling fellowship, mother of many, including half the people you *wouldn't* want to cross in this region. She moved like a blade wrapped in velvet: older than she looked, younger than she let on, with eyes like polished obsidian and a lush voice that could part crowds or silence children mid-scream without altering tone.

"Why have you come to my fire, drenched in accusation, without first offering peace?"

The cleric flinched. It was brief, but I saw it. You always remember your first misstep with Nema. He bowed. It was shallow. He regretted it as soon as the Oathbound did not mirror the gesture.

"My Lady Nema, I am Father Bouwt, and come in holy grievance. Fraud has been committed in the name of the Cathedral of Sacred Ablution. Pilgrims misled. Authority falsified. Sacred rites mocked."

Nema's gaze didn't waver. She simply nodded.

"Then you have questions."

"Yes," the cleric hissed, then held up one of my beautiful forgeries. "And we require *the one who has signed this*."

And I, idiot that I am, laughed. A single, traitorous bark leapt from my lips and danced around the fire yelling, "*Pick me! Pick me!*"

Brin sighed.

Mero slipped behind the fig tree.

My hand flew to my mouth, but it was too late. Betrayed —
by breath, by timing, by my own irrepressible genius. And
in a way, of all the accusations the priest might have
hurled, he'd picked the best. He might not have
appreciated the art, but he'd been drawn to it all the same.
Because that signature? That was the flourish — the chef's
kiss. Entirely unnecessary. Utterly essential.

In florid ink, dutifully impressed upon each pass by the
"assistant," it read: *Magi O'Holy-Balls.*

The Accidental Vow Incident

The cleric was staring at me like I'd just pissed in the baptismal font. One Warden turned slightly — just enough to mark my shape in her periphery. The other remained motionless, measuring my neck for the verbal noose they were about to place around it. Possibly lamenting the interruption of their passionate debate over the use of *and* versus *or* in the statute prohibiting red paint on wooden ladders if they lean *and* fall. Hopefully.

I opened my mouth — to deny, to explain, possibly to hypothetically compliment whoever did the inkwork on the pass.

Nema raised a hand.

Not to strike. Not to scold. Just calm and slow, fingers splayed like she was feeling the heat off a fire she knew too well.

A few Ruanne were wandering back, drawn by curiosity, and the gravitational pull of my impending humiliation.

I knew better than to speak when Nema was angry, exasperated, or deciding where to bury my body. And she was definitely all of those things. I just wasn't sure which one was winning.

She sat. Like a queen. Receiving petitions.

"Father," she said, "do you bring formal charge on behalf of the Cathedral, or merely righteous discomfort?"

Bouwt blinked. Paused. His face twisted as his mind tried

to crawl out of the logical snare she'd wrapped around it.

She turned, just slightly, to the Oathbound. "Do you observe breach of contract? False oath? Violation of doctrinal truth? Speak it aloud, or sheath your posturing."

It wasn't shouting. Nema didn't shout. She unwrapped her sentences like surgical knives — smooth, glinting, and precise. The wind shifted again, just enough to catch the scent of dust and simmering pride.

The Oathbound remained still.

Nema continued, her voice silk strained through iron. "The document in question" — she gestured to the sacredly defaced pass — "is signed on behalf of a Magi O'Holy-Balls, an individual whose ecclesiastical standing I confess myself ignorant of. Perhaps your order has lowered its standards. Or perhaps this is merely doctrinal parody, offered in poor taste."

The cleric's mouth opened. Nema did not stop.

"And Father, I trust you agree that parody of an assistant to a non-existent Magi is no concern of the Cathedral. Surely it would be beneath the dignity of your order to respond in person, rather than with a politely worded screed, sealed in triplicate, and ignored by all."

"Lady Nema — "

She cut him off with a raised brow. "My name is Nema of the Ruanne. I do not accept titles from men who arrive uninvited, unevidenced, and without a single god-blessed offering to my fire. So. Again. Do you bring charge?"

The cleric looked to the Oathbound.

The one on the left — the woman — finally turned. Her hood fell just back enough to reveal a cheekbone sharp enough to cut parchment.

"We observed mockery," she said, low and level. "Of sacred rites. A binding signature on falsified authority. Enough to warrant judgment."

"And?" Nema said.

The Warden stepped forward.

"We will not press formal charge." Her eyes flicked to me. "Yet."

Nema inclined her head. Barely.

"Then we are finished here." She turned slightly back to the fire.

The cleric looked like he wanted to explode. Instead, he sputtered, invoked higher offices, and promised consequences.

Nema ignored him. Thoroughly.

Brin exhaled behind me. Mero emerged from behind the fig tree, chewing something he probably hadn't paid for.

Me? I smiled.

Too soon.

Now, before I explain what happened next, you need to understand: there was something particularly insufferable about Mother Superior Sharpface. She was young. Probably younger than me. But prematurely crone-like from a strict diet of haughty judgment. Skin too flawless for compassion, posture too perfect for comfort. Her robe was immaculate. Her boots: practical. Her eyes were judicial parchment inked with disappointment.

She stood in the ruddy light and looked at me like I was a three-stringed lute—hopeless, useless, and an insult to music.

You know the look. The one that says, *I've never broken a*

rule, but I'd like to break you.

It was on the tip of my tongue: *Let me show you just how ignorant, false, and wrong you are, Mrs. Smugface.*

First—no one could prove anything.

Second—there was no debt. Nothing on the pass promised anything.

Third—I hadn't even demanded payment. I had *refused* it. As a man of devotion, all I could accept were voluntary gifts. The unwashed pilgrims had thanked me. The girl had given me her chicken.

And yet—

Just as these absolutely unassailable defences lined up, ready to be deployed with the fury of a thousand righteous fig-puns, Brilliance returned and took hold of my mouth. What he said was likely the stupidest idea he'd ever had—and it was definitely dragged steaming from his personal favourite path: *What's the worst that could happen?*

I took one step forward. Bowed low before everyone.

One hand on my heart, one in the air, swirling the wind.

My oath: "*I vow to make amends for any sacrilege, perceived or actual, in a manner fitting the dignity of the Sacred Ablution and under the honest guidance of its most esteemed representative.*"

What I thought was: *Suck on that, Sister.*

Now, before you get excited, let's break it down:

First: "*make amends*"—very flexible. Second: "*dignity of the Sacred Ablution*"—questionable. Third: "*honest guidance*"— oh, the comedy of watching Father Butt try that. And finally—and most importantly—it wasn't a real vow. You can't bind yourself to something that doesn't exist.

Only… the Oathbound were both looking at me.

Their eyes?

White.

Not just the whites of the eye. No pupil. No iris. Just white.

Just for a flash.

The woman said, "Done."

And then… nothing.

Of course, nothing. I nearly laughed at myself for worrying. As if *that* had been a real—

But the faces around me—Father Butt: triumphant. Nema: massaging her temple like I was the worst headache she'd ever caught. Mero: shaking his head, full of *I told you so*. Brin—Brin blinked. I think.

The Oathbound woman bowed to me. "I will return at first light. Be ready."

Wait. What?

It was around then that the smell of what I'd stepped into finally hit me.

The "most esteemed representative" was not the cleric.

I mean—*how was I to know?*

She didn't look esteemed. Esteemed people have beards, and ceremonial flatulence, and gold-trimmed hats shaped like theological regrets. Not cheekbones and doom.

At least I said *guidance.*

What does *she* consider guidance?

I tried to open my mouth. Explain the satirical nature of my vow. File a retraction with the universe. Nothing came out. Just a faint pressure, below my ribs. Like someone had tied a ribbon inside me and was slowly pulling.

The Oathbound were already turning away.

She paused—just once—at the edge of the firelight. Looked over her shoulder.

Met my gaze.

And then—I swear to every god I've ever lied about—she smiled.

Not cruel. Worse. The smile of a woman who knew exactly how much pain a promise could inflict—and planned to make it *educational*.

Then she vanished into the dark, and I exhaled a single syllable that summed up my condition perfectly:

"…shit."

Nema stood. Not quickly. She moved like someone who'd already written the eulogy. "That," she said, "was impressively stupid. Even for you."

I rubbed the bridge of my nose. "In my defence, it was extremely funny."

"No, Aen. It wasn't."

She walked off, muttering to herself in a language I didn't recognize, but understood entirely.

Brin clapped a hand on my shoulder. He didn't say anything. He didn't need to.

Mero sighed beside me.

"Well," he said, "I guess we're staying in Nareth."

Enter the Love Interest

What use is a story if it doesn't have a love interest?

Especially a story about me. My autobiography simply wouldn't be believable without swooning maidens, heaving bosoms, and probably a double wedding to share me in the third act.

Sadly, Seren neither swooned, had any bosom to heave, nor showed any interest in weddings—double or otherwise. She was either sworn to celibacy or waiting for someone (likely female) to sweep her off her feet and whisper sections of the *Protocol for Quantification of Damages* like sweet nothings into her ear.

She looked like the gods had started to sketch a woman, got distracted, and forgot to add any softening touches. She had a scholar's build—lean, fine-boned, all edges honed by too many years spent wrestling law scrolls instead of anything human. A face that might make a man reconsider his priorities—paired with eyes that had already weighed, tallied, and filed you under *Irrelevant: See Also, Regrettable Choices*. Slender lips that didn't need to move to say, *Don't bother. You're not my type*. The kind of woman who could set a heart on fire just to study how efficiently it burned.

Worse, she didn't find me funny.

Which is *impossible*.

Honestly, I wasn't even sure she had a pulse.

But I'm getting ahead of myself.

The Black Bird Descends, Stick in Hand, Judgment in Eyes.

It was shortly after my eyes had once again lost their noble battle to drink Brin under the table—and several hours before I was capable of forming a coherent sentence—when she arrived.

As I recall, even the sun seemed afraid to rise that morning.

I should have been scared too. But at the time of the arrival of the pedantic stormcloud, I was incapable of feeling anything at all.

Apparently, she had brought a stick. To beat sense into the lawless. And a face to inform you that the beating was already overdue.

Because the wagon where Brin and I had collapsed was suddenly assaulted by a blunt object, determined to hammer us awake no matter how hard I tried to ignore it.

Brin threw me at the door.

There was another crack. Possibly her staff. Possibly my skull.

I opened the door. My body forgot to stop. The ground tasted like betrayal and cold stone.

To the best of my recollection, our first exchange went something like this:

"You're drunk. And you stink."

"Well, you're boring."

"Put your head in a bucket. And do something about your breath."

"Only if you do something about your face."

Not brilliant. But in my defence, my head was full of cheese and someone was screaming obscenities behind my eyes.

Brin didn't appreciate my attitude. I'm not sure if it was the poor quality of the insult or just that he wanted to go back to sleep. Either way, he *assisted* with the bucket. I think he enjoyed it more than was fair.

"Alright!" I screamed, now fully betrayed and awake.

Brin lumbered off.

I wiped the hair out of my face and lacquered my features with wounded pride.

Seren, meanwhile, regarded me like manure in the myth of the hero's stable-cleaning labour. The sort of mess that makes the gods laugh and mortals weep.

"Aen Marr," she said, "your oath compels you to serve under my direction until you make amends for your wrongdoing — or until it is decided your penance is fulfilled."

I held up a finger.

"First — if we're going with 'it is decided,' how about it decides *now* that I'm sufficiently penance-ized and save everyone the bother. Second — who talks like that?"

She didn't even smile.

Witness Now: The Tragedy of Aen Marr, Struck Down by One Grim Feather.

"You shall be assigned to reparation and re-education…"

There were more words. Many more. Delivered with perfect clarity, immaculate enunciation, and not a single goddamn adjective. The weasel in my brain was screaming again. I started wondering what the long-term effects might be of always speaking in passive voice.

Had *I* been assigning penance, it could have involved making a thousand copies of the verse *I shall only pee standing up*, or cleaning actual pilgrims, or sitting through silent lectures and being required to ask meaningful questions in mime, or enduring a sermon on *The Sanctity of Honest Sentences* delivered in monotone by a monk with a lisp.

Instead, she started talking about *returning the gains* from my pilgrim pass hustle.

"Now let's not get hasty," I said, with genuine horror.

But there was no arguing with the Grim.

She listed names. Dozens. Every poor, gullible soul I'd conned from the pilgrim pass hustle. It was — honestly — impressive. I'd forgotten a few myself.

I waited for her lips to stop moving. I was already assembling the requisite lies to make this penance impossible.

But when I opened my mouth to explain — gently, patiently — that the gains were not ill-gotten, that I hadn't counted them, and that I no longer had them...

Nothing came out.

Well — not *nothing*. A sound emerged. Something soft and meaningless. Entirely composed of vowels.

My mouth shut like a sprung trap. My eyes bulged. I started sweating — despite the dew still on the ground.

"What have you done to me?" I squeaked.

"I've done nothing," she said. Her face utterly impassive. She genuinely seemed confused.

"I can't… talk."

"Well," she replied, "clearly you can."

I tried again.

My mind said, *"We exchanged the coin and spent it on amiable ladies you could learn from, if you ever wanted to try having a personality."*

My mouth bleated.

Seren looked at me like one might regard a man who had suddenly, and for no reason, burst into song. Without words. Without tune.

"Is there something you wish to say?"

I took a breath. Focused.

"There are… so many things I wish to say to you. But I can't seem to say any of them. My words… just stop working."

She studied me. Contemplative. Maybe even intrigued.

"What sorts of things?"

"Ooii." (Nothing.)

"Uahoooaii." (Just trying to explain.)

I proceeded cautiously. "The… explanations… that would be… helpful."

And by *"helpful explanations,"* I meant *"convenient versions of the truth."*

And by *"convenient versions of the truth,"* I meant *lies.*

Oh gods.

I can't lie to her.

The realization hit like a guillotine.

Honest guidance.

Somehow, I had lost the one thing I was actually good at.

And with the worst person possible.

Mero, I thought, frantically. Mero's smart enough to escape anything. Mero might think of something. I left Seren with my bucket, her stick, and her morning cheer, and scuttled off into the camp, every step a painful reminder of my living nightmare.

"Mero, you've got to help me!"

"Bruh."

"I'm serious! Wake up!"

Mero opened one eye. Decided I wasn't worth it, and rolled over. "Brought it on yourself."

"The oath I swore, it's *worse*."

"Don't care."

"She's going to make me give back all the money!"

That got his attention. He sat up, shrieking, "What?!"

My hands waved — *Shh, please* — begging him to keep his voice down. My head!

"What? *My share?*"

"*All* of it." I whispered.

I saw the wheels turning in his eyes as he dragged himself to consciousness. Waited for the obvious conclusion. It wasn't long.

"So, tell her you don't have it."

Bingo.

"*Exactly.* I would. I tried. But...I can't. Physically. Something about the oath. When I try to tell her anything that's not true, I turn into Bingo the talking dog."

He looked at me for a long moment.

"Was it you that ruined my green leather jacket?"

"What?! What does that have to do with—"

"Just answer the question."

There was suddenly too much enthusiasm in his voice.

Mero once had a beautiful leather jacket. The kind sold in high-end shops, found in neighbourhoods where people had people to do things for them—like carry them places, guard them from the sun, or buy expensive, impractical things that others consider the height of fashion.

And I might have borrowed it on occasion without asking. Especially on one occasion involving a buxom redhead, an unpaid entry to a penthouse bedroom, and a hasty departure out a window and into a romantic but filthy canal.

"Me? Absolutely not. I already told you."

Oh, thank gods.

Mero remained unconvinced. And from his wilting expression, he clearly had arrived at the same conclusion as me.

I could still lie. Just not to Seren.

Speaking of whom, She-Who-Must-Be-Obeyed had arrived at Mero's.

"Reparations must be made," said the stick. At least, that's what her voice felt like in my head. "Gather your gains. It is time to leave."

Mero approached her.

"Most honourable Magi," Mero began, hands spread

placatingly, "Aen made the forgeries. I did not. He hired me to keep watch, and to direct traffic. Which I did. An honest contract. Honest service. Surely, you're not..."

She ignored him. Looked at me. "Get them."

None of Mero's entreaties swayed. Brin just nodded.

The sun, relieved that the trouble was all ours, had by this point risen in the east. It rose bright and clear, an honest luminescence that removed all the romanticism of the camp and revealed us to be small, and shabby, and cluttered with sin.

Seren led the way—mounted, of course, on that black-hearted mare of hers, the very picture of righteous judgment given hooves. Mero and Brin followed on foot. A full day's hard-won earnings swayed in a velvet pouch on my belt, and me, already bemoaning its loss.

Except for the chicken. It had already achieved sainthood through sacrifice.

If I could have eaten the silver and kept it too, believe me—I'd have gnawed through it like a condemned man at his last meal.

How to Lose Pilgrims and Alienate Clerics

The Law Complex of Nareth was what happened when a city tried to build Reason out of stone — and then kept building until it resembled a lunatic's chessboard. First came the Hall of Justice: four grim towers judging a battle they no longer understood. Then the endless Hall of Regulatory Administration, the conspiratorial Remand Centre, and brooding behind them all: the Archive — a building designed by people who clearly hated sunlight, fresh air, and ambition.

This was the world of the Oathbound. Seren lived in the Chamber of the Magi — small private quarters behind the courts — and spent her days in the Archive, combing statutes until her eyes turned into ledger entries.

The Archive was exactly what it sounded like: solemn, silent, and deeply committed to its core principles: public misery, incomprehensibility, and its own importance. The building loomed like a testament carved from sun-bleached stone, its arched windows frowning down on the square below. The kind of place that took pride in how little joy left its doors.

Inside, it was worse.

The walls were lined with scrolls and ledgers. Shelves groaned under the weight of doctrine. A statue of Oren the Judicious loomed over us, one hand raised, the other clenching a book thick enough to be a table.

Mero's eyes, as usual, were casing the joint for items of value. I saw none. Unless your market was exclusively masochistic insomniacs.

"Don't touch anything," Seren said, gliding ahead in that infuriating, effortless way she had. Her boots made no sound on the polished stone. Mine, of course, squeaked. Repeatedly.

A scribe waited for us behind a dais taller than necessary. He was the colour of the faded parchment around him, and about as animated. His quill moved with the speed of molasses and all the joy of being stuck in traffic. His robe bore the insignia of the *Third Archive of Minor Offences and Associated Compensations* — a department whose very name screamed prestige.

Seren bowed her head. "Oathbound Warden Seren Vey, bearing restitution Order seventy-three-dash-Lumen-nine."

The scribe blinked. Once. Then slowly reached for a scroll.

I cleared my throat. "Does this mean I'm officially famous?"

No one responded.

He cracked the scroll open and read with all the emotion of a drying sponge. "Claimant is one Aen Marr. Crime: fraud by forged sacramental permit. Seventy-two counts. Fourteen faiths affected. Compensatory path: verbal admission of guilt, full restitution of ill-gotten gain, and a temple tour."

"Tour?" I said, hopefully. "Do I get a stage name?"

Again, nothing.

Seren turned to me with her usual glacial composure. "You will apologise. Formally. Publicly. At each temple you defrauded. Your words will be recorded and witnessed by clerics and Oathbound alike. The process is called the restitution tour."

I nodded solemnly. "So... what I'm hearing is: this is a publicity opportunity."

"You will also return the coin," she added, ignoring me entirely. "Each apology will be appended to a penitent register and attested by Oathbound scribes for bureaucratic purity."

"Because the only thing purer than a public flogging is a flogging *with paperwork*," I muttered.

Brin exhaled through his nose. Possibly a laugh.

Mero failed entirely to hide a snort.

Seren did not smile.

The scribe handed her a stack of parchment—names, dates, locations. "Each institution has confirmed receipt of the schedule. They will provide ceremonial scripts to be read aloud. Adherence is compulsory."

"Compulsory like 'aggressively recommended,' or compulsory like 'you will spontaneously combust if you ad-lib'?"

Seren stared. I stared back.

We both knew the answer.

She held out a scroll. The sample apology was longer than the kind of sermon where you start wondering if anyone is still listening, even the one woman still nodding along. And twice as boring.

"I, Aen Marr, Ruanne, without fixed address, having acted in contravention of the sacred order and in deception of the pilgrim faithful, do offer solemn regret for my wrongful actions, which may have, if not explicitly, then by necessary implication, caused spiritual harm, and/or monetary injury, to those whom the gods

in their wisdom have seen fit to guide here..."

I stopped reading. "*Who wrote this?* I can't decide if it's an apology, or a sentence that wandered off, got lost in the wild, forgot language, and was found years later playing with its lips and rambling incoherently."

"You will memorise it," Seren said.

I continued unrolling the scroll. There was no period. Just despair. "Memorize? I might need heirs."

Here is how the apology tour started. (Hint: Poorly)

The Temple of the Everwake sat in domed opulence at the end of a broad avenue that promised grandeur but delivered disappointment. Its doors were carved with sleepless eyes and scriptural warnings about laziness. Inside, it smelled of dry incense, penance, and false protestations. Everything was dim. Heavy. The light came from tiny lanterns arranged in vigil circles. No torches. No candles. Just the slow burn of eternal regret.

I hated it immediately.

The clerics of the Everwake were not a fun-loving bunch. These were people who believed rest was for the weak and naps were a moral failing. Their highest sacrament was staying awake through a three-day recitation of the "*Litanies of Continual Witness.*" Without blinking.

I shuffled to the centre of the room, robed in the ceremonial browns that screamed, *poor fashion choice,* to anyone who would listen. Not only was it too large, it smelled like it had been stored next to a camel, or inside a camel, and caused me to itch in parts of my body it wasn't even touching.

A line of monks looked down on me with bloodshot eyes

from high back chairs on a raised dais. I'm pretty sure the one at the end had painted eyes over his eyes, because they did not look real. No one blinked. I felt an overwhelming urge to blink on their behalf.

Seren stood off to one side, arms folded, face impassive. Brin and Mero loitered near the door. Brin, impassive as always. Mero chewing on something and taking a religious interest in a golden eye decorating the wall.

A clerk cleared his throat.

I stepped forward and unrolled the script.

"I, Aen Marr, Ruanne, without fixed address..."

So far so good.

"...having acted in contravention of the sacred order and in deception of the pilgrim faithful..."

Breathe.

Keep the tone sincere. Imagine you're apologizing to that poor woman whose goose you stole. The one who chased you with the ladle.

"...do offer solemn regret for my wrongful actions, which may have —"

I paused.

This next bit was unnecessarily wordy. I could fix it. Clarify.

"...which may have explicitly or by implication, caused spiritual or monetary harm — and injury — that is, spiritual or monetary — or injury — or harm — and harm..."

Oh no.

I hurried on, "to the gods, in their wisdom, who have fleeced — I mean fit —

The words were a blur. I couldn't find my place.

"...the fit. The gods—fit, of their wisdom—to guide—here..."

Silence.

I tried again.

"—fit to guide through my deceptive—though, some might say, enterprising—No. I mean, my deeply regretful and entirely miscalculated—ah..."

The monks began whispering.

One of them crossed himself with alarming speed. Another picked up a bell and rang it three times. A scribe gasped like I'd just declared war on his mother.

A dried fig hit me in the shoulder.

Hard.

"I would like to apologise for that as well," I said quickly, "and for the fig. Though to be fair, I'm not sure that one was my fault."

A child in the audience leaned toward his mother and whispered, "Is that the man who tried to sell papa the fast-pass to salvation?"

I tried a grin. It came out... unconvincing.

"Right. Yes. That was me. But! The intention was noble. I was trying to make religion more... accessible."

Seren's voice cut across the room: "*Silence.*"

It hit me like a club. My jaw snapped shut mid-gesture. The echoes of my attempted charm clattered to the floor like broken coins.

A beat of silence followed.

Then a slow, disappointed cough.

The head monk rose.

He didn't speak. He didn't have to.

He simply turned to the clerk beside him and intoned: "Recorded. Witnessed. Register amended. May he be guided from here with haste."

Which, I suspected, was polite monk-speak for *"Get him out of here before he breaks anything else."*

We left in silence.

Well—mostly silence. Someone threw another fig at my back on the way out.

Outside, I shed the burlap betrayal masquerading as a robe as quickly as humanly possible.

Mero offered half a date. "One down," he pronounced, jauntily. "Seventy-one to go!"

Brin handed me a skin of water.

Seren, still unreadable, simply unrolled the next name on her list.

Not, mind you, that we could do all the temples in one go. Oh, no. That would be too merciful. Each apology had to be *scheduled*—approved, witnessed, notarized, and entered into the Great Bureaucratic Stomach of Nareth to be digested at its own glacial pace. Some temples only held ceremonies once a week. Some insisted on special penitence days. A few had to wait for visiting dignitaries to properly scowl at me.

Which meant—lucky me—the whole miserable parade would be stretched out over weeks. Months, if the gods truly despised me (and I had reason to think they did).

Seren would return to the Ruanne camp whenever the next temple was ready for its ration of my humiliation. Like an ill-tempered tax collector. Or Death. If Death wore black and had cheekbones sharp enough to invalidate a marriage license.

The Whispering Baths Incident

So... Brin.

I think he's owed a story. He's been lumbering around being strong, faithful, and monosyllabic long enough. It's time you got to know him. Not just the legend, but the real man under all that silence. Even if he might kill me for telling this particular tale—some stories are worth the bruises.

This was back in the good old days in Dararein—our ancestral home. A city of smoke, spice, sandalwood perfume, and a slow-burning hatred for anyone who borrowed without asking, danced without shame, and could turn a dried bone into a work of art. Like the Ruanne. And by "good old days," I mean back before such people decided they'd prefer to just murder us in our sleep.

But on this day? There was sun. There was laughter. And me, dragging Brin to a bathhouse.

You remember Brin fights for coin? Well, he wasn't always the Beast of the Ruanne. There was a time when he suffered defeat. When his jaw got reacquainted with stone floors and his ribs with bootheels. It didn't happen often— Brin was born with a sixth sense for where not to be when opponents attempted to rearrange his limbs—but it happened. There were times when, instead of holding up his hands, he did a convincing impression of a mangled rug.

Yesterday had been one of those days. Mogg the

Merciless, a man named for subtlety, had left Brin dented and broken. There were bite marks. Elbow-shaped bruises. At one point, Mogg had picked Brin up and used him to beat the ground into submission. The match ended with Brin unconscious, facedown in the dirt, one leg twitching like it was trying to escape. Five copper to show for it — collected by me, his loyal manager, mostly because Brin's fingers weren't speaking to him — was more insult than prize.

It was, however, enough for the two of us to go to the baths.

So, rather than let him wallow in pain, welts, and poor life choices, I kindly suggested that we take our prize money and put it to good use.

"Our?" he said. That is, I think that was what he said. It sounded more like "Uuuuhn?"

"Whatever. Let's go. You'll thank me later."

The place was officially called *The Bathing Annex for Male Labourers and Their Dependents* — which I can only assume was the sad result of trying to name a bathhouse by committee. No one called it that. To us, it was simply *The Whispering Baths*. Not because of anything magical — though the mildew might've gained sentience — but because of the acoustics. Saying sound "carried" doesn't quite cover it. Every whisper, groan, or ill-considered comment bounced off the domed ceiling and pinballed through the steam like a gossip-prone delinquent in a confessional booth with no shame and excellent diction. More than one duel had started outside those stone doors because someone had unburdened a secret along with their grime. If you spoke in the *Whispering Baths*, you had better be open to everyone hearing it — and be ready to fight over it in a towel.

A room that could turn whispers into weapons? Naturally, I adored it.

We paid our entrance fee and were issued our "towels" — and I use that term as generously as the towel itself was stingy. Towels in the sense that they were made of cloth, and were approximately rectangular. Imagine a napkin. Now imagine its smaller, more insecure cousin, freshly laundered on the setting called *spite*. Their size left little of the body to the imagination.

Now, I'm built like a poet in exile. Tragic. Wiry. Ideal for dramatic silhouettes. Brin, on the other hand, is carved. Broad shoulders, muscles upon muscles, a chest you could lose an echo in. He raised the towel, turned it sideways, and gave me a look.

I shrugged. "Think of it more as a concept than a coverage."

Inside, the pools steamed and gurgled, thick with the usual stew of grizzled men, preening showoffs, and the mildly contagious. We found a quiet corner, half-shaded by crumbling tiles and mercy. Brin eased into the water like a wounded boulder trying not to offend the surface. Watching him disappear into the steam — bruised, silent, eyes closed — I let myself believe that he could have a little of what others have every day.

Peace.

Which lasted about as long as my ability to shut up — roughly three minutes.

As we relaxed, my attention landed on a pair of young ladies bathing. One with curling black hair, dark eyes, and skin the colour of roasted honey. The other — petite, graceful, with a wink for a laugh. Both dangerous. Both perfect.

And both eyeing us. Well, more accurately, Brin.

Here's the thing about my hulking friend: Brin could make a nun reconsider her vows just by stretching in the sunlight. He's built like a sculptor got bored of chiselling normal bodies and decided to show off. But put him in front of a pretty girl and he forgets how language works. He couldn't ask a woman for directions to the butcher without breaking into a sweat. But women? Women are attracted to him like tigers to bleeding meat. They circle. They close in. And when they do, Brin, bless him, just freezes — like if he doesn't move, maybe he'll just disappear.

They whispered. Giggled. I caught it all.

"Is that him?"

"Look at those shoulders."

Brin, oblivious, soaked in his bruises and self-pity.

I saw opportunity.

Sliding behind him, just out of the girls' sightline, I dropped my voice to Brin-level gravel.

"Aen," I murmured, "Did you see that black-haired beauty? A moonrise in human form."

Brin cracked one eye. "What?"

"Her smile could light the night sky."

He sat up. "What are you doing?"

"Her laugh makes me believe in joy again."

"What are you —" he looked around and saw the girls. Panicked. Looked at me. Shook his head.

"Don't do this," he whispered. "You *know* I can't talk to girls."

I laughed. "Then let me do the talking."

With Brin's body as the bait, and my words the hook, I reeled them in.

They drifted closer.

Brin's eyes darted, seeking escape. Too late.

Dark-eyes paddled up beside Brin. "Hi," she said, smiling with that dangerous mix of nerves and hope. "We heard you ... and just had to ask. Who were you talking about?"

Brin turned the colour of boiled meat.

"I thought it was really beautiful," she added with a smile.

Brin opened his mouth. Nothing came out. His lips formed vague shapes. Possibly words. More likely distress signals.

I stepped in. "Forgive him. Big heart. Small vocabulary."

The golden-haired one turned to me. "You're funny."

Finally. Taste.

I took her hand gently, like a relic too holy to touch, and said, "That's what I've been trying to tell the clerics for years."

She giggled. Her friend kept her eyes on Brin. "Say something else," she asked softly. "I liked what you said before — it was lovely."

Brin looked at me. *Help. My brain is on fire. The words are gone and I'm dying.*

I nodded encouragingly. "Go on, Brin. Say anything." To the lovely thing in my hand, I added conspiratorially, "He was talking about your friend."

The dark-haired beauty smiled wide. "That was about me?"

She placed her hand — delicate, damp, and absolutely intentional — on his bicep.

"Tell me more," she whispered in his ear.

This was it. I had done it. Stage one: seduction by proxy. Triumph secured.

I wanted Brin to win. Just once. To get something he didn't have to fight for. Something warm. Something kind. And maybe, if I was lucky enough, some of that would fall my way too.

I saw the evening roll out before me like a script the gods left lying around and forgot to bury under ten feet of divine bureaucracy. Brin could say something. Anything. The water's nice. *You* seem nice. What's your name? Maybe smile — that slow, shy one he does that looks like a sunrise trying not to wake anyone. Maybe flex, just a little, purely by accident, of course. Maybe — if the stars aligned and his brain didn't short-circuit — she'd touch his hand, and he'd hold it back, gentle, like it was something sacred. The kind of moment people remember.

And then — well, who knows? Maybe she'd laugh at one of his quiet, nervous jokes. Maybe they'd leave the baths together. Maybe he wouldn't come back to the caravan that night.

And — gods willing — her friend would be curious, bored, and equally generous with her time. I'm nothing if not a supportive wingman. I imagined the four of us, warm from the baths, walking barefoot through the lantern-lit alleys of Dararein, her fingers brushing mine, Brin with a smile he didn't know he could make. For once, a night where neither of us ended up bruised, bloodied, or running from an authority figure with strong opinions on forgery. A night that belonged to us. A small, stupid, beautiful thing we might remember when everything else fell apart.

All Brin had to do was open his mouth.

Instead, his brain quietly resigned.

Panic staged a coup.

And in the absence of leadership, his body made a decision.

Specifically, his legs.

Brin stood.

The towel, alas, did not.

I swear on every minor deity in Tahl'Vareth: time stopped.

Her eyes widened. Mine did too. Golden-hair made a little "oh" with her mouth. Brin let out a breath that might have been a whimper. Or a final prayer.

Their gazes dropped.

Down.

And down.

And stayed down.

Then Brin fled.

Didn't shout. Didn't argue. Just turned and sprinted, wet feet slapping tile, dignity flapping somewhere behind him like a broken flag.

And even in his retreat, his butt—curse him—was magnificent. Sculpted. Heroic. The kind of rear end that makes statues jealous. The kind you could use to start a war or win one.

I sat there, towel intact, dignity questionable, surrounded by the ripples of his departure.

The girls laughed. Oh, how they laughed.

Then they swam away.

Leaving me unclaimed. Untouched.

I sighed and sank lower.

"You think they'll come back?" I asked a passing boy.

He glanced at me. Shook his head. "Not for you."

And as my dreams were washed away, the Baths lived up to their name. A whisper cut through the steam — clear, delighted, and absolutely unholy: "Did you see it?"

Lessons in Dignity (We Failed All of Them)

> *"Easy to cheer when your blood's not on the floor."*
> — *ancient Ruanne proverb.*

Our camp is beautiful. Magical. A little battered around the edges, like a beloved old coat you can throw over your shoulders, wear through a storm, and still come out laughing. Hope stitched to canvas. Music tucked between wagon wheels. Home you can roll up, sling over your shoulder, and carry into the next disaster. Most nights, when the fig trees rustle and the wine blurs our memories soft, it feels safe.

Unless, of course, life happened.

Which, predicably, it had.

Again.

Brin sat slumped, one arm cradling his ribs, a storm of bruises blooming beneath his tunic. His lip was split, his brow swollen, and his right eye was working its way shut. I had a sore back, scraped palms, and a ringing in my ears that made Mero's smug humming sound like distant bees. My pride? Flattened. My brilliant idea had begun with lunch and ended with a public thumping. Mero — of course — looked immaculate. Not a scratch. He even whistled as he counted our "recovered" coin. The bastard.

If you're wondering how a simple check-in at the Hall of Justice led to this tableau of pain, regret, and stolen coin — pull up a chair. I promise poor judgment, daring nonsense, and enough levity to keep us from openly weeping.

The morning began as they often do in our little camp

outside Nareth: damp canvas, stubborn goats, and the smell of last night's wine trying to reclaim its dignity.

A messenger had arrived the previous afternoon — one of the city's scribes, stiff as parchment and exactly as cheerful. He'd announced (in tones normally reserved for death sentences) that Seren would collect me at dawn for my next round of temple apologies.I nodded, smiled, signed whatever scrap of paper he shoved at me — and promptly did nothing about it.

Dawn came. I did not.

Brin had been up for hours by the time I stumbled out of my wagon, blinking against the sun. Probably doing push-ups with boulders for fun. Mero was still cocooned in his blanket, dreaming of unsecured treasures.

Now you'd think Seren's non-appearance would be grounds for celebration.

You'd be right.

Except.

Except for gods-damned oaths.

Even as I lay emerging from what had begun as a pleasantly disordered mind and had now hardened into a dry, aching husk of regret, I felt an unfamiliar tug in my chest. At first, I thought it was the hangover auditioning for a promotion. But no. It was like a conscience — if a conscience had grown fangs, mutated into a goblin, and taken up xylophone lessons on my ribs. And we Ruanne don't grow consciences. We *borrow* them at best. Preferably after heavy bargaining and a refundable deposit.

No matter what I did — staring heroically at a patch of tent canvas until it blinked first, apologizing to the fig tree I'd accidentally kicked yesterday, contemplating whether leftover flatbread could declare national independence — there was that drum, banging away inside me, growing louder and louder, until it sounded suspiciously like Seren herself, ordering me to march my sorry backside into the Hall of Justice before someone else marched it for me.

Also, Seren had made it quite clear — several times and without using small words — that if I failed to comply, I would be bureaucratically drawn and quartered. Which might not have been a metaphor.

I kicked Mero's bedroll until he emerged, squinting like a feral cat dragged into sunlight.

"We're late," I announced.

"For what?" he grumbled.

"Official dignity-loss duty. Get up."

The capital bustled as we trudged in. Cobblestones, street hawkers, and a perfume of meat, sweat, and miracle tonic that smelled like damp horse. The usual.

People stared. They always do. Ruanne don't blend. Loose, colourful clothing, homemade jewellery, the kind of flair that says, "We know exactly how unwelcome we are and have decided to look fantastic anyway." Brin, towering and tattooed, didn't help matters. But we weren't trying to cause trouble — we just weren't willing to vanish.

Seren lived at the Hall of Justice — small private quarters tucked behind the courtrooms — but she worked out of the Archive. Which presented me with a choice.

We could look for her within the four grim towers of the Hall itself — great white slabs of stone, arranged around a courtyard like ancient judges long since fossilized. Just stroll in, announce ourselves, and wait to find out exactly which bland variety of punishment was today's order: death by paperweight, stoning by judicial tablet, or bolted into stocks to recite bad poetry. Slowly. And without expression.

Even I wasn't quite suicidal enough to show up without compulsion.

Which left the Archive. A more cheerful name for a building that looked like someone had weaponized the concept of filing cabinets and then given them a minor in architecture. We'd been once before — during the first stages of my illustrious apology tour — and the memory still itched like a bad sunburn. Still, it beat death-by-Magi-glare.

I steered us across the courtyard, Brin plodding beside me like a wary ox and Mero quietly sketching out a five-point escape plan for when (not if) this all collapsed around us.

The Archive's front loomed ahead — two enormous stone doors, towering twice the height of a man, framed by an arch so heavy with carving and solemn inscriptions it practically sagged under its own righteousness. Script ran over the arch: *KNOWLEDGE IS THE FOUNDATION OF CIVILIZATION.* Which sounded noble until you realized they had forgotten the basic foundation of a door — namely, that it should open.

After a moment of confused loitering, we remembered. The real entry was a small, scuffed door tucked humbly beside the grand monstrosity — no sign, no ceremony, just a weary drip of bureaucrats wafting through like smoke escaping a dying fire.

We filed in behind them, swallowed by the musty hush of the Archive's interior: a sea of parchment-scented gloom, broken only by the dry rustle of dead whispers and the faint suicidal creaking of ancient floorboards.

It took a few minutes of cautious navigation — past rows of scribes hunched like dying spiders over endless scrolls — before we found him.

Master Paperweight. As I had dubbed him in my personal taxonomy of Nareth's more regrettable lifeforms.

Still thin. Still ink-stained. Still radiating the quiet, inevitable despair of someone born to suffer through other people's paperwork until the end of days or until the next public holiday, whichever came last. He looked, if anything, even more like a loaf of bland bread left too long in the sun — only now with the added seasoning of bitter resignation.

His eyes lifted at our approach. Glacially slow. Like two tectonic plates finally giving up and deciding to blink.

"Name and business?" he intoned, like it pained him to acknowledge our continued existence.

I put on my best winning smile. "Aen Marr. Ruanne auxiliary. Seeking audience with Magi Seren Vey."

The quill didn't move. "Magi Vey is not present."

I blinked. "Not present where? Here? Nareth? This plane of existence?"

He blinked once, magnificently unimpressed. "Assigned to external duty. No schedule available. You may requisition an appointment, should you need to appear before her."

He didn't say *don't steal anything while you're loitering,* but I heard it loud and clear.

Mero shifted like a man contemplating larceny purely out

of boredom. Brin grunted—either pleased, disappointed, or confirming he was awake. I, however, did an internal jig. Unsupervised day in the city? Yes, please.

Outside, under the dull noon sky, I turned to the lads. "Seren's off, we're free, and the city awaits. Ideas?"

Brin rolled his shoulders—crack, crack. Stretching or warning. Hard to say.

"We could see where our feet take us," Mero offered. "Visit the market, mingle with the locals, maybe liberate a few unattended valuables." He wiggled his fingers innocently.

I waved it off. "Let's aim higher than petty theft. Something memorable. Or at least mildly chaotic."

I led the way down the street. Brin fell in beside me, the crowd parting like he was an oncoming cart.

"Food first," he rumbled.

Brin always had his priorities straight: food, rest, company. The holy trinity of contentment.

"Food," Mero and I chorused. That, we could afford to agree on. Well—almost. We had a collective coin pouch that could maybe bribe a thirsty dog. Penance had bled my funds dry, and Brin and Mero had been too busy watching my disgrace to earn any coin themselves. Between the three of us, we couldn't afford the promise of lunch.

We followed our noses to the market district, lured by the sizzle of street food. A vendor stood over a grill, skewers sizzling with something that might've once been goat. Or chicken. Possibly rat. With the right spices, who cares? Our mouths watered. Our coin might buy one skewer—if we pooled it and haggled hard.

Then we noticed Mero was gone.

I swear, you can be looking *right at him* and still lose him. One blink and — poof. Gone.

Brin and I exchanged a look and drifted to a shaded corner to wait. We'd learned long ago: when Mero vanishes, you don't chase — just loiter discreetly, preferably out of sight of any nearby guards. Sure enough, less than ten minutes later, he reappeared, crunching an apple like he'd just popped out for groceries. He strolled up and slid a small pouch into my hand. Five silver Nareth marks inside.

I raised an eyebrow. "We should probably eat fast — before someone realizes their purse is missing."

Mero looked affronted. "What do you take me for? Theft is both immoral and terribly risky." He took another bite. "Besides, it was just lying beside a drunk by the fountain. Practically abandoned. I rescued it."

His ethics were, as ever, interpretive. But hunger is clarifying. We had coin. That was enough.

Soon we were perched on a low stone wall overlooking the square, skewers in hand, flatbread in lap, devouring food like it was our first meal in days. For a few moments, we just watched the city exhale beneath the sun.

Here it comes.

Our attempt at flying. Without wings. Without feathers. Possibly with a very hard floor.

My gaze snagged on Nareth's coliseum, squatting across the square like some ancient beast fat with the bones of better men. A flash of inspiration hit — one part brilliance, two parts catastrophic self-sabotage. I glanced at Brin, blissfully chewing, grease on his chin, eyes half-lidded in contentment. Brin, who hadn't lost a fight in years. Sweet, dangerous Brin, who could dismantle a man in less time than it took me to finish a sentence — or apologise for it afterward.

"You know," I began, slipping into my best conspirator's whisper — the kind that meant trouble was not just coming but had already packed a lunch — "there's a way to make more coin than this."

I jingled the pouch of silver for effect. A pitiful sound.

Mero shot me a sideways look — already calculating how many steps it would take to abandon us. "Go on," he said, around a mouthful of bread.

Brin was frowning. Never a great sign.

I pointed toward the coliseum with the grand, sweeping optimism of a man about to lie to himself and his friends. "What if you went big, Brin? You already make a few silvers knocking heads outside the city. But in there?" — I jabbed my finger like I was personally accusing the arena — "that's the real deal. People pay to see blood. Especially when it's not exactly fair."

(If there's anything Ruanne understand, it's surviving unfairness.)

Mero's eyes narrowed. "You mean the arena."

I snapped my fingers. "Exactly! Nareth's legendary coliseum of clobbering! You go in, win a match, we get a cut of the bets. Better yet — if they set the odds against you? And you win?" I grinned wide enough to shame a shark. "We clean up."

Brin stared at the arena across the square, chewing slower and slower, like his jaw was trying to buy him time.

"Not my kind of fighting," he said at last, low and certain.

He wasn't wrong. It was a stupid idea. I should have shut up. Instead—

"You've trained with a sword," I pressed. "You're good. You'd get better training. Maybe even the best." (Even I didn't believe that one.)

Mero shook his head, sharp and quick. "This is insane. Those fighters live for this. They dream of this. Brin could get seriously hurt."

"Fights aren't to the death," I said breezily, the desperation leaking through anyway. "We'd make that clear. First-timer match. No stakes but pride. Pride and possibly a few teeth."

Brin kept staring at the arena. Unmoving. Thinking. That scared me more than shouting would have.

"It's not just the coin," I added, softer now. "It's showing them. These city folk"—I jerked my chin at the square full of people—"who treat us like background noise. Sing for them, cook for them, bleed somewhere else." I swallowed. "But if you step into that pit and win? They'd have to see you."

Brin didn't answer. But he didn't walk away either.

Mero, now doing his best impression of a very tired conscience, tapped his chin. "Couple problems. One: the arena's not exactly a haven of inclusion. They don't let just anyone in. Especially not..."

"...Ruanne," Brin finished.

There it was. The line they never said out loud but always meant.

I held up my hands. "Sure. But the arena master's a businessman. You show him a profit? He'll squint past the tattoos."

Mero waited, praying, I think, for either divine intervention or a massive sinkhole.

Brin sighed. Set down the last of his skewer. Wiped his hands on his trousers. Stood. Towered. And said, in that soft, immovable way that made armies nervous:

"I'll do it."

I blinked once.

Grinned twice.

And immediately began planning our future as Brin's entourage, counting the wagons of gold I was definitely going to mismanage.

Brin stood, rolling his shoulders. He towered over both of us by a head. "We need coin. I'm not afraid to fight. If they'll let me in, I'll prove I belong."

His voice held a quiet resolve I hadn't heard since Dararien. Part of him wanted this — maybe to show them, maybe to show himself.

Suddenly, it wasn't just a joke. Brin wasn't just a brawler from the back alleys. He was the Beast of the Ruanne. If anyone could walk into a pit and walk back out, it was him.

"Then it's settled," I said, leaping down from the wall. "To the arena, gentlemen. Let's make Brin famous."

The Nareth City Arena isn't hard to find — just follow the noise and the faint scent of bloodlust and cheap ale. It rose at the edge of the entertainment quarter, all stone arches and aging banners from tournaments past. Even midday, it bustled with hawkers, gamblers, and retired gladiators bragging to wide-eyed fans.

We pushed into the entrance hall, greeted by the aroma of sweat, metal, and trampled straw. A few workers swept the stands. A bored clerk manned the front desk, mechanically stacking betting slips.

I approached with Brin and Mero at my sides — our usual formation for making trouble.

The clerk, thin and ink-fingered, didn't look up. "Next fights are this evening. Betting opens an hour before."

"Actually, we're here to see the arena master," I said cheerfully. "Holgren, right? Baron of Beatdowns? Emperor of Elbows? I'm fuzzy on the formalities."

That earned a glance. The clerk's eyes traveled over Brin — his bulk, his height, and especially his tattoos. His expression curdled. "Holgren's busy. No petitions today."

I leaned in. "Maybe let him know a promising fighter wants a word." I gestured grandly at Brin. "Trust me — he'll want to see this one throw a punch."

The clerk's lip curled. "We don't take boys off the street. And certainly not — " He paused, eyes flicking back to the ink on Brin's skin. " — not unproven fighters."

Brin's jaw clenched, but he stayed silent. Professional, stoic. Terrifying, if you didn't know him.

I kept it light. "Everyone starts unproven. But come on — nothing sells tickets like an underdog story. The house wins either way."

The clerk sniffed. "We have standards. Licensing. This isn't a back-alley brawl pit."

I resisted pointing out that half their 'licensed' fighters probably came straight from back alleys. "Fine. Tell Holgren we've got a Ruanne fighter willing to take on impossible odds. Two opponents, even. Crowd'll eat it up."

That finally made him blink. "Two at once?"

Brin shot me a look: *Two? Really?*

I gave him a tiny shrug and an even tinier nod. *Trust me.*

"Ruanne are strong, but they're slow," I added, flashing a grin. "Makes things more balanced. And think of the betting frenzy — one man versus two, maybe even three! The house takes a cut either way. Bigger spectacle, bigger profit."

The clerk didn't bite, but he didn't walk away either. He chewed his lip, sighed, and finally muttered, "Wait here."

He slid off his stool and disappeared through a side door.

Mero exhaled. "Bold strategy — promising a gauntlet match. You trying to get Brin killed before he even gets a fanbase?"

His tone was light, but his eyes weren't.

I clapped Brin's arm. "Come on. Look at this thing — bigger than my leg." Which was true. "He can handle a couple of amateurs." I said it for Mero's sake. And mine. "Besides, it's just a pitch. Holgren won't really go full gauntlet... probably."

Brin grunted. "If he does, I'll still stand."

Brave. Or, worse, believing in me.

We waited under the disapproving stares of passing arena staff. After what felt like a week, the side door banged open and out came Holgren himself.

He was everything I'd been warned about: broad, balding, scar down one cheek, and rings on every finger — each likely worth more than my horse (assuming I could afford a horse, which I couldn't). He moved like a man used to yelling orders just to see people scramble. The clerk scurried after him like a nervous dog.

Holgren stopped a few paces away, arms folded. He gave Brin a long, slow look—from face to boots, lingering on the tattoos. His expression didn't move, but the sneer was audible.

"This the Ruanne pup wants to fight?" he said, directing the question at me—as if Brin were a crate of turnips.

I smiled with teeth. "Yes, sir. Brin's strong as they come. Took down half a gang solo." (Okay, it was two guys. And Meroa and I might've helped. But Holgren didn't need the footnotes.) "He'll put on a good show."

Holgren grunted. "Ruanne are tough, I'll grant. Heard you lot wrestle bears for fun."

"Only on weekends," I said. His mouth twitched. Progress.

He circled Brin slowly, like assessing livestock. Brin didn't flinch, didn't speak. Just watched him, calm as a storm cloud.

Holgren came back around. "Problem is, the crowd's jumpy. Some think your kind fights with curses. Or turns into wolves under moonlight." He chuckled, clearly delighted with himself. "Bad for business if people think the match is rigged."

I clenched my jaw, then smiled smooth. "Which is exactly why it'll pack the stands. They'll come to see Brin sprout claws and breathe fire."

Holgren raised an eyebrow, considering.

Holgren rubbed his chin. "And you said he'd take on multiple opponents. Feeling confident, are you?" This time, the question was aimed at Brin.

Brin straightened, rising to full height—taller even than Holgren. "I'll fight whoever you put in front of me." No boast. Just a plain, solid fact. If you didn't know him, you might've heard arrogance. I heard commitment.

Holgren stared for a moment, then barked a laugh. "Gutsy. Alright, Ruanne. You want a stage? You've got one."

My heart did a somersault. It was happening. I tried not to look too shocked. "Excellent! When do we—"

"Follow me," Holgren said, already turning. We trailed him down a corridor into the prep area behind the arena floor: packed dirt underfoot, weapons racked along the walls, a few training dummies with straw spilling from their bellies.

Brin eyed the weapons. Holgren caught it and waved dismissively. "No steel. House rules. First-timers fight with what they bring." He offered a smile with no warmth. "Wouldn't want anyone thinking I allowed a Ruanne to fight with an enchanted blade."

I cleared my throat. "Actually—we should probably set expectations. This isn't a death match. Bare hands, maybe—"

Holgren didn't break stride. He pointed to a side door. "Wait in there. Medic'll check your man, get him ready. We'll draw a decent crowd in a couple hours."

I blinked. "A couple hours? And the training, and the terms we—"

Holgren turned and smiled, all teeth, no mirth. He clapped a heavy hand on Brin's shoulder. Brin didn't flinch, but his jaw tightened.

"You wanted a shot. You've got it. Don't move." He

turned again, barking to his aide about "rounding up the lads."

A door creaked open nearby — just a narrow room with a bench, a basin, and a few pegs on the wall.

I moved to follow, but the clerk slid in front of me with a pleasant smile that somehow made me want to kick his teeth in.

"Only fighters," he said, chipper. "You and the other one can wait here. We'll fetch you when it's time."

My instincts flared. "I'd prefer to stay with my friend."

The clerk raised a hand. "Procedure."

Something was off.

"Holgren didn't answer my question," I said. "We're not staying if Brin's bare-handed and they're swinging swords."

The clerk offered a syrupy smile. "Of course. No real weapons. We'll take good care of him."

Brin, catching the stall, turned at the doorway. "It's fine, Aen. I can wait."

I didn't like it. But he gave me a nod — the kind that said *let it go for now.* He didn't sense danger, or at least thought the odds were still worth it.

Reluctantly, I stepped back. "We'll be just outside if you need anything." It sounded silly. What was I going to do, yell through the walls?

Brin ducked inside. The door closed. A lock clicked.

A lock.

I exchanged a glance with Mero. He caught it too.

The clerk nodded once, then vanished after his boss. Mero

and I were left in the prep area, alone.

"They locked him in," I muttered.

Mero's usual smirk had vanished. His eyes were cold. "Yeah. They did. That's not normal."

"Maybe they're worried he'll bolt?"

"Brin's not a runner."

No. More likely, they didn't want us poking around — or listening too closely.

I started pacing.

Mero tilted his head toward the corridor Holgren had taken. "I'll go snoop."

"I'm coming — "

He cut me off with a hand. "No. You stay. If they open that door early, Brin might need you."

I hated that he was right. Mero moved like smoke in the dark. I moved like someone being chased by a drumline.

"Be careful," I said.

He grinned. "Always." And slipped away, quiet as breath.

So there I was. Alone in a half-empty prep corridor. Brin locked in a closet. Mero off on a stealth mission. Perfect. Definitely not ominous at all.

I leaned toward the door. "Everything alright in there?"

"Fine," Brin replied. A pause. Then, more quietly: "You sure about this, Aen?"

Guilt tightened in my chest. But I made my voice bright. "Trust me. You'll be brilliant. The crowd'll go wild. We'll be rich and slightly famous before sunset."

He didn't answer. Which meant he didn't believe me. Or

worse — he did.

I could picture him on the bench, still as stone, chewing over every bad look, every closed door. Brin never said much about it, but I knew the sting. Knew how much it cost him, pretending it didn't matter. Maybe — just maybe — a win here would change something. Earn him a shred of the respect he deserved. Or at least make someone think twice before looking down their nose.

Footsteps echoed.

I straightened as Holgren's voice boomed down the corridor: "Alright, bring them in!"

Rough laughter followed. Never a good sign.

The far prep door burst open. Holgren strode in, flanked by three gladiators. No steel, but no doubt what they were — bare-chested, scarred, arms thick as fenceposts. One carried a wooden practice sword.

Holgren didn't look at me. He barked over his shoulder, "Secure the exits. No interruptions."

Two guards in leather stepped into position at the main doors, casual but firm.

The prep area suddenly felt smaller. And very, very private.

This might be a good time to mention that in some places in Tahl'Vareth, it's not against the law to kill a Ruanne. I'm not making this up.

"Hey!" I said, stepping forward, hands up. "I thought this was scheduled for later?"

Holgren finally turned. His earlier smirk was gone — replaced with flat contempt. "Change of plans. We don't put animals on the main stage. But don't worry — you'll still get your show."

He waved toward Brin's door.

One of the gladiators threw it open.

Brin barely had time to rise before all three men crowded into the small room, cutting off my view.

It happened fast. Holgren threw out an arm, blocking me as I stepped forward. Rage flared up fast—white hot.

"You snake," I spat. "That wasn't the deal."

Holgren looked down at me, entirely unmoved. "Deal's changed. You lot need reminding where you stand. No one embarrasses Holgren in his own house."

Inside the room, I heard the thud of movement. A grunt—Brin, sizing up the ambush.

Holgren raised his voice. "You wanted a fight, Ruanne? Let's see if you can take one."

The first attacker lunged.

Damn it. This wasn't a match. This was a message. And the message was: *Know your place, Ruanne.*

My brain spun uselessly. I had nothing but my mouth, and that only made things worse half the time.

I couldn't charge in— because then Brin would have had to protect *me*.

Holgren stood between us, arm outstretched, watching the chaos with the casual amusement of someone inspecting livestock.

Inside the room: movement, thuds, a shout. I edged sideways to peer around Holgren.

Brin was already in motion—fast, brutal, efficient. One of the thugs was on the ground, clutching a bloody nose and making wounded dog noises. The other two circled, smarter now.

Brin swung at one, who ducked. The third came from behind, jabbing with a wooden sword. Brin took it in the side, grunted, and kicked backward — caught the man in the knee. That earned a yelp.

"That's it, Brin!" I shouted, which earned me a shove from Holgren's massive forearm.

"Shut it, runt," he growled.

I lost my temper and took a wild swing. Clipped his ear.

He blinked, then laughed. "Sit down before you get hurt."

He caught my wrist, twisted, and dropped me like a sack of laundry. I landed hard. The world spun for a second.

Inside the room, Brin threw one of them into a wall. Two down? Maybe. But he was slowing. Breath ragged.

The third fighter circled wide, then slammed a wooden blade across Brin's skull. I shouted — too late. Brin dropped to one knee.

That did it. I charged — no plan, just fury.

Holgren was faster than he looked. He grabbed the back of my tunic and hauled me off my feet.

"Watch," he hissed, slamming me against the wall like a schoolteacher correcting a particularly loud desk. "This is what happens when scum forgets its place."

I struggled, but he pinned me there — watching as the beating continued.

Brin, still on one knee, swung wide — but he was moving slower now, like the whole room had turned to sludge.

The last standing fighter slipped in and cracked a wooden blade across Brin's arm. It dropped limp. Another hit to the gut bent him double.

The first two were back up—one limping, one still bleeding. They grabbed his arms, yanked them behind him. One took the opportunity to punch Brin square in the face.

I shouted something incoherent. Brin sagged, blood trickling from his brow—but he didn't make a sound.

Then they started dragging it out. A show beating. A lesson.

Holgren finally let go of me and stepped into the room.

He raised a hand. The fighters froze, holding Brin kneeling between them.

Holgren surveyed the damage like a craftsman inspecting a flawed product. "Stupid Ruanne," he muttered. "You think I'd let you sully my arena? You're not entertainment. You're a warning."

He nodded to the thugs. "Toss him. The rest too."

They hauled Brin out. I moved to follow, but one of the guards stepped in, spear angled just enough to make a point. I froze.

The gladiators dragged Brin across the prep area, toward a back door now standing open. Sunlight streamed in like nothing was wrong.

I followed close, fists clenched and useless.

They swung Brin once, twice, and flung him into the alley beyond. He hit the dirt hard and let out a sharp exhale.

I was beside him in an instant.

Holgren lingered just long enough to loom in the doorway. "Next time I see any of you here, you won't be walking out." Then the door slammed shut behind him, sealing the stink of that place inside.

For a moment, all I could hear was our breathing. And beyond that — the market, the city, oblivious.

I touched Brin's shoulder, my hands shaking. "Brin. Talk to me."

He coughed and rolled onto his back with a wince. "Feel like I got trampled by a war mammoth," he croaked. Then — somehow — a crooked smile. "But I'm here."

Relief washed over me, chased quickly by self-loathing. This had been my idea. My brilliant, lunchtime brainwave. I bit back the apology clawing its way up — Brin didn't want it. Not yet.

Instead, I helped him sit up. "Easy now. Let's see..."

Bumps and bruises everywhere. Lump on his head, cut above the eye, arms and ribs a mess of swelling. Split lip. Nothing obviously broken. Probably. Hopefully.

Brin noticed my scowl. "Don't blame yourself," he muttered, reading my thoughts like a map.

I barked a bitter laugh. "Sure. I only led you into catastrophe, with a side order of sadism. Why should I feel bad?"

He reached out and gave my shoulder a squeeze — firm, grounding. "We all agreed. I chose to fight." His voice cracked a little. "But this... just a joke to them."

I blinked hard and forced a smile. He didn't need to see pity.

"Well, if it's any comfort," I said, voice rough, "I think you broke two of them. The one with the nose? Might actually look better now."

Brin chuckled — then winced and clutched his ribs. "Don't

make me laugh."

"Laughter's the only medicine I'm licensed to administer."

A shadow fell over us. I tensed—then relaxed as Mero stepped into view, expression flickering between concern and outrage.

"You two look... awful," he said, tone light but tight. "I was almost halfway through planning a rescue when I saw them toss you out."

I helped Brin lean back against the wall. "Stellar timing," I muttered—more sharply than intended.

Mero opened his mouth, thought better of it, and instead held up a leather pouch. He gave it a shake. It clinked.

"Thought I'd salvage *something*," he said. "Lifted it off Holgren while he was busy playing tyrant."

My eyes widened. "You what?"

Mero shrugged, smirking. "The man was distracted. And frankly, he owed us a payout for Brin's fight."

He tossed me the pouch. I caught it—and nearly dropped it. Heavy.

Brin managed a weary grin. "Little thief," he muttered fondly.

I peeked inside: gold and silver, a glittering mess of it. More than we'd seen in months. I let out a low whistle. Leave it to Mero to turn disaster into profit.

"Well, I'll be damned," I breathed. "Holgren pays himself well."

Mero cracked his knuckles. "I might've helped myself to the arena's cashbox on the way out."

For a moment, I could only stare. Then a laugh bubbled

up—sharp, bright, and unexpected. We got the coin after all. Just... not quite the way I'd planned.

Brin chuckled too—then winced, pressing a hand to his ribs. "Careful. They'll be after us for trespassing *and* theft."

"We were invited until they changed the deal," I said, putting on my best innocent face. "Call it compensation for injuries and emotional distress."

I helped Brin up. He swayed once, then set his feet and shrugged me off with a nod. Stubborn as sunrise. "We should move," he said. "Before Holgren checks his pockets."

The three of us limped down the alley—bruised, battered, but intact. Brin refused help after the first few steps, though I hovered anyway. Guilt and loyalty make terrible travel companions.

"Next time," Mero said dryly, "let's just get lunch and take a nap."

I snorted. "Where's the fun in that? No bruises, no stolen fortunes, no gladiatorial betrayal. Just boring relaxation."

We emerged onto a bustling street and melted into the crowd as best we could—three very sore Ruanne with one very heavy secret. People stared, but Nareth had seen stranger things.

The adrenaline was fading, and pain was setting in—every place Holgren had introduced me to a wall. Still, we moved, one step at a time, toward the city gates. Toward home.

As we walked, I cleared my throat. "Brin... I'm sor—"

He cut me off by slinging an arm over my shoulders and yanking me into a half-suffocating hug—an *I'm-not-crying-you're-crying* embrace from a battered bear. "Stop.

You meant well. We tried. It went wrong." He let me go with a nod—almost a bow. "Thanks for standing with me."

That nearly broke me. He was thanking me. *Me.*

I swallowed hard. "Always, brother."

Mero drifted to Brin's other side, patting his back gently. "Besides, we're rich fools now. Upgrade."

Brin smiled—bloodied lip and all. "Nema's going to be suspicious when we start eating twice a day."

I grinned. "We'll tell her we bet on a knife-fighting urchin."

It was a terrible lie. But we'd come up with something better later.

For now, we had coin in our pockets, a half-decent story, and each other.

In my book, that counts as a win.

Where the Ruanne Dance, Trouble Follows

You recall how, after Brin subjected himself to a gauntlet of gladiators — and, against all sense, probability, and the laws of natural decency, emerged victorious? How I also helped at a key moment, heroically and with impeccable timing? And how the King of Nareth himself (I think Nareth has a king. Or maybe it's a Master Bean Counter. Anyway — that guy!) showered us with riches, crowning us the glorious conquerors of the day?

It just happened.

Surely, you've not forgotten already.

I know we said we'd hide it from Nema. We did not plan to get caught. Made promises to lie well, to hoard the gold to ourselves. But gold in the hands of teenage Ruanne slips through the fingers like hot goats through a busted fence during courting season. (Or something. I'm still workshopping the metaphor.)

The point is: we were rich.

Loaded with gold like desert sultans after a particularly fruitful festival of miscalculation.

And we would not spend frugally. We would not save prudently. We would not, under any circumstances, exercise restraint. No — we spent lavishly, immediately, competitively.

Mero and I accidentally fell into a contest — as we do about everything — to see who could spend the fastest and most awesomely. It escalated. Rapidly. Heroically. Disastrously.

Until Nema caught on. Which took about a day.

Also, I might have told the story to the entire Family. Dramatically. With embellishments. Possibly including sound effects.

Anyway.

After *The Great Arena Escapade* — as it became immortalized in song, story, and several inaccurate murals — the Family was rich. Not just *in spirit*, mind you. Actually rich.

Ish.

Now, the Ruanne, if you don't know, have a particular philosophy about good fortune: If life hands you a feast, you eat until your ribs creak and your neighbours start taking bets on when you'll pop. Saving for tomorrow? Suspicious behaviour. Only fools believe tomorrow won't have its own miracles (or disasters — but miracles are more fun to plan for).

So we partied.

We feasted.

There was bread for everyone. New pots. New spoons. A wagon wheel — an extravagance! And mounds of coloured cloth for reasons no one could adequately explain but everyone agreed were urgent and necessary.

And then — as fast as it had come — the time of arena gold was gone. Replaced by the soft, throbbing headaches of arena gold hangovers. Because while we had been dancing, and eating, and buying hats shaped like animals (a necessary investment, by the way), no one had been making any actual money.

So.

Broke.

Now, there's broke, and then there's Ruanne broke.

Broke is when you tighten your belt and start eying your neighbour's goat like it's a particularly juicy roast dinner.

Ruanne broke is when you've eaten all your belts, all your goats, and most of your neighbours, and start wondering if dust might be edible if you add enough salt and lower your standards. Tempers frayed.

Boots wore thin.

The last of the lentils sprouted weevils — and then the weevils, being discerning creatures, packed up and moved somewhere better.

On top of which, the good folk of Nareth — who had once flooded to our camp for cultural immersion and a lively freak show (either of which we could serve up in generous measure) — had slowed to a trickle. Perhaps the temples and the merchant guilds, jealous of our success, had entered into a grand conspiracy to keep customers away. Perhaps it had simply gotten too hot, too dusty, too inconvenient to seek out the Ruanne's ramshackle splendour. Or possibly — and I say this with all due humility — it was because we had very little to offer beyond cobbled-together junk and semi-consensual theft.

Whatever the reason, by any objective measure, it was bad. And when things get bad — truly, spectacularly bad — someone needs to do something spectacularly stupid.

Naturally, I volunteered.

If the good citizens of Nareth were unwilling or unable to come to us, then clearly — *clearly* — it was time for us to go to them. There were markets. There was space. All we needed was a little ambition, a few rickety carts, and the ability to squint at broken junk until it looked like exotic treasure. We would descend upon the city with all the glory and salesmanship of a migrating swarm of peddlers. Better yet, it would be honest work.

Ish.

Of course, our people might work the crowd a little. Smile, flatter, perform minor miracles of persuasion. But our merchant carts would offer spectacular treasures from distant lands — once we assembled them, labelled them creatively, and convinced buyers of their obvious worth. We would entice. We would haggle. We would charm silver from the pockets of the skeptical and the sentimental alike. We would make an honest day's coin, just like every other corrupt merchant in Nareth.

Simple. Genius, even.

I set about taking inventory of our prospective "luxury goods." The offerings of the Family, curated by yours truly, included:

Blacksmithing work: pots and pans hammered from salvaged scrap, slightly uneven but undeniably serviceable.

Basket weaving: a flourishing craft among our younger cousins, producing baskets in vibrant lopsided shapes that no two gods could agree on.

Colourful clothing: vivid stitched-together strips of cloth, forming garments so bright they could blind a man at twenty paces.

Carved trinkets: small animals and figures whittled from bone, wood, or occasionally, stubbornly magical roots that hummed faintly if you licked them. (I advised against advertising that feature.)

Musical performances: drums, pipes, and dancing—loud enough to wake the market square and bold enough to offend the local priests.

Fortunes told: sometimes even accurately, if Macha Mevin's cats agreed to cooperate.

In short, cultural marvels, each and every one.

Now, the small obstacle remained of convincing the Family that this was a good idea. I gave a rousing speech by the firepit—complete with grand gestures, impassioned appeals to tradition, and wild promises about how many pots of stew we'd be able to afford once we dominated the Nareth market scene.

There were doubts. There was heckling. Someone threw a spoon.

But momentum was on my side. Hunger is a persuasive god.

Even Nema, whose patience for my schemes could usually be measured in grains of sand, found herself reluctantly persuaded. Not by my speech, obviously. By necessity. She warned me, as she always did, that the city was not our home, that the law would not be kind to loud, bright, inconvenient Ruanne. That our welcome was thinner than a cartwheel after a bad winter.

I told her—hand over heart, solemn as a priest (though being careful to avoid anything that could be perceived by the gods to be an oath)— that we would be *discreet.* That we would be *careful.* That no trouble would follow us home.

And so, with the full—or at least reluctant—blessing of the Family, the *Ruanne Market Collective* was born. And Nareth, poor unsuspecting city, would soon learn what happened when desperate genius met a public thoroughfare.

The sun was already climbing toward its vicious noon perch by the time we descended on Nareth's Lower Market—a sprawling half-mad tangle of smells, shouting, and stubbornness, set just inside the crumbling south gate. It wasn't the posh part of the city, where silk merchants and jewelers gleamed under awnings embroidered with gold thread. It was the people's market—the honest, grimy, glorious heart where butchers, potters, weavers, tanners, tinkers, swindlers, bakers, drunks, and the occasional missionary all smashed together in noisy, fragrant harmony.

We smashed in. Joyfully.

I had selected our beachhead carefully: an open wedge of space near the broken well at the east end of the square. Technically, the space was "common ground," meant for temporary vendors and public entertainments. In practice, it was a no-man's-land—a place the regular merchants sneered at and occasionally tossed buckets of dishwater into.

Perfect.

Within minutes, we turned that scrap of dust and sun-baked stone into a festival.

Jorann's battered wagon groaned open to reveal pots polished within an inch of their battered lives. Maja's grandsons arranged crooked baskets with solemn pomp. Rue and Sila hung a riot of patchwork cloth like a festival had collided with a paint merchant. Omri bellowed songs to scandalized matrons while Kes baited customers with fortunes, real or invented. Children swarmed, selling invisible goats and fictional miracles. It was chaos, it was beauty, it was the Ruanne.

The city merchants, grim and permanent behind their shaded booths, watched us with the same expression you might give a slowly approaching flood.

Our bright tents strained against the invisible borders of "where you should be" and surged outward, creeping into better, richer territory—elbowing into the cleaner flagstones, the shadier spots, the well-trafficked thoroughfares. Not by force. By charm. By chaos. And by sheer, blinding Ruanne-ness. Our musicians were louder. Our fabrics were brighter. Our children were more persistent, our laughter more shameless, our bargains more bewilderingly compelling.

The city merchants noticed. Their gazes grew heavier, their hands a little tighter on scales and purses. No words yet. Just the tightening of air before a thunderstorm.

Where the regular merchants haggled grimly over the price of onions, Macha Mevin's middle boy was juggling handwoven baskets for an appreciative crowd. Where official vendors mumbled behind counters, Sada was giving five-minute futures for a copper and a whispered prayer.

I—naturally—presided over it all. Master of Operations. Commander of Markets. General of Joy. I directed wagon placement with sweeping gestures. I assigned bards to corners like a battlefield captain deploying artillery. I plucked grubby children from underfoot, dusted them off, handed them scraps of painted cloth, and sent them back into the fray with renewed mission.

And soon, the Lower Market belonged not to Nareth, not to the guilds, not even to the gods— —but to the Ruanne.

Coins started to clink into our hands. Crowds thickened,

drawn by colour, music, and the irresistible gravitational pull of a people who had long ago decided that if you can't outrun your troubles, you might as well dance them into confusion.

It was glorious.

Now, let's just stop here for a moment.

The action is frozen: The Ruanne market blazing like a bonfire — music, laughter, bright fabric snapping in the lazy, dust-choked wind. Children wild, arms full of bright scraps and half-sold trinkets, darting between customers, wagons, and wary goats. Macha Mevin's youngest had somehow acquired a rooster and was mid-auction to an increasingly agitated crowd. ("Goes to the highest bidder! Also bites!"). Tovi and Mira Estrel, solemn-faced as priests, haggling mercilessly over a pile of baskets with a harassed-looking potter. Omri Nuvra serenading a group of matrons near the bread stalls, his battered lute barely audible over the shrill whistle of his enthusiasm.

Even those of us with a more *entrepreneurial approach* weren't hurting anyone. Nobody was getting cheated who didn't deserve it.

I caught sight of Mero once or twice in the crowd — drifting casual as smoke, brushing elbows, offering distracted apologies. He wasn't lifting much. Small things. Purses that hung too loose. Bracelets that had already given up hope.

Harmless, by Ruanne standards.

This story should not end in disaster. But of course, it does.

At first, the heat was the only warning.

The sun, already high, grew heavier—a thick, leaden weight pressing down on the square. The dust rose slower now, clinging to sweat and cloth. The smell of spice, old leather, and ambition thickened into a soup you could almost chew. But the market's mood was shifting. You could feel it if you listened hard enough—under the laughter, under the songs. A tightening. The old merchants, solid and scowling behind their permanent stalls, watched us with narrowed eyes. Their hands clenched harder on their scales, their wares, their purses. Whispers flitted back and forth like gnats under a winter blanke. Not loudly. Not officially. Just enough.

The guards began to prowl—not pushing yet, not shouting. Just watching. Counting. The way butchers eye stock before a slaughter.

A guard noted Rue's bright cloth banners sagging a little too far into neighbouring stalls—and Tovi and Mira's baskets spilled too freely into the thoroughfares. Random Ruanne were told that their children (not bothering to check if they were related) were laughing too loud, too long.

They caught little Kirel slipping a handful of coins from a merchant's distracted pocket. Though, to be fair, he *did* flash a charming smile afterward, which I thought showed excellent manners.

No charges. No steel. But the weight of the guards' gaze—heavy, official, patient—settled over the square like a slow-growing stormcloud.

I noticed, of course.

You don't grow up Ruanne without learning to smell trouble the way other people smell rain. I clocked the guards. Noted the merchants' mutters. Heard how the clinking of coin had turned defensive.

But what could I do?

We were flourishing. The Family was laughing. Eating. *Living*.

And the people of Nareth loved us.

Needed us.

Surely, the good we were doing would buy us a pass. Just for a day.

First, a flicker of black robes. Then the sinking certainty.

Seren.

She moved through the crowd like a blade — untouched, unstoppable. And worse: she was coming straight for us.

Her black robes were crisp despite the heat, her posture infuriatingly upright. She threaded through the crowd with that solemn, unstoppable grace the Oathbound seemed to cultivate, parting vendors and gawkers alike without touching a soul.

Then her gaze caught the edge of Rue's cloth stall — the banners sagging too far into the next merchant's shade — and followed the spill outward, tracing the bright, messy tide of Ruanne occupation.

She didn't blink. Didn't sigh. Just adjusted the angle of her steps and walked straight into the heart of the chaos.

Professional horror first. That much was clear.

Her jaw tightened almost imperceptibly. Her gloved hand hovered briefly at the fold of her sleeve, where the formal charges and writs were usually tucked. Her entire posture screamed *infraction detected, prepare containment measures.*

And then—gods help me—she saw me.

I was, of course, standing in the thick of it. Hands on hips. Cloak artfully flared. Smiling the triumphant, idiot grin of a man presiding over a masterpiece.

Our eyes met across the square.

Professional horror twisted, softened into something worse.

Personal horror.

In my defense, I wasn't running a con. I wasn't pocketing coins or slipping knives. I was trying. Trying to pull my people a little closer to safety, one chaotic festival day at a time.

Be that as it may, she changed direction immediately, cutting through the crowd with a speed that made the guards look like they were wading through mud.

She reached me at the precise moment little Kirel barreled between us, clutching a fistful of pilfered apples and laughing like a victorious godling. A nearby merchant shouted. A guard turned.

Seren didn't flinch. She just tilted her head at me, very slightly, and murmured from the side of her mouth.

"You need to stop this. Now."

I swallowed hard. Smiled, because what else could I do?

"We're thriving," I said. "Loudly."

"Thriving is not a defence," she said. "You're obstructing trade. Inciting disorder."

"Celebrating commerce," I corrected. "Promoting local vibrancy."

She stared at me with that flat, patient look bureaucrats

reserve for repeat offenders.

Then, low and fast, voice all iron and panic beneath the professional calm, she said, "The guards are circling. The merchants are calling for enforcement. If this escalates, I can't shield you."

I shrugged, trying for casual and missing.

"It's honest work," I said. "Mostly."

Her expression flickered — the tiniest crack in the mask.

And then came the moment.

She hesitated — the barest flicker — and then asked, low and raw: *"Is this... your doing?"*

Not an accusation.

A question from someone who already knew the answer — and didn't want it.

Now, the obvious answer to that specific question is, "No."

What? Me? No! I was just passing through. I don't even know these people. How could you —

The lie was on my teeth before I could think.

But there it stopped. Stuck like thorns in my throat. That awful noise was coming out of my mouth again. The one that was all vowels and a giant red flag: *Liar! Liar!*

The oath held me — binding my words to only truth whether I liked it or not.

And so, after a heartbeat of struggle, I exhaled and said — honestly, hopelessly:

"Yes."

For the briefest instant, she looked almost hurt.

Before either of us could say anything else, a sharp voice rang out.

"Magi!"

One of the senior guards was bearing down, scroll in hand, official seal dangling like an executioner's axe.

Trouble was no longer creeping.

It was here.

The senior guard approached at a brisk, unpleasant clip, his tabard straining against the generous outlines of a man who liked his ale more than his paperwork. In his hand, the scroll bobbed and jerked — a fat, official document, red-ribboned and heavy with bureaucratic menace. The city's laws were like that: clumsy when they wanted to be, cruel when they needed to be.

"Magi," the guard said, sketching a bow so shallow it barely qualified as mockery. "I request official sanction to clear unauthorized vendors under Section Twenty-Three, Subclause Nine, on grounds of market disruption and unlicensed assembly."

Seren didn't so much as blink.

Her hands folded calmly at her waist. Her expression remained the serene, soul-crushing neutrality of the bureaucratic elite. Only the faintest tightening around her mouth betrayed her.

"Present your grounds," she said coolly.

The guard thrust the scroll forward.

"Obstruction of trade. Disturbance of peace. Improper occupation of public grounds. Minor thefts. Unauthorized musical performance."

I couldn't help it. "The authorized musical performancers

couldn't make it."

I beamed.

Seren's look stabbed me in the face.

I stopped beaming and became very conscientious.

She took the scroll, scanned it, then lifted her head.

"Incorrect filing," she said.

The guard frowned. "Begging your pardon, Magi, but —"

"You have filed for *expulsion* under Subclause Nine," she said. "Expulsion requires prior warning issued by a magistrate and recorded acknowledgment by the offending parties. You have neither."

The guard shifted, mouth working like a man trying to chew his own embarrassment.

"This... gathering," he tried, "was clearly unauthorized —"

"This," Seren interrupted, her voice cutting across the square like a knife through cloth, "falls under Market Demonstration Clause Twelve."

Several guards and merchants murmured, confused. So did I.

Seren didn't flinch. Didn't even breathe differently.

"During the month of fasting, worship, service, and pilgrimage of the western faiths, and for thirty days thereafter," she recited, voice flat and inevitable as law itself, "temporary market demonstrations may be authorized at magi discretion without prior permit requirements."

She folded the scroll with crisp finality and handed it back.

"I authorize this gathering," she said. "One day only.

Fines to be limited to minor disturbance penalties, to be assessed at close of market."

The guard's face flushed red to the roots of his thinning hair.

"Magi," he hissed under his breath. "This is highly irregular."

"Submit your complaints to the Hall of Justice," Seren said, turning away, already dismissing him from existence.

It was done.

We would not be arrested. We would not be flogged, fined, or hauled before a tribunal.

There would be minor penalties, yes. Coin lost. Pride bruised.

But the Family — my Family — would walk out of this mess upright.

At a cost.

I caught a glimpse of Seren's face — and saw it.

The weight she carried for us, the cost carved into the lines of her mouth.

She had bought us a day of freedom.

And chipped a piece off her soul to pay for it.

I wanted to say something.

I'll learn from this. I'll change my ways.

But the words stuck — not because of the oath, but because we both knew:

I wouldn't.

The Holy Soap Rebellion

"So I was thinking," I said—because thinking was clearly where everything went wrong—"if we divided the apology into four parts and all started at once, we'd finish in a quarter of the time."

Seren led the march toward the Temple of the Sacred Ablution, second stop on my world-famous repentance tour. Her pace hovered somewhere between *'urgent'* and *'vengeance is nigh'*. My feet weren't sure if we were walking or fleeing.

"Add a little music. Call it a quartet. We might even make some honest coin."

That morning, our constipated stormcloud arrived before breakfast.

Breakfast in the Ruanne camp is usually a spirited affair: spiced lentils, shouted insults, and enough flatbread to tile a small roof. Jorann, who handled cooking, could take ingredients that hated each other and arrange food marriages so beautiful they made other foods believe in love. He looked like an ogre but was gentle as a lamb—unless you wasted food. Then he'd rip off your arms. And add them to your next meal.

We were in the middle of a highly strategic argument about who'd stolen the last of the honey when hoofbeats announced doom.

Seren rode in on her black horse—Monarch of

Calamities — a creature so brooding, graveyards looked festive by comparison. Her robes snapped in the dust. Monarch, for his part, surveyed the camp like he was drafting a formal list of grievances.

She dismounted in one smooth motion and planted herself by the table, arms crossed, radiating disapproval — of our banter, our mess, our collective attire, and anything else that didn't involve deadlines or consequences.

Nema, serene behind her tea, offered sweetly, "Join us for breakfast, dear?"

Seren responded like a trebuchet flinging a dead horse over ramparts: "We have a schedule."

I offered her wine from my skin and suggested we review the schedule over a drink. It was barely past dawn. The sun hadn't even rubbed the sleep from its eyes yet.

She turned to me like I'd suggested we bathe in goat's blood. "We leave in five minutes. Be ready."

She didn't tap her foot. She didn't need to — her silence drummed time into our skulls.

When that got boring, I kissed Nema, kissed Jorann for good measure, and sauntered toward Seren with a wink. "Well, we better get going."

A pause. A stare. I looked innocent. She looked constipated.

"Get your robe. And the coin."

I tapped my forehead. "Oh, my gods. I forgot to tell you. Eeoaieiay —"

"Aoeeiaauu —"

I sighed.

Muttering, "I'll get them," I returned a minute later with

the penitential robe, twelve Geth-Harramian silver crowns, four copper, and a deep loathing for oath magic.

Still smarting from the previous tour's public humiliation, I generously suggested that Brin and Mero weren't technically required.

Brin ignored me and grabbed a dozen flatbreads to go.

"We wouldn't miss it," Mero said, falling into step. "Maybe they'll burn you alive this time."

The Temple of the Sacred Ablution

(*Yes, again.*)

Nareth has many wonders. This is not one of them.

A giant circular temple lurked in the lower tier of the city, wedged between a refuse canal and an extremely vocal tannery. The surrounding streets smelled of damp rope, mouldy bread, and despairing wine. The temple was a water-obsessed monolith — ringed with a moat, frothing fountains, and grotesques that spouted water from orifices best left undescribed. None of it was clean.

Father Bouwt waited at the entrance, watching me with greasy anticipation and the smugness of a man who'd written *"see me after class"* one too many times.

I attempted to forget the hirsute robe. Without success.

Inside, we were hit by a waft of humid filth that felt like being slapped by a decomposing tongue. The temple was built in concentric circles — holy pools nested within holier pools. Each bath housed partially submerged believers, bobbing in meditative marinade. The deeper we went, the worse it got. The pools thickened. The air stagnated. The smell... dear gods, the smell. It stopped being a smell; it became a houseguest who shared offensive opinions and insisted on touching you.

At the very centre, in the sanctum where even angels would fear to tread, we arrived at the holiest of holes. It resembled a soup of black eels and pureed cabbage. It gurgled, ominous and unrepentant.

Floating in its depths was the high priest himself — an enormously swollen creature who had transcended hygiene, reason, and most human dignity. He lay there like a holy walrus, his considerable hair floating gently around him like a deranged halo.

"Pilgrims," he rasped. "Welcome to the Seat of Cleansing."

Brin turned visibly green.

Mero stumbled behind a pillar and offered his last meal to the gods.

My eyes watered. "A pleasure," I lied.

The basin blurped solemnly. Either it or the priest was pleased.

"In the ancient rite," he intoned, "we cleanse not only body, but burden. Each possession must be cleansed of sin. Cast them into the Basin of Benediction and let them be baptized."

Seren gave me a nudge that said: *Do it, or I'll drown you myself.*

I stepped forward, drew the silver crowns and copper, and — trying very hard not to pass out — cast them into the pool. They sank without a sound. I'm not entirely convinced they weren't dissolved.

I silently wished for a prophet to arise and preach a gospel of soap.

"Now," Seren commanded, "the apology." She breathed through her teeth. "You may abbreviate."

I cleared my throat. Lifted the scroll dramatically. And then —

— it slipped.

A collective gasp.

For a moment, it floated like a dove. Then — delicately — it settled into the Basin, and disappeared from sight.

Pause.

Then —

A fountain of outrage burst forth.

"A HUNDRED YEARS!" the high priest howled. "A hundred years of holy filtrate! Pilgrim offerings! Sacred particulates! Baptized broth! And now — corrupted!"

Bouwt dropped to his knees beside the basin, wailing and clutching at invisible spirits.

The high priest flailed, sending tsunamis of benediction across the tiles. Acolytes went down like wheat before a scythe: one plowed into a pillar; another vanished into a lower pool with a greasy splash.

Mero yelped as a flying prayer bowl clipped his ear.

Brin, flatbreads held aloft like sacred relics, pirouetted around a tidal wave of sanctified slime.

Seren stood rigid as a statue while holy sludge christened her robes.

The high priest emerged, clutching the scroll — now blank as his expression. He wept. Silent, disbelieving, horrified tears.

I gingerly retrieved the scroll. "Maybe we keep this

incident to ourselves?"

He fixed me with a watery stare. "We cannot lie to the divine essence! The Waters of Life see all!"

"It was just one moment—"

"You cannot fathom it, heretic! This basin is a gateway to transcendence! Touched only by the pure of heart, clean of sin—"

'Clean' is doing a lot of work in that sentence, I thought.

Aloud, I said, "The scroll wasn't mine. It's the Magi's. She's pure of stain. Her stinks don't even stink."

The priest paused. Peered at Seren. Considered. Shook his head sadly. "She's not of the faith."

I felt brilliance blooming in my skull. Mero saw the look on my face and muttered, "Oh no. We're doomed."

"What if..." I said, "she was baptized into the faith?"

Seren's eyes snapped to me, and then to the basin. "Absolutely not."

I ignored her. "What if the Magi became a believer? Even a rough one. Then the taint—of the incident, not her personally—might be lessened? Transcendence... preserved?"

The Walrus considered. Nodded.

Seren looked at me like she was debating which bone to break first.

Father Bouwt had already produced extra prayer beads and was muttering about contingency rites.

I smiled at Seren and shrugged. "I mean, it's a solution."

We left the temple at a brisk pace.

And by "we," I mean Seren stormed ahead, dripping sanctity and mortification in equal measure, while the rest of us trailed behind like guilty acolytes caught sneaking wine.

Her hood hung limp down her back, plastered to her scalp with holy muck, exposing a small face and a scowl large enough for three people. Dark hair, once immaculately coiled, now clung to her scalp in filthy knots. The brown of her imperious eyes had been replaced with fire. And her robes — drenched, dark, and blessed in all the wrong places — clung to her, tracing sharp lines and subtle curves that I absolutely, definitely, resolutely did not notice.

Brin walked beside her, pretending not to exist.

Mero kept a safe distance behind, twirling a souvenir he had liberated from the chaos — a string of prayer beads that might still have been dripping.

"I'd say that went well," I offered.

No one responded.

I tried again. "And mandatory ablutions only come once a year, which is quite…lenient."

Seren didn't turn. "You are very lucky I don't use oaths without authorization."

We crossed through the market, past vendors, jugglers, nut-sellers. For one brief moment, the chaos stilled: every eye fixed on us — the soaking Magi and her doomed companions. Seren marched forward without hesitation, chin high, robes trailing rivulets of muddy sanctity.

A stray cat hissed from atop a crate, took one look at Seren, and slunk away sideways, never breaking eye contact.

When we reached the Archive gates, Seren paused. Turned slowly, boots squelching.

"I'll find you when it's time," she said, flatly.

"Of course," I said, smiling.

She held my gaze a moment longer, as if tallying the full sum of my sins — and finding the debt incalculable.

Then, low enough that only I could hear, she said, "Next time, we scrub the inside of your skull."

And she vanished into the Archive without another word.

Brin shook his head. "She's going to kill you."

"Oh, probably."

Mero twirled his dripping beads. "Next time, let's skip the apology and just start with the part where you get crucified."

"Too late," I said. "We've already cleansed my sins."

Brin gave me a long look. "No, we haven't."

I smiled. "Maybe not. But we did baptize the scroll."

A Canal Is No Place for Love (or Leather)

> *"First the feast, then the fire."*
> — *ancient Ruanne proverb.*

Now this is a story that takes us back to Oltara — jewel of the spice routes, city of bronze domes and bloodstained gutters. A place where every laugh is a dare and every dance is a knife fight waiting for music. We were there in the fall, just before the Festival of the Everfilling Cup — the one time of year when the date palms sag, the air stinks of fermented honey, and even the priests forget how to say no.

I was, as ever, minding my own business. Which is to say: I was in a bar I couldn't afford, wearing a jacket I hadn't technically been allowed to borrow, giving my reflection little approving nods every time I passed a mirror. It was a fabulous jacket. Deep green. Buttery leather. Collar turned just so. Mero's pride and joy. A touch tight in the shoulders, but I could work smug in any size.

That's when she happened to the room.

I think her name was Lily. Or Lolly. Something with an L. What it should have been was a sound between an eruption and a scream. She was generously endowed — by which I mean gravity had surrendered and taken early retirement. Her dress was made of tension and bad decisions. I noticed her. Of course I did. I have eyes. I'm not dead.

She noticed me back.

And then — gods save me — she bought me a drink.

Naturally, I repaid her kindness with wit.

Started with satire. Jabs at public officials. Nothing. Shifted to charm. Blank stares. In desperation, I reached for puns and one-liners like a drowning man grabbing wine corks. That's when it hit — her laugh. Deep. Seismic. It rolled through the bar, dislodging pigeons from the rafters and hope from the walls.

Lesson: know your audience. Sometimes, your audience wants fart jokes in iambic pentameter.

Halfway through a bit involving monks, fermented sheep's milk, and questionable miracles, she grabbed my hand. Her grip had all the subtlety of divine punishment. I smiled — or grimaced. Hard to tell when your fingers are being slowly martyred by lust and alcohol.

She ordered another round.

We drank. We laughed (she laughed, I survived). And — unexpectedly — she told a joke. A terrible one. About a farmer, a goat, and three barrels of honey. She laughed so hard at her own joke she nearly slid off her chair. Something in that moment almost — *almost* — made her human. (Which only made what followed worse.)

Then her friends arrived.

Now, I'm familiar with dubious company. But these folks made "dubious" look like an aspirational lifestyle. They didn't have names — just threats. *Toothless the Brick-Eater. Poison-Face the One-Handed. Blood Moon, Murderer of Puppies.* One had a tattoo of a knife fighting another knife. On her *face*.

The bartender poured without making eye contact.

More drinks arrived. A chair died. A table wept. Patrons fled like mice abandoning a collapsing bakery.

Then she draped an arm around me. Possessive.

Proprietary. Like I was a prize ham and she was a starving butcher's daughter.

I considered greasing myself and sliding under the table like an eel.

Instead, I stayed. Of course.

The drinking contests began. A knife balancing competition. Someone juggled bottles. Someone else juggled knives. A third juggled insults in four languages. It got rowdy. It got personal. It got inevitable.

At some point, she kissed one of her companions full on the mouth, stole the bartender's apron, and declared herself Queen of the Tavern. The bartender and I exchanged a glance of mutual hostagehood. He shrugged. Oltara.

Then she leaned into me, hot breath full of datewine and decisions made without consulting common sense.

"Let's go upstairs," she whispered.

Technically a proposition. Functionally a sentence.

"I'd love to," I said, with the enthusiasm of a man watching the executioner sharpen the blade. "But I just remembered — urgent appointment. Camel races. Very important."

She giggled. Or maybe the ceiling cracked. Hard to say.

And then — exit stage left. Me dragged along behind her, hand welded to hers, my feet doing their best impression of resistance while my dignity surrendered with a whimper.

We climbed the stairs. I glanced back — and met the eyes of two of her chaperones. One had a hook for a hand. The other had "YES PLEASE" tattooed across his forehead —

in blood, or something convincingly similar.

The bedroom door clicked shut.

Just me, Brunhilda, and the dying echo of every good decision I'd ever dodged.

There was no place that wasn't bosom. She played with my hair like it owed her back wages. She leaned in close, whispering sins against my neck, and reached for—I don't know. My soul? My inheritance? My third-best ideas?

Whatever it was, it panicked.

And in that moment—divine inspiration.

I looked her dead in the eye and said, "Would you do me a favour? Slip into something... sexy. Really spice things up."

She grinned—a sight that would have sent braver men to prayer.

"Be right back," she purred. "Don't move."

"Wouldn't dream of it," I lied.

The moment she vanished behind the curtain, I moved.

Straight through the window. Which, for the record, was *not* designed to open.

Two flights down. Into the canal.

It was cold. It was filthy. It smelled like dead fish, dying dreams, and a camel with irritable bowels.

But it was freedom. Wet. Humiliating. Beautiful freedom.

I never told Mero about the jacket.

Not because I hadn't ruined his things before.

Not because it was worth more than either of us.

But because the story was priceless.

And you don't ruin a story like that with confession.

The Sword-Swallower's Son

I promised Mero I would never tell this story. But I'm a liar.

And some lies deserve better company.

If you're thinking, "Ah yes, Mero—the charming pickpocket with the smile of a minor god and the morals of a raccoon loose in a bakery," you'd be right. But what you might not know is that Mero didn't hatch fully formed from a stolen satchel of coin and charisma. No. He was forged. Hammered and tempered in the fire of the knife-wielding, sequined disaster that was his father: Joaquin Vato, Sword-Swallower, ringmaster of Tirnan's Grand Company of Wonders, and professional cautionary tale.

Joaquin, bless his black little heart, travelled with a circus that was one part showmanship, one part organized crime, and one part emotional trauma on wheels. By day, he performed feats of danger and delight: swallowing swords, juggling fire, tossing knives at beautiful living targets while blindfolded. By night, he ran gambling dens, trained feral monkeys to steal jewelry, and—according to rumour—lost Mero in a card game. Twice.

Young Mero—bright-eyed, quick-fingered, and approximately the size of a caffeinated ferret—learned survival the way most kids learn lullabies: early, badly, and with a lot of screaming involved. By eight, he could pick a lock with a butter knife, scale a greased tentpole, and filch a man's coin purse while the man was still holding it—and thank him for the privilege afterward.

Now, people accuse me (maliciously) of exaggeration. But when I tell you Joaquin's parenting style hovered somewhere between "mildly illegal" and "morally indictable," I'm being generous. Affection was something Joaquin treated like taxes: dodgeable whenever possible. If Mero succeeded, Joaquin claimed it. If Mero failed, he fed him to the monkeys. (Not literally. Probably.)

The Family Arrives

It started, as most of our finer disasters do, with a broken wagon and a blessing we immediately regretted.

We were limping along the east road—a procession of mismatched wagons, hand-stitched tarps, and children multiplying like spilled lentils—when Jassa Marnett's front axle let out a noise like a dying accordion and snapped clean through.

We rattled into a clearing just off the trade route, hopes held together by spit and threats—and promptly realized we weren't alone.

Tirnan's Grand Company of Wonders had already claimed the ground.

Now, calling it a "circus" feels rude to both words. This was no village fair with a juggler and a drunk goat (although, to be fair, they had both). This was glamour lacquered in mystery. Their wagons glistened in deep indigos and crimson, the trim picked out in gold like they expected royalty to visit and be impressed. Acrobat lines stretched between trees. Fires danced in coloured lanterns. Exotic animals lounged on rugs that probably cost more than our whole camp. It smelled like incense, wine, and lawsuits waiting to happen.

We were, to put it mildly, underdressed.

Nema sent word with a peace offering: salted dates —
because nothing says 'friendship' like confused taste buds
and desperate preservation methods — and a formal
request to share the clearing.

The reply arrived on two legs, dressed in scandal and silk.

Joaquin Vato.

Sword-Swallower. Ringmaster. Probable illusionist.
Possible minor deity of bad decisions.

He bowed so deep I thought he might snap something
important. "Tell your Matriarch," he purred, voice like
silk soaked in smoke, "that the Company welcomes
beauty and resilience wherever we travel. And should she
wish to share the fire tonight..." He smiled, slow as spilled
molasses, "I would consider it an honour."

Now, Nema does not often blink at men. She has stared
down magistrates, warlords, and at least one cursed
mirror that tried to eat Brin's soul. But when Joaquin
kissed her hand *without asking* and called her *La Sabia* — the
Wise One — in flawless Eldarian...

She blinked.

Once.

I have never, before or since, been more afraid.

That night, the two camps became one — visibly different,
painfully incompatible, like an arranged marriage
between oil, water, and one drunk goat.

Their performers dazzled us. Flame dancers spun fire
from their hips. Contortionists folded into trunks so small
they needed a crowbar to get out again. A fire-eater named
Elatha swallowed an entire torch and then whistled a tune

through her teeth.

We offered songs, stories, and Jorann's lentil stew, which he insisted was a "traditional northern delicacy" and which the circus folk consumed like it might attack if left unsupervised.

But everything circled back to the fire.

Joaquin and Nema, facing each other across the flames like rival kings at a feast. He poured her wine. She declined. He offered her a charm — a silver coin pierced with a black ribbon. She turned it in her hands, considered it the way you consider whether a scorpion might be someone's idea of a pet, then tied it around her wrist without a word.

It wasn't love.

Not yet.

It was that moment at the card table, just before someone flips a knife into the pot and the real game begins.

Brin sat near Nema that night, glaring at Joaquin like he was trying to set him on fire by sheer force of will. The elders whispered. Some said Joaquin's hands were too quick. Some said his smiles had too many teeth. Some said it had been years since Nema smiled back at anyone, and wasn't that worth something?

I, naturally, decided he was the villain and immediately resolved to seduce his daughter in revenge. Unfortunately, he didn't have a daughter. Just a son.

The Boy Who Wasn't There

Some people arrive like storms. Mero arrived like mildew — quiet, stubborn, and already halfway inside before you noticed.

I didn't really meet him until the third day.

By then, we'd more or less wedged ourselves into the clearing. Brin was digging latrines with the tragic dignity of a boy who believed he deserved better. The Tanviros were trying (and failing) to flirt with fire dancers. I had flirted with a woman who juggled knives and earned a demonstration that might technically qualify as an assassination attempt.

It was a good day.

And there, half-crouched in the shadows behind Jorann's stew pot, was a boy.

Thin. Wiry. Skin baked the colour of dusk. Mismatched eyes. Smile like a knife tucked under a napkin.

He was watching the steam rise from the pot like it was telling him secrets.

He didn't belong to the Grand Company. Didn't belong to anyone, far as I could tell. Just... hovered. Drifted. A ghost in a camp full of ghosts that didn't realize they were dead yet.

Naturally, I adopted him on the spot.

I sidled up with all the casual grace of a man who'd been rejected by two knife jugglers and a woman who wrestled goats recreationally.

"You look like a boy who knows how to get things," I said, offering him half a bruised plum I may or may not have liberated from Brin's secret stash.

He sniffed. Bit into the plum. "*You* look like a boy who doesn't know how to shut up."

I beamed. "Guilty. I'm Aen. You got a name?"

He shrugged. Bit the plum again. Said, mouth half-full,

"Not today I don't."

That, as they say, was the beginning of a beautiful friendship.

I learned his habits. He never came when called. He never left when expected. He could steal your apple while you were still chewing it. He never really spoke about himself. But he listened. He listened like he was mapping escape routes in every word.

I told him about the time our spice rack was haunted, and Brin wrestled a wild pig that turned out to be somebody's very irate husband. He told me about a monkey that bit a nobleman and got promoted.

"Is that true?" I asked.

He grinned—a crooked, broken, brilliant thing. "Truer than lots."

Nema noticed him, of course. Nema notices everything. Especially things that try not to be noticed. One evening, as the sun was coughing its last across the treetops, she murmured beside me, "He doesn't walk like the others."

I squinted at Mero, who was currently helping Rue Lohre with her herb pouches like he hadn't personally stolen half her onions yesterday.

"Walks fine to me," I said. "Bit lurky. Very mysterious."

She didn't smile. "Walks too carefully. Too light."

"He's nice," I said defensively. "For a lurking urchin."

She nodded once, slow. "He's hungry."

"That's why I feed him," I said. "I'm raising him to be my henchman."

Nema gave me a long, hard look. The kind of look that says: Even your jokes are dangerous, you beautiful idiot. Then she handed me a slice of bread. "Give him this," she said. "Tell him I'm watching."

I did.

He took it, tore a piece off with his teeth like a starving wolf trying to look casual.

"Tell her," he said around the bread, "I'm watching back."

The nights grew heavier. *Tirnan's Grand Company of Wonders* unfurled like a slick, glittering spider. Canvas tents glowing with firelight. Drums throbbing. Laughter and lies spinning in smoke.

And the main event? Joaquin Vato's signature act: Blindfolded knife-throwing at live targets.

Because why merely endanger yourself when you can endanger a pretty woman for applause?

There he was — Joaquin — standing bare-chested in the center ring, knives gleaming in both hands, a silk blindfold tied with the flourish of a man who thought death was a punchline.

The assistant — red dress, excellent posture, even better nerves — took her place against the spinning wheel.

The drums beat faster.

The crowd leaned forward like crops bending before a storm.

The first knife flew. *Thwack.*

A gasp.

The second. *Thwack.*

The third. Closer. Closer. Until the final blade spun through the air like a silver swear word — landing an inch from the woman's ear.

Silence.

And then —

"THIEF!"

It ripped the hush apart like a hawk through a flock of doves.

A man near the back — silks, rings, ego — had a boy by the wrist.

Mero.

Caught red-handed, or at least pink-wristed, with a coin purse halfway between the mark and his own pocket.

The wheel stopped spinning. The crowd stopped breathing.

Joaquin tore off his blindfold. The knives clattered to the ground.

The mark bellowed, "Caught him! Gods-damned street rat tried to rob me!"

The twins — Joaquin's private mooks — hauled Mero forward. He didn't struggle. Of course he didn't. He didn't fight when it wouldn't help.

Joaquin's smile sharpened like a butcher's hook.

"To the Company's honoured guests," he said, bowing low, "I apologize for the disruption. We do not tolerate vermin among our wonders."

He turned to the crowd.

"And what better entertainment than swift justice?"

He slapped Mero across the face. Twice. Once for the crowd. Once for himself.

The sound cracked the night open like a rotten egg.

The crowd roared. Because nothing fills a man faster than feeling bigger than a boy half his size.

Nema didn't move. Didn't speak. Just sat there, hands clenched so tightly in her lap I half-expected the bones to splinter.

Backstage, Mero bled into the straw.

I found him behind the tent near the whipping post— really just a broken ladder tied to a fence and given a fancy name, like pain got tired of pretending.

He looked like somebody had tried to turn a child into a cautionary tale, then got bored halfway through. One eye was swollen shut. His lip was split so wide it whistled when he breathed. Welts ran down his back in crooked rivers.

He grinned when he saw me.

That was the kind of idiot he was.

"Did you like the show?" he asked, teeth red.

"You're not supposed to perform during the performance," I muttered, crouching down beside him. "The act was knives, not light theft and a public flogging."

He shrugged. Winced.

"I'm not supposed to be seen at all," he said.

"You certainly know how to make an exit."

He coughed a laugh. Then flinched.

"I didn't mean to get caught," he mumbled. "It's just—the purse was right there. Not even tied. That's on him."

"Still," I said, voice thick with a joke I couldn't quite choke out, "you certainly picked a crowd that appreciates the classics. Blindfolds, knives, and beating the help."

Mero didn't answer.

Just sat there, bleeding, grinning, breaking and pretending he wasn't.

After the show, the Grand Company's fires burned brighter than ever. Laughter rolled through the clearing like thunder with a knife hidden in its pocket. Joaquin took his bows, drank his wine, and pretended the night hadn't cracked open and bled at his feet.

We pretended, too. Because what else do you do when the man smiling across the fire is the one who teaches you how sharp the world can be?

Nema began whispering.

To Brin's mother. To old Omri. To me.

"We're leaving," she said, voice soft as a blade slipping free of a sheath.

I blinked. "Leaving leaving?"

"Yes."

"But—" I flapped a hand at the carnival of felonies around us "—we're the life of the party."

Her gaze slid to Joaquin's tent, where lights burned late and too many shadows moved inside.

"It's time," she said. "Before he decides I'm part of the act."

I straightened. "Should I steal something important before

we go? His teeth, maybe?"

She almost smiled. Almost. "Steal his dignity."

I clapped a hand over my heart. "So nothing, then."

The Family moved fast when it had to.

The wagons creaked into formation under the bruised sky. Brin walked beside the lead horse, jaw set hard enough to crack walnuts. Jorann's kitchen tent collapsed like a dying spider. Melina clutched her geese—Pickle and Plum—tight against her chest like feathery hostages.

No music. No goodbyes.

Just the steady, grim shuffle of people who knew too well what it meant to leave first.

Behind us, the Big Tent roared—drums, applause, wonder.

Ahead of us, just the road, and whatever came after.

And then— there he was.

Mero.

Leaning against a broken wagon wheel, arms folded, blood crusted at his mouth. He wasn't crying. Just stood there like he didn't know how.

He didn't call out. Didn't plead.

He just watched. Small and silent and stubborn as a nail hammered too deep to pry loose.

The first wagon passed him.

Then the second.

Then Nema's.

And Nema—who could stare down kings and curses and the end of the world— she stopped.

The whole caravan shuddered to a halt behind her.

Wheels locking. Dust rising. Breath held.

She leaned out the door, studying him like a map that might still get you lost.

Mero stared back.

"I've got nothing," he said.

Voice flat. Like facts were safer than hope.

Nema tilted her head, slow and deliberate.

"Good," she said. "Lighter that way."

He didn't move for a heartbeat. Two.

Then he climbed into the wagon without another word.

The door swung shut.

The wheels creaked forward.

And just like that, Mero Vato left behind a name that had never meant safety, and joined a Family that didn't ask questions it didn't want answered.

Behind us, the circus roared and glittered and swallowed itself alive.

Ahead of us, there was nothing but the long road and whatever mercy we could cobble together.

And Mero—ours now.

Not because he asked.

Not because we offered.

Sometimes you don't need a welcome. Just a door that doesn't slam shut.

The Cloister of Perpetual Shushing

It was at the Cloister of Perpetual Shushing that our tragicomedy tipped from shameless to deranged. And, as in all great disasters, I blame Mero.

The Cloister belonged to an order of nuns who had taken a lifelong vow of silence. And as everyone knows, oaths are binding. Once sworn, there's no un-oathing, unswearing, or taking-backsies. The sisters were struck mute, bound to silence, and spent their remaining days in contemplation, regret, or both. They mostly kept to themselves, save for the occasional appearance in the city — scowling at anyone who dared speak above a whisper.

There were two kinds of sisters. A rare few had joined willingly: women without tongues, women who loved reading and hated interruptions, and women whose families had enjoyed political debate a little too enthusiastically. The larger group was less voluntary — women silenced for having opinions inconvenient to the men around them. Which is to say, women with opinions at all.

We arrived midmorning. The Cloister rose from the earth in a slab of solemnity — square, heavy, and flat, like a tomb built to mourn the death of imagination itself. It bled drab.

Before the great double doors loomed a statue: a nun carved in stone, clutching a massive tablet as if she intended to hurl it at the next person who coughed. The sculptor had captured a blend of religious fervour and barely restrained violence with disturbing accuracy.

One of the sisters waited at the threshold. Her habit draped over her like water over stone, offering no clues beyond the tilt of her lashes, the fine line of her brows, and the small stubborn angle of her chin. Paladin that I am, I recognized a damsel in desperate need of rescuing.

The great doors opened on hinges so silent they might have been greased with guilt. Inside, the Cloister spread like a warren: corridors of stone, lined with dusty tomes, the shuffling whisper of sandals, and the sweet-sharp scent of lavender and dust. Every door bore a granite plaque stamped proudly with the letters *SH*.

The silence wasn't peaceful. It was the kind of silence you get after someone says, *"Trust me!"* and then jumps off a roof. Heavy, bruised, and very, very final. The air was thick enough to chew. Every wall looked like it wanted to file a noise complaint. Even the sandals shuffled like guilty conspirators. It wasn't reverent. It wasn't serene. It was the sort of silence that made you want to break it on principle — and if you couldn't break it, at least tap dance loudly on top of it.

That would be my cue to stave off the horrors of silence with a not-at-all self-interested skill: flirting.

I fell in step beside our guide.

"Blink if you consent to being whisked away into a life of laughter, bad dancing, and light-to-moderate criminal activity," I whispered.

She kept her gaze demurely on the floor, but the corner of her eye twitched — almost a smile.

Gods. She was like chocolate.

"Tell me," I went on, "you wouldn't happen to stock *A*

Beginner's Guide to Meditations on Forgetfulness, would you? Always seems to be on loan."

Behind me, I could feel Seren's eye-roll punch the air like a thrown brick.

"Or perhaps," I said, "you are the guardian of the Restricted Section. Ever laid eyes on *The Complete Catalogue of Forbidden Catalogues?*"

She said nothing, but her hands tightened slightly on the folds of her robe, as if physically holding back a laugh.

Even here, in the Cloister's deadened heart, a little rebellion survived.

Mero sidled closer. "Ask her where they keep the books with dirty pictures."

The Sister froze, scandalized.

I elbowed him sharply.

"Forgive my lewd companion," I said solemnly. "He has no appreciation for the printed word."

At last, the Sister gestured delicately toward a door marked by a sign: *Sister Melancholera.* Then she glided away.

Inside, the Mother Superior rose from behind her desk. And I do mean rose — like a tidal wave gathering mass. She was built on the same architectural principles as the Cloister itself: broad, towering, immovable. Her silence hung around her like a crown of iron.

Then her gaze fell upon Brin.

Her cheeks flushed. Her pupils widened. She swept from behind her desk with all the subtlety of a hunting hawk and gestured — not to all of us — but directly, and only, to Brin, to sit.

"I think you have a fan," I murmured.

Brin didn't hear me. He was trapped in a wide-eyed opera of panic — and was that arousal? Gods help us all.

We sat down, Brin last, as if led to the gallows.

"Mother Superior," Seren said crisply, "these are the individuals responsible for deceiving your congregants."

Melancholera didn't react. Language itself had become an inadequate tool. She stared at Brin as though memorizing the shape of his jawline for a future sonnet written in silence.

Seren cleared her throat. Loudly.

"Mother Superior," she repeated, raising the volume to a level just shy of blasphemy.

Melancholera blinked, shook herself loose, and nodded — barely.

Seren fixed me with a look that could have curdled butter. "Aen, your penance is to remain at the Cloister until you have copied the Mother Superior's chosen reprimand. One thousand times."

I groaned theatrically.

"If the Cloister hasn't drafted a reprimand," Seren added darkly, "I will."

Melancholera raised a commanding hand. She led us through a labyrinth of stone stairwells until we arrived at a low door labeled: *Records: Nonconforming and Uncatalogable.* Inside sprawled a vast underground chamber, half eaten by shadows. Dusty benches, forgotten crates, and a single splintering table crowded with parchment filled the space.

The Mother Superior dipped a quill and wrote in an

immaculate, iron hand:

I shall not prey on the foolish.

She paused. Then added, after a wicked heartbeat:

unless they deserve it.

She handed the parchment to me — and winked.

Seren opened her mouth, ready to object, but Melancholera silenced her with a single, masterful slice of her hand. It was more than a gesture; it was artistry. A slam of authority, honed over decades of ruling an empire of silence. Seren faltered, visibly out-glared.

I bowed over the parchment. "Your wisdom, Mother, is a gift to all who err."

With a crook of her finger, Melancholera invited Brin to join her for a walk together. Possibly for a tour of the Cloister, possibly something more intimate. It was hard to tell. Brin floated away like a man who had glimpsed heaven and refused to come back.

Mero loitered for a moment, then wandered off into the explore the abandoned depth of the room.

It was a massive task. My hand ached just imagining it. But my heart? Light as a feather.

I got to work.

I scratched out the first few lines with noble determination, but enthusiasm waned somewhere around line fourteen. Seren loomed nearby, arms crossed, supervising like a prison warden who deeply regretted her life choices.

"So, come here often?"

Seren unfolded her arms, brandishing a ledger she must have stolen from some poor sister's desk. No response.

A few more diligent scribbles by me.

I smiled at my favourite crow. "No need to stand. There's space here and lots of quills. It's super fun. Grab a quill. We'd be done a lot faster."

She sat.

"Focus on your penance. It's not mine to serve."

"More wrist injury than penance."

I started whistling. Badly.

"Please stop."

Scribble scribble. I work studiously. By the time my hand was about to fall off—literally—I asked, "How many is that?"

"Twenty."

"What?!"

I got back to work. *I shall not prey on the foolish, unless they deserve it. I shall not prey on the foolish, unless they deserve it. I shall not prey on the foolish, unless they deserve it.*

The silence was maddening. I filled it.

"Got any hobbies?"

"Reading."

"Any *actually* interesting hobbies?"

"Reading *is* interesting."

"What about singing? Dancing? Puppetry? What does a frisky Magi do for excitement?"

"You are not writing."

I scribbled. The margins were boring. I added a little flourish.

"You know," I said, "some cultures reward scribes with foot massages and wine."

She looked like she wanted to vomit. It was almost tragic, how valiantly she resisted.

"Just saying," I muttered. "Could be missing out on a rich cultural tradition here."

"You are not writing."

I scratched another line. To keep things interesting, I modified the sizing. Then the orientation. Then the direction of the script. The ink splotched.

Seren squinted at my work. "What is that?"

"It's art." I held it up, beaming.

She pinched her nose. "It's not art. It's correction. And if you don't write in straight lines, we won't be able to properly count them. No art."

My wrist got tired. I switched the quill to my right hand. The words came out as approximates.

"Ok," I said brightly, adding little feet to the letters. "Forget the cultural exploration. What about your family? Is there a Dada Magi? Mama Magi?"

She whacked me over the head with the ledger.

"Ow," I said, rubbing the spot. "Careful. You're going to dent the merchandise."

She sighed, exasperated. I returned the quill to my left hand.

"No, no, I get it," I said grandly. "It's classic misdirected passion. Perfectly natural."

She hit me again. Harder.

I grinned. Progress.

By sunset, the deed was done. Ink smudged my sleeves, my fingers, and parts of my face I didn't know could hold ink.

We gathered once more at the Cloister gates. Seren delivered a crisp farewell on behalf of the Magi.

I, meanwhile, found my sweet silent sister lingering shyly nearby. She smiled — an almost-smile — and I, fool that I am, kept talking. I could have talked forever.

Brin and Melancholera stood apart, hands brushing like characters in a forbidden play. It was beautiful. Tragic. Completely doomed. A single tear slid down her broad cheek as she turned back toward her life of silence. Then, turning back to her chose life, she summoned a scowl of such magnitude that my poor Sister fled — though not before flashing me the ghost of a wave.

Seren rubbed her temples. "I don't think you learned anything whatsoever."

"Not true," I said. "I learned not to judge a book by its cover."

She stalked off.

Brin sighed. "What a woman," he murmured.

Ah, love.

Later, with the stars overhead and the fire guttering low, Mero and I sat nursing a battered flask between us. Brin wandered off, presumably to compose silent poetry.

Mero drank deep and grinned. From a fold of his jacket, he produced a slim white book.

"It was humming," he said by way of explanation.

I took it reverently. The cover gleamed faintly in the

firelight: *The Everything, Including Nothing.*

Inside, the pages were a madman's daydream: scribbles, loops, inverted margins, words stacked like drunken acrobats. Some pages contained only the word YES, repeated wildly at different sizes. And as I turned the pages, I heard it — a whisper, part hum, part sigh.

"I love it," I said.

"I think it's alive," Mero muttered.

I flipped to a blank page. Slowly, words surfaced from the parchment like something rising through water.

"In the beginning was the Word. And she swam."

The wineskin in my hand turned into a fish.

Mero shrieked and hurled it into the fire.

The fish flopped, sizzled, and expired. It did not turn back.

"Put it down," Mero hissed. "And never read it again."

I cradled the little book like a sacred sin.

"I don't know," I said. "I think it likes me."

"Of course it does," Mero muttered darkly. "All the worst things do."

Absolutely Not Touching Everything and Nothing

"The gods bait the hook with luck."

— ancient Ruanne proverb.

"No," Mero said, staring at me like I'd just suggested kissing a Warden. "Absolutely not."

We were seated around the embers of our campfire, its glow soft, flickering off the half-burnt logs like a nervous confession. The night was quiet. The stars blinked above, unimpressed.

Since the night Mero had pulled it from his coat like a magician, and I'd accidentally transformed a wineskin into a gasping, flopping fish, the book had remained closed. Not because I wanted it that way. Mero had hidden it. Somewhere. Somehow. Despite my best efforts, I couldn't find it.

Mero insisted that because he had "liberated" *The Everything, Including Nothing* — ethically, he maintained — from the uncatalogable records room at the Cloister of Perpetual Shushing, it belonged to him. Therefore, he got to decide when, how, and if it was opened again.

"A weak argument," I muttered, poking the fire. "I don't see you asserting ownership over every suspicious rash you've caught."

Brin grunted. Which might've meant agreement. Or indigestion. Hard to say.

"Come on," I pressed. "Real magic, Mero. Think of the possibilities."

Mero crossed his arms. "Your plans are always fine until we're running through alleyways, pursued by nuns."

"That happened once."

"Three times," he replied.

"Four," said Brin, "if you count Order of Loaves."

I rolled my eyes. "That's not even a real Order. They were a fraud!"

Dismissing the issue entirely, I turned to Brin, "Come on, back me up here!"

Brin hadn't been there to see the divine transformation of wineskin to fish. Even after he had seen the burnt fish, he claimed he didn't believe it.

Brin grunted again. This one sounded vaguely judgmental.

"You see? Brin's intrigued."

Brin frowned, as if reevaluating his life choices.

I turned to Mero with my best earnest expression. "Just flipping pages. No reading. A little innocent page fondling."

He squinted at me like I was a particularly dishonest street urchin. "You can't flip pages without reading. Your ego reads through osmosis."

"I am a noble vessel of curiosity," I said, hand to heart.

"You are a pipe leaking disaster." Then he threw up his hands. "Fine! You want to humiliate yourself? Go ahead. But if you ignite, I'm not putting you out."

"Agreed."

He produced the little white book from somewhere in his jacket, holding it between two fingers like a venomous insect.

It vibrated faintly. Or maybe that was me.

Brin leaned in, curious.

"Ground rules," Mero said, offering the book just out of reach. "No reading. No chanting. No spontaneous oaths. And not near camp."

"Just flipping," I promised, solemn as a priest and twice as sincere.

We crept a little ways. Found a clearing. No witnesses. The moon was bright. The air held the scent of possibility and dry dirt.

Mero opened the book. Flipped a page. "It's just scribbles."

Another.

Still nothing—only blank parchment and erratic loops, like the drunken afterthoughts of a spider.

Mero frowned. "Dead."

He tossed it to Brin.

Brin turned a page. Squinted. Shrugged. "Garbage."

My turn.

The second my fingers touched the paper, the ink stirred.

I turned a page.

Words bloomed: *A duel lost reveals breeches.*

Without thinking, I read it aloud.

POP.

"Hey!" Mero shrieked.

Brin covered himself with a stick.

I collapsed laughing, gasping for air.

"This is harassment!" Mero shouted.

"Beautiful!" I managed, still wheezing.

Brin scowled. "I liked those pants."

"Undo it!" Mero demanded.

I shrugged, still laughing. "How?"

"I don't know," he barked. "Read the words backwards, or something!"

I tried. "Forget your pants, don't!"

Nothing happened.

Mero's expression turned murderous. "Do it properly!"

The book just quivered, clearly delighted by our suffering. I didn't know who was laughing harder — me or the book. I smiled beatifically, flipped another page.

New words surfaced: *If you're gonna hang, make it a performance.*

Without warning, our shadows sprang up and began pirouetting madly across the clearing — stomping, spinning, colliding into trees.

Brin nearly dropped his stick.

Mero looked ready to weep.

"STOP IT!" he shrieked, lunging for the book.

I skipped backward, laughing harder than I had in weeks.

Another page. Another whisper.

"*Everything tastes better with regrets,*" I announced.

At first, nothing happened. Then the ground twitched — once, twice, like something underneath was trying to breathe through the dirt. Tiny clods jerked loose and began to shudder in place, trembling like wet dogs. Before we could move, the clods began clumping, fusing into hissing, lumpy shapes.

The first one rose—a misshapen mass of cracked earth and pebbles, shaped vaguely like a dinner roll that had lost a fight with a gravel path. It grew legs. Then teeth. Then a second mouth. It stumbled forward, dripping dust, and bit down on Brin's boot. He kicked it off. It hit the dirt, shuddered, and giggled—a wet, gurgling sound like a throat gargling pebbles—then lurched back for more.

All around us, dirt-mounds sprang up—snapping jaws, gnashing pebbly teeth, shrieking in voices too small for bodies that were that eager to kill.

One latched onto Mero's bare leg and started gnawing, drawing blood. The thing that bit him spasmed, shuddered, and swelled—doubling in size in a heartbeat. New limbs sprouted, malformed and frantic, as if Mero's blood had fed it something it had been starving for.

Brin's stick came down hard, splitting it in two with a sickening crunch—but the halves kept wriggling until Mero stomped them into paste.

Brin swung his stick like he was harvesting rage. Dirt-buns exploded under his blows, spitting pebbles and dust like furious seeds.

Mero fought differently—wild-eyed, flailing, stomping anything that moved with the desperation of a man trying to un-make bad decisions with sheer foot violence. Every time he crushed one, another seemed to leap for his ankles, giggling like drunk goblins.

Me? I laughed like an idiot, dodging and weaving and throwing kicks at anything that looked bitey. The ground bucked underfoot, alive and treacherous. A half-squashed bun hurled itself at my calf—I yelped, stumbled, nearly cracked heads with Brin, who didn't even look up as he methodically shattered another two.

They weren't dying easy. Even smashed flat, some of them twitched, dragging themselves forward on broken legs, jaws snapping mindlessly at air, at boots, at anything that smelled like meat. The worst ones didn't shriek anymore — they gurgled, low and wet, a noise that made the back of my neck crawl. We fought like idiots in a bakery possessed by devils, and even then, we barely kept up.

Finally, they were properly pulverized. A few survivors skittered into the dark — laughing.

That finished it. Mostly.

Before I could try another spell, Mero tackled me like a man trying to stop a house fire with his jacket.

"BRIN!" he shouted, tossing it like a cursed stone.

Brin caught it midair, clutching it like a man accepting the worst inheritance imaginable.

I flopped on the ground, giggling, shirt twisted around my ribs, entirely untroubled by my lack of trousers.

Mero glared at me, panting. "You. Are. Banned."

A sliver of cold slid through me — a prickling certainty that we'd only barely won, and next time we might not. I bared my teeth in a wider grin and shoved the feeling down. Better to laugh while you still had breath for it.

"Banned from joy?" I asked sweetly.

"Banned from touching sentient objects ever again."

Brin, silent and judicious, stalked toward camp with the book firmly held like a sacred relic — or possibly a feral cat.

We followed, shivering and dignity-free.

But deep inside, warming my ribs like stolen sunshine, the truth curled and settled: the book *liked* me. I was doomed. It was perfect.

The Great Cart Tragedy (And Other Inconveniences)

> *"The desert does not mourn the footprints it buries."*
> —*ancient Ruanne proverb.*

Question: What's worse than being sentenced to penance rounds with a stone-faced Oathbound woman who considers "mirth" an indictable offence?

Answer: Coming back to camp afterward and finding it *quiet*. Not nap-under-a-fig-tree quiet. Not lazy-goat-in-the-sun quiet. No—*the bad kind of quiet*. The everyone's-staring, don't-breathe-too-loud kind of quiet. The kind of quiet that says: *something went wrong*. And now we're just waiting to see who steps in it first.

Let me back up.

We'd just left the *Temple of the Ascendant Balance*. Don't worry, this isn't a temple story. It was boring. We showed up, I delivered a half-baked apology, they sniffed at it, I didn't steal anything (probably), and they let us leave without a single fire breaking out. By our standards, it was a roaring success.

Whatever.

We got back to camp. The wind was still warm. The soup still smelled vaguely edible, if you squinted at it sideways. Everything looked normal. Except it wasn't.

Mero noticed first. He always does. He slowed near the cookfire, scanning faces, like a dog smelling a storm.

Brin was next to catch it. He nudged me, sharp and subtle, then tipped his chin toward the far side of camp.

That's when we saw her.

Shevra.

Sitting beside what used to be her cart—or maybe what was left after someone fed it through a very angry elephant. Splintered wood. Bent axles.

Even before the market disaster, some of the Family were working quietly in the Lower Market—Shevra first among them. No banners, no songs. Just old tables, frayed cloth, and magic you had to stop and see. Unlike me, they hadn't marched into the city like a parade. They just quietly found a place, slipping in like raindrops, setting up wherever they could.

Shevra had found a place and been gently hawking her wares for months. It wasn't much, not at first glance: an old folding table draped in a fraying blue cloth, a few battered crates stacked like crooked teeth to catch the light. Just a corner of the Lower Market, tucked by the cracked fountain where the pigeons fought over breadcrumbs and lost buttons.

But if you looked closer—*if you stopped*—you'd see it. A small world spun from scraps and patience. Wire twisted into miniature dancers. Birds cut from broken glass, their wings sharp and shining, catching the sun like a blessing. Tiny animals fashioned from bottle caps and bone, stitched together with such cleverness they almost seemed to breathe.

It wasn't loud, the way Shevra sold. No shouting. No haggling. No bold cries about miracle cures or enchanted trinkets. Only the quiet invitation to notice. The kind of magic that lived in small things. The kind that asked you to slow down, lean in, and see the wonder stitched into the cracks of the world.

If you hurried past, you missed it. But if you stopped — If

you really *looked*— It could break your heart with how much it mattered.

"They smashed it," Mero muttered.

I blinked. "What?"

He nodded at the wreckage. "The city guard. Or the vendor herself. Doesn't matter. They kicked Shevra out. Someone else claimed the spot."

I went over to talk to her and find out what happened.

Shevra was sitting by the wreckage of her stall, sorting broken bits of wire into neat little piles. Her youngest perched beside her, solemn as a priest, clutching a bent scrap-glass bird with both hands. She looked up when I approached, and smiled. A real smile, somehow. Like nothing was wrong.

"Good selling day?" I asked.

She nodded brightly. "Good-good," she said. "Little slow, maybe. But good."

Behind her, the tablecloth was torn. The crates were smashed. Half her wares were missing. I crouched beside her, lowering my voice. "Shevra. What happened?"

She hesitated, fingers twisting a bit of wire into tighter knots. "Just... busy-busy," she said. "Market change."

"Change," I repeated. "Like a new stall?"

She nodded again, still too fast, too eager. "New lady. Pretty clothes. Big paper." She mimed waving something over her head, laughing a little. "She says, 'Mine!' Very big voice."

My stomach turned. "Did anyone help you?" I asked, sharper than I meant to.

Shevra looked puzzled. "Help?" she echoed, like she

didn't understand the question. Or maybe wished she didn't.

I switched to Ruanne, soft and low. *"Did anyone stand with you, Shevra?"*

Her smile faltered. Just for a breath. Then she bent over her wire again, voice light. *"Many eyes watched. No mouths opened."* She shrugged, as if it were the weather, or spilled milk. *"It's nothing. A new spot will come."*

I stared at the wreckage around her, the broken magic scattered like forgotten promises. *"You had a good place. You earned it."*

Shevra smiled. *"But she had the paper."* Then—gentler, sadder this time, *"We are Ruanne, my pet. We must move like the sand. I'll find a new place."*

I hated how easy she made it sound.

Like it was nothing. Like getting shoved aside was just another part of living.

But it wasn't nothing.

And maybe— maybe if I hadn't stormed into the market like a one-man parade with a stolen rooster and a questionable grasp of city ordinances—maybe they wouldn't have started looking so closely. Maybe someone would have come to her defense. Maybe Shevra would still have her place.

Her eldest, Teren, tightened a bolt on the remains of her cart, tightening bolts like if he tightened enough, the world might give it back.

I stood there a moment longer, fists clenching uselessly at my sides. Because there was nothing noble about it. No dignity in being swept aside by a scrap of paper and a sharper tongue.

Only Shevra's kindness making it look softer than it was.

I walked back to the boys. "Maybe we visit the lady with her high and mighty permit. Maybe a wheel falls off of her cart. Maybe a flock of angry ducks holds a sit-in. Maybe gravity takes an inconvenient interest in her new stall."

They didn't smile. And they didn't say no.

But before we could start planning civil disobedience via poultry, Nema's voice snapped us up straight.

"No."

We turned.

She sat at the fire, arms folded, face carved from stone.

"You can't fight their paper with sabotage," she said. "Go fix it properly."

Properly.

I hated that word.

So now here I am.

Marching, with a heart full of righteous indignation and absolutely no plan, to the *worst* place in Nareth: the Hall of Justice. I stomped in through the front doors like a man with purpose (and possibly a mild head injury). I wasn't going to leave until someone paid attention. Even if I had to shout myself hoarse doing it.

"I need Seren Vey," I told the clerk.

He looked up like I'd asked him to bless a goat in public. "*Magi* Vey is currently reviewing scrollwork. In the Archives."

"Good," I said. "I hope she likes words. She's about to get several. Loudly."

Ten minutes later, I was pacing outside the Archive's eastern stacks, trailing candle wax and indignation. When Seren finally emerged, her robes were crisp, her expression unreadable, and her posture insufferably vertical.

I unloaded.

Told her everything. About Shevra. The wrecked cart. The smug vendor. The permit. The silence of the market. About Teren trying to earn back his mother's dignity with a wrench.

I didn't shout. Just... stacked words like bricks. If she wanted scrollwork, I'd give her something worth binding.

Seren, as ever, didn't interrupt. Just listened. I hate how good she is at that.

Turns out the permit was real. Of course it was. Neatly filed. Dated. Sealed.

Then came the hunt through the scrolls.

I helped. Which is to say I pointed at random clauses and made snide comments while Seren systematically excavated five centuries of bureaucratic sediment.

Eventually, she found it.

"Market Square Zoning Addendum, Clause Twelve, Subsection H," she read aloud. "'In years bearing three moonfeasts, a temporary stall permit may be granted with approval from either a minor magistrate or two unanimous vendor signatures, valid for the duration of a market season.'"

She glanced up. "It's obscure. I didn't even know it existed."

I stared at her. "So she found a rule no one's heard of, used it to displace a Ruanne family who can't read the local script, and everyone else just *let her*?"

Seren's face didn't move. "She operated within the law."

I laughed once. Loud and ugly. "Of course she did. The law's *very* tidy that way."

She stiffened. "You came here for justice, Aen. Not vengeance."

"No," I said. "I came here thinking maybe justice could read a permit. Apparently not."

She crossed her arms. "What do you want me to do?"

I shrugged. "Declare a Festival of Basic Decency. Outlaw smugness. Burn the Archive to the ground."

Her expression twitched. Not quite a flinch. But close.

I turned to leave.

Behind me, she said, "I'll look into it further."

I didn't stop walking. Because I already knew what she'd find.

Nothing that would give Shevra her place back.

That night, I told the story around the fire.

The *funnier* version.

We invented new departments—like the "Office of Opportunistic Loopholes," the "Bureau of Permit Interpretation and Shrugging," and the "Ministry of Stall Occupancy in Years with Three Moonfeasts."

People laughed. Even Shevra, as she sat by the fire, tying bent wire into the wing of a little glass bird. Carefully.

Quietly. Like maybe — if she just got it right this time — the world would let it fly. It wouldn't, of course. But she worked anyway.

We always do.

Of Ducks, Ledgers, and Other Lost Causes

> *"A good lie holds better than a true name."*
>
> — *ancient Ruanne proverb.*

The Ruanne Family camp sprawled just outside the city of Nareth, alive and kicking with its usual delightful bedlam. Twelve brightly painted wagons groaned in the noon sun like old grandmothers complaining about their joints. Goats bleated, chickens squawked, and a pair of lean hounds dozed under a wagon, one eye open in case something edible fell their way. Children darted everywhere — grubby-faced wildlings whooping between the wagons, tripping over dogs and crashing into the cooking fires with alarming regularity.

By the central fire, an argument over soup had reached heroic proportions. Nalia Vashari stirred the pot with the air of a witch brewing mischief, while Omri Nuvra hollered beside her, waving a wooden spoon like a sword.

"You call that soup?" Omri grumbled. "I swear I saw that carrot try to swim for it!"

"It's herb soup, you cabbage-head," Nalia shot back. "If you helped pick greens instead of picking fights, you'd know that!"

The two of them bickered while the rest of us lounged nearby, tossing in commentary like helpful hecklers.

"Needs more salt!" shouted Lasha Kelrani from a wagon roof where she was mending a blanket.

"Needs less Omri!" someone else retorted.

Omri flicked a droplet of soup upward; it landed on old Ferrick's bald head as he passed, earning a startled yelp and a fresh round of laughter.

It was casual chaos, the kind that felt like home.

Women scrubbed clothes in basins. Men cursed at wagon wheels bent by too many potholes. Children staged a riotous potato-peeling contest that ended with skins flying through the air and a small boy wearing a basket like a helmet. Somewhere near the fire, Grandpa Ilan snored in a rocking chair that creaked along with his every breath, punctuating the din like a drunken drumbeat.

And of course, there was singing. There's always singing.

Teo Berrov sawed away at his fiddle, perched atop a barrel, banging out a lopsided jig while a circle of children spun clumsily to the beat. Aunt Salla clapped along, deliberately off-rhythm to torment him.

We shouted the chorus of a ridiculous camp song at the tops of our lungs:

"Hey-ho, the pie's in the fox, and the fox is on the run!"

The noise sent birds scattering from nearby trees and, undoubtedly, made the city of Nareth consider raising the walls a few feet higher. Someone pounded a pot in rhythm, possibly to remind the soup-makers not to burn lunch.

This was life with the Ruanne: boisterous, irreverent, loud enough to rattle the bones of the saints.

A missing shoe became camp theatre — the toddler Bren Estrel waddling past wearing it on his head. A washing mishap near the barrels turned into an impromptu water fight, soaking both the combatants and anyone unlucky enough to wander too close. Every chore was a game. Every disaster was a story.

I moved through it all grinning like a fool, heart thudding

with love for the beautiful mess we made together. With so much clatter and laughter stitched into the day, it seemed nothing short of a divine intervention could possibly quiet us.

I almost didn't notice the intruders at first. It was old Goro, lifting his head with a growl, and little Jessa, squinting from atop a wagon, that gave the first warnings.

Out on the road, a small knot of riders and walkers approached—moving with grim purpose, like a storm marching across a bright sky. They stuck out horribly against our riotous camp: stiff, starched, and dripping authority from a mile off.

At their head rode Seren, spine bolt-straight, chin high, robes of black stitched with the crest of Nareth. She sat her black stallion—Sour Applesauce—like it was part of her spine. Beside her marched two guards, armour gleaming, hands resting, casually-but-not-casually, on their sword hilts. Behind them struggled two dusty bureaucrats, faces red, ledgers and quills poking out of every pocket like hedgehog spines. One already had ink smeared across his nose. They looked exactly like the sort of people who thought rules were more real than people.

The camp's energy shifted as the procession drew near. One by one, our noise tapered off.

The fiddle let out a screech as Teo missed a note—and a step—tumbling off his bucket.

Children froze mid-chase and bolted for their mothers' skirts. Granny Olya stiffened at the soup pot, ladle dripping greenish broth. Murmurs rippled through the camp like the first cold breath of a cold wind.

Seren guided her horse a few paces into the clearing. The guards flanked her like heavy bookends; the bureaucrats fanned out, flipping through their ledgers, tallying us like livestock.

Seren cleared her throat—a sharp, official sound—and announced, "By order of the city of Nareth, we are here to conduct the official census of all persons present."

"Persons" sounded like something scraped off a boot.

Nobody answered.

The Ruanne are rarely formal and never quiet, but now a heavy, prickling silence fell over us.

I realized I was still holding a dripping cloth. Mari froze halfway through folding her mended blanket. Even the dogs stood hackle-raised and silent.

Around the fire, I caught Granny Olya's eye. She gave a tiny shake of her head: Stay still. Stay smart.

Breff looked like he was about to explode from the effort of not cracking a joke. Aunt Salla, bless her, had the same sarcastic glint she always did, but even she pressed her lips tight.

The bureaucrats began scribbling immediately—probably notating "one suspicious fiddle, two barefoot thieves, three barrels of questionable soup"—while the guards watched us like they expected a riot. The wind died. Even the fire seemed to crouch low.

And under it all, I could feel it—the old, deep distrust rising from the bones of the camp.

The Ruanne have never liked being listed, counted, or pinned down. We didn't trust ledgers any more than we trusted fences. And here they were, waving both at once.

No one moved. No one spoke.

The joy of moments before—the music, the laughter, the

glorious, stupid song about a pie-thieving fox—vanished into smoke.

We stood there, a Family caught between old survival instincts and the fresh insult of being treated like cargo.

Seren didn't look bothered by the silence. She stood tall, arms folded neatly behind her back, radiating the calm certainty of someone who expected obedience—whether today, tomorrow, or when we keeled over from sheer stubbornness.

Beside her, the census bureaucrats began their little ritual. One produced a ledger thick enough to brain a goat and a quill so sharp it probably had a body count. He cleared his throat—the international call sign for "prepare to be bored senseless."

"In accordance with the Vagrancy and Settlement Compliance Act, Section Four," he droned, "all persons of itinerant habit must submit to census accounting. You will provide your full name, year of birth, family grouping, number of dependents, special talents, and any distinguishing marks."

He finished with a brisk nod, like he expected applause.

Across the fire, we stared back, faces blank with the horror of it. Full name? Half of us had at least three, depending on who we were lying to. Year of birth? Somewhere between "a spring flood" and "that night the chickens rioted." Family grouping? We didn't come in tidy units with matching surnames and folding chairs. Special talents? Avoiding taxes? Escaping persecution?

The bureaucrat smiled encouragingly. The ledger lay open, quill poised, ready to trap us into tidy, poisonous little rows.

Finally, Granny Olya shuffled forward. She wiped her

hands on her apron and peered up at Seren and the scribe like she was weighing the exact size of the trouble they were worth.

"You want my age too?" she asked, sweet as vinegar.

The quill-wielder beamed. "Yes, honoured citizen."

Olya's eyes twinkled. "Somewhere between seventy and go to hell," she said, with a beatific smile.

A ripple of laughter ran through the Family — suppressed, but only barely.

Seren's jaw tightened. The bureaucrats sputtered. The guards shifted, visibly reassessing how many of us they could realistically club into cooperation if things got exciting.

That was our opening move.

If we had to be counted, we would be counted on our terms: slowly, sideways, and with as much trouble as we could muster without giving them an excuse to start swinging swords.

I folded my arms and grinned. The game had officially begun.

The census-takers tried to rally after Granny Olya's opening salvo. They adjusted their spectacles, cleared their throats again — the last weapon of men who'd never fought a real battle but once filed a complaint about rain being "too aggressive" — and called the next name on their ledger.

Which was a problem.

Because they didn't have the names yet.

Because nobody was giving them.

Instead, we offered up helpful information like:

- "I'm Mira, daughter of Tovi, niece of Sada, but only on Tuesdays."
- "My name's Bren… unless you ask my father, then it's 'You Little Bastard,' and I answer to both."
- "My special talent is 'singing poorly and stealing your spoons.'" (That one was technically true.)

Every time the poor scribe tried to anchor someone to a page, they slipped away like minnows in a muddy river.

And the family groups? Saints preserve us.

Every time they asked for one, it turned into a collaborative fiction project:

"I belong to Wagon Four, but I sleep behind Wagon One because of the snoring. My uncle is my mother's second cousin's ex-brother-in-law's apprentice, and he once promised to adopt me if his goat didn't object. The goat did object, loudly, so I'm technically a free agent until further notice."

At some point, the lead bureaucrat realized the numbers weren't adding up. Because while he was counting heads, half the heads were moving.

Children played tag around the wagons, deliberately swapping hats and shawls to confuse the counters. Mothers passed babies from lap to lap like trading cards. Brin walked calmly through the same spot three different times wearing three different coats, nodding solemnly each time when asked if he had already been counted.

It wasn't open rebellion.

It wasn't shouting or throwing rocks.

It was worse.

It was cooperation with malice.

Seren's lips pressed into a line sharp enough to cut parchment. I caught her eye once — and grinned, teeth and all.

She gave me a look like she was calculating the legal punishment for spontaneous combustion.

(If she ever figured out how to light me on fire by glaring, I'd be charcoal by now.)

But to her credit, she didn't order the guards to start dragging us into line. She just watched. Measured.

And maybe, just maybe, under all that exasperation and duty, there was the faintest flicker of admiration.

Or maybe she was just planning where to bury me later.

Either way, the day was looking up.

After an hour of gathering increasingly useless answers, Seren stepped forward herself. She didn't shout. She didn't threaten. She did something far worse.

She got calm.

"Alright," she said, voice clipped but even. "New procedure. One wagon at a time. Stand with your family head. State your names clearly. Once counted, you may sit."

Then she turned to me — because of course she turned to me — and added, in a tone normally reserved for chronic pickpockets and people who skip temple offerings:

"You. Help organize them. Or I will find a task even less dignified for you."

Now, I should tell you: Being put in charge of organizing the Family is like being asked to herd soap. Slippery. Uncooperative. Smells faintly of rebellion.

Still, I clapped my hands, gave a theatrical bow, and

announced, "Form a line, lovely people! Neatest wagon wins a prize! Possibly my respect, but I make no guarantees!"

The Family laughed — and promptly did exactly what they always do: They organized themselves in the most disorganized way imaginable.

Wagon One — Nema's — formed up first, naturally, out of some combination of respect and terror. Nema stood at the head like a queen in patched skirts, Brin looming silently behind her like the world's most patient thundercloud. Mero slouched beside them, looking like he might dissolve into the dust at any moment just to avoid paperwork.

Wagon Two — the Vashari and Tanviros families — ambled into place, but Kiro Vashari and Laro Vashari immediately started bickering over who was technically taller, which apparently affected order of listing.

Wagon Three — the Kelranis — showed up holding hands with half of Wagon Four, because young Tovi Ralen had dared Mira to swap places and then declared it a sacred pact.

Wagons Four through Seven staggered into something that might generously be called a line if you squinted hard enough and ignored the small scuffle over who was hogging the ink pot.

Wagons Eight through Twelve? They gave up entirely and started a makeshift market off to the side — trading bread, bent spoons, and scandalous gossip while very pointedly not being counted.

The tent and lean-to residents — Riv Talleny's lot and Lena Vier — floated freely, "visiting cousins," "stretching their legs," and "checking on the soup" whenever the census-takers got too close.

The scribe looked like he was praying for a small, localized plague. One of the guards developed a twitch under his left eye.

Meanwhile, I leaned casually against a wagon wheel and watched it all unfold like a proud artist admiring his masterpiece. Sure, maybe my "herding soap" technique wasn't perfect. But you had to admire the sheer, vibrant anarchy of it.

At least until Seren turned her glacial gaze back on me and said — so quietly I felt it in my ribs —

"Fix. It."

And saints help me, I tried.

Seren cleared her throat for the tenth time in an hour. It was the kind of prim cough that said, "I'm still in charge here," but by now it sounded more like she was trying to dislodge one of our stray goose feathers from her dignity. We Ruanne had that effect on officials: a tickle of confusion that only got worse the longer they tried to ignore it.

I leaned casually against the side of Nema's wagon — the big one with the bright red wheels and the suspiciously wobbling axle — and flashed Seren my sunniest smile. It was taking all my willpower not to burst out laughing at her expression: equal parts determination and the dawning realization that this census might just be the death of her.

"Alright," Seren said, adjusting the quill in her hand like a weapon, "once more. How many people are currently residing in this... household?" She gestured broadly at our entire camp — a cheerful tangle of wagons, crates, geese, cats, and the occasional uncooperative goat.

I opened my mouth, but Nema beat me to it.

"Twelve families!" she called from beside the fire, hands on her hips like a general surveying a battlefield.

"No, thirteen!" corrected old Maja Estrel from the shade of her wagon, squinting suspiciously at a group of teenagers wrestling over a loaf of bread.

"Fourteen if you count the cat wagon!" piped in Cousin Miv Kelrani, holding up Darsa Mevin's fat orange tomcat like a banner of rebellion.

Seren blinked at us, her quill hesitating an inch above the ledger.

"Families," she repeated carefully. "I'm asking for people."

"Depends," said Brin, deadpan from where he leaned against the side of Nema's wagon. "Some days the cats outnumber us."

Beside him, Mero gave an exaggerated nod. "And the cats are more law-abiding."

There was a ripple of laughter from the camp — stifled quickly, but not quickly enough.

Seren's jaw tightened almost imperceptibly. "All human family members, assemble here, please."

At this command, the camp erupted into motion like someone had kicked an anthill (a very disorganized, opinionated anthill).

Tovi Ralen immediately started gathering the younger children like a harried sheepdog. Kiro Vashari and Laro Vashari somehow ended up arguing over who was technically taller again. Darsa Mevin, bless her, attempted to corral her cats into a neat group — until she realized they didn't count, at which point she simply herded them off with muttered curses.

From the communal kitchen wagon, Ferrick Nuvra woke from a snoring nap with a startled, "Eh, what? Are we under attack?" — promptly knocking over a barrel of water and sending three shrieking ducks and our most nervous cat scattering in all directions.

One particularly fat duck took flight — straight past Seren's head, molting a feather that drifted down to land squarely on the bridge of her nose.

She sneezed with dignified fury.

I bit my lip hard. If I laughed now, I might not stop — and then they'd probably have to count me as two people: one sensible, one hysterical.

One by one, my kin lined up in front of Seren. Well, "line" might be a generous term. It was more like a squiggly knot, each person subtly trying to stand behind someone bigger, louder, or more confusing.

I sidled up beside Seren, trying to look helpful (and failing spectacularly).

She raised her quill and pointed it at Nema Al'Faerin, who stood like a patched-skirt queen at the front.

"Name?" Seren asked.

Nema smiled thinly. "Nema Al'Faerin."

"Relation to head of household?"

Nema's mouth twitched. "Head of household."

Seren scribbled grimly.

Next up was Brin Al'Faerin, standing so still he looked carved from stone.

"Name?" Seren prompted.

"Brin Al'Faerin," Brin rumbled.

"Relation?"

Nema cut in smoothly: "Bodyguard. Unofficial. Irreplaceable."

Brin just shrugged.

Then came Mero Vato, slouching like a boy trying to merge with the ground.

"Mero Vato," he said, flashing his most innocent *I didn't do it (but I would)* smile.

"Relation?"

"Depends who you ask," Mero said. "Let's say... honorary younger brother, frequent headache."

Seren paused for a long, slow second before writing it down.

Now came the children. First was Bren Estrel, dragged forward by Maja Estrel.

Bren puffed out his chest dramatically. "Bartholomew Ignatius Montague Estrel the Third!" he announced, throwing up a dramatic three-finger salute.

Seren blinked. "The third what?"

Bren beamed. "Third time lucky!"

I coughed loudly to cover my laughter.

When little Mira Ralen's turn came, she curtsied — badly — and lisped, "Mira. Cat herder. Good at hide-and-seek."

Sir Quacksalot, her duck-in-crime, waddled by as if in endorsement.

Then it was Tovi Ralen's turn. He bowed low and

whispered dramatically, "Supreme Commander of Wagon Four's Potato Supply."

Seren closed her eyes for a long moment — and pinched the bridge of her nose so hard I thought she might remove it entirely.

Across the camp, a chicken squawked indignantly as someone tripped over it.

We weren't even halfway through.

When it was little Tamar Drennik's turn, she popped up from behind Seren's leg, clinging like a barnacle.

I pried her off gently. "Come on, love, tell the nice lady your name."

Tamar tucked her head under my chin shyly, then shouted with sudden glee, "Princess Supreme Sunshine Duck-Wrangler Tamar!"

Seren crouched — impressively, given the armour of bureaucratic frustration she wore — and asked, with a perfectly straight face, "And your relation to head of household?"

"I'm the special-est one," Tamar announced. "Also, I wrangle ducks."

As if on cue, Sir Quacksalot honked and strutted by again.

Seren sighed, noted something illegible in her ledger, and stood back up. She sneezed again as another duck feather floated down to land on her nose.

I grinned at her as she glared, as if weighing whether the paperwork for my execution would be worth it.

Still, to her credit, Seren kept going — even as half the camp seemed to be sprouting extra cousins, disputed adoptions, and suspicious quantities of ducks.

I leaned against a wagon wheel, beaming with pride. The Family might have been an absolute disaster for a census, but by all the saints, we were our disaster.

At that moment, Pickle the goose, who had been waddling with great purpose at the edge of our chaotic "line," decided she too needed to be counted.

Pickle flapped up onto a crate and quacked authoritatively at Seren.

Seren stared at the goose. "That's... not a person."

Nema moved forward calmly, plucking Pickle off the crate and cradling her like a slightly irritable baby. "Don't mind her. She thinks she's management."

I couldn't resist. "Technically, she does have seniority over half the camp."

Seren gave me a look that could have ignited tinder. I smiled innocently. Pickle pecked idly at my sleeve.

Finally, Seren turned to me — the last, the crown jewel of this disaster.

She looked as though she were bracing herself.

I swept into a bow. "Aen Marr, at your service, O Supreme Quill-Wielder."

Seren raised an eyebrow. "Relation to head of household?"

"Adopted son of Nema Al'Faerin. Occasional cause of heart palpitations. Rescuer of stray ducks. Raconteur. Troublemaker. It's a very full resume."

"I'll just put 'son,'" Seren said, without even blinking this time.

She scribbled, then frowned at the list. Her finger ran down the names in her ledger: "Nema... Brin... Mero...

Mira... Bren... Tovi... Aen..." She paused. "That's seven."

She looked up sharply. "You said there were eight residents here."

Nema smiled her warm, infuriating smile. "There are."

Seren's eyes narrowed. "Where is the eighth?"

A long, uncomfortable pause.

I helpfully gestured toward Wagon Eight—the one painted with lizards, where the Marnetts and Shivaris lived.

"Jassa Marnett's inside," I said brightly. "Bit shy. Sometimes bites when startled."

Seren's face did something very interesting: a twitch between resignation and despair.

"She must be counted," she said grimly.

"By all means," I said, waving her forward like a court herald. "You'll want to knock politely. And maybe offer a bribe."

Seren, gathering the last shreds of her dignity, strode toward Wagon Eight.

I followed at a safe distance.

At the bright green door, she paused, cleared her throat, and said in her best reassuring official voice: "Miss Marnett? I am here only to record your presence for the city's census. No harm will come to you."

Silence.

Then—from somewhere behind the wagon: a distinct creak. From under the wagon: a scuttling noise.

I craned my neck and spotted Jassa herself wriggling out from under the far side, covered in dust and wearing the most guilty expression I'd ever seen on a human face.

She spotted me spotting her. I grinned and gave her a big, obvious wink.

She bolted into the maze of wagons before Seren even noticed.

Before Seren could react, the door of Gran Carys's wagon—the battered sky-blue one with the crooked axle—swung open with a BANG loud enough to wake the dead.

Out hobbled Gran Carys herself, wrapped in her patchwork shawl and brandishing—saints save us—her ancient crossbow, the one she swore she'd fire if the Purge ever came for us again.

I slapped my hand over my face.

This was definitely not part of our carefully orchestrated, passive-aggressive non-cooperation.

Gran Carys, nearly deaf as a wagon wheel and twice as stubborn, raised her (thankfully unloaded) crossbow toward the sky.

"No government rat's taking my grandson or my goats to be 're-educated'!" she hollered at absolutely no one in particular.

Seren gave a distinctly un-Oathbound yelp and ducked, her ledger flying from her hands as she dropped into a crouch.

Ferrick lunged in and, with the calm of a man who had wrestled this exact crossbow a hundred times before, gently redirected the weapon toward the clouds.

"Gran!" I exclaimed, hurrying forward with both hands raised in the universal 'please don't shoot' gesture.

"Nobody's taking anybody! This isn't a Purge inspection!"

Gran squinted down at Seren, who was crouched awkwardly near the fire. "Then what's that skinny sparrow sneakin' around my wagons for? She don't look like no baker!"

Seren, to her credit, managed to pop her head up just enough to stammer, "C-census, madam! Just a census!"

Gran paused, considering this deeply, as if calculating whether a census was a new kind of weapon.

"We said census, Gran," Ferrick added soothingly, prying the crossbow away from her grip with the delicacy of a man diffusing a barrel of gunpowder.

Gran Carys grumbled but relented, hobbling back toward her wagon while muttering dark threats about what would happen if the ducks weren't properly counted too.

As if summoned, Pickle and Plum—Nalina's half-tame geese—waddled into the clearing, honking furiously and scattering a trail of feathers.

Pickle immediately lunged at Seren's boots, perhaps in defense of civil liberties.

Seren scrambled backward—and stepped squarely into a puddle of something profoundly unfortunate.

Her boot slid.

Her arms windmilled.

"Whoa—!"

Without thinking, I lunged forward and caught her by the elbow just as she tipped backwards toward a mound of duck leavings.

For a breathless second, we stood there frozen: Me gripping Seren's arm, her hand instinctively gripping my shoulder for balance. Ducks milling around our ankles like tiny judgmental witnesses.

"Steady on," I murmured, feeling my heart hammer for reasons that had nothing to do with poultry.

Up close, Seren's face was inches from mine. Her dark hair was loose, her eyes wide, her mouth slightly parted in shock.

And for the first time since she marched into our camp looking like the physical manifestation of a statute, she looked... human.

Real.

Just a girl, not much older than me, trying desperately to hold her footing in a world that didn't want to be measured.

She cleared her throat (again—I've honestly lost track of the coughs at this point) and straightened herself, brushing off her robes with a sharp, flustered motion.

"Thank you," she said, voice low but earnest.

I let go of her elbow—maybe a beat later than necessary—and offered a lopsided smile.

"Anytime, my lady of ledgers."

Her lips twitched. For a half-second, I thought she might smile. Might.

Then the shutters slammed down behind her eyes again, and she turned away, gathering what remained of her official dignity.

Still—

I'd seen it.

The tiny crack in her armour.

And some foolish, traitorous part of me very much wanted to find it again.

"Anytime," I added softly, watching her.

She stooped to retrieve her fallen ledger, brushing dirt and a stray duck feather off the battered leather cover. With a snap, she flipped it open and checked her notes, breathing deeply as she fought to reassemble her professional façade.

"We still have one small person to account for," she said, brisk but notably gentler.

"Ah yes," I said solemnly, flourishing a hand toward the yellow wagon, "the elusive Princess Tansy, Sovereign of Mischief."

Seren shot me a sideways glance. Was that the barest hint of a smirk?

"Proceed."

I cleared my throat dramatically and turned to the wagon like a herald announcing royalty.

"O fairest Tansy! O terror of duck and duckling! O vanquisher of naptime!" I bellowed. "Come forth, that you might be blessed into the sacred pages of Bureaucracy Eternal!"

Behind me, I heard a suspicious noise from Seren — halfway between a cough and a stifled laugh.

The yellow wagon door creaked open.

Tansy appeared, her cheeks flushed pink, clutching her battered wooden duck toy in one hand and a suspiciously stolen biscuit in the other.

"I was busy," she said solemnly, brushing straw from her skirt with great dignity.

Seren crouched slightly, managing a patience I didn't know she possessed.

"And your name, young lady?"

"Tansy Ralen," she said proudly.

"Relation?"

"I'm everybody's favourite. And I herd ducks better than Brin does people."

Seren dutifully wrote it down. I saw her shoulders shake once — very subtly — with silent laughter.

"And how old are you, Miss Tansy?"

Tansy lifted five very sticky fingers into the air.

"Five and three-quarters!" she announced. "Almost six. That's when you're allowed to boss the chickens."

Seren blinked, solemn as a magistrate, and wrote: Age: 5 (and three-quarters).

Sir Quacksalot honked in agreement from somewhere near the soup barrel.

When Seren finally tucked her quill away, she straightened and surveyed the camp — our wagons, our cats, our ducks, our woven chaos of humanity.

"You have a… remarkable family," she said carefully, the warmth slipping through despite herself.

I swept a ridiculous bow.

"Thank you. We'll have that etched into a plaque."

That earned me a small, startled huff of laughter.

Then, smoothing her robes with the dignity of a woman who had survived worse, Seren announced more formally:

"The Crown thanks you for your cooperation."

Somehow, nobody laughed out loud. (Though Mero did mime a dramatic swoon behind her.)

Seren turned back to me.

Unexpectedly, she extended her hand.

No scrolls, no threats—just a hand, offered plain and simple.

I stared at it for half a beat longer than was dignified, then clasped it firmly.

For a moment, everything else—the Family, the ducks, the persistent scent of overcooked soup—faded into a distant murmur.

"Thank you, Aen," she said, voice pitched low, for my ears alone. "For helping to keep things... civil."

I raised an eyebrow. "Civil, my lady? Why, I've been the very soul of restraint."

That earned a genuine smirk, brief and bright.

"Until next time," she said, her voice a low promise—and maybe a warning.

I gave a theatrical salute.

"Safe travels, brave Census Knight. Our door is always open."

I paused. She waited for it.

"Mostly because it won't stay on its hinges."

Seren almost smiled, swung into her saddle, and gathered the reins.

Before she rode out, she lifted two fingers in a casual salute.

I stood there grinning like an idiot as she disappeared down the dusty road, her robes trailing behind her, a duck feather still clinging to her shoulder.

I lingered a moment longer, a lone Ruanne in the settling dust, still holding one of Sir Quacksalot's rogue feathers that had somehow ended up in my hand. I twirled it between my fingers, replaying that moment—Seren's hand in mine, the look we'd shared, the tiny crack in her armour I wasn't supposed to notice.

Behind me, the Family began to erupt back into noisy, glorious life.

Uncle Ryll was the first to break, clapping me on the back so hard I nearly staggered into the firepit.

"Well done, lad! Had that poor girl spinning like a weathervane in a tornado! Ha! The way she jumped when Carys came out—priceless!"

Mama shook her head as she gathered the scattered laundry, though a proud little smile pulled at her mouth.

"I almost pity the poor thing," she said. "Almost."

Cousin Mira was already chasing ducks again, gleefully reenacting Seren's arm-flailing tumble for the younger kids, who shrieked with laughter. Little Tansy, now perched triumphantly on Grandpa Bramwell's shoulders, conducted the chaos like a tiny, tyrannical general.

Mero sauntered over, arms folded, smirking like a cat with feathers stuck in his teeth.

"So," he drawled just low enough for only me to hear, "are we inviting the census knight to dinner next time? Or straight to the wedding?"

I choked on nothing. "Shut up," I hissed, focusing very hard on the feather in my hand.

Mero raised an eyebrow, the picture of insufferable innocence.

"You're blushing," he said.

"I am not."

"You are."

"It was duck muck," I muttered, flushing hotter under his stare. "I was saving her from duck muck."

"Sure," Mero said with an exaggerated nod that dripped disbelief. "Duck muck. Entirely selfless."

He ambled off, probably to start a betting pool.

I stood there a moment longer, breathing in the familiar, messy, perfect noise of home—the scent of burnt soup, damp wagons, woodsmoke, and laughter.

Opening my hand, I looked down at the feather again: a tiny ink smudge stained one side, from Seren's fallen ledger when I caught her.

With a helpless little laugh, I tucked the feather into my shirt pocket, close to my heart.

Maybe—just maybe—we hadn't scared her off entirely.

And maybe, just maybe, that ridiculous, exhausting afternoon had left the whole world just a little bit brighter.

A Tent, Two Geese, and an Extremely Misunderstood Marriage Proposal

> *"A love unbroken is as dangerous as a sword untested."*
>
> — *ancient Ruanne proverb.*

To understand this story, you first need to understand the life we had before we left Dararien.

Back then — before the true madness began — the Ruanne were held together by tradition, history, and a shared hunger for life lived loudly. We laughed, we fought, we loved each other with the kind of passion that usually warmed but occasionally burned. Disagreements were storms: they blew fierce, they broke things, but they passed. Among the Ruanne, a true friend was someone you'd screamed at, maybe even struck, but never let go.

Family was sacred. Parents didn't just raise children — they shaped them, protected them, and watched for the moment their thread could be woven into the larger story of the Ruanne people. Songs, dances, stories, and customs were passed down like heirlooms. And from the moment a child was born, so too began the quiet search for a worthy partner. Strong men for daughters. Loving women for sons. Dowries were generous. Weddings were legend.

None of us imagined what came next.

Fleeing in the night.

Losing homes, kin, and the only kind of life we'd ever known.

But the Ruanne — we don't let something as small as a kingdom rewriting history without us stop our song. We found new ways to dance. New stories to tell.

This is one of them.

Family. Blessing, curse, full-contact sport. Let me explain.

Ours wasn't family by blood. Not always. Not usually. Family was whoever survived the bad times with you — and still laughed at your cooking. About two dozen families, all stitched together by luck, stubbornness, and Nema's particular way of watching you like a hawk watches a half-plucked chicken.

Some were Ruanne, like me. Some joined us along the road — when cities smiled at us and slammed the gates, when bargains turned bitter, when home was a memory you packed in the bottom of a wagon and promised you'd unpack someday.

Twelve wagons, a few tents, and more people pretending they didn't snore than honesty could reasonably support.

Space was scarce. Secrets even scarcer. Every wagon shared. Every breath borrowed. The Ralens whispered more than they spoke, like words cost money. The Shivaris and Marnetts shared a wagon painted in lizards and armed truce. The Mevins raised cats the way other people raised crops — wild, plentiful, and occasionally inside your shoes. And then there was Maja Estrel, who was either everyone's grandmother or nobody's, depending on whether you were due a scolding or a sweet.

Children belonged to all of us. If one misbehaved, twelve adults took turns explaining why that was a poor life choice. If one cried, twenty voices promised the world would look better after soup. If you needed a shoulder, well — good news. We were a people rich in shoulders, and not half bad at leaning.

Our code was simple: We protect our own. We share what we have. We remember.

And we did. Especially the parts you'd prefer we forgot.

The Family gave us food. It gave us music. It gave us safety. It also gave us problems. Mostly if you were young. And stupid. And in love.

You see, among the many ancient traditions we dragged behind us like badly-packed trunks, one of the favourites was matchmaking. Parents plotted pairings with the solemnity of high priests and the accuracy of drunken archers. So-and-so's daughter might make a fine match for so-and-so's son. Quiet grandchildren! Dowries! Stability! All the thrilling promises a teenager in heat dreams of.

Naturally, we had our own ideas. The notion of settling down with the first girl who agreed to dance with you? It felt less like romance and more like a sentencing.

Back in Dararien, it was understood that boys—and the smarter girls—were supposed to test the waters before tying their ankles together for life. Sneak out. Sneak back. Try not to get caught—or at least try to be funny about it if you did.

But even if you were feeling rebellious and charming, there was one tiny, unbearable problem:

There weren't a lot of options.

You could count the number of eligible teenagers on one hand. Two hands if you squinted and ignored things like *deep personal incompatibility* or *threats of minor violence*. Some were already "spoken for" in the vague, wishful way old people liked to talk about the future. Some were cousins you couldn't explain away. Some were so emotionally combustible they ought to have been stored under wet blankets.

That left a few possibilities. Some were uninterested. Some were terrifying. Some were *interested and terrifying*, which I assure you is worse.

So we flirted. We teased. We dared. Mostly, we speculated. And watched each other like gamblers sweating over a rigged deck.

And — of course — some of the Family made a whole sport of watching us back.

For example, Tressa Drennik. Our unblinking sentinel. Not prudish — Tressa had been caught kissing behind a water barrel not three years ago — but obsessive about *propriety*. Her main concern wasn't if someone was sneaking around. It was how well they did it.

"If you're going to fumble around like wild dogs," she once said, "at least have the decency to fumble somewhere out of earshot."

She could smell stolen wine at twenty paces.

She tracked eye contact like a hawk.

She took notes. *Literal notes.*

Enter the tent.

Not a proper tent, mind you. Not the kind a respectable merchant might unfold with a dramatic flourish and three assistants. No, ours was half a canvas, two guilty ropes, one bent pole, and a lot of stubborn faith. It stank of feet, sulked in the rain, and had long since given up any pretensions about being waterproof — or dignified.

But it was ours. The only place we weren't being watched. No aunt lurking to measure the distance between knees. No uncle peering in like a goat judging a fence. Inside the tent, we could be loud, or quiet, or stupid, or ourselves. Usually all at once.

And that's how Nalina, Elwen, Mero, and I ended up together — four half-broken kids jammed into one sagging excuse for a shelter by fate, stubbornness, and a slight misunderstanding with the goat pen. Two boys. Two girls. Each of us carrying fresh scars from Dararein's slow collapse. I was the eldest, self-appointed captain of our sad little shipwreck. Sarcasm was my sword against the dark, and trust me, I swung it like a drunk fencing master.

Across from me sat Nalina, legs tucked under her, stitching scraps of fabric into what might someday, possibly, if we prayed hard enough, become a blanket.

Beside her curled Elwen — quiet as dusk. She always looked smaller than she was, like the world had been trying to fold her away but hadn't quite finished.

And there, stretched across the tent entrance like a sacrificial offering nobody had asked for, was Mero — snoring so loud the canvas gave serious thought to collapsing. My cousin in everything but blood. His nightly gifts included strategic insults, regrettable smells, and sleep-mutterings so incoherent they could have been spells. A master of slipping through life without ever being caught, Mero was everything I wasn't: quick where I was loud, clever where I was stubborn, and just lucky enough to make it all look easy.

"Only ninety-nine more scraps to go," I said, watching Nalina wrestle her needle through a particularly rebellious patch. "At this rate, we'll have a full blanket by midsummer. Just in time to tear it up and start again."

She gave me a half-smile. A real one. The kind you could

plant your feet on, if you were careful. Even Elwen's lips twitched before she tucked her face down.

Outside, one of the geese let out a low, judgmental quack. Probably Plum. That goose had opinions about everything.

We drifted into silence. The wind pushed against the canvas. The ropes groaned. It was the kind of quiet you don't find much in the world—fragile, and stubborn, and stitched together out of sheer spite.

Then Elwen spoke. Soft. Careful. And the tent listened.

"Do you remember the spring fair in Dararein?" she said. "Before everything... went wrong?"

Nalina and I both nodded. Of course we did.

"My mother used to take me to the puppet shows," Elwen said, voice barely more than a thread. "I always wanted to dance the Maypole. With the ribbons, you know?"

Nalina's needle paused. Her face went soft around the edges.

"We had something like that after harvest," she said. "Bonfires, music. Papa would spin Mama around until they both fell over like drunks." She laughed—small, broken around the edges—but still a laugh. "I used to think... I'd have a dance like that at my wedding."

It hit me then—the ache. Not pity. Nalina would gut me for pity. Just that sharp, raw thing that lived under your ribs when you realized how much hope was still fighting inside the people you loved. Even now. Even here. Even under a leaking tent with geese for an audience.

Mero snorted in his sleep. "...no more bread... please..." he mumbled piteously.

All three of us broke at once, laughter slipping out before the sadness could lock us up again. Nalina actually smiled. A full, shameless smile. It hit like sunlight in a dark room.

"Always food with you boys," she teased, nudging my foot with hers.

I clutched my chest like a dying hero. "Slander! I'll have you know I dine only on the finest vintage field mice and artisan tree bark."

Elwen giggled, quiet and lovely. "With a side of wild mushroom stew," she added. "And beetle garnish. For texture."

We laughed. Laughed the way you laugh when you're stealing something precious right out of the jaws of the world. Just for that moment, we weren't refugees. We weren't orphans. We weren't anything the world called us. We were just four idiots in a collapsing tent, dreaming about ribbons and weddings and soup, while a goose plotted our downfall outside.

And for that night, it was enough.

One more thing: Nalina.

Nalina Al'tiera had arrived with one shoe, two geese, and the kind of thousand-yard stare usually reserved for soldiers and people who've tried to fix a leaking wagon in the rain.

Her family had lived in a lopsided cottage just outside Dararein. Her grandfather built it. Her mother kept it warm. Her father painted clouds on the ceilings because he believed every room ought to remember the sky. When the purge came, he tried to distract the guards with a puppet show so awful it might have been classified as an act of war. He died before the punchline. Her mother disappeared into the smoke. Her little brother, Lio, was last seen being carried away by a stranger who mistook him for luggage.

All that remained was Melina. One shoe. Two geese— Pickle and Plum—who followed her out of the city like feathered grief. Blistered feet, empty hands, and a heart stitched together by sheer, bloody-minded refusal to die.

She didn't beg. She didn't cry. She just marched into our camp like a ghost with strong opinions, collapsed by the fire, and refused to move. The geese settled on either side of her like trauma wearing feathers.

Enter the Berrovs of Wagon #5. Garron Berrov, a candle-maker turned philosopher—literally. He once spent a month trying to invent a scent called "melancholy flame." Sella Berrov, nocturnal, suspicious, and shaped like someone who had survived more midnight patrols than was strictly reasonable. And their daughter, Elwen—soft-voiced, sharp-eyed, and doomed by the lethal Ruanne trait of caring too much.

At first, they tried ignoring her. Sella said, "We can't adopt every stray with a tragic aura." Elwen brought her bread anyway. When the geese lined up politely for their share, Sella reconsidered: "Anyone who can civilize poultry deserves a roof."

They gave her a bedroll and cupboard space. She gave them silence, survival instincts, and once—accidentally— a boot, which Pickle promptly converted into a nesting site. Over time, she added murmured thanks. Small, wary smiles. And, eventually—dangerously—laughter.

Garron made her a goose-shaped candle. She didn't

throw it away. Sella started regularly making extra food. Elwen braided her hair.

They weren't just stitched together. They were the kind of broken that fits.

Okay. Ready or not, here we go.

Outside the tent, Elwen's mother called the girls. We said our goodnights, and the two of them slipped away toward their wagon, arm-in-arm.

Later that night, I couldn't sleep. Maybe it was my stomach growling. Maybe the wind scratching at the canvas. Or maybe it was the echo of Nalina's voice from earlier — the way she'd spoken about wedding dances, like they still belonged to her. I wasn't sure. But I needed air.

I crept out of the tent, wrapping my coat tight around my ribs. The camp was quiet, lit only by a waning sliver of moon. Clouds chased each other across the sky. Near the edge of camp, I passed the goose pen. Pickle and Plum shifted and grumbled, soft feathered protests.

"Sorry, ladies," I whispered. Plum gave me a disapproving quack and tucked her head back under her wing.

We'd made camp on common land off the east road to Nareth, our twelve wagons parked in a loose semi-circle. Nearby stood an old well, and beside it, a solitary willow tree — its drooping branches brushing the dirt like it, too, had grown tired of standing.

I wandered toward the well, thinking I'd get a sip of water, but paused when I heard voices — soft, private, on the other side of the willow.

My first thought: bandits.

Second: run.

Third: listen.

I crept forward, parting the willow's curtain of leaves. Moonlight caught two familiar shapes seated on a fallen log. I relaxed, but I didn't step out. Not yet. The way Elwen's body curled into Nalina's side, the hush of her voice—I knew I was intruding.

"I try to be strong," Nalina whispered, voice raw. "But I can't. There's nothing left. I've lost everything."

My chest ached. Nalina rarely let anyone see her brokenness.

"You won't lose me," Elwen murmured, gathering Nalina in her arms. "Not ever. I promise."

They sat there, woven tight under the willow's drooping branches. Quiet. Close. Grieving the way only people who'd lost everything could.

I tried to sneak away, but as I turned, my boot caught a bramble. It snapped loudly.

They broke apart like startled birds.

"Who's there?" Nalina called, voice sharp with fear.

I stepped into the clearing with hands raised. "Just me," I said, trying not to look like a ghost or a spy. "Didn't mean to interrupt. I, uh... had to pee."

Elwen turned away. Nalina faced me—flushed, teary, wary. For a second, she looked like she expected me to shout, or tease, or worse.

I smiled instead. "Didn't mean to spook you. I thought everyone was asleep. Otherwise, I would've invited myself to the late-night gossip circle."

Nalina tried to smile. It wobbled at the edges. "We just couldn't sleep."

"Too many dreams of beetle stew," I said, stepping back toward the camp. "I understand."

Elwen finally looked at me, her eyes shy but grateful. "Sorry, Aen," she said. "We'll save you a log next time."

I gave a theatrical bow. "Much appreciated."

"But really," I added, "it's cold. We should get back. If Mero wakes and finds all three of us gone, he'll think we were kidnapped or — worse — started breakfast without him."

That earned me a real laugh from Elwen. Nalina let out a shaky breath that might've been a chuckle.

Mero was still asleep when we returned, snoring with the dedication of someone who knew no shame.

I curled under my ragged blanket and stared up at the dark canvas ceiling.

Under the willow tree, I'd seen something fragile and real.

Nalina — so guarded, so fierce — had let herself fall apart. And Elwen, quiet and steady, had held her through it. There was a kind of love in that. Not the loud kind. Not the easy kind. But the kind you carry, even when the world has burned.

Morning stumbled in grey and drizzly, like even the sky regretted last night's decisions. By the time I emerged from the tent, Mero had already coaxed the fire back to life and was humming something cheerful and off-key while toasting yesterday's bread over a flat stone. Elwen stood nearby, sleeves damp from the grass, feeding Pickle and Plum handfuls of precious grain like some kind of sainted poultry goddess.

Nalina was nowhere in sight.

Mero looked up and grinned the grin of a man who had seen something and was never, ever going to let it die. His eyebrows waggled like they were trying to wriggle off his face and escape the shame. "Morning, lover boy," he muttered.

I blinked. "Morning, what?" I hissed, glancing quickly at Elwen to make sure she was out of earshot.

"She's busy seducing the poultry," Mero said, jerking his chin toward Elwen. "You're safe. For now."

I rubbed my face, like that could scrub the last thirty seconds out of history. "Mero. What are you talking about."

He elbowed me playfully. "Don't play innocent. I saw you. Midnight Stroll himself, creeping out of the tent like a lovesick ghost. Off to murmur poetry under the willow, was it?"

Realization hit me like a thrown sandal. "Oh gods. No. Mero, you idiot — it wasn't like that." I dropped my voice. "I did go out, yeah, but I wasn't meeting anyone. I needed air. I stumbled across Nalina and Elwen talking. That's it. No poetry. No ghosting."

Mero folded his arms, wearing the smug satisfaction of a cat that had just found the cream, the pie, and the key to the larder. "Uh huh. And you just happened to wander under the most romantic tree in camp? By accident?"

I groaned and raked a hand through my hair, somehow making it worse. "It wasn't romantic. She was upset.

Elwen was comforting her. I stayed for maybe thirty seconds. Then I stepped on a bramble and screamed like a cursed soul. It was extremely dignified, I assure you."

Mero gave a sage nod, as if recording my shame for future blackmail. "Classic."

"I'm serious," I said, which would have been more convincing if my voice hadn't cracked.

He raised his hands, palms out, the universal Ruanne signal for *I'm wrong, but I'm still winning.* "Fine, fine. Just saying — if you're sweet on one of them, don't wait around until somebody faster gets there first."

Before I could improve my argument with violence, Nalina appeared, two heavy water buckets hooked over her arms. Mero, the opportunistic coward, trotted off to help her, whistling like innocence itself.

I turned back to the fire and busied myself tearing the stale bread into four ragged, definitely-not-symbolic chunks. I was so focused on not thinking that I didn't notice Elwen watching me until she spoke.

"Everything alright, Aen?"

I startled so badly I nearly threw the bread in the fire. "Oh! Yeah. Fine," I said in the voice of a person very much not fine.

She raised an eyebrow. Silently. Devastatingly.

I winced. "Mero was just... being Mero," I mumbled.

Her lips twitched at the edges. She didn't push. But I caught the faint flush rising in her cheeks, and suddenly I forgot how to hold a piece of bread without looking like I was trying to strangle it.

Thankfully, Nalina and Mero clattered back with the

water, and the moment crumpled mercifully into the noise.

That day, something felt off.

At first, I blamed the drizzle, or the general inconvenience of being a teenager in a camp full of adults who treated your existence like a suspicious noise in the dark. But then I noticed the glances. Just a few, at first. Older Family members, turning their heads. Whispering behind hands. Nothing dramatic. Just little shifts. A name carried on a hush it wasn't meant to ride.

I was hauling firewood from the stack near the Vasharis' wagon when I passed close enough to hear Tressa Drennik whispering with Elwen's mother, Sella. They didn't notice me. Or they did, and wanted me to hear.

"...saw Aen sneaking off, bold as brass, after midnight," Tressa murmured, lips barely moving. Her sharp eyes flicked toward me. I froze, pretending I was deeply, spiritually invested in the condition of a split log.

Sella's voice came next, low and tight. "You think he's trifling with one of them? My Elwen? Or Nalina?"

"Nalina," Tressa said, with the smug certainty of someone who had already edited the truth for publication. "Looked right distraught this morning, didn't she? Pale as a sheet when I spotted her by the well. And I saw him coming out not long after her last night. Mark my words, Sella, there's mischief there."

I felt my stomach turn over. *Mischief. Trifled.* They made it sound like I'd stolen something sacred.

"If he's compromised the girl," Tressa went on, "he ought to do right by her."

There was a pause. Then Sella said, serious as a hanging judge, "We'll need to talk to Nema."

I nearly dropped the firewood. They were talking about me. About Nalina. About a thing that never happened.

I wanted to march over, wanted to tell them they were wrong, that I hadn't touched her, hadn't *trifled* with anything. But I couldn't. Because to explain would be to drag Nalina's hurt into the open, and that wasn't mine to drag.

So instead, I turned and ran. Firewood forgotten. Heart hammering loud enough to wake the whole camp.

I found Mero near the far wagons, playing some kind of dice game with a cluster of younger kids and winning all their pebbles. I grabbed his shoulder and yanked him aside.

"What's got your trousers in a twist?" he asked, frowning as I pulled him behind a tent.

"Gossip," I hissed. "Somebody saw me sneaking around last night. And Nalina looked upset this morning. Now they think I—" I dropped my voice even lower, " — messed with her honour."

Mero blinked, then grinned. "You scandalous rogue."

I scowled. "This isn't funny."

"They think you seduced her under the willow?"

"They think I compromised her," I spat. "And now they're talking about going to Nema about her and I. Like we are something that needs *organizing*."

The grin dropped off his face. "Oh. That's... not ideal."

"You think?" I ran a hand through my hair. "If this gets to Nalina or Elwen, they'll be horrified. And if some elder corners Nalina to 'have a word' about it…"

Mero winced. "She'll panic. She's barely holding things together as it is."

We found Nalina or Elwen near the wash line, folding linens together.

Nalina looked up, saw our faces, and straightened. All instincts alert. "Is everything alright?" she asked.

"Not exactly," I said, glancing around. A few of the kids were nearby, playing with a stick and some unfortunate frog.

"Let's walk," I murmured.

Elwen nodded. Nalina hesitated for half a second before following.

We stepped out past the wagons, toward the scrub at the edge of camp, where no one could overhear.

The sky was still heavy with rainclouds. The wind tugged at the edges of our clothes. We walked in silence for a few beats.

And then I turned, looked Nalina in the eye, and said: "You're not going to like this."

As the four of us walked beyond the reach of curious ears, I laid it out.

The whispers. The assumptions. The "compromise." The impending scandal.

Nalina's expression shifted from confusion to horror in slow motion. "They think… you and I — ?"

I nodded grimly.

"Oh gods," she whispered, face flushing. "Knowing

Tressa, she's probably told the entire camp already."

Elwen's hand found hers and squeezed tight. "And my family will believe it," she said quietly, fury threading her voice. "Especially with us sneaking out. They'll assume..." She couldn't finish.

Nalina stood still, her jaw clenched. "I'll say it's not true. I'll tell them nothing happened."

"They won't believe you," Elwen said gently.

"They'll think you're covering," I added. "To protect me."

And that's when the idea hit me. Now, a sane man—or even just a moderately bruised one—might recognize the warning signs. A sudden flash of brilliance? Most likely a snare set by the gods to make sure I impale myself doing something theatrical and stupid. But did I ignore it? Did I smile politely and back away like a man who knows better? Of course not. I charged straight at it, arms wide, shouting, "*This'll end well!*"

"Or," I said slowly, "maybe we don't deny it."

Three pairs of eyes turned on me like I'd suggested we elope with the geese and start a theatre troupe.

Mero looked alarmed. "Aen. No. This is not the time for one of your plans."

"Are you seriously suggesting," Nalina said, eyes wide, "that we pretend we're—what?"

I smiled winningly. "We declare our undying love."

They stared.

"I'm serious," I continued. "We lean into it. Loudly. Publicly. We say it's love—star-crossed, inconvenient, impulsive love. And if the Family thinks it's love, they'll drop the accusations. Maybe even approve."

Mero blinked. "That is the stupidest plan I've ever heard."

"It'll work," I said, "It's true love. Presto – no scandal."

Elwen bit her lip. "What if they say you must 'do right by her'? Like propose?"

"We'll deal with that later," I said, waving off anything resembling caution. "This isn't about a proposal. It's about control. We take their gossip and turn the tables."

Sure enough, the Family moved with the speed of a priceless vase falling off a table.

That evening, Elwen and Nalina got hauled in by and a flock of aunties for Question Time. They denied everything. Swore up, down, and sideways that nothing had happened.

Which, obviously, meant it absolutely had. Or so the Family decided. By dawn, the rumour had grown legs, sprouted wings, stolen someone's hat, and was flapping around the camp screaming scandal in twelve dialects and at least three musical scales.

By afternoon, Nema summoned me. And Nalina. Waiting for us were Sella, Tressa, and a scattering of elders all wearing the sort of grim faces usually reserved for funerals or inventory day. Nema sat at the centre, flanked by tea and judgment, sipping calmly enough to make you wish for an earthquake.

"Aen," she said, far too calmly. "You may be young. But youth is no excuse for dishonour. If you've behaved improperly with this girl, there will be consequences."

I stepped forward, placed a hand dramatically over my heart, and announced in my finest, most tragic-hero voice: "It's true love."

The room buzzed like a stone thrown through a beehive.

"Nalina deserves love," I declared, pitching my voice for maximum tragedy. "She is brave, she walked through fire to get here. She keeps geese, and secrets, and dreams of a world that doesn't spit on people like us. She laughs like it doesn't hurt and fights like she's already lost too much."

Tressa narrowed her eyes into knife-slits. Sella clutched her necklace like it might save her soul. Nema blinked once. Slowly.

"You're too young to know what love is," she said, in the careful tone you use when debating whether to smack a fool or pray for him.

"I see beauty," I said, full of foolish courage, "and I know it to be true."

Nema turned to Nalina. "And you?" she asked. "Is this true?"

Nalina's back went straight as a bowstring. Her fists clenched in the folds of her skirt, but her voice was steady when she said: "I do. I feel it too."

Somewhere behind me, someone gasped. Possibly a fainting chicken. I refused to turn around and check.

Nema studied us both for a long, heavy moment. Then she nodded. "Very well," she said. "We will consider this."

With that, we were dismissed.

The wagon door creaked open behind us, and I stepped

out into a wall of cheerful voices. Campfires crackled. A pot somewhere boiled over with lentils and anticipation. The sky was still grey, but the air had changed — like someone had lit a match in a room full of old papers.

Behind me, Elwen's parents lingered in Nema's wagon, their voices low, reverent. I paused, glanced back, and saw it: the look on Sella's face. Not suspicion. Not relief.

Joy.

The kind of joy reserved for when your daughter is about to be folded safely into the arms of tradition.

And just like that, my stomach bottomed out.

I'd meant to stall a rumour.

Distract a few nosy elders.

Buy the girls time.

Instead, I'd authored a fairy tale. And they were writing the ending for me.

It didn't take long. That evening, Nema called the Family to the fire circle. She spoke in that calm, heavy voice she saved for decrees — and executions.

"Nalina and Aen have declared their love before the Family," she said. "And as we are a people who treasure both tradition and truth, we will honour their bond. A wedding will be held. Not one day, but soon. Let joy rise among us."

For a second, the camp froze. You could've heard a bean drop. And then —

Applause. Cheers. Someone actually sobbed. A flower garland got shoved onto my head. I think a toddler blessed me with a bean. Somebody else slapped me on the back hard enough to dislodge a tooth.

I stood there grinning like a drunk goat at its own wedding feast, while the catastrophic weight of what I'd done dropped onto my spine like a dung wagon falling downhill.

Across the circle, I caught sight of Nalina.

She wasn't smiling.

By morning, it was official. The Family was planning the celebration of the season. Old linen was being dyed with crushed berries. Someone had started carving a ceremonial spoon. The Vasharis began prepping a "blessing feast" that required no fewer than three goats. The Mevin cats wore ribbons they clearly despised. Even the lizard-wagon got painted.

I spent the morning trying to find Nema. I had half-formed plans of pleading for a delay, citing some made-up illness or tragic case of second thoughts. But Nema was busy. She'd vanished into the machinery of matrimony — discussing ceremonies, blessing stones, and flower paths. Her lieutenants flanked her like saints guarding a shrine.

Everywhere I turned, people were smiling at me.

I found them huddled behind the drying racks near the cook tent. Nalina was pacing like a cat in a snare. Elwen sat perched on a barrel, arms wrapped so tight around herself she looked ready to vanish. Mero leaned against a crate, watching me with the expression of a man who'd just found something unspeakable on his boots.

"You're a genius," Nalina snapped. "An oath-breaking, goose-cursed genius."

"I didn't think they'd take it literally!" I protested.

"You declared your love!"

"Yes," I said, desperate. "And love is famously slippery! Vague! Interpretive!"

Elwen looked up, voice quiet but slicing clean. "They're not treating it like a story, Aen. They're treating it like a sacrament."

Mero shrugged. "On the bright side, the fish stew's going to be excellent. The Berrovs have already dug out their good pots."

Nalina rounded on him. "Mero. Not helping."

"Wasn't trying to," he muttered.

"We can't let this happen," I said. "We'll go to Nema. Tell her it was a misunderstanding. Clear it up."

"And she'll ask why we lied," Nalina shot back, arms folded like shields. "Or worse — why *I* changed my mind."

The words hit me like a sack of wet flour. Right. I could back out and still be the fool, the boy who panicked. But Nalina — the girl who spoke her heart in front of the Family — She'd be a stain. A shame. A warning.

"I'll take the blame," I said. "I'll tell them I panicked. Made it up. Got confused by... I don't know, heatstroke."

"No one will believe you," Elwen said gently.

"Not after all this," Mero added. "You've got a goat named after you now, Aen. A literal wedding goat."

Nalina let out a strangled sound — half laugh, half sob. "They named a goat after him. Of course they did."

Silence settled like dust. Heavy. Relentless.

Then Elwen stood, moving like a decision. "Okay. We stall. We delay. We smile and play along until we find a way out."

"Or until they get tired of planning and move on," I offered, hopefully, idiotically.

Mero raised an eyebrow so dry it could have started a fire. "When," he said, "have the Family ever moved on?"

No one answered. Because we all knew the truth.

They never did.

By dusk, the camp had transformed.

Children rehearsed songs. Aunties debated cake fillings. Someone was embroidering Nalina's name into a scrap of veil.

Everywhere I went, people clapped me on the shoulder, winked, whispered blessings. I smiled. I bowed. I lied through my teeth.

That night, at the fire circle, I was asked to tell the story of how I'd "proposed." I panicked. Invented a saga involving a goose chase, an accidental pie, and a heartfelt speech under the stars. People loved it. Tressa wept openly. A child tried to hug me. I think I'm now the reason "goose blessings" are going to be a thing.

From the edge of the firelight, I caught Nalina watching me.

Not with hatred.

Not with anger.

Just a quiet, exhausted sorrow.

And that was worse.

The night before the wedding, Nema gave me a jacket.

It was beautiful. Deep blue with scarlet trim, patched in places but lined with golden thread. Too fine for a thief. Too fine for a liar. It must have belonged to someone important once — maybe a merchant or a priest. But now it was mine. It fit almost perfectly, like it had been waiting for me.

"I found it years ago," she said. "Saved it for someone who might wear it with meaning."

I didn't know what to say. It was the kind of gift that made you feel seen and undeserving at the same time.

"Mama," I said, voice catching.

She only smiled and adjusted the collar with both hands. "Don't slouch in it. And try not to spill anything."

I didn't spill anything.

But I did ruin everything.

By midday, the camp was vibrating with joy.

Streamers hung from the wagon wheels. Ribbons wound around poles. Two children from Wagon Seven had been taught a short recitation about eternal union, which they kept mispronouncing as "eternal onion." Elwen's family, radiant with pride, prepared honeyed bread and roasted vegetables. A pair of cats escaped with a ceremonial flower garland and were promptly chased.

Brin helped me brush dust from my boots.

"You look ridiculous," he said, deadpan. "Like a noble's mistake."

"Thanks," I muttered. "You're a great best man."

Mero passed me a wilted bouquet with a wink. "It's not too late to fake your own death."

"I'm considering it."

Nalina, when I glimpsed her across camp, looked like someone carved from silence. She wore a white dress — retooled from an older one, hastily adjusted — and a soft crown of dried flowers. Elwen stood beside her, pale and focused on her feet. They hadn't spoken to me since yesterday's rehearsal.

We lined up beneath the willow.

Nema stood at the centre, her blessing stone cradled in her palms. Elders gathered in a semicircle. Children sat cross-legged in front. Even Jorann, the cook, wore a clean shirt and had prepared a feast that smelled like it could bribe the gods.

I stood beside Nalina under the bright patchwork wedding canopy, sweat prickling at my collar despite the cool autumn breeze. Around us, the Family had gathered in all their colourful finery, eager, expectant. I was supposed to be smiling. Instead, my stomach churned like I'd swallowed a nest of bees. Gods, give me strength, I thought. I'm about to upend my own wedding.

I risked a glance at Nalina. She looked perfect — borrowed ivory gown, wildflowers in her hair, the very image of a radiant bride. But her eyes didn't see me. They were fixed on something far away, or maybe someone. She hadn't looked at me once. My heart twisted. I knew why. That smile she was wearing? It wasn't for me. It belonged to someone standing just out of reach.

My gaze found Elwen near the front, beside her parents. Dressed in blue, hands clenched around a handkerchief, she looked like glass: rigid, fragile, already cracking. Tears shimmered in her eyes. She was trying not to let them fall, and that hurt more than if she had. Watching her broke something open in me. This had gone far enough.

Nema stood in front of us, steady as always, reciting the rites in her clear, strong voice. I heard none of it. My pulse pounded in my ears. The moment for the vows came. My moment. I swallowed, hard. There was no going back now.

When Nema turned to me, eyes steady, waiting for my vow, I cleared my throat. "I... I have a confession," I said, and even I heard the crack in my voice.

A confused murmur spread through the crowd like a sudden wind through the tents. This wasn't in the script. Nalina turned to me, alarm flashing in her eyes. I gave her a small, sad nod. I knew what I was doing. I hoped she'd forgive me for it.

Nema's brow creased, but I pushed forward, trying to steady my voice. "Before we continue," I said, "everyone should know the truth." I managed a smile—thin, bitter. "This wedding... it's built on a lie."

Gasps erupted. Nalina's free hand flew to her mouth. I felt the heat of a hundred stares slam into me. My heart pounded, but I kept going. "I cannot marry Nalina, because she does not love me."

Silence. The heavy kind, like the moment before a storm hits. Nalina let out a soft sob—I didn't know if it was fear, relief, or both. Mouths were hanging open all around us. People exchanged stunned looks. Garron—Elwen's father—went stiff, his face darkening. Elwen stood frozen, and then her tears began to fall.

For a moment, no one dared move. Then Nalina stepped away from me, walking alone into the center of the storm.

Her cheeks were wet, but she lifted her chin. Her voice shook, but she spoke anyway. "I do not love him," she said. Then she drew a breath and said it louder: "I do not love Aen!"

Uproar. A wave of whispers and gasps tore through the crowd like a gust through dry leaves. Sella pressed a hand to her chest. Garron's face twisted in outrage. And Nalina—gods—she glanced toward Elwen. Just for a second. But it was subtle. Too subtle for most of the Family to catch. They saw scandal, yes—but not *that* scandal. Not yet.

"It's a trick," someone hissed nearby. "He's got cold feet!"

"No respect for the rites!" another muttered.

Heads turned, but it was all confusion, outrage, suspicion—not understanding.

I could feel the weight of it bearing down. And because I'm me, and I never know when to keep my mouth shut, I tried to lighten it.

I spread my arms wide, gave a crooked grin, and said, "Well, if it's any comfort—I'm just as surprised as you are."

It was meant to be funny.

It wasn't.

Garron's face went dark as a thunderhead. He stormed up the dais in three strides, and before I could blink, his hand came swinging.

The slap cracked across my face, sharp and furious, knocking the joke right out of me.

I stumbled back, pain bursting across my cheek like fire. Nalina screamed—"No!"—and grabbed my arm before I went down completely.

"You LIED to us!" Garron roared, fury twisting his face into something unrecognizable. "You disgrace my family with this spectacle!" He lunged again, hand raised like he meant to finish the job.

I didn't move. Didn't block. Didn't speak. I was frozen — too stunned, too guilty, too everything. Blood touched the corner of my mouth. I tasted metal. "I — I'm sorry," I rasped, blinking through the sting behind my eyes.

Elwen rushed forward, sobbing, "Father, stop!" Sella had both hands on his arm, trying to hold him back. "Garron, enough!" she begged. I saw two of my cousins and one of the elders break from the crowd and move in, grabbing Garron just in time.

Nalina threw herself between us, arms out like she could block a mountain. "It's not his fault!" she shouted. Her voice cracked. "Please, I — "

Garron, still straining against the hands holding him, turned that furious glare on Nalina. "Not his fault? We took you in, girl!" he spat, his voice ragged with rage. "We gave you a home, treated you like our own — and you repay us by making a mockery of it?" His words lashed out like a whip. Nalina cringed.

"ENOUGH!" Nema's voice cracked across the camp like a staff on stone. She stepped between us all, small but absolutely immovable. A heavy, stunned silence fell again, broken only by Nalina's muffled sobs and Elwen's quiet weeping.

Nema swept her gaze around the circle like she was daring anyone to argue. "This ceremony is over," she said. "What's done is done. We will not resolve it with shouting and blows." She faced Garron squarely, and only when he finally sagged and dropped his gaze did she move.

Drawing a breath, Nema lifted her voice to the whole camp. "Family — we have prepared a feast. We will not waste it. We will eat and drink together, as planned. This matter will be handled privately." She raised her hand. There would be no argument. "Come now. Music! Let us eat. We are still Family tonight."

For a moment, no one moved. Then old Elior, the fiddler, gods bless him, lifted his bow and struck a quick, lively note. It broke the spell. Slowly, the Family began to drift toward the tables and benches. First a few voices sang along with the tune, cautious. Then an uncle lifted a cup and shouted a toast. Then a few sisters started clapping out a rhythm. Before long, mugs were clinking and the camp was singing like nothing had ever gone wrong.

While the Family forced themselves back into revelry, Nema stepped off the dais and lowered her voice. "Nalina. Aen. Garron, Sella, and Elwen — come with me, now," she said. She didn't wait to see if we obeyed. She just turned and started walking toward her wagon at the edge of camp.

We exchanged looks — anxious, guilty, miserable — and followed. Garron shook off the hands that had been restraining him and strode after Nema, jaw tight, his eyes still burning. Sella guided Elwen, who was sobbing quietly, her arm around her daughter's shaking shoulders. Nalina stayed close beside me, her fingers brushing mine in a quick, trembling squeeze. My cheek throbbed from Garron's slap, but honestly, I barely felt it. I was too numb.

Inside Nema's wagon, the air was thick with incense and the kind of silence that makes you want to shrink into yourself. A single lantern threw soft gold light across shelves stacked with herbs and battered trinkets. Nema stood at the head of the little wooden table. The rest of us crowded in however we could: Garron and Sella by the door with Elwen between them, me and Nalina a few steps in front of Nema. Someone pulled the door shut behind us, muffling the sounds of the feast outside.

Nema's stern gaze traveled over all of us. She pressed her lips together, disappointment thick enough to taste. "What a mess," she said quietly, shaking her head. "We'll speak plainly here, as Family."

Garron's nostrils flared, but he didn't say a word, his chest rising and falling like he was trying to hold the rage inside. Sella sniffled and kept an arm around Elwen, who was still trembling.

Nema's eyes locked on me first. "Aen," she said, and there was so much disappointment in that one word I almost flinched. "Explain yourself. You started this with a lie — why?"

I swallowed. My mouth was dry as dust. I stepped forward a little, under Nema's gaze, feeling like I was about to be flayed alive.

"I didn't lie," I said, rough and hoarse. "Not exactly."

That earned a few sharp looks, but I pressed on.

"I said there was love. And there was. There is." I glanced sideways, not daring to look at Nalina or Elwen. "I just… let everyone think it was between me and Nalina."

I forced myself to meet Nema's eyes. "I should've corrected it. Right then. I should've told the truth. But I didn't. Because I didn't want to shame anyone. I didn't want to expose something that wasn't mine to tell. Honestly, I thought, if I let everyone think what they wanted, the story would pass. The gossip would move on. That nobody would get hurt." I gave a hollow laugh.

"Instead, suddenly they were sewing a jacket for me and picking flowers for a wedding feast."

Silence followed my confession.

Sella's eyes held some compassion, but Garron's face didn't soften a bit. If anything, it got harder.

"So you admit you deceived us," he said, voice cold enough to frost windows. "You made fools of my family in front of everyone." His arm locked tighter around Elwen's shoulders. She kept her face buried in her mother's sleeve, tears still slipping free.

I nodded. "I did," I said. "I'm sorry. I thought it was the right thing at the time... but it wasn't."

Garron's jaw clenched tight enough I thought his teeth might crack. His glare shifted from me to Nalina. "And you," he growled. "We welcomed you into our home. Treated you like our own daughter. And you..." He couldn't finish.

Nalina flinched under Garron's glare, but then I felt her gathering herself. She wiped her face with the back of her hand, trembling all over, and stepped a little away from me. She raised her chin, even though I could see the fear in her eyes.

"I never wanted to betray you," she said, small but clear. "You and Sella have been like parents to me since the day you took me in. I'm grateful for everything. I tried—I really tried—to be the daughter you deserved."

She swallowed hard and looked between them. "I thought if I married Aen, like you wanted, maybe I could bury what I felt. Maybe with time, I could be happy, and you would be proud." Her voice cracked right down the middle. "But when it came to it... I couldn't do it."

Garron's face twisted between pain and anger. "Is there someone else, then?" he asked, voice bitter enough to curdle milk. "Someone you truly care for? Or was this just about defying us?"

I saw Nalina hesitate. Her eyes flickered—just for a second—toward Elwen. That was all it took. Garron's gaze followed and darkened like a stormcloud. "Elwen," he snarled, low and poisonous, like the name itself was filth. Elwen whimpered and pressed herself tighter against her mother.

Nalina straightened her shoulders. There was no hiding anymore. "I do not love Aen," she said, clear and shaking. "I... I want to build a life with Elwen."

The wagon went dead still. Elwen broke into a soft sob, and Sella wrapped her arms around her like she could shield her from the words. I felt my chest twist painfully. I had known, of course. But hearing Nalina say it aloud— here, now—landed like a hammer blow.

Garron's face drained pale, then flushed to an ugly red. "Under my roof," he said, hoarse and shaking. "All this time... you and my daughter?" His fists trembled at his sides. "We showed you nothing but kindness, raised you like our own—and this is how you repay us? By leading Elwen into... into disgrace?"

"Please, Father," Elwen cried, twisting against her mother's hold. "It's not like that... I—I love her." Her voice broke into a wail, and Sella hushed her softly, her own face streaked with tears.

Nalina took a tiny step forward, like she wanted to reach out, though she stopped herself. "I know I've shamed the family. And I'll accept whatever punishment you think is fair."

She straightened, trembling but fierce. "I'll do anything—anything—to make this right."

Garron let out a harsh, disbelieving laugh. "Make it right?" he spat. "How could you possibly make this right, girl?"

Nalina flinched like he'd struck her, but somehow she stayed standing. I saw something shift in her—something stubborn and desperate all at once. She drew a shaky breath, wiped her palms against her skirt, and lifted her chin.

"With a dowry," she said.

For a second, no one spoke. I blinked, sure I'd misheard her. Garron frowned in confusion. Even Sella tilted her head slightly, like the words hadn't quite made sense.

Nalina pressed on, her voice trembling but clear. "I have nothing. No gold, no land, no jewels." She swallowed. "But I have Pickle and Plum."

I felt my breath catch. The geese. Saints, her geese.

Nalina squared her shoulders. "They're good geese. Strong. They lay fine eggs. They could start a whole flock." Her voice quivered, but she kept going. "They're all I have. They're everything I have. And I offer them to you. In exchange for your forgiveness. In exchange for a chance... for Elwen and me."

Tears welled in her eyes, but she stood. Fierce. Desperate. Broken.

Across the wagon, Elwen let out a soft, broken sound. "No," she whispered, shaking her head, tears spilling. "Nalina, no—you don't have to do that for me."

Nalina turned toward her, that fierce little smile breaking through the wreckage of her face. "I would," she said simply.

Garron stared at Nalina like she had just grown a second head. Then he let out a sound—a half-snarl, half-bitter laugh. "You think two geese can pay for what you've done?" His voice was low and ugly. "Keep your damn geese."

Nalina's body appeared to crumple. She stood there, shaking, while the last of her pride slipped away.

Sella's voice, soft but firm, cut through Garron's anger. "Oh, Nalina," she murmured, tears bright in her eyes. "We don't want your geese. We never wanted your things. We only wanted your honesty."

Nalina nodded once, tightly, as though every word was a blow.

Nema, who had been silent through it all, finally stepped forward. She laid a hand gently on Nalina's shoulder. "Your offer shows courage, child," she said. "But this is not a debt that can be paid in feathers."

Nema's voice shifted, losing its warmth and settling into something firm—final. She looked between Nalina and Elwen. "It's clear there's deep feeling between you two," she said, and her gaze softened a little when it landed on Elwen's tear-streaked face. "But the way it's been handled—the secrecy, the way it exploded into public scandal—has caused real harm to the Family that took you in."

Nalina just nodded, her tears falling in quiet surrender. Elwen squeezed her hand tight, both of them standing there like one broken body held together by sheer will.

Nema drew herself up, straight-backed and solemn.

"Here is what will happen now," she said. "Nalina will

not be cast out of our Family," Nema continued, turning to Nalina. "But you can't stay with Garron's family anymore. Tonight, you'll sleep here, in my wagon, under my care. We'll figure out a more permanent arrangement later." She looked to Elwen, and her tone gentled. "For now... a bit of distance is necessary."

Garron gave a curt little nod. Elwen made a soft, pained sound.

Nalina bowed her head. "Yes, Matriarch," she whispered. I could see the way her shoulders hunched in quiet grief — but there was something grateful in her tone, too. Nema wasn't casting her out. Just giving her a place to breathe, to not be hated. It was mercy, even if it hurt.

Nema's voice was calm, almost soft, but it carried finality like a blade. "None of this is easy. But there will be consequences. And time to think about the future." She turned toward Garron and Sella. "Take Elwen back to your wagon."

Garron still looked like he wanted to break something, but he was tired now — tired and red-eyed and done. He nodded once, stiffly. "Come, Elwen," he said, low and rough.

Sella wrapped an arm around Elwen and gently started steering her toward the door. Elwen fought it, her feet dragging, her eyes locked on Nalina like she could hold her in place just by looking.

Sella guided Elwen out after Garron, murmuring soft, broken words none of us could quite hear. The door swung open, letting in a burst of cold night air and the tinny sound of fiddles and laughter from the feast outside — so sharp, so wrong it made my teeth hurt. Then the door shut again, and it was just me, Nalina, Mero, and

Nema, left behind in the thick, heavy silence.

Nalina sagged where she stood, like her bones had forgotten how to hold her up. I wanted to reach for her, to say something — anything — but the words tangled up and died in my throat.

Nema moved first. She stepped close and laid a hand on Nalina's shaking back. "Gather your things, child," she said quietly. "You'll stay here tonight."

Nalina nodded, a tiny, broken movement, and went to the corner where her few belongings had been piled in preparation for a wedding that would never happen. She picked up her shawl, her blanket, a little wooden comb. She clutched them to her chest like they were armor.

Outside, the camp was still pretending everything was fine.

The fire blazed high. Mugs clinked. Someone was leading a half-hearted song, and others were shouting along, the way you do when you're trying not to cry. Laughter rang out — too loud, too brittle, cracking at the edges if you listened closely enough.

The Family, gods bless them, had decided to feast anyway.

That's what we did. When things were unbearable, when storms broke everything apart, we danced harder. We drank deeper. We made so much noise that maybe, just maybe, we wouldn't hear the pieces breaking.

I didn't join them. I stayed at the edge of the firelight, half in shadow, where the songs couldn't reach me properly. A few people spotted me standing there and raised their mugs in awkward salutes. I managed a crooked smile back, but I couldn't make my legs move toward them.

Across the fire, Garron's wagon stood closed and dark.

And five doors down, in Nema's wagon, Nalina sat alone, wrapped in the blanket we were supposed to have shared on our wedding night.

I sat down on a stray log, feeling a hundred years old, and watched the Family eat and drink and sing over the ruins. The fire crackled, and the fiddler played, and people clapped and shouted. And me — I just sat and listened to it all, and told myself that tomorrow would come anyway, whether we were ready for it or not.

It took months.

You'd think after a scandal like that, the Family would tear itself apart — or at least keep tearing at Nalina and Elwen like fresh wounds. But no. We're Ruanne. We don't heal pretty, but we do heal.

At first, Nalina stayed with Nema. For weeks, she barely left the wagon unless she had to. She did her chores. She kept her head down. She smiled when spoken to and learned to make herself small, invisible, harmless. Elwen kept her distance too — or at least, made a show of it. The two of them didn't speak much where anyone could see. Gods, you could almost believe there was nothing left between them but shared shame.

But anyone with eyes could see it wasn't gone. Just buried. Tucked away, the way you tuck away precious things when you know the world isn't ready for them.

Behind the scenes, Nema and the elder women must have worked some kind of magic — lots of quiet talks, lots of heavy silences and careful bargains. I wasn't privy to it, but I heard the ripples. Heard the way Garron's voice softened when he talked about Nalina again. Heard Sella telling someone in Jorran's kitchen that "a child once loved is a child forever."

Maybe it wasn't forgiveness, not exactly. But it was close enough.

And so, one damp, gray morning, without fanfare, Nalina moved back into Wagon #5. Garron and Sella welcomed her — not with open arms, but with quiet hands that lifted her trunk inside and made space for her by the stove again. No speeches. No apologies. Just a place made for her, like there had always been.

There were rules, of course. Nobody said them out loud, but we all knew them. Nalina and Elwen weren't left alone together much. There were always extra eyes nearby, casually lingering a little too long. If they hugged, it was brief. If they looked at each other too long, someone cleared their throat. It was... a truce.

The Family didn't bless what they didn't understand. Didn't celebrate it. But they didn't tear it apart either. As long as Nalina and Elwen kept their love quiet — small enough to fit into the cracks between what the Family was willing to see — they could stay.

It wasn't perfect. It wasn't even fair.

But it was survival.

And in our world, sometimes that was the closest thing to a happy ending we ever get.

I said once that we Ruanne love like storms.

We come in loud. We break things. We shout. We fight. We cry. But the storm always passes. And when it does, we don't waste time counting the broken things. We just gather up what's still standing, pull each other close, and keep walking.

Family isn't about getting it right. It's about staying. Staying when it's ugly. Staying when it's hard. Staying when you don't know how to fix it, but you show up anyway.

Nalina and Elwen didn't get a fairytale ending. Not the kind with dances and songs and easy smiles. But they got something better, maybe: a place. A place where storms are allowed. A place where love—wild, messy, stubborn love—doesn't have to ask permission to exist.

And the Family? We're still here. Still singing. Still fighting. Still loving in the only way we know how—loudly, fiercely, and badly enough to make the saints wince.

It's not perfect.

It's us.

And gods willing, that'll always be enough.

The Law of Unreasonable Harmony

> *"Let the stones break their teeth, not your dance."*
>
> — *ancient Ruanne proverb.*

Let me tell you a story.

This is the Ruanne creation myth. One version of it. Our stories are... flexible.

Before Tahl'Vareth. Before the sand. Before even the sky got its act together—there was Aiyalae, the great mother.

Aiyalae had dirty feet, wild hair, and a heartbeat loud enough to make the stars sit up straight.

And she danced. Not neatly. Not prettily. She danced the way storms argue with the sea. Pregnant. Sweating. Stomping life into existence.

She twirled, shuffled, spun, and stomped—for three days, or maybe seven, depending how grandmothers remember it.

She stomped down the mountains, every peak a thump of her heel. She swirled the soles of her feet against the nothingness and made deserts bloom in the dust. She shook out her hair, and oceans poured from it, wild and roaring. She lifted her skirts, and her waters spilled out, flooding valleys, filling rivers, coaxing green from the mud.

Life burst out in all directions—flapping, slithering, sprouting—because she danced, and the world had no choice but to dance with her.

She clapped her hands and made men and women—

barefoot, laughing, chasing each other across the new earth — until the world was stuffed to the rafters with wild, reckless joy.

Then she breathed once — just once — and the world spun into motion. The winds whirled and howled and did cartwheels across the sand, because how else do you honour a mother who dances the universe into being?

And when she was finished, when her feet ached and her heart was full, she rested.

For a time, the world danced as she meant it to.

The sun rose, and the people played. The sun set, and they held each other close and sang thanks into the cooling sky.

It was good. Wild. Beautiful. Free.

Until —

(And there's always an until.)

The firstborn among men happened.

Depending who's telling it, he's a short greasy fellow with grubby fingers and a hook for a nose, or a tall gargoyle of a man with fingers like snakes, or a goat masquerading as a man — with compensation issues. Whatever the description, you know the type. The kind who can take a perfectly good party and turn it into a brick — and then turn the brick into a weapon.

He decided his dance was better than everyone else's.

(Hint: it wasn't.)

Then he persuaded a bunch of like-minded idiots to agree.

Before you know it, these party-crashers are telling everyone that their way of stomping the ground is the only way. Line up. Stomp like us — or get stomped. And where the lines didn't work, they brought chains. And where the chains didn't work, they brought spears.

Then the firstborn—who had the biggest spear (I'm just saying)—jabbed it into the earth.

And the dancing stopped.

The world grew silent.

The people forgot the songs. Forgot the steps. Forgot that the ground was meant for more than marching and dying.

Until there were only two dancers left: one man, and one woman.

They went to Aiyalae and begged her to wake. And when she woke, she looked at the earth—and her heart broke at what the people had done to the beautiful world she had made for them. Her tears fell, and the last two dancers caught them. The rhythm took root in their bones, in their blood, in their children's children. A beat the world could wound, but never break.

This is how the Ruanne were brought into the world.

And this is how it has been ever since.

So.

They arrested Teyra and Elior for dancing.

Not fighting. Not stealing. Not singing bawdy songs about magistrates and turnips (which, I'll admit, was a close second). No—*dancing*.

Apparently, while performing in the city square, wearing traditional Ruanne scarves, they drew a crowd that was *"interfering with pedestrian flow and civic tone."*

That was the charge.

I found out when Gala Joranni woke me up with a ladle to

the ribs.

"They took them," she said.

"Who?"

"The twins."

I blinked. "Musical twins or firebug twins?"

She glared.

"Right. Musical. Should've guessed by the lack of smoke."

I dragged myself to the Archive (which still smells like burned parchment and moral ambiguity) and barged into Seren's office without knocking, as is my God-given right as a nuisance and occasional penitent.

Seren didn't even look up. "You're supposed to knock."

"You're supposed to stop evil."

That got her attention. Her quill paused mid-sentence, hovering above a scroll as if deciding whether it was worth bludgeoning me with it.

"What now?" she asked, already sounding exhausted.

I strode in, dripping theatrical outrage with every step, and planted myself dramatically in front of her desk.

"They arrested Teyra and Elior," I said.

That got a frown. A real one.

"For what?"

"Excessive joy in a public space. Weaponized rhythm. Dancery with intent."

She blinked. "First, you are just saying random things for flamboyant effect. Second, none of those things, assuming

I understand them, are a crime."

"Ah!" I said, wagging a triumphant finger. "It wasn't."

I reached into my coat and unfolded a battered, slightly soup-stained proclamation like a man offering sacred wisdom written on a napkin

"Behold!" I intoned. "The Official Justification for the Criminalization of Happiness."

I slammed it onto her desk, where it promptly curled pathetically at the corners.

Seren regarded the document like it might give her fleas.

"Where did you get this?" she asked, pinching the edge with two fingers.

"Borrowed it," I said innocently.

"From where?"

"The Notice Board of Cultural Suppression and General Bad Ideas," I said. "Technically, the market square. Right after Gala hit me with a ladle."

Her eyebrow climbed. "You stole it off a public board."

"I prefer 'liberated' — For the cause of truth and slightly better font choices." Then more seriously, "Seren, these are my Family. I needed you to see."

She sighed, set down her quill, and skimmed the page.

Her brow twitched about halfway through.

"Cultural Expression Regulation..." she muttered. "Subsection three... 'Behaviours disruptive to societal harmony'... including, but not limited to, unlicensed public displays of music, dance, chant, or communal noise-making likely to impede pedestrian flow or alter civic tone..."

She looked up, pinning me with a flat stare.

"That's us," I said brightly. "We're disharmony in scarves."

To her credit, she stood. "Come with me."

"To the jail?"

"To the magistrate. If this is a real law, I want to know who drafted it."

"And if it's fake?"

"Then we're breaking someone out."

I grinned. "You say the most romantic things."

She sighed. "You're still bound by your oath, Aen. Try not to lie. Or seduce anyone."

"No promises."

The Office of Public Harmony Enforcement was wedged between the Archive's storage annex and the Bureau of Pigeon-Related Ordinances. It smelled like wet parchment and smothered complaints.

Inside, a clerk named Dorlo sat behind a desk so tall it needed stairs. He had the serene expression of someone who took joy in suffering — as long as it was correctly notarized — and a moustache so neat it looked issued by decree.

"We're here about the Cultural Expression Regulation," Seren began, crisp and professional. "There was an arrest of two Ruanne citizens yesterday — "

"Non-citizens," Dorlo corrected without blinking.

Seren's jaw twitched. "Two *individuals*, then. On charges related to music and dance?"

Dorlo slid a stack of forms toward her.

"Form 74-B for release requests. Form 12-A if you wish to dispute the arrest. Form 9-C to request an official translation of the regulation into Common. And Form 44-Delta if you intend to submit a motion for cultural exemption under Subclause Three, Sect—"

I leaned forward. "Do you have a form for stopping injustice? Or do we need to fill out a preliminary application for that?"

Dorlo blinked. "That would be Form 88."

"Of course it would."

Seren took the forms, brows furrowing.

"What happens if we just pay the fine and take them home?" I asked.

"You'd be admitting guilt on their behalf," Dorlo said.

"But they're not guilty."

"Then you'll need to request a hearing."

"How long?"

He checked his notes. "Standard scheduling is six weeks."

I looked at Seren.

She didn't flinch. "We'll escalate."

He smiled thinly. "Of course."

Back outside, Seren was silent. I didn't press. Not yet.

We reached the bottom of the stairs before she muttered, "I didn't know about the regulation."

"I know."

"It should've crossed my desk."

"It didn't."

"It's wrong."

I stopped. "You said that out loud."

She turned. "Don't quote me."

"Too late. Etched it into metaphor already."

"Aen."

I stepped closer. "You're a good person stuck in a bad machine. I see it. So do they. And, I bet, so do your bosses, which may be why they keep handing you mop duty — like managing unmanageable Ruanne." I smiled, but it broke a bit.

A pause.

She looked at me. Something unreadable flickered.

Then: "Let's go get them back."

The magistrate's office looked like someone had tried to convert a stable into a temple, failed, and then decided to fill it with paperwork until everyone forgot. Teyra and Elior were seated on a bench in the corner, shackled not by iron but by sheer bureaucratic boredom.

Teyra waved at me. Elior was composing an opera in passive-aggressive throat clicks.

A sour-faced assistant appeared. "You have five minutes. The magistrate is currently observing a silence fast to protest noise-based dissent."

I blinked. "He's not *speaking* because someone else *sang*?"

"Correct."

I turned to Seren. "This place is a temple to irony."

She nodded. "And bad acoustics."

We were ushered into a dim chamber where a statue of Justice wept into a cracked teacup.

The magistrate—a damp-looking man in a silk hat—gestured solemnly. He did not speak.

A parchment was slid toward us. *Public Apology Required. Performed Verbally. Tone: Contrite. Phrasing: Pre-Approved.*

I read it. Seren read it. Then we both looked at each other.

"No chance," I whispered.

She sighed. "I'll do it."

"No." I stepped forward. "Let me."

I stood in front of the human statue, cleared my throat, and began to read.

"I, Aen Marr, acting representative of the Ruanne people and licensed humiliation sponge, do hereby solemnly apologize for the grievous cultural indecency committed by my kin, who dared to wear colour in public, and move rhythmically without municipal supervision."

The magistrate's eyebrows rose.

"We now understand that spontaneous joy is a threat to civic unity, and that our tribal scarves cause migraines to the spiritually fragile. We further regret that our harmonies clashed with the dominant tonal expectations of the sidewalk."

Seren's mouth twitched.

I pressed on. "In future, we promise to suppress all visible joy, communicate only in beige, and clap on one and three, never on two and four."

Elior clapped sarcastically on two and four.

The magistrate scribbled something, rang a bell, and the hearing was declared concluded.

Outside, papers were stamped. Teyra and Elior were released. Teyra hugged me. Elior kissed the air in every direction.

Seren lingered at the gate.

"You didn't have to go that far," she said.

"Did I go too far?" I said, sweetly.

She looked at me. For a moment, not with disdain. Not quite.

Something that made the air between us feel a little less like a fight, and a little more like a dance.

The Noblewoman, the Murder-Lord, and the Fertility Conspiracy

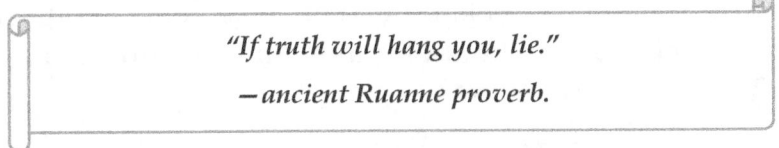

"If truth will hang you, lie."

— *ancient Ruanne proverb.*

She came to us veiled.

Not just veiled — *cloaked, hooded, hunched.* Every inch of her wrapped in shadows and panic. She wore the kind of veil that said, "Please do not look at me," and shoes that said, "If you recognize me, I'll deny everything." Her footsteps were soft, furtive things — the walk of someone who had much to lose and even more to hide.

Because visiting the Ruanne — us wagon-dwellers, fortune-sellers, miracle-peddlers — was a risk. We were tolerated at best, despised at worst. No noblewoman wanted to be seen haggling over hope with the likes of us. And certainly not one married to a man like hers. A man whose suspicions were said to be sharper than his sword, and whose sword had already retired several wives.

You can always spot them — the ones married to titles and tombstones. She was married to a Murder-Lord. They probably pinned a dozen titles on him: *Duke, Lord of the Fifth Meridian, Warden of Three Rivers, Supreme Commander of Bad Decisions* — but when your household staff changes every full moon and your previous wives fall off balconies with suspicious regularity, you earn new titles. The kind whispered behind hands.

It was said the Duke had a gardener executed because the man's rosebushes bloomed out of season. Another rumour insisted his second wife died of a tragic hunting accident: namely, she was mistaken for a stag. No one quite believed it, but nobody dared say otherwise.

The lesson was simple: if Lord Venison-and-Falconry was unhappy with you, sooner or later you found yourself experiencing a fatal bout of gravity, misidentification, or tragic misunderstanding.

And now, here was Lady Vervena, risking all that just by breathing the same air as us.

And she? She was recently elevated Wife Number One.

Because after a couple "unfortunate accidents," the harem had dwindled. She alone held the coveted spot—the first wife, the titled one, the politically valuable one. A position with all the glamour of a noose made from gold-threaded silk.

Her name—and I swear I'm not making this up—was Lady Vervena de Istral-Morne. Yes, *Vervena*. Like something you'd gargle to cure a chest cold.

"My lady," I said, bowing just low enough to be legally offensive. "You have the look of a woman with secrets—and possibly an ulcer."

She didn't laugh.

Instead of laughing, she twisted her fingers together under the table, knuckles whitening, shoulders hunched against a blow that hadn't yet fallen. It was the look of a woman who had learned that bruises weren't always visible—and that smiles could be deadlier than knives.

Whatever hope had carried her here had been stitched together out of desperation and defiance, threadbare already, fraying before our eyes.

She'd heard of Nema. Everyone has. When the rich want their miracles dirtied by plausible deniability, they come to us.

Vervena lifted her veil. I swear, the air itself held its breath. Pale skin, dark eyes, lips like a dying prayer. She was beautiful in the way fragile things are — beautiful and in terrible danger.

"I cannot bear children," she said, politely sipping the foul brew Jorann optimistically labeled "tea" — clearly not tasting a drop.

"And your husband —" Nema said.

"Will kill me," Vervena said simply.

"Because you're barren?"

"Because I'm no longer..." She hesitated. "...useful."

Cue the kind of silence normally reserved for botched executions and bad marriage proposals.

Now, Nema — may she reign in fury and maternal judgement — cannot *technically* conjure babies out of thin air. But she knows things. Deep things. Old things. The kind of things whispered by grandmothers when the fire is low and the doors are barred.

"I can help," she said, voice low. "But I'll need three things: a lock of his hair, something from his favourite meal, and a likeness."

"Why?" asked Lady Vervena.

"Because if Lord Venison-and-Falconry happens to suffer a slight and entirely coincidental case of internal combustion," Nema said sweetly, "we'll want to know which nose to draw on the curse bowl."

Was she joking?

Probably.

Maybe.

(Absolutely not.)

Vervena came back the next night, and the next, and the next.

First came the Ritual of Womb Blessing. Which involved: (a) a full-body bath in rosemary and goat's milk, (b) Being smudged vigorously with campfire ash and Nema's sharp opinions, and (c) Listening to Brin chant rhythmically while shirtless.

(Because, as Nema said: "*Fertility spirits appreciate a good view.*")

Nema, of course, did not stop at shirtless drumming. Oh no. There were ancient rites to observe—ancient, in the sense that Nema might have made them up three days ago.

On the second night, she declared that Brin had to wear a ceremonial sash. No one knew where the sash came from. It was purple, glittering, and suspiciously resembled a curtain tieback from the mayor's house two villages ago.

"Symbolizes virility," Nema said with an absolutely straight face.

On the third night, we added incense—heavy, cloying, and smoke-thick. So much incense that Brin nearly choked mid-chant and I had to heroically slap his back until he coughed up a lung. "Strength leaving the body," Nema declared solemnly. "Very auspicious."

On the fourth night, someone (Jorann) slipped a sacred fertility dance into the ritual. Brin did *not* dance. Brin stomped in place, looking like a bear swatting at invisible bees while the women of the camp applauded with unseemly enthusiasm.

Brin, dear Brin—our monosyllabic mountain of muscle—

stood there grimly thumping a drum while women sighed and men resolved to work out more frequently.

"You look tense," I told him once.

"Focusing," he grunted.

"On fertility?" I asked.

He hit the drum harder.

It was around the fourth night — I for one was surprised it took that long — and after one particularly spirited smudging session — that Vervena's eyes started drifting.

Specifically, toward Brin.

She watched him with the kind of expression usually reserved for miracle healers and expensive desserts.

Brin is many things: brave, loyal, built like a siege engine. But, as you may recall, he is catastrophically bad at women. Women terrify him. He treats flirtation like a battle charge — one you duck and roll away from. So when Vervena began lingering, brushing "accidentally" against his arm, smiling up at him with those heavy-lidded, come-hither eyes... Brin's ears turned a shade of red normally reserved for emergency beacons.

By the fifth night, Vervena wasn't even pretending. She invented reasons to linger: fetching water she didn't need, asking deeply unnecessary questions about the ritual ("Should the drum be played faster for... quicker results?"). She managed to brush his hand. Then his arm. Then his chest. Each time Brin reacted as if physically struck, flinching and backing away with the stiff misery of a condemned man walking to the scaffold.

At one point, he tried to hide behind a goat. The goat, who had long since committed fully to the role of scandalized bystander, sneezed directly into Brin's face.

Vervena only laughed—a soft, dangerous sound that tightened every muscle in Brin's body.

"I'm doomed," he hissed to me as he wiped goat snot from his eyes. "She's hunting me."

"You're a fertility spirit now," I said cheerfully. "It's your sacred duty."

"She's staring at me," he hissed at me behind the water barrels.

"Of course she is," I said. "You're half-naked and built like the answer to this lonely woman's prayer."

"What do I do?"

"Smile," I advised. "And for the love of the gods, don't say anything complicated."

"Smile."

"Yes."

"Complicated," he muttered darkly.

Of course, the first attempt went... poorly.

On the sixth night, after a particularly vigorous round of chanting, Vervena cornered Brin behind the water barrels. (It's always the water barrels.) She leaned close, eyes shining with a mix of desperation, determination, and something perilously close to hope.

"I feel... blessed already," she whispered, fingertips brushing his wrist.

Brin, champion of subtlety and wit, stared at her for a solid three seconds—then bolted.

He didn't just walk away. He *ran*. Through the camp. Through a laundry line. Through a goat pen. He crashed through a henhouse, left a trail of outraged chickens, tripped over the stew pot, and finally crashed straight into Mero, who promptly fell into a fish barrel, cursing him in three languages.

Vervena stood blinking after him, dazed but undeterred. I decided to count that as a warm-up attempt.

Now — let's be honest — it wasn't *only* hormones at work. Vervena was practical. She preferred a future. She wanted an heir. She hoped to live long enough to complain about her arthritis. And Brin — well, Brin looked close enough to her Murder-Lord husband that a baby could plausibly pass. Same broad shoulders. Same hard jaw. Same "I could end you, but I'd rather nap" energy.

This was Nema's magic plan.

One crafted with centuries of Ruanne experience. Gently. Carefully. With the tact and discretion of a brick through a stained-glass window.

But honestly, it was the sort of keep-it-simple-stupid plan that works.

On the seventh night, Vervena "slipped."

Brin "caught" her.

Her dress "tore."

Brin "shielded" her modesty.

The goats (and I) witnessed everything and promised solemnly not to gossip. (I lied.)

Success! Lady Vervena's honour was *deeply* compromised and Brin looked like he'd survived an assassination attempt.

The camp exploded with gossip by morning. The goats bleated suggestively. The cats sat in judgment. Jorann started carving a fertility idol that bore an *unmistakable* resemblance to Brin.

Rue Lohre composed a bawdy ballad titled *The Blessed Brin and the Lady of Longing*, which was immediately banned by Nema for "impropriety and too many agricultural metaphors." (We sang it anyway.) By midday, Brin couldn't walk across the clearing without being blessed, winked at, or patted on the back. Someone started offering "Blessed Brin" fertility charms—twigs wrapped in goat hair and optimism—which sold out before noon.

"Drink this," Jorann said, handing him something that smelled like vinegar and goat droppings.

"What is it?" Brin asked, sniffing.

"Post-miracle tonic."

Brin drank it. Immediately gagged. Looked betrayed all over again.

I have no idea what it was, or why Jorann made him drink it. I don't think there was a reason.

Four moons later, a servant arrived with a very generous donation from the Lady Vervena, who had apparently heard that our little camp was not being treated well by the authorities and wanted to provide a discreet contribution for our people.

We also heard that the Lady Vervena was glowing. Radiant.

Pregnant.

And when a son was born, the Murder-Lord hosted a banquet to end all banquets. Toasted the gods. Named the child after himself. Slept easy. Never dreaming that his heir may have been begotten under a wagon tarp while a goat with sinus issues sneezed in rhythm.

Or, possibly, it was Nema's miracle Ruanne tonic.

Either way, I say it was real magic. And a little luck. Life's like that.

And we?

When the news arrived — riches from Lady Vervena's "private gratitude" — the camp threw a feast that lasted three nights. We sang. We danced. We raised our mugs to Nema, to Brin, to miracles made the old-fashioned way — with hope, trickery, and a dash of extravagant debauchery.

Brin was crowned with a wreath of dried rosemary and forcibly seated at the head of the long table. Babies were pressed into his arms. Married couples threw rice at his head "for luck." Mero painted a goat gold (badly) and led it around proclaiming it "the Blessed Offspring of the Great Seed-Bringer."

Brin took it all with the same stoic misery he reserved for tax collectors, sword drills, and my storytelling.

"It'll die down," he muttered darkly into his stew.

"It'll get worse," I assured him.

Because you see — among the Ruanne, a good story never dies. It breeds. It multiplies. It spawns sequels. By winter, Brin's legend would be recounted with drumbeats, puppet shows, and deeply inaccurate murals. By spring, mothers would threaten unruly children with, "Behave, or Blessed Brin will smudge you with goat ash!"

And honestly? He deserved every minute of it.

Somewhere in the noble hills of Nareth, there's a little Ruanne princeling growing up — with his mother's cunning and Brin's nose — and one day he'll look in the mirror, flex experimentally, and wonder why he keeps craving goat stew.

But that, my friends, is the thing about miracles: they only need to be believed once.

The rest — is just good storytelling.

Maja and the Bitter Leaf

Maja wasn't just old. She was gloriously, indecently, obscenely old. Old enough to remember Eldania as a country, not a cautionary tale. Old enough to have outlasted one mostly decorative and one vaguely useful husband, a nuisance son-in-law (Hinna's husband, who loved her enough to survive her complaints), three children (two of whom were barely tolerable, the third, considerably worse), and enough grandchildren to start her own petty little kingdom.

Which she did, by the way. She ruled it through a tangled system of favours, debts, and threats so subtle you didn't realize you'd lost until three years later, at your own wedding.

She smoked the bitter leaf. Not because it brought her peace, or pleasure, or any of those other ridiculous reasons people poison themselves — but because it offended people. She puffed it after breakfast. She chewed and spat it liberally between meals. She stuffed it in her cheek like a personal insult aimed directly at the concept of moderation. It blackened her teeth. It blued her lips. Her farts — *gods!* — could strip paint off a wagon wheel, and kill small plants at twenty paces. And she cackled like a witch every time she cleared a room.

Maja remembered everything. *Everything.* Especially the things you prayed she'd forget — your mistakes, your missteps. That time you wet yourself during Festival. When you drunkenly slept with a maiden and awoke to find her a goat, and that the two of you were cuddled in the middle of the camp. Naked. She filed these treasures away like a miser hoarding coins, ready to spend them when your dignity was low and her audience was high.

When she died, it wasn't a grand affair. No dramatic collapse. No final curse that cracked the sky. No — she simply didn't get up one morning. Her cough had hollowed her out. Her laughter had worn her thin as old cloth.

True to form, she left without warning, without permission, without so much as a by-your-leave.

Because Maja never owed anyone the courtesy of goodbye.

We washed her body — arms, legs, her long silver hair that shimmered like someone had forged moonlight into thread. Her teeth, though. Those lips. *Gods forgive us*, we tried. We scrubbed, we polished, we whispered apologies to the air. But bitter leaf stains deeper than soap can reach, and honestly, she probably laughed herself sick watching us.

We placed cold coins on her eyes — not to pay some mythical ferryman (please, the Ruanne don't bribe the dead; if they can't find their own way, they're not worth the trip) — but to weigh her soul just enough to keep her moving. Not that it would help. If anyone could out-stubborn the laws of death, it was Maja. If anyone could haunt a camp with nothing but sarcasm and a drafty breeze, it was her.

We gathered at twilight.

No one plans these things. The sun just sort of dips low enough that everyone looks around and, without speaking, decides: *Now. Now is the time.*

The sky burned low, a bruise-coloured thing, purples bleeding into rust-reds, streaked with the last stubborn light clawing at the horizon. The air smelled of smoke and dust and the faint copper tang of the river beyond the fields. Campfires dozed across the wagon circle, their smoke trailing lazy prayers into the night.

Everyone came. Even Darsa, herded along by ten cats, each howling their own mournful sermon. Even gruff old Jorann, who hadn't left his soup pot in four years without the promise of either a brawl or a miracle. Even Nema, who almost never cried—who tonight looked like a cracked pot just barely holding bitter tea inside.

The Lohres arrived arm in arm, silent for once. Omri Nuvra limped in and sat, cradling his battered old lute like a lover he was afraid to wake. The Gelloris whispered like undertakers swapping gossip. Children clung to skirts and trouser legs. Goats bleated in the distance, restless, as if they, too, knew some piece of the world had gone missing.

And, naturally, the Calix twins showed up late, skidding into the circle like a pair of drunken spirits. They had spent the walk arguing over what colour was most respectful for the dead—and both, in the end, wore stubborn, defiant red. Bright, bloody red. They looked like they'd mugged a jester at knifepoint and stolen his dignity for the occasion.

We gathered to mourn Maja Estrel—Mother of Mischief, Matriarch of Memory, Belcher of All Things Unholy. The old woman who had seen more winters than the desert had dunes. Who carried more grudges than most carried children. Who could conjure a curse sharper than a blade and a laugh louder than a thunderclap.

Maja had been laid out with care: hair combed until it shone like silver flame, body shrouded in cotton stitched by old, careful hands. The wagon behind her stood quiet, draped in worn banners—scraps of cloaks, festival ribbons, embroidered prayers stitched by fingers long gone to dust. The wheels were chalked with Ruanne runes to keep spirits moving forward—not lingering, not looking back.

Her daughter, Hinna, sat crumpled by the body, hands trembling in her lap, her mouth open like she was trying to catch a word that had already fled. All that came out was silence—thick and strangling as smoke.

The air felt thick. Heavy. The sky breathed raggedly.

I was asked, politely—and when I say politely, I mean that Nema fixed me with the full, crushing weight of every terrible idea I had ever had, catalogued and alphabetized like a murderous librarian—not to speak.

Not tonight. Not at Maja's farewell. Not when grief hung so thick you could have sliced it into hunks and served it beside the lentils at supper.

And for a heartbeat, I meant to listen. I really did.

But then I looked at Hinna—poor, broken Hinna—and knew the way forward was mine to carve. Badly. Probably with a bent knife and a map drawn in goat spit. But mine all the same.

It's not my fault. I blame the gods.

When the Powers That Be were handing out talents, they must have wandered off mid-roll call to smite a village. Then, realizing they'd left one soul unassigned, they grabbed a handful of scraps—songbird, fire scroll, something that definitely wasn't legal—and shoved it into my mouth.

The result was me: a walking bonfire of ill-advised declarations.

I stood anyway.

Because someone had to. Because there are moments when silence isn't reverence — it's betrayal. Because Maja Estrel deserved a send-off hot enough to crack the sky.

So here it is, Maja. The eulogy you never asked for. The best one I can tell.

I knew Maja Estrel the way a rabbit knows the shadow of a hawk. Not through kindness — though she had some, buried deep and sharp-edged — but through sheer *presence*. Fierce. Certain. Entirely disinterested in anyone's comfort but her own."

You didn't meet Maja. You *survived* her.

She had a voice like broken bells — cracked, battered, but ringing anyway — and a mouth like a bear trap baited with promises. She once told me I had the soul of a politician and the charm of a moldy boot. Which, coming from Maja, was practically a love letter.

Tonight, it should've been someone else standing here. Someone respectable. Someone careful. Someone who knew how to mourn with dignity instead of... whatever it is I'm about to do.

But grief doesn't wait for permission. And Maja would've spat on the idea of dignity anyway.

So here I am.

You know, she once chased off a tax collector with nothing but a soup ladle and a string of insults so inventive the chickens stopped laying just to listen. She bribed the gods—never with prayers (too slow, too slippery)—but with steaming spiced lentils left on stones at the crossroads. *"If you want something done,"* she said, *"feed them first. Pray later."*

And she used to hum lullabies while darning socks—her fingers nimble, her lips sweet—plotting vengeance as tenderly as sewing stitches.

That was Maja. Fierce. Terrible. Ours.

But those stories are easy to tell. The ones we've wrapped in laughter until they've worn smooth.

The story she *wouldn't* let me tell—the one she glared me into silence over more times than I can count—that's the one I'll tell tonight.

Because if you're going to get cursed by a ghost, it might as well be for a crime worth committing.

She would've thrown something at me for this. A shoe. A ladle. A curse so vicious it would wilt my grandchildren.

And she would have *loved it.*

Because now is not the time for politeness. Or quiet. Or tame respect for the dead.

Now is the time for life. And blood. And spit. And betrayal. And laughter.

So gather round. Let me get cursed for you. And let's remember Maja the right way—through a story about a handsome husband, a useful lover, and the time she was very nearly murdered.

The Handsome Husband, the Useful Lover, and the Very Nearly Murdered Bride

Maja was married twice. Once by arrangement. Once by

accident. And both times by sheer force of her terrifying personality.

Her first husband — may his name be forgotten and his casseroles curdle — was a *very* handsome man. Truly. His jawline could slice cheese. His eyebrows were carved by minor gods. His smile once convinced a nun to take off her wimple.

He was also as useful as a chocolate saucepan in a sandstorm.

An ornamental husband. Couldn't cook. Couldn't fix a wheel. Couldn't pitch a tent without three servants and an emotional support wine.

Maja was married to him at the age of nine — which, in those days, was cheerfully the height of romance. For ten long years, she endured him. She made the meals. She managed the household. She smoked her bitter leaf and made snide comments at parties. And eventually — inevitably — she got bored.

Enter: Thornik. No last name. When you have a face like a blighted potato and arms like siege weapons, you don't *need* a surname.

He was strong. He was quiet. He could split a log with his bare hands and once repaired a wagon axle using only spit, prayer, and pure stubbornness.

And most importantly — he was *helpful*.

Maja met Thornik at a funeral. (Naturally.) He was carrying the coffin. With *one hand*.

She took one look at his enormous, scar-slashed forearms and said, *"Now that's a man who could kill my husband."*

Which, it turned out, was prophetic.

Because one thing led to another—ladders were climbed, skirts were lifted, marital expectations were pointedly ignored—and lo and behold, Maja ended up pregnant. With Thornik's child.

Now, Mr. Decorative—Mr. Useless—Mr. I-Need-A-Spoon-To-Button-My-Shirt—was outraged. Outraged, mind you. Not because he loved her. But because her womb had dared produce something without his royal contribution.

He demanded justice. And, being the charming patriarchal dung-pile he was, he asked Maja's father to have her killed.

As one does.

Her father agreed. Because nothing says "family values" like murdering your daughter for getting bored of a walking haircut.

But Maja—Maja didn't flinch. She lit a bitter leaf, spat into the fire, and said, *"Tell him to try."*

He didn't have to. Because Thornik did it for him. On the night they came for her, Thornik broke in—*through a wall*—and murdered Mr. Prettyface. With a *ladle*. Because swords were too dignified. And kitchenware is poetic.

Then he grabbed Maja—who stopped to grab her satchel, her smokes, and three jars of preserved lemons—and they ran. Together. Into the night. Into legend.

They were never caught. Because no one wanted to find them. Because, as Maja would later say, *"We left behind the one thing no one wants returned: shame."*

Thus began the second marriage of Maja Estrel. Forged not in ceremony, but in action. In daring. In a choice made by a woman who refused to be ornamental.

So yes. She was a grudge-holder. A gossip. A smoker of infernal plants and a swearer of vicious truths. But she was also a survivor. A rebel. A lover of competence over convention. And if you ask me — which no one did — that's how we should all be remembered. By our better mistakes. By the fire we fled toward, not from. By the ladles we chose to lift.

Rest well, Maja. May your husbands remain exactly where you put them.

When I finished, the Family sat still. No one coughed. No one shifted. Not even the goats, who normally considered silence an act of war.

The fire between us crackled low — small, tired pops and sighs, like an embered heartbeat refusing to give up. Above us, the stars blinked awake one by one — timid at first, then all at once, scattering across the sky like spilled salt.

For a long moment, it was just fire, and sky, and the hollow shape of the heart we'd lost.

Then Nema rose. Slowly. Deliberately. Like an old tree bracing against a storm.

She stood there, outlined in firelight, her shadow long and patient across the ground. She looked at Hinna — still clutching herself together. At the children, sniffling into sleeves. At all of us, gathered ragged and raw and stubborn.

When she spoke, her voice was low, but it carried. It always did.

"She was a blade, that one," Nema said. "A sharp edge on an old truth." She paused, letting it hang there, letting the night catch it and turn it over like a prayer. "May we all be so lucky."

And somehow, just like that, the ground beneath us steadied. The loss didn't shrink. But it shifted. Made room. Made space for grief that didn't drown you, but shaped you into something fierce enough to survive.

Then the songs began.

Mero brought out his flute. Tovi banged a drum, off-beat but determined. Mira sang first—high and clear and shaking. Then others joined, their voices rising rough and beautiful into the night.

We danced. Because that's how we grieve.

We tell stories. We laugh too loudly. We drink just enough. And then some more after that. We dance — not in spite of the pain, but because of it. We burned a little bitter leaf for her. Not because she needed it. But because the stink would have made her grin, scold us, and demand a proper drink.

This is how we carry the dead. With rhythm. With memory. With enough laughter to keep their ghosts amused.

And just as the fire burned low, and I was slipping away — maybe to be alone with my thoughts, maybe just to steal a pastry — *she* arrived.

Seren. With news. Always with news.

Another temple. Another summons. Another weight to drag us back into the long, grinding business of survival.

"Can't it wait?" I asked, even knowing the answer.

"No, it can't," she said. But there was something different in her eyes. Something almost soft.

Maybe it was the grief. Maybe the smoke had gentled me, blurred my sharper angles. Maybe—for once—I was less exhausting to love.

Whatever it was, she stayed.

For the fire. For the food. For the dancing.

Because the Family, gods bless our stubborn bones, danced. We danced the way the Ruanne always have—when the sky falls, when the road vanishes, when the world stitches up its heart without us. We spun and clapped and stomped, flinging ourselves against the night with bare feet and ragged hearts, daring the stars to burn us down.

It wasn't for Maja, exactly. It was *because* of her. Because the truest tribute to a woman like Maja Estrel was not silence, or mourning, or neat little prayers. It was reckless, shameless, joyful life.

And when I pulled Seren into a spin—half invitation, half dare— she didn't say no. For a moment, she forgot to be made of rules and ice. For a moment, she laughed—a real laugh, loose and bright, like a string snapping free. For a moment, it felt like maybe, just maybe, this story could find a softer ending than the others.

So naturally, I ruined it.

I said something charming. Something clever. Something just slightly false—because that's what I do, when something is too good to trust.

I said, lightly, "Careful. If you smile too much, they'll think you belong here." A joke. A lie. A shield thrown up too fast.

And even as the words left my mouth, I felt it—the clench, the wrongness, the little death of something delicate and real.

Her smile faltered. Faded. Died.

"You'll never make anything real if you're always lying," she said.

Not angry.

Not cruel.

Just tired.

And then she walked away. Leaving me spinning alone, under a sky that was too big, too bright, and far too empty.

The Last Stop on the Repentance Tour

> *"Some sins are worth the stain."*
>
> — *ancient Ruanne proverb.*

My friends, I regret to inform you that we've reached the final stop on my glorious penance tour. No more dives into Nareth's sanctimonious underworld. Just two silver coins left in my purse, and only one temple remained to scandalize. One last shrine, one final bow, a quick kiss on a holy relic — and then, exit stage left.

With Seren's return (having presumably wrestled a dragon's worth of bureaucratic scheduling and paperwork), and my apology delivered, my debt would be cleared, my record reduced to a respectable grey smear, and my career as a legally tolerated menace could resume. Freedom. I was thrilled. Completely, totally, and absolutely thrilled. Except.

That morning, my heart sagged. Like an old tent left out in the rain and forgotten by everyone but the mildew.

Now, I'm not saying I'd developed a fondness for Seren. That was impossible. She was the human equivalent of a locked door in a burning building. The sort who alphabetized her threats. Arguing with her was like debating a mountain — unyielding, faintly condescending, and entirely likely to kill you if you stood in the wrong place. Fluent in six dialects of *No.* My emotional opposite in every way: where I was sun, she was glacier; where I was charm, she was law; where I was whimsy, she carried a warrant.

Still, there were her feelings to consider. And she was completely, totally, and absolutely into me. I mean — she hadn't executed me yet. That's basically a confession. She remembered my name. *Out loud.* In *public.* With *inflection.* Her glares lingered—longingly. She sighed when I spoke. Heavily. She heard everything I said, despite devout attempts otherwise—sometimes with fingers pressed to her ears and screaming *"la la la la."* Once, she almost smiled. Or maybe she had gas. Either way: *a moment.* And let's not forget, she *loved* writing my name on official documents. In ink.

Today was the last time I'd get to squabble, spar, and—if the stars aligned—flirt shamelessly with the most terrifying woman in Nareth. Seren of the Black Robes. Or, as the Family muttered behind cupped hands: *that poor boy's doom on horseback.*

And I had plans. Good ones. I'd composed a poem. Practised an exaggerated bow. Saved a particularly obscene joke about sacred yoghurt rituals. It was going to be magnificent.

The Ruanne camp bloomed in full morning chaos: the air thick with lentil steam, shouted insults, and Jorann's bready curses floating from the kitchen tent. Children shrieked after goats. Chickens plotted sedition. The sun clambered up the sky, drunk and belligerent.

Then the dust cloud rose. Off toward the walls of Nareth. Low at first. Just a huff. Just an angry dust mote crawling across the flatlands.

The Family slowed, feeling the wind turn. Gossip ignited like brushfire.

"That's her," muttered Elen Shivari.

"Poor boy," sighed Rue Lohre, cutting a glance at me. "We'll remember him."

"Sounds like a right storm coming. What you done this

time, boy?" said Darsa Mevin, squinting from her perch atop a creaky barrel.

I ignored them. Mostly.

And then she was there—riding like Judgment Day had been rescheduled without her permission and she'd come to enforce the new deadline. Her horse—*Majesty of Passive Aggression*—charged toward us, hooves devouring earth, black as spilled ink and twice as mean-looking. It suited her. Seren rode high in the saddle, black robes whipping like smoke, her face carved from the same pitiless stone they use for tribunal steps and gravestones. A satchel bounced at her hip, heavy enough to dent skulls and probably packed with forms in triplicate.

She didn't slow. Didn't look left or right. Just thundered into camp like she meant to write citations on our souls.

The Family scattered. Kids bolted. Women vanished into wagons. Even the goats—who, while roughly as intelligent as fermented dishwater, still possess a well-honed fear of divine retribution—sprinted for the hills.

I, fool that I am, decided to intercept her.

I sprang forward. Dusting off my best shirt (the one with *one* wine stain, plus *two* sexy rips enticing all to my emasculated masculinity), running a hand through my hair, and planting myself squarely in her path, I bowed dramatically. Flashed a roguish smile. Began to recite the world's worst poem.

But before I could finish my first stanza (a limerick glued to an epic couplet), her horse snorted, veered, and nearly trampled me. Seren rode past without even a flicker of acknowledgement, like I was nothing more than an unfortunate shrub. Her satchel hit the ground a moment later with a thud that shook nearby tents. The impact was... concerning. So was her face when she slid off the saddle and turned.

I smiled winningly. "Lovely weather for mass executions, don't you think?"

"Not today, Marr," she said. Flat. Sharp. Like a gavel slamming shut.

Something was wrong. Wrong beyond the usual bureaucratic fury, wrong beyond the stiff shoulders and black looks. Something hollow rang inside her words. Something cracked.

The Family—who could sniff out drama from a quarter mile—pretended not to listen while leaning conspicuously on wagon wheels and laundry lines. I opened my mouth to say something better. Something helpful. Nothing came out.

And then, mercifully or cruelly, Brin and Mero appeared.

Mero lounged against the nearest wagon, smirking like a man who enjoyed watching housefires he didn't have to put out. "Ten coppers says he flirts anyway and gets stabbed," he offered, voice low. Brin just crossed his arms like a wall eying a battering ram soaked in oil. "No bet."

I saluted them both with a very rude gesture, turned, and jogged over to Seren.

She barked the order without looking up: "Get your things. We leave now."

So much for my poem.

I grabbed my satchel—one suspiciously flexible relic, three half-broken quills, a vial of suspect ink, and two dented silver coins—and followed. One last temple. One last apology. One last chance to slip through the noose before it closed.

I looked back at the camp—the wagons, the gossips, the smoke curling lazy prayers to the sky—and thought, not for the first time: *How bad could it be?*

The last stop on my sold-out, world-famous Nareth repentance tour was The Temple of the Seeded Womb. A place of ancient fertility rites, venerated by scholars, farmers, and anyone who'd ever desperately prayed for rain, healthy crops, or marginally less disappointing children. In Tahl'Vareth, it wasn't just *a* temple—it was *the* temple: the blessed belly-button of the nation, where gods, goats, and grain all got cozy in the name of survival. Even the city folk, who liked to pretend they'd outgrown such rustic nonsense, still whispered about it during hard seasons, hoping the old gods might throw in a good harvest out of pity.

The day was hot, and our journey into the city was a dust-choked ordeal that smelled faintly of goat, dried regret, and whatever Brin kept in his boots to discourage conversation. Not that it started badly. At first, we made good time. Brin took point—broad, silent, lumbering along with such force that trouble declined preemptively. Mero drifted behind, hands deep in his pockets, whistling a tune so off-key that a passing crow lost the will to live and crashed into a bush.

Seren rode in the centre. High atop Doom Nibbler, her not-at-all compensatory black steed, she looked like justice dressed for a funeral. Her face was unreadable, jaw clenched tight as if holding in something sharp. The wind caught her robes, making her look like a banner of outraged mourning.

I jogged along behind her like an afterthought with legs. After the third helping of kicked-up road dust, I cupped my hands and called forward: "Any chance of a ride?"

"No." She didn't look back.

I picked up my pace, managing to jog beside Chaos Repressed's flank long enough to catch a whiff of leather, sweat, and righteous fury. "Come now," I said, flashing what I hoped was a charming smile. "You wouldn't leave your favourite criminal to die of heatstroke and dust inhalation, would you?"

Her gaze flicked to me—just a fraction, but enough to sting. "If only," she muttered.

I let the silence sit there awhile, hoping it would go stale and blow away. It didn't.

And because I have the survival instincts of a boiled turnip, I cleared my throat. "For the record," I said, "if you're angry—and I'm not saying you are—but if you *were*… it's not because of something I've done yet?"

This time she turned. Not the full, dramatic stare I deserved—just a slow, tired swivel of the head, like someone trying to remember why they still bothered with gravity. Her voice, when it came, was quiet. Cold. "If I were angry about you, Aen… you'd be walking back to Nareth with your teeth in a pouch."

There wasn't fire behind it, though. Just ash.

I dropped back a step, hands raised in surrender. Which turned out to be wise, because Storm Redundancy picked that moment to snap at my shoulder. Probably in sympathy.

The road unspooled ahead of us, cracked and brittle, winding through forgotten fig trees and shepherd posts. The sun hammered down without mercy. Dust rose in lazy, cursing spirals around our boots. Mero whistled, paused only to hurl a rock at a particularly judgmental goat statue, then carried on, tuneless and cheerful.

And Seren... Seren was a fortress. Closed. Impenetrable. Crumbing somewhere deep inside where I couldn't follow.

I hated it. I hated the stiff set of her shoulders. I hated the silence coiling tighter around her until even breathing felt like trespass. And most of all, I hated how useless I was — me, Aen Marr: bard of Ruanne legends, breaker of hearts (mostly my own), sun-kissed disaster of the southern roads — reduced to nothing in the face of a grief she wouldn't even name.

The Temple of the Seeded Womb didn't so much loom as *insist*. Tucked into one of Nareth's cleaner districts — where fountains still trickled and the city guards wore matching shoes — it rose from the noise and filth like a sanctified pastry: tall, frosted in pink and white stucco, and entirely too ornate for a place promising moral clarity. The temple towered before us like an apology cake baked by a drunk god. Pink marble. White domes. Silk banners drooping from every archway, printed with fertility symbols so enthusiastic they'd get you arrested in polite company.

We threaded through the crush of bodies and barrows, past spice vendors, street criers, and one extremely enthusiastic man selling fertility charms shaped like confused vegetables.

Our quartet didn't exactly match the neighbourhood. Brin looked like a bouncer at a temple-sponsored knife fight. Mero had just stolen something. Seren radiated sanctity so fierce the cobblestones flinched. And I, of course, brought shame, sweat, and a dazzling smile.

We stopped at the foot of the temple steps.

Now, you'll have to excuse the interruption, but — as is sometimes (read: always) the case — there's a tiny, negligible, barely-worth-mentioning detail I may have... strategically omitted... about my relationship with this particular sacred religious order.

You see, unlike at the other temples — where I merely redistributed a few minor valuables, whispered persuasive nonsense, and collected modest tithes — my sins here were somewhat more... extravagant.

Yes, I was paid two silver for a handful of forged pilgrimage passes. That part is true.

However, I might also have stolen the pilgrims.

In my defense, she was very, *very* pretty.

She — a beautiful devotee with come-hither eyes and the figure of a fertility statue gone to finishing school — and her girlfriends, were meant to pray, purify, and be filled with a deeper sense of fertile purpose. Instead, the sale of a couple of fast passes turned, as things tend to do, into coquettish banter, laughter, and a genuine interest in following us home for... alternative explorations of fertile purpose with the Ruanne.

I would argue we assisted the Temple's noble purpose. We danced. We drank. We serenaded. Romanced. Possibly bedded. Possibly more than once.

They left spiritually fulfilled and thoroughly satisfied. Which is more than I can say for most temple visits.

Point is, by the time they sobered up and realised they'd

never made it to the temple, their week of abstinence was already up—and they had nothing to show for it but sore legs, fond memories, and a deep suspicion they might now be pregnant with joy. Possibly just with joy. Hopefully.

And for some reason, despite their official commitment to fertility, the Temple of the Seeded Womb took issue with our contributions.

Hence... grudge. Vilification. Penance.

But I digress.

The heat sharpened. Ahead, the temple doors gaped wide, framed by statues worn down to featureless lumps— fertility gods reduced to ghostly warnings.

Mero drew up beside me, shielding his eyes. "You sure you want to go through with this?" he asked. "Plenty of nice prisons that smell better than yoghurt."

"Where's your spirit of adventure?" I asked.

"Probably back there," he said, jerking his thumb toward the camp, "selling tickets to your funeral."

Brin grunted. Agreement. Or sympathy. Or realising he'd forgotten to pack a snack. As always, Brin's language was one of nuance and infinite variation.

A pair of priestesses waited at the gate, draped in flowing robes the colour of hope and bad decisions. Their faces were serene—in the way a thunderstorm is serene before it rips off your roof.

The older one, wrinkled as a raisin and twice as sour, stepped forward and banged her staff once on the ground. "Pilgrims of repentance," she intoned. "Approach with reverence."

Mero leaned sideways. "She means you, idiot."

I placed a hand over my heart and affected a penitential limp. Brin and Mero were told to wait. Brin nodded. Unbothered. Mero smirked and slunk behind him like a small, sarcastic shadow.

"But you," the priestess glared, making the word *you* sound like an indictment, "will proceed. And are forbidden from speaking unless spoken to."

I bowed deeply. "As you command, O Vessel of Womb-ly Wisdom."

Seren, dismounted now, found my ribs with an elbow. Deadly precision.

The priestess squinted, suspecting mockery but unable to prove it. She gestured curtly. "You will proceed to the Antechamber of Cleansing. You will disrobe, cleanse yourself in the Waters of Purity, and don the white robe provided." Her voice dropped to a tone normally reserved for sentencing war criminals. "No deviation."

I nodded solemnly.

I was already planning five minor deviations and one major scandal.

Seren, to her credit, merely muttered, "*Behave,*" under her breath as we were ushered through the main gate.

Now, the Temple of the Seeded Womb wasn't just one big open hall where anyone could stroll in, slap down a prayer, and expect results. Oh no. It had *layers.*

There were outer courtyards for general blessings — public gardens, fountains, shrines for rain, fertility, safe births, healthy harvests, moderately competent husbands. You name it. Anyone could visit those parts: men, women, children, even the occasional goat seeking divine intervention for a difficult kidding.

But deeper in — past the banners and the priestesses and the increasingly disapproving looks — you reached the sacred places. The places *only* women were permitted to enter.

At the very heart of it all, behind veils and carved doors and more ceremony than a noblewoman's wedding dress, lay the Basin. The Holiest of Holies. The Sacred Seat of Life.

What happened inside the Basin was a mystery carefully guarded by generations of women and utterly unfathomable to the male imagination.

We — meaning men — knew only what we were allowed to know: that it had something to do with fertility, blessings, and the ancient, unbroken thread of life that tied the past to the future.

Also: that under no circumstances, ever, were we to set foot inside it. Not by invitation. Not by accident. Not even in our dreams, if we knew what was good for us.

Which, naturally, made it irresistible.

Not that I would ever dream of sneaking in. Not even I am that stupid. (*Probably.*)

The temple smelled like incense, spoiled milk, and aggressive sanctity. Pink silk clung to every surface like an overfriendly octopus at a lingerie sale. We passed statues of fertility goddesses: generous hips, smug smiles. Murals depicted rituals involving various fluids I refused to think too hard about. The further we went, the hotter it got.

Steam clung to my skin. The air vibrated with low, droning chants.

At a branching hallway, another priestess materialized — pale, severe — and gestured with two fingers toward the left archway. "Antechamber," she said, though her hand hovered oddly, somewhere between left and forward, like even she wasn't sure where the holy parts began.

Seren didn't wait. Still radiating enough fury to curdle milk, she strode hard to the left, black robes hissing behind her like angry ink.

I followed, of course. That's what I do. Also: left looked less crowded.

About three steps in, the floor tiles changed — delicate pink-and-gold mosaics in shapes I refused to interpret. The steam thickened. The air smelled like flowers, salt, and old secrets.

"Uh," I said, "Seren — "

"Not now."

"No, but — are you sure this is the — "

She spun on me. "I said not now."

I held up both hands. "Right. Of course. You lead. I trespass."

We kept walking.

The corridor narrowed, darkened... then opened again.

Into a vast marble chamber. A vision. A nightmare vision.

A massive circular pool dominated the space — carved from pale stone, filled nearly to the brim with something white, glistening, and faintly steaming. It looked like yoghurt. It smelled like yoghurt. It wobbled like something that remembered being alive.

Oh gods. The Basin. The Holiest of Holies. The sacred Seat of Life.

Around the Basin moved figures — women, dozens of them, draped in clinging silks or nothing at all. They sang low prayers. They anointed each other with glistening handfuls of sacred cream. They glowed in the candlelight like a fever dream of goddesses. At the far end of the pool, atop a dais draped in ivory, stood the High Priestess herself. Tall. Bare. Wreathed in steam and righteous authority. She was in the middle of anointing a young woman at the forehead, murmuring blessings.

The air itself hummed. I froze. Seren froze. Too late.

One of the women by the pool turned. Smiled at me. Another winked. A third licked her lips in a way that suggested theological error. I took an instinctive step backward —

— and stepped directly on Seren's trailing robe.

She jerked. Arms pinwheeled. Body twisted midair like a particularly furious cat.

There was a glorious splash.

And Seren, magistrate of the Hall, enforcer of order, breaker of fools — plunged face-first into the sacred yoghurt.

Time dilated.

Seren flailed, emerging half-submerged, a dripping, steaming, mortified wreck. Her robe, traitorous fabric that it was, tore at the seams.

For one hideous moment, she bobbed there, sputtering, clothed in nothing but scandal.

And me? I, fool that I am, lunged forward to help.

And promptly slipped. And toppled. And tumbled.

Straight into the Basin after her.

Sacred yoghurt slopped over the marble lip in fat, glistening ropes. Steam rose in embarrassed clouds. The women encircling the pool froze mid-blessing, their mouths forming perfect O's of horror. Somewhere, a candle guttered and died.

I surfaced with a gasp, blinking away curdled divinity, and found Seren thrashing nearby, half-sunk, half-drowned, wholly mortified. Her hair plastered to her face. Her shoulders bare. Her robe clung like wet betrayal. Even the candles blushed.

Across the Basin, the High Priestess drew herself up to her full, appalling height. Her naked skin gleamed under the candlelight like a vengeful goddess, and her mouth twisted into a snarl fit to curdle fresh milk.

"A *man*," she hissed. "A *man* in the Basin."

Some women in the pool recoiled — — but not all of them.

Some edged closer. One, still glistening with anointing oil, smiled at me in a way that suggested she was open to *new interpretations* of sacred ritual. Another beckoned. A third, bold as thunder, waded through the yoghurt and reached for my arm.

I blinked.

My body suggested we stay.

My brain shrieked flight.

The High Priestess's voice cracked across the chamber: "*Defiler! Desecrator! Polluter of sacred rites! You have profaned the Holy Basin! You have corrupted the line of blessing!*"

She pointed— Not at me. At Seren.

"You brought him here. *You* will answer."

Seren, gasping, tried to stand. "No—" she croaked.

"*Silence!*" thundered the Priestess. "You will answer before the Hall. Before the Magi. Your crimes will be written in ash and blood—"

And still the women pressed closer to me.

Another hand brushed my shoulder. Another whispered, "Are you... *blessed?*"

Blessed? Cursed, more like.

With great difficulty, I ripped free—yoghurt spraying in holy arcs—and climbed onto the slick marble. Every step squelched.

The High Priestess turned now to *me*, spitting venom.

"You will *both* be cast out. You will carry this shame forever."

Seren sagged, robe wrapped around her (mostly), hands holding what was left of her drowned dignity. Ruined. Her career, her reputation, her place in the Hall—smashed to slurry with one stupid, stupid accident.

So, with all the conviction of a fool asking to be struck by lightning, I said:

"Forgive her. She did nothing wrong."

The High Priestess sneered. "You entered the Basin. *She* is responsible."

"No." I stepped forward, squelching nobly.

"She tried to stop me. She warned me. She fought to protect your rites. But I—" I drew a dramatic breath, thick with damp cheese aroma— "I was drawn. Drawn by the sacred call. The fertility. The mystery. The—" I faltered only slightly— "—the sacred cream."

The crowd gasped. Even Mero, somewhere beyond the doors, probably facepalmed hard enough to sprain something.

"I," I said, thumping my yoghurt-slick chest, "am cursed with overwhelming virility and catastrophic judgement. I tricked her. I seduced destiny itself. This desecration is mine. *Only* mine."

The High Priestess narrowed her eyes, assessing the sheer, uncut idiocy before her.

"You'll both be cast out," she snapped. "Nothing can cleanse the Basin now."

"Cast me *twice*, then," I said, smiling through a mouthful of terror. "But she's innocent."

A long, ugly silence stretched between us. Then the Priestess turned her back. Silk banners flared like a drawn blade.

"Guards," she barked. "Eject them."

The temple guards were thorough.

We were seized, stripped of dignity (though Seren was issued a new robe), and marched to the outer gates— dripping sacred yoghurt from every possible orifice. No trial. No ceremony. Just one final, squelching, humiliating walk into the sun.

Behind us, the Temple doors slammed shut with a boom

that rattled my teeth.

Ahead lay the empty road back to Nareth. It baked under the noon sun, stretching long and merciless and notably lacking any convenient holes for me to crawl into and die.

Brin and Mero — saints that they were — had not waited.

We walked away together. Seren led her horse, face carved from salt and stone, bare feet brushing the thoroughfare. It wasn't far to the city gates, but it felt long. And sticky. Very, very sticky.

Every step *squelched*. Every gust of wind stirred a fresh miasma of sour milk and regret. Somewhere behind us, the Temple doors remained shut — barring us forever from sacred mystery and complimentary anointings.

Ahead: dust, stone, blistering sun.

Even the goats in distant fields seemed to have decided this wasn't worth heckling.

It gave me time to think. (*Always* dangerous.)

By most rational standards, I had just ruined my life.

The High Priestess hadn't been bluffing. The Hall would hear of this. Seren's superiors would hear. The city gossips would hear. And I? I would be immortalized as the idiot who defiled a basin of sacred fertility yoghurt.

Maybe they'd name a cautionary tale after me. *Beware, children: tread lightly, or you too shall fall like Aen Marr into the Cream of Sorrow.*

But it wasn't the yoghurt clinging to my knees or the sting of scraped pride that hurt most. It was the silence.

Bleeding something raw and real into the dust.

I watched Seren's back. So straight. So rigid. Like she was holding herself together with the last threads of law and willpower.

I followed, quiet for once, yoghurt dripping from my elbows, and thought: *Well. It was worth it.* Even if she never forgave me. Even if the Family laughed until the stars burned out. Even if I died alone, sticky, and universally mocked.

Because sometimes a fool has to pick his moment to be sacred, too. Even if all it gets him is cast out into the dust.

We reached the edge of the city just as the sun hammered its zenith. The dust turned to gravel. Low stone walls marked the outskirts — fields of wilted crops and forgotten promises.

Seren slowed. Stopped. For a heartbeat, she just stood there, facing away. I held my breath.

Finally, she turned.

The yoghurt had dried to sour crusts on her sleeves. Her hair was a wreck. Her face — tired, furious, devastated — was the most beautiful thing I'd ever seen.

"You made it worse," she said, voice ragged.

I nodded.

"You humiliated me."

Nod.

"You desecrated a sacred site. Mocked a faith. Ruined a ritual older than the city itself."

"Technically," I said carefully, "the *floor* did most of the desecrating. I merely — "

Her glare cut me dead. I shut up.

She crossed her arms — *squelch* — and stared at me. Hard.

And then... something shifted.

The iron in her spine softened. The rage in her shoulders sagged. The judgment in her eyes dulled into something quieter.

Understanding.

"You knew," she said, low. "You knew what it meant. What it would cost me."

I didn't answer.

"So you made yourself the villain."

I shrugged. "Didn't have to try very hard."

For a moment—just a moment—the corner of her mouth twitched. Not a smile. Not exactly. More like the memory of one.

She looked down, wiped one sticky hand across her face, and sighed.

"You're an idiot," she muttered.

"Professionally."

"A selfish, arrogant, insufferable idiot."

"Independent contractor rates available."

Another long silence. The wind kicked dust across the road, rustling the dry fig trees like skeletal applause.

Finally, she looked up. Met my eyes. Held them.

And in a voice so soft I almost missed it, she said:

"Thank you."

Two words. No armour. No sarcasm. No walls.

Just Seren.

I swallowed. Tried to think of something clever. Failed.

Instead, I just nodded.

I left her at the gates.

And as I limped toward the Ruanne camp—where the goats would surely mock us, the gossips would feast, and Mero would invent ballads of unholy yoghurt anointments—I felt lighter than I had in years.

Because sometimes the sacred thing isn't the Basin.

It's what you pull out of it.

Absolutely Not Touching Everything and Nothing (Again)

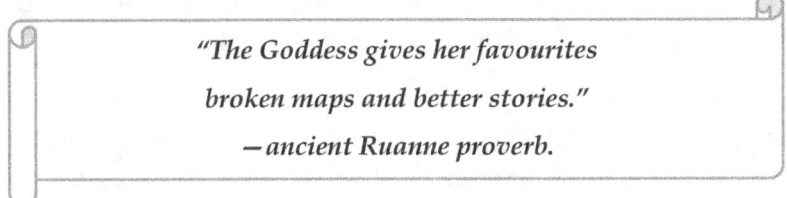

> *"The Goddess gives her favourites*
> *broken maps and better stories."*
> *— ancient Ruanne proverb.*

This one is weird.

And that means something, coming from me.

I've lied to kings, seduced the unseducable, and once convinced an entire courthouse that I was a visiting ambassador from a country I made up halfway through the trial. (The proud Republic of Vardh. Our national animal was a disappointed goat. Our anthem was mostly sighing.)

So when I say this one is strange, I mean it punched through my usual nonsense and came out the other side whistling.

It started, as all dangerous things do, with boredom, curiosity, and Mero's deeply flawed belief that he can keep anything hidden from me.

You remember the book. *The Everything, Including Nothing.* Slim, white, smug. A little disaster bound in fine linen and terrible judgment. It turned a wineskin into a flopping trout, played with our shadows, and perhaps most famously — bit Mero. (There was only a little blood.)

Mero being the big baby that he is, and born with a survival instinct entirely foreign to me, hid it away like a terrible secret. He claimed it was for our protection. I claimed he was being a joyless ferret.

I searched. Gods, I searched. I rifled through bags, cloaks, secret pouches. I once spent forty minutes dismantling his hammock on the theory he'd woven it into the fabric. (He hadn't. But I did find a handful of dried figs and a drawing of Brin in a dress. Still unclear on the context.)

I checked under cooking pots, behind soup barrels, inside Brin's boots (don't do that), and even sweet-talked a goat into sniffing out magic. The goat ate my sleeve and headbutted a tree. Jury's out on whether it helped.

Days passed. Nothing.

And then, one evening, while Mero was out relieving himself against a tree and I was scouring his tent for any sign of it—again—I found it.

Or rather, it found me.

I was elbow-deep in his laundry pile, lifting his so-called "bedding" (which smelled like regret and feet), when I felt something hard press against the underside of my thigh.

It was not there before. I'm sure of it. But then it was.

Not glowing. Not humming. Just sitting. Smugly. Like it had always been there, and I was the fool for ever doubting it.

I stared at it.

"You weren't there before," I said aloud.

Because apparently, I talk to objects now.

The book did not reply. Which, frankly, was suspicious.

Now, a reasonable person—if one of those accidentally wandered into my skin—would have shouted for Mero. Or Brin. Or Nema. Or maybe doused the thing in blessed vinegar, locked it up in a chest, and lit the chest on fire. But as we all know, I am not a reasonable person. I am an enthusiastically unreasonable person. I'd like to think of myself as devotee to the broken, curious, and the chaotic.

So I wrapped the book in a spare shirt, tucked it into my coat like it was a stolen pastry, and crept out of the tent.

Then the camp.

Silent as guilt. Swift as tossed cat. Grinning at the moon like it was my co-conspirator.

The grove I chose was more a forgotten corner of the world where the land had decided to stop trying. The trees were fig, allegedly. Their trunks twisted like they'd been caught mid-scream, their leaves sparse and clawed. They danced — not in the usual wind, but in something unseen, something that moved between the branches like breath through a cracked reed. The ground was a chaos of scrub brush, growing in no particular order, like a drunk gardener had had a grudge against symmetry. The sky above was... wrong. Brighter than usual. The stars blinked like they were trying to send a distress signal, only to be smothered mid-blink by invisible clouds that coiled and uncoiled like smoke pretending to be sky. The moon flickered behind them — now bright, now swallowed, now bright again, as if deciding whether this scene deserved illumination or discretion.

Shadows played across the earth with no source, no reason. They weaved and darted like gossip at a wake — too lively, too misplaced.

At the center of it all sat a boulder. Or maybe it was a fossil. Or an altar abandoned by a very confused cult. Cracked sandstone, pitted and striped in patterns that almost meant something if you stared too long — but never quite. Like a language you almost knew, or a joke you were just a hair too slow to catch.

I sat beside it, feeling appropriately heretical. The kind of place where a man could commit a small cosmic error and feel proud of it.

Blank.

Then—ink. Slow, swirling, deliberate. Like it was thinking. Like it wanted me to watch.

To Aen Marr, Delightful Disaster, Thief of Meanings, Moon's Favourite Mistake, and Patron Saint of Improvisation,

Did you miss me?

I snorted. "No. Not even a little."

Liar.

I grinned. Then after a moment, I asked, "What are you?"

Mirror. Voice. Seed. Song.

I grinned wider. My heart lurched and swayed. I wanted to hug the book to my heart. This was my kind of magic. It didn't need to make sense. I didn't want it to. I gazed up at the sky, and for a moment, it felt like the world tilted. Like I had been spinning wildly and just sat down. Like I was wonderfully drunk.

I looked back to the magic in my hand.

You've forgotten.

"I forget a lot of things," I said.

Here we go.

And then the page bled.

I don't mean the ink ran. I mean it *bled*—black with flecks of stardust, seeping through the page like the book had veins. It poured over my hands like viscous liquid. I was so shocked I forgot to scream. Just sat there as liquid sky ran over my skin and a strong smell rose up into my nose and mouth. It smell like warm earth. Or crushed leaves?

Or salt.

And then I wasn't in the grove anymore.

I tried to look away. I didn't want this. But the book wasn't asking.

It was dark as pitch. There was nothing. No sky. No ground. Nothing.

Something moved in the dark. I squinted.

There you go, she said. *Here we go. Do you see him?*

Then there was light and colour, and I saw... me. Years ago. In Dararein.

With a terror sliding into my heart, I remembered.

Yes, she whispered. *Look at him. So small. Broken.*

Somehow, she was taking me back to something I never wanted to remember. There I was hiding at the bullfight. Watching as a man beat young Brin bloody. And I hid in the corner, unable to move.

"No. Please," I heard myself say.

Shh, she cooed. *It's just a story, darling. A little story to stitch the cracks. A little story that sings, that dances in the fire.*

This story takes place once upon a time in Dararein.

It was hot that day, the kind of hot that makes your clothes hate you. Two Ruanne women were trying very hard not to kill each other in public. Nema, fierce and furious, screaming that Ana, all hips and honey, had decided that monogamy was a suggestion, not a commandment. And young Altrein, poor thing, standing guard with his helmet askew and his future unwritten, got an eyeful of everything. Especially Ana.

There are women who mostly want what other's have. Ana was one of such women. And Nema's Juro was strong and proud and vain. So, Ana had flicked her teeth at Nema, and had hated her, and coveted. Then she spat on the ground before Nema, crowing that she had claimed Juro as Nema was too small, too dry, too worthless.

Nema's loathing for all thing Ana cannot be overstated.

Hair was pulled. Curses were flung. A wooden spoon may have been involved.

Altrein was ordered to arrest Ana, but when she leaned close – close enough to smell like summer and scandal – he melted like butter on a furnace and let her go. She parted, leaving him with a flower, red as blood. In return, though he did not know it then, he gave to her a child. You, Aen.

Altrein was smitten. But soldiers do not claim their own fate, and so off to war he went, poor fool. Six years murdering to prove for once and for all that a certain patch of dirt was claimed by one petty tyrant, and not another. Until the next dance of spears. Entirely justified and righteous, just like the last. And the next.

Altrein sat in the sun. Killed dutifully. Starved when required. Cowered when arrows rained death. Prayed to all the gods that he might live. Six years of nightmare and ruin and death. And through it all, he carried that blood rose, folded and pressed close to his heart, and dreamt of Ana eyes. And soft hands. And playful hips.

And against all reason, and mostly by chance, he did live.

He came back, scarred and victorious, and sought Ana out with the kind of romantic intensity usually reserved for those who had lived on prayers. But sweet Ana? Moved on. She had a new flame: Rodrello the bullfighter, with thighs like a statue and a smile that could part oceans. He was coveted by thousands, and so Ana had to have him. Rodrello had lots of time for Ana's curves and smiles. Not so much a child that was not his.

Your flower, Altrein said, holding out the little thing she'd once given him. Dried, pressed, war-worn. She laughed. And he heard in that laugh a chance. And he saw a child that looked like him.

But small, wiry, with quick eyes, and the look of neglect.

You belong to me, he said. She didn't deny it — not the child, not the past — but she refused him all the same.

To pursue her, he quit the army. He chased. She laughed like the wind. He spent his saving on gifts, offerings of love. She accepted the gift but refused the love.

He festered. He obsessed. He twisted into the dark. Even in his dreams, Ana's laughter sounded like mockery.

Ana stayed radiant. You toddled beside her.

Nema — Nema watched from a distance. She warned her son, Brin, who had his mother's frown and a silence sharper than steel, of the dark places in the heart of the world of men. Of dangerous women, and dangerous men. Of those for whom family has not meaning. Those who think only of the sun on their skin, and gifts to themselves.

The waters were rising, but none of them saw it. Not yet.

Rodrello's bullfight. The world attended.

And as luck would have it — though there is no such a things as luck, only me — Ana (with you) and Nema (with Brin) were both in attendance. The old hatred between the women still lurked, but it did not touch you boys. And so, while the crowd waited, you two puzzle pieces discovered each other.

Of course I was there. Because already you were mine.

The crown roared. Trumpets blared.

And into the scene walked fate wearing Altrein's face.

He had murder in his eye. And a knife in his coat.

Nema saw it. Ran. Screamed. Tried to fetch Rodrello.

But it was too late.

Ana turned, saw him. A last smile.

Blood and fate and madness. And she fell.

And you would have been next if Brin — tiny, furious Brin — had not flung himself at Altrein with a fury that belonged in sagas. He fought. Twelve years old. All elbows and rage. Altrein beat him bloody. But he didn't reach you before Rodrello was there, and the bull fighter killed the rabid bull that was Altrien.

But why have I told you this tale, my sweet?

I told you all that to show you this.

This is my gift. The remembering.

Because he never told you.

I saw it then. I saw the scene in that magic place the book had created.

Everything slowed. There's no sound.

Ana's blood on the arena stones. Altrein breathing his last. Nema's hatred draining, replaced by shock and horror. Rodrello victorious, sad, but already looking for a safe opportunity to walk away. Crowds descending. And in the heart of it, me, small and broken. The truth I had worked so hard to forget.

Nema taking Brin, covered in blood, trying to lead him away, but Brin won't go.

Won't leave me.

And then, with a soft wave of sound, I heard the oath he swore. *We have to take him, mama. I will watch over him. I will take care of him. Forever. Swear to the gods. I swear it.*

And just like a blink, the magic world was gone, and I was back in the grove.

The Everything, Including Nothing open on my lap. Pulsing like a heartbeat.

I took a long breath.

Tears were on my face.

"I will take care of him. Forever."

I repeated it aloud, testing the shape.

It didn't feel like a memory. It felt like a promise I'd borrowed.

But it was the strangest thing. A moment ago, I was there, and I was remembering it all. It was all true. And now —

"I don't remember any of that," I said to the book.

A shame, she scribbled, *how truth slips away when you aren't looking.*

The page crinkled. It felt like a wink.

I took another long breath. Wiped my eyes.

"True enough?" I teased.

On the page in front of me, a word bubbled up:

Garnish.

A ripple ran up my neck. I felt my hair rising up to the sky.

Her nonsense wasn't water, it was fire — ridiculous, bright, and holy in the worst possible way.

I laughed then. And howled at the moon.

Of Grief and Other Dangerous Magic

We steal babies.

We curse the crops.

Bewitch the cattle, seduce the sons, hex the daughters, and make the milk sour with a glance. They say if you so much as shake hands with a Ruanne, your chickens will forget how to lay eggs and your mother-in-law will move in forever.

They say our women sleep under the moon to learn its secrets, our men whisper to fire, and our children learn to steal before they learn to walk.

To all that, I say: *only the milk thing is true,* and even that depends on the cow.

Let's get one thing straight. Ruanne magic is real. It is *inconveniently* real, *irritatingly* real, real in the way lightning is real — unpredictable, unruly, and prone to striking when you're already wet. Real like grief. Real like hope. Real like the moment before a kiss when everything holds its breath and forgets how to be afraid.

But here's the thing no one tells you — especially not the historians, who are mostly cowards, and definitely not the priests, who are mostly wrong: *Ruanne magic doesn't take unless you flirt with it a little first.*

It needs theatre. It needs rhythm. It needs flour tossed into lamplight and an audience willing to believe, or at least too desperate not to. It's an old, wild thing, like a dog that remembers being a wolf, and if you want it to sit and stay and shake hands like a respectable mutt, you're liable to be bitten.

No. If you want to coax the fae, you need to sing to it in the old language and dance on one foot under a sky full of half-forgotten stars.

Magi? Ha! That's a city word, heavy with flounces, hats, handkerchiefs and people sawing each other in half. With words. We're not sorcerers. We don't have towers or contracts or schools that teach you how to incinerate your classmates. What we have is older than that. Dirtier than that. *Truer* than that. What we have is stories, handed down mouth to mouth, heart to heart, sometimes whispered, sometimes sung, sometimes screamed at full volume during an argument over whether ghosts can get drunk. (They can. We've checked.)

You see, our magic doesn't come with rules. It comes with *reasons*. Reasons like: she died too soon. He never got to say goodbye. The baby won't stop crying. The rain won't come. The world is a cruel, bloody mess, and someone needs something *impossible* to get through the day without collapsing. And when that happens—when someone needs something so badly their soul goes knocking—they come to us.

And we help. Sort of.

Not always. Not perfectly. Not without a fair amount of smoke, mirrors, and a very uncooperative lantern. But sometimes? Sometimes the dead speak. Sometimes the grief opens wide enough to let the magic in. Sometimes the sky listens. And when that happens, we don't ask why. We don't poke it or prod it or write it down for the scholars to misunderstand.

We just bow our heads, light the fire, and let the moment

pass through us like a song no one remembers learning.

So yes. Ruanne magic is real.

It just needs a little encouragement.

Preferably with good lighting, a cracked mirror, and a friend named Brin ready to shake the floorboards when the dead arrive.

Queue the mood lighting. Here we go.

It started the way these things usually did — with a man who needed something impossible, and a Family stubborn enough to give it to him anyway.

He wasn't the first. Probably wouldn't be the last. But he was the saddest thing I'd seen in a long while: stoop-shouldered, hollow-eyed, wearing grief like a second skin. Even his boots sagged, and they were new. City-made. Probably cost a month's wages, but no amount of fine stitching could hide the fact he didn't know where he was walking anymore.

His wife had died birthing their daughter, and from the look of him, it might as well have been his whole world that bled out that day. He came to us, to Nema, because that's what people did when polite prayers and proper priests weren't enough. Somewhere between fear and hope, between stories of Ruanne "magic" and Ruanne "lies," there was a space wide enough for real miracles — or at least, for a good enough imitation to keep a man breathing.

Nema listened to him carefully, patiently, flour still on her forearms from baking, and said: "We will do what we can."

Which was how I ended up wedged into the back of her

wagon with a cracked mirror, a bucket of flour, three lanterns of questionable reliability, and Mero sitting cross-legged beside me, knotting invisible fishing lines like a very sullen spider.

Out front, Nema was setting the stage. No lies. No tricks. Just the right words, the right lighting, the right pause between breaths. Mood mattered. Ceremony mattered. If you wanted someone to open their heart to the impossible, you had to give them a door to walk through. And that was our job: I was in charge of whispering the right words at the right moments, stirring the mirror's reflection, tossing a pinch of flour through the lamplight. Mero ran the wires, pulling lanterns and curtains in slow, careful rhythms. Brin, stationed outside, would rock the wagon just enough to make the floor shiver when the dead were near.

People say the Ruanne wield dark magic. Maybe we do. There are old ways that have been passed down through generations. And there are so many things that we don't yet understand in this world. Yes, we performed. But what really matters is that, sometimes, when we did our magic just right, the ones the broken needed to hear would find a way to answer.

I wiped my hands on my trousers and checked the mirror's angle one more time. Mero muttered a few dire predictions under his breath, because optimism has never been Mero's strong suit.

"Ready?" I whispered.

"No," he muttered back.

Which, for us, meant: Yes. Gods help us.

The man sat stiff and shaking on the little stool Nema set out for him, hands clenched so tight around his knees I thought he might splinter the wood. He was dressed too fine for our camp: polished boots, crisp tunic, a heavy silver ring that kept catching the firelight and stabbing it into our eyes. Grief makes people dress up, I've noticed. Like they think mourning is something you can impress your way through.

Nema worked around him in slow, careful circles. Lighting the lamps. Tending the brazier. Soft little rituals, half-seen, half-heard. She wore her best shawl — the indigo one stitched with the old patterns — and let the silence stretch long enough to make the air itself start to ache.

Mero gave a sharp little tug on the fishing line, and one of the lanterns swayed, casting a shadow that stretched and clawed along the wagon wall. I tossed a pinch of flour through the brazier's smoke. It caught the firelight and bloomed into drifting, ghostly shapes. The man shivered. Good. He should be afraid.

Nema knelt by the fire and murmured words in Old Ruanne — our language, full of broken syllables and swallowed vowels, old as dust and stubborn as roots. Most of the Family didn't use it much anymore, but in moments like this, when you needed the world to listen, it still had weight.

Outside, Brin leaned his full weight into the wagon's side, slow and rhythmic, like a heartbeat. The floorboards creaked under us. The brazier flickered. Somewhere overhead, a lantern chain groaned. The man's eyes darted from shadow to shadow. I waited. Timing was everything. Too soon and you spoiled it. Too late and the fear curdled into doubt. When his breathing hit that ragged, gasping edge — the place where terror and longing meet — I leaned close to the cracked mirror and whispered, just loud enough for him to hear: "She is near." He flinched like I'd struck him. His mouth opened, closed. His whole body leaned forward, desperate.

Nema rose from her kneeling place, her shawl swirling around her like smoke, and faced him squarely. "Tell her what weighs on you," she said. Her voice wasn't grand. It wasn't theatrical. It was steady. The kind of voice that could make even the dead listen, if they were lingering nearby.

The man swallowed hard. His whole face crumpled. "I—I can't do this alone," he choked. "I don't know how to raise her. Our daughter. She's only a babe. And you—" He broke off, head bowing under the weight of it.

"Speak," Nema said softly. "She will hear you."

Outside, Brin shifted his weight again. The floor gave a long, low moan.

The man's gaze fell. He didn't lift his eyes as he began to speak. It wasn't entirely coherent; the emotion was too pressed down, too buried beneath a year trying to lock it away, paper it over with routine. Broken apologies, pleas, promises—everything he'd never gotten to say before death slammed the door shut. And through it all, Nema stood steady, a quiet shore against the storm. When the words ran dry, she moved closer, and bent her head as if listening. "Your love is with us. She listens," she said, "and shares your sorrow. She does not blame you. She says you are stronger than you know. You will raise her daughter well. You will teach her to laugh again. And when you do, your beloved will be near."

The words hung in the smoky air.

The man lifted his head, trembling, broken open. The room felt full—heavy—with something more than smoke and whispers. I felt it. Even Mero, miserable bastard that he was, stilled. Nema's words drew forth the old magic. Or perhaps the man's grief was the match that lit the magic and brought it forth. I don't know. But in that moment, the dead were close.

Nema's voice was low and steady, woven through the smoke. "She sees you," she said, voice heavier than the wagon air. "She watches still. She holds you in her heart."

The man trembled. His shoulders hitched. His mouth twisted. I could almost see it happening: The part of him that wanted to believe—and the part of him that hated believing.

The smoke thickened. The shadows shivered. Outside, Brin shifted the wagon just so, creaking the boards, tapping the lanterns, making the air dance the way the dead were supposed to dance. Inside, I gave the brazier a little flick, sent the flames fluttering higher—painting ghost-light across the walls.

The man gasped. "Is that—?" he croaked. His hands rose, reaching toward the wavering shapes like he could catch her in his fists.

Nema closed her eyes for a beat. When she spoke again, her voice was different—softer, thinner. "My love," she said, her voice shaped like grief itself. "I see you. I am proud of you. You must go on. You must raise her well. You must forgive yourself."

The man let out a noise that wasn't human. Half sob. Half animal. He staggered forward, almost toppling the brazier. Caught himself on the edge of the stool. His face was broken open with pain. He heard. Gods help us, his wife spoke to him there in our little wagon.

Her presence was too much for him to bear. Like a wave crashing, his grief suddenly broke, but not to sadness, into uncontrollable anger. He swayed on his feet. Suddenly, he was screaming. "You left me!" he shouted, voice cracking like a tree splitting in a storm. "You LEFT me here with nothing — with her — alone!"

Nema opened her arms, calm as a still lake. "You are not alone," she said, in that same soft, ghost-voice. "You were never alone."

The man howled. And before I could even move — before anyone could — he lunged. Not at the fire. Not at the air. At her. At Nema. At the woman he thought was wearing his wife's face. He hit her square in the chest, shoving with both hands.

Nema stumbled back, barely catching herself on the wagon wall.

I scrambled forward, heart clawing up my throat.

Outside, the wagon gave a lurch — Brin already moving. The man stumbled wildly forward, pulling back for another strike — this one harder, wilder, the kind of blow meant to break something that wouldn't bleed enough the first time — and Brin hit the door like a battering ram. He didn't shout. He didn't ask questions. He just grabbed the man like a sack of bad onions and hurled him out the door into the mud. Mero was right behind him, arms up, ready for a fight that never came because the man hit the ground and stayed there, sobbing, clutching his chest like it was caving in.

Inside the wagon, I knelt beside Nema. She wasn't hurt — thank all the gods and half the demons — but she looked... tired. Worn thinner than I'd ever seen her. Like something had been drained right out of her with that shove.

She touched my face — gently, lightly, like I was the one who might shatter.

"It's alright, Aen," she said, and her voice was still the voice of a woman who could talk to ghosts if she wanted.

But me? I didn't feel alright. Not even a little. Not because of the danger. Because for one awful second, when he screamed at her — I think Nema really was carrying the dead woman's sadness and loss. Her soul, not quite departed. I know what I heard and what I felt there in that small room, and I will go to my grave swearing that the dead woman was there that night, reaching out to comfort the husband she had been forced to leave behind.

The man didn't run. Didn't even get up. Just lay there, face down in the mud, breathing painfully, like the whole sky was falling on him.

Brin hovered nearby — big, stone-faced, fists clenched — ready to hammer him back into the earth if he so much as twitched wrong. Mero leaned against the wagon, arms crossed, looking about as sympathetic as a cat watching a drowning mouse. And me? I stayed in the doorway, one hand braced on the jamb, breathing hard, feeling way too small for the size of the world all of a sudden.

Nema stepped out. She didn't push me aside. Didn't bark orders. Just touched my shoulder lightly, the way you nudge a bird off a branch when you're afraid it'll fall.

I wanted to stop her. Gods, I wanted to. The man had attacked her. He'd shoved her so hard she still had a handprint blooming on her chest like a slow bruise. But Nema — gods bless her bloody stubborn bones — she just knelt down beside him in the mud.

"You loved her greatly," she said, voice soft as a lullaby. "I know."

The man lifted his head, blinking through tears and grime and rage, and for a second — just a second — I thought he was going to swing again. But he didn't. He broke. Collapsed forward with a sound like ripping cloth, grabbing at her skirts, weeping like a child lost in a storm. I don't know what he said. He was speaking, but the grief poured out so hard that the words came out wrong; misshapen and broken.

Nema let him cry. Didn't flinch. Didn't scold. Didn't wipe the mud off her skirts. Just sat there, her hand on his shaking back, murmuring things too soft for me to hear. Maybe prayers. Maybe nothing but breath.

I don't know how long they stayed like that. Long enough that the other Family members nearby stopped pretending they weren't looking. Long enough for even Mero to shift awkwardly, muttering something under his breath about needing to check the wagon wheels. Brin stayed like a statue. And me? I watched. And hated it. And loved it. And hated myself for loving it. Because somehow, in all the smoke, shaken lanterns, creaking boards, and rattling chains, something real had slipped through.

Ghosts are real. Magic is real. But so too is grief. And whatever Nema had pulled out of that man — it wasn't an illusion. It wasn't a trick. It was him. Naked and bleeding on the inside, for the first time since his whole world had gone up in fire and screaming. And somehow — magically — Nema had caught it. Held it like it wouldn't burn her.

Later that night, after the man had gone — staggered off with Nema's blessing ringing in his ears and my bruised ribs aching just from watching Brin throw him — we sat around the dying cookfire, lost in our own thoughts. Mero was plucking burrs out of his cloak, muttering curses under his breath. Brin was busy pretending he wasn't still vibrating with leftover fury, sharpening a knife that already could've shaved a saint bald. I was poking the fire with a stick, watching the embers collapse into themselves like tiny red stars burning out.

"So," I said at last, to no one in particular. "We're definitely adding a hazard surcharge to the séance package, right?"

Brin grunted. Mero flicked a burr into the flames.

"Maybe," Mero said. "Maybe we just stop playing with the dead altogether."

I snorted. "Sure. And maybe pigs will start writing poetry."

He shrugged. "One tried last month. Wrote better than you."

I lobbed a pebble at him. Missed.

Nema emerged from the dark a few minutes later, quiet as a wraith. She settled onto a crate beside us, wrapping a shawl around her shoulders like armour. For a long time, none of us spoke. The fire crackled and spat. Somewhere in the deeper camp, a baby wailed once, then fell quiet again.

Finally, Mero cleared his throat. "Isn't right, what he did," he muttered.

Nema gave one of those tired little smiles she saved for when people asked questions with no easy answers. "I'm fine."

I wanted to believe her. Gods, I wanted to. But I kept seeing the way her body jerked when he shoved her. The way her hands had trembled when she brushed mud off her skirt.

"You didn't have to forgive him," I said, voice rough. "We

could've handled it."

She looked at me, and her gaze was steady and warm and utterly unbreakable. "I did what he needed," she said. "Not what I needed."

Mero looked away. Brin stabbed the knife deeper into the whetstone. I just kept poking the fire, wishing it would tell me something useful.

"Was it real?" I blurted before I could stop myself. "The… you know. The wife. The voice."

Nema smiled again. Not tired, this time. Sad.

"Yes," she said. "In the all the ways that matter."

I sat with that for a while, feeling the way the night folded in closer around us. I had thought we made magic with trick mirrors and shaking walls and whispers from under floorboards. Magic with sleight of hand and clever lies. But what Nemat ought me is that we made magic because people needed it. And sometimes—just sometimes—it becomes real. Not because of the props. Not because of the tricks. Because people carried their own magic inside them. All we did was give it a door by which to enter.

The fire burned lower. Nema stood, kissed the top of my head like she had when I was little and scraped my knees trying to fly, and drifted back into the night.

Mero yawned. Brin stretched and cracked his neck.

I stayed a little longer by the coals, watching the last light sputter and die. And maybe it was the cold. Maybe it was exhaustion. But just before I finally dragged myself to bed, I could've sworn I heard a woman's voice—soft, laughing, familiar—singing out across the empty night.

And What, Exactly, Do You Call That?

A city official with a nervous moustache and a degree in Missing the Point will ask what happened that night. He'll want names. Timelines. Neatly labeled explanations with brass plaques that say things like *illusion, coercion, trauma response.*

And we'll smile. Sweet as sin.

And we won't explain.

Let them talk.

And if they scoff—if they say, *"That's not real magic,"*—we'll raise an eyebrow, tuck our hands into our sleeves like a street prophet or a drunk uncle, and say: *That's what you say.*

Then they'll press. They'll splutter. They'll wave their clipboards and try to legislate the wild out of the world.

And we'll just shrug and say what we've always said:

It doesn't matter what you call it, so long as it helps the broken find their way home.

They'll hate us for that. Of course they will.

They always have.

They'll cast words like *sorcery, sin, corruption* at our backs like stones, as if naming a thing can unmake it.

But we don't claim anything. We don't brand it. We just hum the old songs while whatever-it-is rises in our blood like smoke from a wet fire.

Not tidy. Not safe. Not for sale.

But real. Gods help us, it's real.

Even when it shouldn't be. *Especially* when it shouldn't be.

And if you don't believe me?

That's fine.

Just don't say it too loud.

The wind might be listening.

The Eviction That Wasn't (But Somehow Still Is)

> *"In the judge's garden, even the snake wears a crown."*
> — *ancient Ruanne proverb.*

After my vision under the stars, I crept back into the camp, the *Everything, Including Nothing* clutched to my chest, and curled myself under a blanket by the main firepit — half-buried in cooling ash, half-convinced the flames might protect me. It wasn't the worst spot. Jorann's cookfire still threw a little warmth, and the smell of charred lentils masked my guilt. Almost.

I hid the book beneath my blanket. Pressed it to my ribs. Slept curled around it like a dragon around a single stolen jewel.

And I *dreamed.*

Dreams that were too large to hold. Red and gold and wild, full of strange voices, old songs, women laughing under broken stars.

I woke up to the distinct, terrible feeling that I was being observed.

Not by the gods — I've long since made my peace with their voyeurism — but by something far more unsettling.

By children.

I opened one eye to find myself entirely *surrounded* by a gaggle of wide eyed, scruffy, curious camp rats. They multiplied in silence like guilt in a church — standing around me in a ragged ring. There were at least eight, not counting Brin looming behind them, or Mero standing off to the side with the expression of someone who'd bitten into a fruit and discovered it was full of wasps.

One of the younger ones knelt nearby, stick in hand, as if she had just poked me.

"Maybe he *molted*," said another, in a tone of profound scientific interest.

I sat up, bleary and suspicious. Something felt... off. The world looked a touch brighter, maybe. The air smelled faintly of burnt cinnamon.

"Look!" another one squeaked. "It's glowing again!"

"Poke it," hissed a third.

"Do *not* poke me," I croaked, rising from the blanket.

And then I saw the curl.

Just one. Hanging in front of my face.

Red.

Flaming, unrepentant, impossible red.

I blinked. Blinked again. Pulled the curl into full view. It remained a furious ribbon.

A copper pot stood nearby. I scrambled out of the cocoon of my blanket and crawled clumsily over to it. Raised it up.

My head — my *entire* head — had apparently been replaced in the night by a flaming shrubbery.

"What the —" I began.

The twins screamed with delight.

"Oh gods," I croaked. "Tell me it's dye. Tell me Mero finally snapped and painted me in my sleep."

"It's not dye," Mero said, too calmly.

I groaned and buried my face in my hands. My hands — still tragically mine — offered no protection against cosmic embarrassment.

"It wasn't this bad last night," I muttered. "It was only a little... warm."

"It's beautiful!" cried one of the girls, starry-eyed. "You look like a phoenix!"

"I look like a *fruit*," I grumbled.

"You look," Mero said, "like someone who should explain what you were doing with a certain demonic book."

"It's not..." I started. Then stopped. My heart dropped. I patted my coat. My belt. The place under my blanket where I definitely, definitely didn't keep forbidden magical tomes.

Empty.

Gone.

Vanished like virtue in a brothel.

"You *took* it," I said, scandalized. "You absolute *thieves*."

"Correct," said Mero.

"*Confiscated*," said Brin, jabbing a large thumb toward wagon #1.

"*You took it to Nema?*"

A beat of silence answered me.

And that silence said, *Yes.*

And also, *You're in so much trouble the dead are taking notes.*

I collapsed back into my blanket.

"Oh gods," I moaned. "I'm going to be cursed *and* banished."

"You're not cursed," said a small voice beside me. "Just... extremely bright."

Nema was waiting for us.

The wagon smelled like old cedar, ink, and disappointment.

She didn't speak right away. She didn't have to. Her silence was the kind that came with altitude — the high, rarefied silence of someone surveying a disaster from above and deciding which parts were worth salvaging.

I shuffled awkwardly inside, resisting the urge to bow, kneel, or hide behind a cushion. Brin lumbered in a sat, tilting the wagon. I felt Mero behind me, slouching at the door like an idle shadow.

She looked at me. Not surprised. Not alarmed. Just tired in a way that suggested she'd already rehearsed several possible murder scenarios and found them all too time-consuming.

I stood there, sheepish. "Before you say anything," I began, "it was like this when I woke up."

"Brin told me his version," she said at last. "Mero's too."

"Then you already know it wasn't my fault."

"I do," she said.

Pause.

"Oh," I said, relaxing.

"I also know you made it worse."

"...Right."

Another pause.

"You've been playing with a fire scroll, or worse, and calling it a toy," she said. "I should throw you into the river."

"But you won't?" I suggested, hopefully.

"Not today." Her tone made it clear that tomorrow had options.

"Aen, I love you like the sun itself. And I think about murdering you at least three times each day."

"Fair. If it's any consolation, that at least five times less than most everyone else."

"The book's been put away. For your own good."

I wilted inside, but couldn't say anything. First, she was using the Voice. The matriarch Voice that ordered the world to line up with no back talk. Second — well, permanently being doused with flame for hair had put a slight pause on my enthusiasm for pure chaos.

I nodded.

Nema took a deep breath, as if to say, I've successful not murdered you. Now, we have more important matters to attend to than your idiocy.

And she was right.

She walked over, plucked a scroll from a sideboard, and handed it to me.

Six seals gleamed in the light of the wagon, each more unnecessary than the last. Seventeen signatures cluttered the margins like drunken ants. And at the very bottom, just above a flourish of legalese that resembled either a penstroke or an unfortunate jam incident, it read:

Notice of Revocation of Unauthorized Property Possession Pursuant to the Property Ownership Limitation Act, Subsection 12-A, Revised Charter Addendum VII.

Nema tapped the scroll once, twice, as if daring it to

explain itself.

"That," I said, "is a lot of words to say absolutely nothing."

"They're evicting me," Nema said, in the tone of a woman informing you that your house was on fire and it was somehow your fault.

"From land you don't own," I clarified.

"Never claimed to own," she added.

"Never wanted to own," Brin offered.

She arched an eyebrow. "And yet."

We bent closer. The scroll's middle portion resembled a particularly vindictive recipe:

> *Thirty days to vacate.*
>
> *Failure to comply would result in sanctions, fines, asset seizure, and mandatory relocation.*
>
> *Relocation to an approved site, unnamed and unspecified.*
>
> *Further information available at the Bureau of Discretionary Enforcement and Voluntary Conformance, address hand-corrected three times in different inks.*

"The Bureau of Voluntary Conformance," I said slowly. "That's new."

"Nothing voluntary about it," Nema muttered. "Look at the fine print."

I squinted. The letters grew smaller the longer you looked at them, like some malevolent optical illusion.

"Voluntary compliance shall be interpreted in accordance with Subsection 9-B (mandatory compliance protocol, enforcement mechanisms at discretion of local authorities or delegated administrative bodies)."

Translation: march, or be marched.

"Who signed this?" I asked.

Nema jabbed a finger at the final seal, a bloated thing stamped so hard it had puckered the parchment.

Minister of Societal Alignment.

The same hand that had rewritten the laws in the first place. The same hand tightening around our throats, inch by inch, smile by smile.

Nema didn't curse. She didn't sigh. She didn't rage. She simply folded the scroll, neatly, like a letter to an old enemy.

"Fix it," she said.

Because, of course, when the sky fell, it fell on Aen Marr's very deserving head.

I straightened my (only slightly wine-stained) shirt and flashed her a grin so reckless it could've been arrested for public indecency.

"Gladly," I said. "But if we're doing this, we're doing it properly."

She looked at me, expression carved from granite.

"We're going to the Hall of Justice," I declared, already regretting it. "Because if they want absurdity, we'll give them a show."

She handed me the scroll as if handing me the fuse to a lit bomb.

Behind me, Brin and Mero exchanged a look.

It was the look of two men who had seen this particular movie before—and knew exactly how many punches, bruises, and miraculous survival stories it would take to reach the credits.

The Law Complex was what happened when a city tried to build Reason out of stone — and then kept adding wings, halls, and sub-committees until the whole thing resembled a lunatic's chessboard.

First came the Hall of Justice: four grim towers squatting around a central courtyard like elderly generals judging a battle they no longer understood.

Then the Hall of Regulatory Administration, a place so labyrinthine the architects had given up on blueprints and started using string.

Beyond that, the Remand Centre and the Temporary Holding Cells huddled together like conspirators in some grim fairy tale.

And then, lurking behind it all, the Archive: a building that looked like it had been designed by someone who hated sunlight, fresh air, and human ambition.

We pushed through the crush of law clerks, petitioners, and despairing litigants to the steps of the Archive, where Seren was seated on a worn stone bench, her arms full of scrolls, her hair slightly mussed, and her expression already halfway to homicide.

She held up a hand.

She stood there for a moment, transported by what had happened to my head. Behind her eyes, I saw it — the spiralling collapse of all higher brain function. First, confusion. Then recognition. Then a brief but furious debate about whether arson was still illegal if it was directed at a person. Then, what I could only describe as spiritual resignation.

Her mouth opened. Closed. Opened again.

She blinked. Once. Twice. Then: "You know what? I'm not even going to ask."

Her gaze swept slowly from my glowing red curls to the scroll I was brandishing like a drunken prophet, then back to my face, which I was fairly certain had "trust me" written on it in several dialects of disaster.

"If you're here, it's already bad," she said.

"Bad is a strong word," I said. "Let's say... creatively challenging."

She narrowed her eyes. "Alright, give it to me."

I solemnly handed her the scroll.

Mero produced a slightly bruised apple from somewhere and began polishing it against his sleeve, the universal gesture of someone preparing for a show.

Seren unfurled the scroll, skimmed the heading—and froze.

Then she frowned.

Then she frowned harder.

Then she made the small, desperate noise of a woman realizing she might need to set herself on fire to escape her day.

"This..." she said slowly, "is a Notice of Revocation of Unauthorized Property Possession."

"Yes!" I said brightly. "Good start."

"...Pursuant to the Property Ownership Limitation Act, Subsection Twelve-A, Revised Charter Addendum Seven?"

"Very good," I encouraged. "You're a natural at legal incantations."

She shot me a look. "This law applies to existing property owners within the City of Nareth's chartered limits."

"Indeed," I said.

"But Nema Al'Faerin doesn't own land inside Nareth."

"Nope."

"She hasn't filed any ownership claims."

"Nuh-uh."

"She hasn't registered any title deeds, squatters' notices, or property transfer oaths?"

"Not unless she's been moonlighting behind our backs," Mero added around a mouthful of apple.

Seren's fingers tightened around the scroll. "Then this doesn't apply."

"Well," I said, reaching over her shoulder, "except for that bit."

I pointed.

She squinted. "'Occupancy in Lieu of Title'... shall constitute de facto possession... in cases deemed prejudicial to community alignment objectives... as defined by the Ministry of Societal Alignment?"

Her voice rose slightly with each clause, like a violin being tuned by an enraged monkey.

Brin rumbled a quiet, warning chuckle.

She shook her head. "No, no. That's an amendment to the amendment. That shouldn't have cleared the Review Council. That's not how property law —"

"Check the compliance deadline!" Mero chirped.

She found it. Her mouth compressed into a line that could have sliced glass.

Thirty days to vacate.

Failure to comply would trigger sanctions, fines, and asset forfeiture, followed by mandatory relocation to an approved site to be determined by the Department of Discretionary Enforcement and Voluntary Conformance.

Seren stared at the final clauses like she might actually murder the paper.

"There's no relocation address," she said slowly. "They're... relocating you to nowhere."

"Efficient," I said. "Saves on printing costs."

"And if we want to find out more," Brin rumbled, "we go where?"

Seren flipped the scroll. Tiny text squatted at the bottom like it was ashamed of itself.

"For inquiries, refer to the Bureau of Discretionary Enforcement and Voluntary Conformance," she read. Then frowned. "Address corrected... twice."

Mero leaned in. "Last correction's in a different handwriting."

"Different ink, too," I noted. "Really adds to the aesthetic of barely repressed panic."

Seren folded the scroll with violent precision.

"You're right," she said, glaring at me.

I blinked. "I am?"

"You're the sense-maker," I said modestly.

"You're a menace," she corrected. Then, sighing, "But we'll get to the bottom of it."

We set off toward the Registry Office, which, if tradition held, would either be precisely where it was supposed to be—or relocated by committee to somewhere between tragic and hilarious.

The Registry Office, in theory, lived in the east wing of the Hall of Regulatory Administration, third floor, past the terrifying statue of Oren the Dutiful (who, legend said, once died of paperwork injuries).

In practice, when we arrived, the office was missing.

Not closed.

Not relocated.

Simply gone—as if it had packed up its scrolls and wandered off in search of better working conditions.

Instead, we found a desk.

One desk.

Occupying the centre of an echoing marble hall like a shipwreck in a dry ocean.

Behind it sat a girl of about fourteen, half-buried in ledgers, balancing a quill behind each ear, and exuding all the enthusiasm of someone waiting for the end of the world and mildly disappointed it was taking so long.

Seren stepped forward, radiating that thin, dangerous calm unique to people who still believe in systems.

"We're here about an unlawful eviction order. Registry Office, please."

The girl didn't look up.

"Moved."

Seren blinked. "Since when?"

The girl consulted a scrap of parchment, as if she might find the answer written there in runes.

"Three weeks ago. Realignment orders. They're in the Temporary Administrative Annex now."

I leaned over Seren's shoulder. "Temporary?"

The girl shrugged. "Technically."

Mero whispered loudly, "That's government for never."

Seren inhaled sharply. "And where is this Temporary Administrative Annex?"

The girl brightened slightly, like a corpse that briefly remembered taxes.

"Old transit station. Past the statue with no nose. Left of the pigeon garden. Behind the Public Fountain of Moderate Triumph."

She delivered this without blinking.

Seren closed her eyes for a dangerous second.

"Thank you," she said, in the voice of a woman calculating the paperwork penalty for murder.

We left quickly, before either could make a decision they'd regret.

The old transit station had seen better centuries.

What had once been a hub of civic pride was now a warehouse of sad banners, half-collapsed stairwells, and a smell that hinted darkly at wet pigeons and lost hope.

A hand-painted sign sagged over the entrance:

Temporary Administrative Annex.

Below that, in smaller, more desperate handwriting:

Please Form An Orderly Queue (Or Just Scream).

We stepped inside.

The floor was a chessboard of water stains.

Desks sprawled everywhere, none matching, staffed by clerks who seemed to be competing for Most Visibly Defeated Employee.

At the far side, a man was aggressively re-filing the same sheet of paper into the same drawer. Over and over. Possibly forever.

We approached.

Seren, still clinging to the wreckage of protocol, cleared her throat. "We're here about an eviction order issued under the Property Ownership Limitation Act."

The man sighed, a long, slow exhale like the death of a civilization.

"Not us anymore."

Seren stiffened. "It was yesterday."

He shrugged. "Realignment. Authority transferred. You want the Subcommittee on Mobile Populations."

"And where would we find them?" I asked, fully expecting the answer to involve a map, a donkey, and three riddles.

The man handed us a flyer.

For a sandwich shop.

Seren stared at it.

Then at him.

He shrugged again, heavier this time, as if the first shrug had somehow failed to convey the appropriate level of existential defeat.

"They sublet," he said.

The sandwich shop stood halfway down a street of crumbling tenements, tucked between a laundress and a pawn shop offering "ethical discounts" (a claim I had serious doubts about).

Its sign read:

Fred's Fabulous Sandwiches & Bureau of Temporary Populational Affairs.

Inside, two tables were occupied by actual sandwich-eaters.

The third, tucked in the back behind a barrel of pickles, had been colonized by a young woman in half-armour, surrounded by parchment, inkpots, and the raw, naked scent of despair.

We approached warily.

"Eviction order," Seren said crisply, presenting the scroll like a knight offering a severed dragon's head.

The woman sighed and reached for a ledger so thick it had visible gravitational effects.

"Ah, Property Limitation Act. Classic. You'll need Form I-38-Temporary, Application for Relocation Request while Appealing Unlawful Designation of Land Occupancy."

"Wonderful," Seren said through gritted teeth. "How long to process?"

The woman flipped pages. "Forty to sixty days. Standard."

Mero whistled low. "We've got thirty."

"Oh!" She smiled brightly, as if he'd complimented her boots. "You can expedite it."

Seren leaned forward. "How?"

The woman's smile grew strained.

"You just need a waiver."

Mero muttered, "Of course we do."

"And where," Seren said slowly, "would we find this waiver?"

The woman gestured vaguely.

"Waiver Office. Two blocks north. Look for Iago."

At the name, my stomach did a very specific, very familiar somersault of dread.

I closed my eyes.

Mero elbowed me. "You know him?"

I sighed. "Let's just say... history was made. Poorly."

Brin cracked his knuckles. Seren tucked the scroll under her arm with grim determination.

We had our next destination.

We had thirty days.

We had a bureaucracy that hated us on principle.

And somehow, impossibly, things were about to get worse.

The Waiver Office lived — if that's the word for it — two blocks north of the sandwich shop, behind a blacksmith's that specialized in ornamental locks and very judgmental signs.

Its plaque read:

Official Office of Waiver Review, Processing, and Discretionary Approval.

(In much smaller lettering beneath: Please knock politely. Broom closet in use.)

Mero stared at the door, then at me.

"Sure this is the place?" he asked.

I pointed at the plaque.

"Official as anything else we've seen today."

Seren looked like she wanted to walk into traffic.

Brin just pushed the door open.

Inside was a broom closet.

A literal, honest-to-gods broom closet.

One shelf sagged under the weight of tangled waivers and abandoned mops. A cracked lantern dangled from a nail.

And perched behind a rickety fold-out desk was Iago.

I hadn't seen Iago since the Great Municipal Music Licensing Fiasco—a story that involved one stolen harp, two angry goats, and the temporary outlawing of spontaneous whistling.

Judging by his expression, Iago remembered everything.

His shoulders slumped the moment he saw me.

"Oh no," he said. "Not you."

"Hello again, Iago," I beamed. "I see you've been promoted."

He gestured wearily at the brooms.

"I supervise custodial waivers now."

"A vital role," I said. "Essential to the dignity of the Realm."

Seren stepped in before Iago could commit something regrettable with a mop.

"We've been issued a thirty-day eviction order under the Property Ownership Limitation Act," she said crisply, producing the battered scroll. "We were told we need a waiver to file a delay request while appealing the designation."

Iago grimaced as if she'd asked him to personally gnaw off his own foot.

He thumbed through a heap of battered forms, muttering to himself, and eventually produced a five-page document held together by what appeared to be either hope or mildew.

"This is your waiver."

Seren scanned it. Her jaw clenched.

"It requires approval from the Office of Land Management," she said. "And from the Archive's Adjudicator of Unclaimed Holdings. And from the Department of Public Tranquility."

"Correct," Iago said, dead inside.

"Which one of them issued the eviction order?"

Iago stared at the ceiling as if it might offer absolution.

"None," he said.

Pause.

"Excuse me?" Seren said, dangerously polite.

Iago fiddled with his quill. "The order came straight from

the Ministry."

Seren paled.

"The central Ministry?" she whispered.

Iago nodded miserably. "Signature stamp. Minister of Societal Alignment."

Even Brin flinched—a tiny muscle tic at the corner of his eye, but for him, it was basically a scream.

We stood there, in the broom closet of broken dreams, absorbing the truth.

This wasn't some paperwork error.

This wasn't some overzealous local administrator.

This was the Ministry itself, reaching down with all the casual malice of a giant flicking ants off a picnic blanket.

They didn't just want us off the land.

They wanted it official, legal, and irrefutable.

They wanted it to look like it was our fault.

Seren folded the waiver with mechanical precision.

Mero tossed his half-eaten apple core into a broom bucket.

Brin simply turned and left, the door creaking behind him.

I lingered a second longer.

"You know," I said to Iago, smiling sadly, "if the Ministry ever tires of being terrible, you might make an excellent frontman."

Iago flipped me off without enthusiasm.

I took that as a fond farewell.

Outside, the afternoon sun was a cruel, cheerful thing,

bouncing off the stone and blinding us.

The camp was visible across the canal, a sprawl of wagons, canvas, and smoke curls rising lazy against the sky.

Home.

And the target on our backs.

"They want us gone," I said quietly.

"Yes," Seren answered. "And they want to make it look like law."

Mero kicked a loose pebble into the water. "So no appeal, then. Just delay."

Brin turned to me.

"What now?"

For once, I didn't have a speech ready.

For once, the weight of it all—the stupid cruelty of it—pressed down hard enough to silence even me.

I looked to Seren.

And this time, she didn't look away.

Her hand was clenched so tightly around the scroll that the wax seal cracked and crumbled away.

"I'll stall them," she said.

"You'll help?" I asked, careful.

"I'll delay," she said, voice sharp enough to cut stone. "You'll find the loophole."

I grinned.

"I'm a Ruanne," I said. "Loopholes are our folk art."

Together, we turned toward the setting sun.

Toward the camp.

Toward whatever madness would come next.

And for once, Seren's steps fell into rhythm beside mine.

Not walking away.

Not yet.

> *"A fool answers questions the way they're asked."*
> — *ancient Ruanne proverb.*

We regrouped in the alley behind the Waiver Office, which smelled like pickles, burnt paper, and the crushed hopes of minor civil servants. Brin leaned against a cracked wall, arms crossed, radiating the sort of calm usually reserved for bomb squads and condemned men. Mero perched on an overturned crate, flicking a stolen coin into the air and watching it spin as if waiting for fate to slap him across the face.

I paced.

"We can't just wait," I said. "Waiting is for people with options. Which, in case you haven't noticed, we're a little short on."

Brin grunted — a sound with the emotional depth of a falling guillotine.

Mero caught the coin midair and gave me a hairy eyeball. "You've got that look again."

"What look?"

"The look that says you have a plan, and we're about to end up running, bleeding, or on fire."

I smiled winningly. "That's only happened, what, five times?"

"Seven," Mero said.

"Nine," Brin rumbled.

I cleared my throat. "Regardless. I have a plan. A good one."

Mero closed his eyes briefly, as if searching for strength from the gods, the stones, or possibly the bottom of a wine jug.

"We don't beat this eviction by arguing about waivers and appeals," I said. "We go to the source."

"Meaning?" Mero asked warily.

"We find this Minister of Societal Alignment. Get his name. Find where he lives. And then we—"

I mimed knocking on a door, then making a very persuasive punching motion.

Mero groaned. "You want to just show up at his house?"

"Exactly!" I beamed. "Nice and personal. None of this hiding behind scrolls and seals. Just us, a polite conversation, and, if necessary, Brin putting him through a tasteful end table."

Brin cracked his knuckles thoughtfully. I took that as approval.

Mero swung his legs off the crate and stood. "You're insane."

I shrugged. "I've never denied it."

He pointed accusingly. "You're going to get us killed."

I spread my arms wide. "Maybe. But heroically."

Mero looked at Brin.

Brin shrugged.

Mero sighed. "Fine. Let's go get a name. But if this ends with us bleeding in a drainage ditch, I'm haunting you."

"Deal," I said, offering my hand.

He ignored it.

We headed out into the maze of Nareth's government quarter, where the Law Complex sprawled across the hillside like a sleeping bureaucratic dragon — stone towers, arched bridges, and windowless archives stitched together with the purest spite of three centuries of lawmakers.

Somewhere in there, tucked behind paperwork and signatures, or a regrettable fountain, was the name we needed.

We just had to find it.

And then we could pay the good Minister a very personal visit.

The Office of Ministerial Correspondence squatted at the east end of the Law Complex, wedged between the Hall of Regulatory Administration and the Remand Centre, as if it had been too timid to pick a side and instead huddled in perpetual bureaucratic purgatory.

The building was shaped like a letter no one wanted to open.

Its doors hung slightly crooked.

Its plaque had been polished so aggressively that half the words had vanished.

Inside, the atmosphere was thick with dust, old paper, and the kind of institutional despair that leaves a permanent brown ring around your soul.

We approached the front desk, which was manned — if that's the word — by a clerk so ancient he looked like he might have been carbon-dated for tax purposes. He wore a vest several sizes too large, spectacles perched at an angle best described as "wishful," and an expression of profound regret at every life choice that had brought him here.

"Good afternoon," I said, deploying my best smile, which had previously sold counterfeit relics to actual priests. "We're hoping to obtain some information regarding the Minister of Societal Alignment."

The clerk peered at me over the edge of his glasses.

"Name?"

"That's precisely what we're after," I said brightly. "The name of the Minister."

The clerk squinted harder, as if trying to bring me into focus through sheer willpower.

"Form?"

I blinked. "Sorry?"

He sighed.

"You'll need Form 17-G. Request for Ministerial Identity Confirmation."

I looked at Mero, who shrugged.

Brin crossed his arms.

"And where would we find this... Form 17-G?" I asked carefully.

"Discontinued," said the clerk.

"Right," I said, adjusting course. "Then perhaps you could just tell us who currently holds the office?"

The clerk shuffled through a stack of forms so weathered they might have been written in blood and good intentions.

Finally, he produced a brittle scrap of parchment and

jabbed a finger at a line near the top.

"The Deputy Under-Minister of Administrative Affairs," he announced with the air of someone delivering a death sentence. "You'll need to speak to him."

"And where might we find this Deputy Under-Minister?" I asked.

"Temporary location," the clerk said, coughing into his sleeve. "Assigned to the Department of Moral Harmonization. Second tower, fourth floor, just past the Hall of Mild Correction."

Mero muttered, "Second tower, fourth floor, mild correction... sounds promising."

Brin loomed a little closer to the desk.

The clerk looked up at him and immediately became more helpful.

"Take the main stair, turn left at the statue missing its face, follow the yellow tiles until they run out, then knock three times on the third door you see."

I gave him a sunny, professional nod. "Thank you kindly."

He waved a hand at us as if shooing away a cloud of flies, then immediately resumed a staring contest with his inkwell.

We stepped back into the hallway.

Mero was the first to speak. "So. We're chasing a Deputy Under-Minister through a building designed by mad poets."

"I don't see what could possibly go wrong," I said.

"Your optimism terrifies me," Mero said.

"It should," Brin added.

We set off, following the trail of bureaucratic breadcrumbs, hearts full of courage, heads full of bad ideas.

The first step on any grand adventure, after all, is the delusion that you know what you're doing.

The Department of Moral Harmonization perched on the second tower of the Law Complex like a pigeon that had given up on life. Its motto, etched above the doors in cracked stone, read:

"Unity Through Correct Thought and Pleasant Facial Expressions."

I knocked three times, as instructed.

Immediately, a voice from within called out, unnervingly cheerful:

"Enter, friends! Your journey toward harmonious compliance awaits!"

Mero gave me a look that suggested he was about five seconds from setting something on fire.

Brin simply shoved open the door.

Inside, the place smelled aggressively of lavender and wet optimism.

A woman in a lemon-yellow robe beamed at us from her seat behind the reception desk, beaming like a saint on market day.

"Welcome to the Department of Moral Harmonization," she sang. "How may we assist in your ethical realignment?"

"We're here to see the Deputy Under-Minister of Administrative Affairs," I said, flashing a smile that had previously closed deals, opened doors, and on one unfortunate occasion, started a brawl.

Her face brightened even more, dangerously close to combustion.

"Of course you are!" she chirped. "One moment, please!"

She vanished behind a curtain of pastel drapery.

Mero sidled up beside me. "Want to place a bet he's not here?"

"Don't be ridiculous," I said. "Of course he's not here. The question is how creatively they'll lie about it."

A moment later, the clerk returned, still beaming — but with a visible crack around the edges.

"I'm terribly sorry," she said, voice syrupy enough to cause dental damage. "The Deputy is currently unavailable."

"When will he be available?" I asked.

She hesitated. "Soon."

"Today?"

"Possibly."

"Is he out for lunch?"

"It's hard to say."

Mero leaned forward. "When did you last see him?"

She opened her mouth. Closed it. Shrugged.

"And how long have you been working here?" I asked.

She lit up. "Oh, twenty-two years!"

We all stared.

"If the deputy is not in charge of this department," Mero

asked, casually flipping through a pamphlet about the virtues of internal compliance, "who is?"

She looked perplexed. "Of course the Deputy is in charge. He's the Deputy."

"Wait. How do you take instructions from someone you've never seen?" I asked scratching my head.

"Oh, we receive written orders," she said. "Every week. Delivered by courier. Sealed and stamped."

"From the deputy?" I pressed.

"Yes. From Central office," she chirped.

I blinked. "There's a Central Office?"

"That's just our name for it."

"I see. And if we were wanting to find this central office, what would we look for?"

she smiled again, eager to help. "Its proper title takes a little while to say. Perhaps you would like to take a seat?" And then, "I'll get the paperwork."

She began to shuffle around on her desk. After a moment, she produced what appeared to be one of this week's instructions delivered by courier. She began to read from the top of the missive: "The Bureau of Executive Direction, Procedural Oversight, Administrative Orders, Alignment, and Guidance..."

"Please stop, "I interrupted.

She stopped.

My mind was spinning. Then a thought hit me. "Just out of curiosity," I said, "does the Deputy minister have an office here?"

"Of course."

"Wonderful," I said, stepping past her.

"Wait—!" she called. "If you go in their without permission, I'll have to call the guard!"

But we were already moving. Quickly.

The Department's interior was a fever dream of pastel corridors, motivational slogans, and tiny shrines to bureaucratic virtue.

Plaques lined the walls bearing wisdom like:

"Freedom in Compliance."

"Only *YOU* can eradicate privacy!"

"Today is compulsory cheerfulness day!"

We found the Deputy's office easily enough. It had a brass plaque read:

> DEPUTY UNDER-MINISTER OF ADMINISTRATIVE AFFAIRS
>
> (IN HARMONIOUS SERVICE SINCE Time Immemorial)

The door was unlocked.

The office beyond was a mausoleum of abandoned paperwork and lavender potpourri. Dust cloaked every surface. A stack of unopened mail sagged dangerously on the desk. On the wall hung a large framed portrait of a smiling silhouette—no face, just a blank oval where a human being should be.

"Comforting," Mero said.

Brin grunted.

While I stood marveling at the artistic representation of

existential despair, Mero slipped around the desk and rifled through a pile of dispatches. With a satisfied hum, he plucked out a crumpled multi-page memo.

I leaned in.

Across the top, in ornate, officious lettering, it began: *The Bureau of Executive Direction, Procedural Oversight, Administrative Orders, Alignment, and Guidance, Enforcement Division of Codified Norms, Exceptional Measures...* There was more, but I stopped reading.

Flipped a page.

Still going. An unholy parade of nouns, none of which had ever done a day's work. Possibly designed just to outlive the reader.

I flipped to the last page.

At the very bottom, in fine, almost invisible ink, it read: *Authorized Signatory: Director Velen Dharis.*

Mero waved the paper like a victory banner.

Behind us, someone cleared their throat.

Not a cough. Not a warning. A polite *ahem* — the kind that suggested *someone was about to ruin your life in the nicest possible way.*

We turned.

A man in soothing grey robes stood in the doorway. Middle-aged. Immaculate. Serene in the way cliffs are serene — right before you fall off them. He held a folder labeled *Tranquility Enforcement Incident Reports*, which I found personally offensive.

"I must politely request," he said, with the vocal warmth of a tepid bath, "that you cease unauthorized exploration of departmental spaces. Your continued presence may cause emotional misalignment."

Brin cracked his knuckles.

The man smiled. *Gently.* As if inviting us to a picnic. A picnic where the sandwiches were made of regret and the wine was vinegar and consequences.

"If you would be so kind," he continued, "as to return to reception for Harmonious Reprocessing, we would all benefit from restored inner equilibrium."

This was the guard. Of course she'd called security.

There was a long moment.

Then, because none of us could quite figure out how to punch serenity without getting a wellness citation, we let ourselves be herded back down the corridor by the enforcement monk of smiling doom.

Back at the reception desk, the lemon-clad clerk fluttered forward eagerly, relieved to have us back under "guidance."

At the door I turned and I smiled my brightest, most predatory smile.

"One more thing," I said. "If a concerned citizen wanted to send a gift to a loyal public servant—say, a pie, or a bouquet of strongly worded suggestions—is there an office that keeps addresses for officials like... Director Velen Dharis?"

The clerk lit up like a devotional candle.

"Of course!" she said brightly. "Personnel Archives! North wing, past the Office of Lost Possessions, third floor!"

"Thank you so much," I said, bowing slightly. "You've been very...harmonious."

Her chest visibly swelled with pride.

Mero rolled his eyes so hard I feared for his balance.

Brin simply turned and started walking.

I saluted the Department of Moral Harmonization one last time, savoring the faint smell of lavender failure, and followed my brothers-in-misadventure out into the labyrinth of law.

The Personnel Archives lived at the far end of the Law Complex's north wing, past the Office of Lost Possessions, two abandoned kiosks, and what appeared to be a spontaneous gathering of feral pigeons arguing over constitutional law.

The door was a slab of peeling wood with a plaque so tarnished it was mostly suggestion:

Personnel Archives (Inquiries Welcome by Appointment)

Brin pushed the door open.

Inside, the air smelled of mildew, ancient ink, and despair that had given up even trying to ferment into rage. Filing cabinets drooped against the walls. Stacks of brittle scrolls teetered in alarming piles. At the centre, perched behind a listing desk, sat a woman who looked like she'd been filed herself sometime around the last dynasty and forgotten.

She peered at us through spectacles thicker than the hull of a galley.

I straightened my shirt, summoned my most dazzling grin, and approached like a man preparing to sell wine to a drowning man.

"Good afternoon, venerable custodian of our bureaucratic heritage," I said, bowing just slightly. "We come bearing only the purest of civic intentions."

She blinked.

I pressed onward. "We're seeking the residential address of one Director Velen Dharis. For...uh...purposes of loyal citizen engagement. Possibly involving baked goods."

She blinked again, slower this time.

I resisted the urge to check if she was still breathing.

Finally, she squawked, "Form?"

I turned on the charm. "We were hoping to bypass minor technicalities for the sake of speed and public happiness."

Behind me, Brin shifted his weight. The sound was subtle but ominous—the whisper of a landslide considering whether it might like to visit your living room. The woman flinched.

"Name?" she rasped.

"Director Velen Dharis," I repeated.

She wheezed upright and began rummaging through an ancient filing system that appeared to be based on the concept of alphabetical chaos. While she was occupied, Mero slid along the wall like an affectionate shadow, cracking open a nearby cabinet and slipping a thin folio into his coat. Never let it be said we relied on just one strategy.

Finally, with a triumphant grunt, the archivist produced a battered personnel file, tied with a bit of fraying twine.

"Here," she said, thumping it onto the desk hard enough to rattle the past loose.

I untied the file with reverence usually reserved for holy relics or particularly stubborn knots.

Inside was a thin sheaf of parchment listing assignments, commendations, and, near the bottom, the golden prize: Residential Address.

I read it once.

Then again.

Then a third time, hoping the words would arrange themselves into something sane.

They did not.

It read:

> Director Velen Dharis—Residential Quarters, Archive Sub-Basement Level 9B, Vault Section 3

I stared at the page.

Mero peered over my shoulder and let out a low whistle.

"Cozy."

Brin grunted, the kind of grunt that might accompany the discovery of a very large, very stupid bear sleeping in your tent.

I cleared my throat.

"Just to clarify," I said, turning back to the archivist, "this is… underground."

She nodded once, solemn as a judge.

"Deep underground."

"In the Archive," I pressed.

Another nod.

"In a vault."

Third nod.

Brin muttered something that might have been either

"figures" or "fun."

I forced a smile. "You've been very helpful."

The archivist beamed, visibly thrilled at the compliment, and immediately began stamping something at random to celebrate.

We beat a dignified retreat before she could find forms that needed our blood types.

Back outside, in the narrow alley between the Personnel Archives and the old carriage yard, we huddled around the file.

"Well," Mero said, "not exactly the cushy manor house I was imagining."

"Nothing says luxury like living next to the rat archives," I agreed.

Brin just stared down the alley toward the looming bulk of the Archive proper.

Its towers rose into the darkening sky like blackened fingers.

Its lowest foundations, hidden deep below street level, had long since slipped from public memory into rumour.

If the Minister of Societal Alignment had quarters down there...

We weren't hunting a bureaucrat anymore.

We were descending into the system's rotten heart. And it had a name.

Velen Dharis.

Into the Depths, Through the Laundry Room

> *"The deeper the cellar, the older the ghosts."*
>
> — *ancient Ruanne proverb.*

We found Seren exactly where fate preferred her when disaster loomed: on the steps of the Archive, halfway between fury and resignation. She spotted us immediately and frowned — though to be fair, that was her standard greeting.

"We're victorious," I announced, sweeping a bow so low I nearly cracked my skull on the stone railing. "Choose your emotions accordingly."

She folded her arms.

Brin stepped forward and handed her the battered folio we'd pilfered from the Personnel Archives.

Seren flipped it open with the grim precision of a woman expecting disappointment and finding it early. Her eyes landed on the address.

"Sub-Basement 9B, Vault Section Three," she read aloud.

Then again, slower.

She looked up, expression flattened into polite disbelief. "That doesn't exist."

I grinned. "And yet! Printed. Stamped. On official parchment. Probably sacred."

"There are only three known sublevels," she said, more to herself than us. "Level Nine isn't on any Archive map. It shouldn't exist."

Then her gaze caught on the name.

"Velen Dharis," she said. Her brow furrowed, just slightly. "I know that name."

Mero leaned forward. "Famous villain?"

She shook her head. "Minor bureaucrat. Clerk's assistant, I think. Department of Executive Directions."

My spine stiffened. Heat crept up my throat.

"No," I said, sharper than intended. "He's not a nobody."

Seren's look was careful. Too careful. "Aen—"

"He's the one behind this. All of it. The eviction. The surprise inspections. The shifting codes that only ever snare us."

Brin grunted in agreement.

Mero shrugged. "Paper-pushers make the deadliest traps."

Seren hesitated—just for a breath—but tucked the folio under her arm like a loaded weapon. "I'll make inquiries."

She turned for the Chamber of the Magi.

We started to follow.

She raised a hand without turning. "No. You're not coming."

I raised an eyebrow.

"The Chamber is restricted. Where I'm going, I do not need—"

"Aen blowing everything up in your face," Mero finished helpfully.

Brin gave me a sympathetic pat on the shoulder. I affected offense. Slightly.

But I wasn't done.

Reaching into my coat, I drew out a slightly crumpled but still mostly-presentable handkerchief, pressed it into Seren's hand with courtly solemnity, and intoned:

"Since you ride into peril alone, noble champion, accept this humble token—that you may remember us should you fall in your quest for truth."

Brin closed his eyes.

Mero gagged theatrically.

Seren examined the handkerchief like it might burst into spontaneous sonnet.

"You're an idiot," she said flatly.

"And you," I replied with my most tragic bow, "are our last hope."

She didn't throw it back.

Instead, with a tiny shake of her head and a muttered curse I pretended not to hear, she tucked it into her sleeve.

"Stay here. Don't talk to anyone. Don't steal anything."

She didn't bother waiting for promises. She vanished up the Archive steps.

The second she was gone, Mero collapsed onto a bench and began whittling a stick into something that could be a snake. Or a depressed fish.

Brin leaned against the wall, arms folded, patient as a mountain with a grudge.

I paced.

Tapping rhythms against the stone railing.

Scouting hiding spots. Eyeing exits. Worrying my lip.

Because Seren was wrong.

Velen Dharis wasn't just a petty paper-mouse. You don't sign eviction notices, settle bans, limit property rights, and enforce curfews with surgical cruelty unless you *mean* it. You don't hide an entire sub-basement unless you know what waits at the bottom.

No.

We weren't hunting a clerk.

We were hunting a dragon.

And if you're going to confront a dragon, you don't show up empty-handed.

You bring Excalibur.

I stopped pacing.

Mero glanced up. "I liked it better when you were pacing. Now you're thinking."

"The dangerous kind," I confirmed.

And turned on my heel.

Brin sighed behind me.

Mero muttered, "Someone's about to get arrested."

The Ruanne camp sprawled under the afternoon sun, wagons clustered in colourful defiance of dust and stone. Smoke curled lazily from cookfires. Goats bleated at nothing, everything, and possibly existential despair.

I made a beeline for Nema's wagon.

Which, unfortunately, posed a small problem.

As you may recall, Nema Al'Faerin—matriarch, fortune-teller, and collector of unfortunate secrets—had confiscated my book.

But caution was for people with fewer ambitions. And less excellent hair.

I loitered near the wagon, whistling with the subtlety of a badly disguised thief. Cracked the door. Peered inside.

Empty.

I slipped in.

The air hit me like a wall of incense and spilled memories. Sunlight filtered through strips of dyed silk hung over the windows, turning the cramped space into a stained-glass dream: amber, crimson, violet. Fabric was everywhere. As were smells. Sweet smoke. Bitter herbs. Dust and wax and too many secrets.

Every surface was covered with something, and most of the somethings were *watching* me.

Tarot bones in a chipped teacup. A rusted blade laid gently across a sheaf of mourning veils. A shelf of tiny jars lined one wall like gossiping judges, each labelled in Nema's curling script: *Ash of Husband #1 Unforgivable Salt Truthberries (Dry)*

Tapestries layered the walls, stitched and restitched until the stories blurred together, myth on top of memory on top of threadbare thread.

Two cracked mirrors flanked the central support beam, each reflecting a different angle of regret.

I searched her usual hiding places.

Nothing.

I searched the hiding place she *thought* I didn't know about.

Still nothing.

"Come on," I muttered, panic nibbling at the edges.

Then I heard it—a faint whistle, like a kettle just starting to boil. Then a hiccuping gurgle, as if a teapot were attempting jazz.

I stepped closer.

The sound grew louder, more insistent. I pressed a hand to the wall.

A panel shivered.

Of course.

Not hidden *in* something.

Hidden *as* something.

The panel popped open. Inside, nestled among dried herbs and old letters, was my book.

My beautiful, smug, reality-warping disaster of a book.

The Everything, Including Nothing.

I picked it up. It purred.

I tucked it inside my coat, the weight familiar against my ribs.

"Miss me?" I whispered.

It burped.

Which I took as a yes.

By the time I made it back to the Archive steps, Brin and Mero were still exactly where I'd left them—Brin meditating on vengeance, Mero carving his stick into what now looked like a very determined worm.

And just in time.

Seren was already striding back across the courtyard, her robes streaked with dust, her expression caught somewhere between righteous fury and exhausted triumph. In her hands, she carried a book the size of a small, particularly judgmental dog.

The Compendium of Restricted Holdings.

She dropped it onto the bench with a *thunk* that made the paving stones reconsider their career choices.

"I found something," she said grimly.

Brin straightened.

Mero pocketed his whittling knife.

I clutched *The Everything, Including Nothing* tighter under my coat. The air buzzed around us, like the moment before a thunderclap.

Because now —

Now we had our sword.

Now we had our map.

And dragons?

Dragons were optional.

Victory was mandatory.

Seren flipped the Compendium open. It belched a puff of dust and the vague scent of mildew and bureaucratic shame. The spine cracked like an ancient joint. Pages rustled in protest.

"This," she said, "is everything that officially doesn't exist."

It was divided into sections. Horrifying, hilarious sections.

- *Vaults of Questionable Ancestry*

- *Chambers of Special Adjustment (Closed Pending Review)*

- *Emergency Mourning Cells (For Events of Excessive National Sadness)*

- *Room of Mandatory Sigh Correction (Two Sighs Per Citizen Allowed Daily)*

Each page listed rooms too absurd to be real, too real to be unintentional, and somehow all too *official.*

Seren flipped faster now, her fingers growing more aggressive with each absurdity.

"There," Brin said, tapping a page with a thick, calloused finger.

We all leaned in.

Near the bottom of a neglected column, in script so small it looked embarrassed to exist:

Auxiliary Storage Wing B (Laundry and Linen Distribution—Staff Only) Access: Authorized Personnel or Ministerial Directive Only

There was a silence that tasted like dust and dawning horror.

Mero spoke first. "Laundry?"

"It's a cover," I said brightly. "Nothing says 'secret lair' like abandoned linen closets."

Brin grunted. Possibly agreement. Possibly deep, existential regret.

Seren ran her finger along the line.

"There's a utility corridor. Off the staff wing. Supposed to be condemned. Beyond that..." She frowned. "The Compendium says it links to older foundations."

Mero narrowed his eyes. "Older than the Archive?"

She nodded once. "Older than *anything* aboveground."

I grinned.

Mero cracked his knuckles.

Brin shifted his stance like a mountain preparing to fall on something.

Seren, to her credit, simply closed her eyes and breathed.

Then, with the air of a woman about to break every rule she ever memorized, she said, "Right. We plan."

"We sneak carefully," I corrected, already walking.

She closed the Compendium with a *thud* that threatened local stability.

"If we're caught trespassing in the Chambers of the Magi—"

"Expulsion?" Mero guessed.

"Imprisonment?" Brin offered.

"Execution?" I said, ever helpful.

Seren gave me a withering look.

"Administrative review," she said.

We all winced.

For a moment, none of us moved. The Compendium sat at our feet like a judgment from the gods. The sun dragged long shadows across the stones.

Somewhere below us, past forgotten linen closets and condemned corridors, the truth waited.

I straightened my coat.

"Time to do something extremely stupid," I said.

Brin nodded once.

Mero smiled like a man preparing a dagger for polite

conversation.

Seren just sighed and started walking.

We followed.

Because loyalty is many things.

And sometimes, it's very bad ideas, executed with excellent company.

The Chambers of the Magi were supposed to be a sanctum of legal wisdom and solemn authority. What we found was... less impressive.

Marble columns. Vaulted ceilings. A hush only broken by snoring, arguing, and the slap of expensive boots on polished stone.

We crept through the shadows, but—honestly?—stealth felt almost insulting. No one was watching.

At the first rotunda, two magistrates were locked in mortal verbal combat over the classification of sighs.

"Voluntary sighs," one wheezed, "reflect contempt for the court!"

"Only if they exceed the prescribed depth!" the other countered, brandishing a scroll like a cudgel. "All sighs must be weighed and found wanting!"

Brin stepped past them in silence.

Mero, ever the collector, swiped a gavel off a nearby bench and twirled it experimentally.

Farther on, a trio of junior judges bickered over judicial wig standards.

"Gold trim is mandatory for internal *and* external appeals," one insisted. "Silver is for hybrid proceedings.

Except leave hearings — then it's jade."

"Rubbish," said the second, wearing a blue wig with its *own* wig. "Two wigs minimum! The people demand opulence."

The third — who wore a wig so tall it deserved its own title — intoned gravely, "Judicial grace begins with wig height."

We slinked by unnoticed.

Officially, Magi robes were mandated black. Unofficially? Every robe was a personal opera.

Black with gold-threaded legal maxims. Feathered epaulettes. Patent leather boots with "VERDICT" stamped in gilt across the toes.

We passed a judge asleep against a column, mouth open, a small scroll jammed up one nostril.

Brin stepped over him.

Mero lifted the man's coin pouch. Reflexively, I think.

Two judges further down were arguing about the legal status of jury coughing.

I dropped back beside Seren.

She was tense.

Too tense.

Eyes scanning. Shoulders tight.

"You know," I said quietly, "you don't fit here."

She didn't answer.

Just kept walking, jaw clenched.

"You don't belong with them," I said. "And that's not an insult."

Her pace slowed.

Then — quiet, bitter — she said, "I know."

She glanced sideways, shadows slipping across her cheekbones.

"I never have."

We paused behind a collapsed tapestry rack. The others moved ahead. A stolen moment of quiet.

She twisted the edge of her sleeve. "I was seven. When it happened. I used oath-magic — real magic — in public. I hurt someone."

I waited.

"The Magi called it a miracle. A prodigy. They said I'd be protected. Honoured. Educated." Her voice turned sharp. "They never let me go home."

My chest ached.

I wanted to say something clever. Something noble.

Instead, I said the one thing that wasn't either:

"If we get out of this... you should leave. Come with us. Find your family. Or make a new one."

She turned sharply. "You don't just *fix* things like that."

"No," I said. "But among the Ruanne, we believe bad things happen. You don't let them own you. You pick yourself up, you put it behind you, and you dance anyway."

She blinked at me.

And — so fast I might've imagined it — her expression softened.

"You," she said dryly, "are dangerously optimistic. And

you still look ridiculous."

I flounced my magically red hair. "I prefer 'enthusiastic.'"

She rolled her eyes.

But she didn't say no.

And that was enough.

The others had reached the end of the staff wing. A door slouched in the shadows, neglected and unimpressive. Grime dulled the plaque until we wiped it clean:

Laundry and Linen Distribution — Staff Only

I straightened my jacket. Adopted my best narrator's tone.

"This is it. The final barrier. The impenetrable threshold. A seal forged by — "

"It's locked," Seren said.

Mero rattled the handle. Locked, indeed.

Of course it was.

"We have fought, stolen, lied, and trespassed our way through half the Archive," Seren said. "And now we are defeated. By a door."

We stared at it.

The final boss.

A door.

"Maybe," I offered, "we knock it down."

Brin cracked his knuckles, intrigued.

"No," Seren hissed. "Every Oathbound in a mile would come running."

I patted my coat.

"Okay. If smashing is out—there's always... this."

I drew *The Everything, Including Nothing* like a gambler revealing a forbidden ace.

It practically vibrated.

Seren narrowed her eyes. "What is *that*?"

"Magic book," I said cheerfully.

"Magic?" she repeated.

"Experimental. Some side effects. Mild to moderate reality warping."

Mero, who up until this point had been content to supervise our idiocy with the detachment of a man watching a parade of ducks crash into walls, sprang into action.

"Nope," he said. "Absolutely not."

He dropped to one knee. Lockpicks flicked from his sleeve.

Click.

"Not locked," he announced.

Seren closed her eyes and muttered something about divine patience.

Beyond the door, a spiral staircase wound downward into blackness. It wasn't the polite darkness of night or a closed room. It was a heavy dark. The kind of dark that felt like it might reach up and pull you down by the ankles if you lingered too long. The stairs curved sharply out of sight, stone slick with ancient dust. The air that drifted up was cold and stale, carrying with it the dry whisper of secrets no one had spoken aloud in centuries.

We stood at the threshold.

I clutched the book tighter.

Mero rolled his shoulders.

Brin readied himself.

Seren adjusted her robes.

"Well," I said. "Downward is the only way."

And we stepped through.

In Triplicate, With Blood

The stairwell narrowed. The air grew colder, heavier, tasting of old dust and older ink. Our boots scraped against worn stone steps as we spiraled downward, the darkness pressing closer with every turn. Finally, the stairs spilled us into a chamber — a low, circular room lined floor-to-ceiling with filing cabinets, broken quills, and reams upon reams of parchment. There were no windows. No doors leading onward. Just the faint, maddening rustle of paper shifting in unseen currents. And sitting at the center, behind a desk precariously buried in scrolls, was a man — or at least something shaped like one.

He wore threadbare robes stitched with official seals, his face pale and smiling with the placid delight of a man surrounded entirely by his favourite paperwork. He folded his hands as we approached, beaming like a host welcoming very slow guests to a very boring party.

"Welcome, travellers!" he chirped. "I am Adjudicator Feldrix, Assistant Coordinator of Transit Permissions and Sub-Level Access Review."

None of us moved.

"You are expected," he said, as if we'd been invited to afternoon tea.

"Before proceeding, you must complete the standard documentation for traversal into restricted zones."

He gestured to four enormous stacks of forms that had not

been there a moment ago. Each pile towered higher than Brin. Each was topped with a battered quill and an inkwell that smelled faintly of despair.

"You will each begin with Form 117-B," Feldrix explained cheerfully.

"The Notice of Intent to Commence Movement Through Restricted Access Points."

He beamed.

"Followed by Form 117-C, the Addendum of Intent Clarification, Form 117-C2, the Sub-Addendum of Modified Clarification, and Form 117-D, the Reaffirmation of Non-Malicious Motivation."

Mero stared at the nearest pile.

Brin flexed his fingers, possibly evaluating how many forms he could tear in half at once.

I cleared my throat. "And once we've filled those out?"

"Oh," said Feldrix, eyes twinkling.

"Then we shall proceed to the necessary Supplemental Attachments!"

He waved a hand. Another stack of forms materialized, nearly toppling a cabinet.

"Begin!" he said brightly.

We sat. We wrote. We scribbled until our fingers cramped, until ink stained our sleeves and sweat beaded on our foreheads. Form after form after form.

Each question more demented than the last:

"Please describe the intent of your intent to clarify your intent."

"Are you now, or have you ever been, in possession of a

sentiment inconsistent with approved feelings?"

"If yes, explain in no fewer than 700 words."

Every time we completed a form, Feldrix produced two more. Each stamped with some minor discrepancy requiring immediate rectification. Each slightly more infuriating. It didn't matter how fast we wrote. The forms multiplied faster. It was an avalanche. A drowning. A slow, papery death.

"This is impossible," Seren muttered, snapping a quill in frustration.

Mero wiped his forehead with the back of his hand. "They're breeding."

I stared at my most recent form, which seemed to be accusing me of "malicious eyebrow deployment," and felt something inside me give way.

There was no way through. Not like this.

Which meant— I glanced sideways. Mero's eyes met mine. He gave a minute nod and melted away from the desk.

While Feldrix was busy humming happily to himself and producing another wheelbarrow of addendums, Mero sidled around behind the desk.

Quick fingers.

Steady hands.

A flicker of motion—and he palmed something small and metallic off Feldrix's belt.

He tossed it to me under the desk with a flick of the wrist.

I caught it.

A universal seal. An official stamp of bureaucratic

approval.

I grinned. Dipping the seal into the nearest inkpot, I began forging approvals like a man possessed.

Form 117-B? Approved.

Form 117-C? Approved.

Form 999-Z? Whatever that was — approved.

Declaration of Spontaneous Contrition for Unforeseen Misjudgments? Approved thrice over.

In two minutes, we "completed" more paperwork than an entire mid-sized court system processes in a decade.

I stacked the stamped forms neatly.

Cleared my throat.

And presented them to Feldrix with a flourish.

The demon took the stack, blinking. His eyes glazed as he rifled through them — stamp after stamp of glorious, unimpeachable approval. Slowly, reverently, he smiled.

"Excellent," he whispered. He snapped his fingers.

With a grinding noise and a gust of stale, ink-scented air, a door materialized in the far wall — where before there had been only blank stone.

"Proceed," Feldrix said warmly. "And congratulations on your unwavering commitment to procedural excellence."

We didn't wait for a second invitation.

Brin all but dragged me toward the door.

Mero sauntered after, whistling.

Seren grabbed my sleeve and muttered something about punching me if I ever forged her signature again.

The door swung open.

And once more, we descended.

The stairs spat us out into another chamber—this one grander, older, and far more broken. Cracked marble floors stretched out before us, veined with dust. Massive, corroded pillars leaned precariously under the weight of forgotten judgments. At the center stood a great set of weighing scales, big enough to measure a man—or his sins. And beside them, smiling with the weary cheer of a man condemned to run an endless line at a bakery, stood a demon.

Senior Metricator Jaspin.

His robes were faded grey, his scales embroidered with dozens of minor legal insignias, each more pointless than the last.

He bowed to us with bureaucratic grace. "Welcome, travellers!" he said brightly.

"I am Jaspin, Senior Metricator of Weights, Measures, and Moral Rectification.

Congratulations on reaching the second stage of processing."

None of us spoke.

He clapped his hands. "You are expected," he said.

Jaspin gestured toward the scales, which groaned ominously in response.

"Per the Ministry's Provisional Protocol on Civic Integrity," he intoned, "each of you must undergo a formal weighing of guilt and contrition."

He smiled wider. "For each infraction, a corresponding waiting period shall be assigned, during which you must complete corrective purgatorial tasks. Once your cumulative sentences have been fulfilled, you will be permitted to proceed."

He produced a cracked ledger the size of a tombstone and a quill that wept black ink. "Shall we begin?"

We didn't answer.

Which he took as enthusiastic consent.

First, Seren.

He adjusted a monocle over one yellowed eye and read aloud:

"Infraction: Emotional withholding during mandatory vulnerability sessions — two days."

"Infraction: Improper filing of Rebuttal Petitions — one day."

"Infraction: Refusal to participate in institutional morale celebrations — three days."

"Total: six days. Penitential tasks: cataloguing obsolete litigation codes."

Seren ground her teeth audibly.

Next, Mero.

"Infraction: Theft of minor valuables — five days."

"Infraction: Unauthorized sarcasm — two days."

"Infraction: Smirking in the presence of authority — four days."

"Total: eleven days. Penitential tasks: re-alphabetizing the Department of Misplaced Records."

Mero muttered something profoundly unprintable under his breath.

Then, Brin.

"Infraction: Excessive looming — three days."

"Infraction: Incomprehensible grunting — Five days."

"Total: eight days. Penitential tasks: restoring ceremonial bench cushions."

Brin stared at him with a look that could have sundered continents.

Jaspin, oblivious, turned the page.

The Catastrophe of Ian Marr

"And now — " He smiled at me. " — Ian Marr."

He cleared his throat.

"Infraction: Unauthorized charm deployment."

"Infraction: Weaponized storytelling."

"Infraction: Distribution of unlicensed hope."

"Infraction: Malicious wit."

"Infraction: Reckless fraternization with noble bloodlines."

"Infraction: Conspiratorial eyebrow activity."

"Infraction: Disrespectful silence while being judged."

I winced.

He kept going. And going. The list stretched on — sin after minor, absurd sin, each demanding days, tasks, re-education sessions, emotional sincerity essays, mandatory group contrition outings. At this rate, I was racking up decades of purgatory.

Mero edged closer to the wall, looking for exits.

Seren muttered furious calculations under her breath.

Brin's fists tightened at his sides.

Jaspin, cheerful as a funeral clown, flipped to another page.

"And finally —"

Brin's Brilliant Violence

Brin moved. Smooth as an avalanche. I barely saw him cross the space. One moment, Jaspin was happily reciting my list of conversational misdemeanours. The next, he was airborne. Brin grabbed the demon by the scruff and bodily hurled him onto the colossal weighing scales.

There was a tremendous CRACK.

The scales shuddered.

Wobbled.

Collapsed in a glorious spray of fractured metal and splintered judgment.

Parchment rained from the ceiling. The ledger snapped shut with a noise like a bone breaking.

Jaspin lay sprawled atop the wreckage, looking deeply betrayed by physics.

I blinked. "Was that allowed?" I asked.

Brin shrugged. "He was weighing guilt. I weighed him instead."

Mero snorted.

Seren just rubbed her temples.

Jaspin staggered to his feet, brushing dust from his ruined robes. "Per the Subsection of Non-Operational Apparatus and Incidentally Compromised Weighing Rituals," he said, voice dazed but automatic, "this proceeding is now considered void."

A door appeared at the far side of the chamber, shimmering into existence like an apology.

Jaspin bowed, swaying slightly. "You may proceed."

We didn't need to be told twice.

As we hurried toward the exit, I glanced at Brin.

"You know," I said, "you technically owe about eight more days for violence against an official."

He grunted. "I'll pay it."

And somehow, that simple promise—so blunt, so certain—felt heavier than all the bureaucratic nonsense in the world.

Because in the end, real loyalty isn't about avoiding the weight. It's about carrying it anyway.

The stairwell narrowed again, the air turning sharp with the smell of burnt paper and scorched promises. Each step down grew hotter, the stone underfoot warm enough to prickle through our boots. When we finally emerged into the third chamber, it was like stepping into the mouth of a forge.

The room was vast, circular, and choked with acrid smoke. Cracks in the floor wept thin streams of flame. Ash floated in the air like dying snowflakes. And directly ahead: A doorless archway—completely filled with a roaring sheet of fire. The only way forward.

Standing between us and the inferno was a man—or at least, something shaped like one. Compliance Director Revoth.

He wore the fine, crinkled robes of a mid-level administrator promoted just enough to be dangerous.

Slick hair. Sharp teeth. A smile stretched taut over some older, more patient hunger.

He bowed as we approached. "Welcome, honoured travellers," he purred. "You are expected."

Of course we were.

Revoth gestured elegantly toward a marble table at the center of the chamber. Upon it lay a tome so thick it had to be chained down at the corners — The Contract of Passage.

"Per Subterranean Code 7.5-A, Revised Charters of Transit," he said smoothly, "all individuals seeking unauthorized descent must first execute this binding agreement."

He tapped the cover.

"Upon signing, you will be granted safe passage through the flames beyond."

Mero eyed the wall of fire dubiously.

"And if we don't sign?"

Revoth's smile widened. "You may attempt to cross unaided. Survival projections are... suboptimal."

I leaned closer.

Written in elegant, predatory script along the contract's margin was a cheerful clause: "Signatures must be affixed in blood to validate compliance."

Of course they must.

Because normal ink would be far too sensible.

Seren stepped forward, eyes sharp. "This contract," she said carefully. "It contains protections?"

Revoth inclined his head. "Naturally."

"And no obligations beyond transit?"

There was the faintest flicker at the corner of his mouth.

That was all the warning we needed.

Seren drew herself up. Voice clear. Voice sure. She spoke an Oath.

"In the presence of binding terms," she said, her voice threading with a subtle, powerful resonance, "I command: You will act as our legal advocate. You will disclose fully and without omission any clause, sub-clause, or hidden obligation which would materially obstruct our safe passage, or bind our persons, wills, or futures to any external authority."

The air shifted. Revoth stiffened — twitched — but the Oath took.

He bowed low, sweat beading at his temples. "Very well," he said through gritted teeth.

And then the real nightmare began. Revoth started reading.

Buried on page 17, sub-clause 42-A: "Signatories waive the right to future self-determination."

Page 113, footnote 9: "Passage protections void upon incidental expressions of dissatisfaction."

Page 224: "Signatories may be harvested for administrative resources if transit is deemed incomplete."

Page 537: "Fireproofing effective only between the hours of 2 and 4 a.m."

Page 712, appendix G: "Definitions of 'fire' are subject to reinterpretation."

Mero's mouth twisted. "Definitions of fire?"

"Indeed," Revoth said silkily. "In some cases, your flesh could be reclassified as a flammable material requiring mandatory cleansing."

Brin made a noise low in his throat that might have shattered less stubborn demons.

"Right," I said, cracking my knuckles. "New plan."

Under Seren's direction—and much to Revoth's visible agony—we set to work. Crossing out paragraphs. Striking through footnotes. Writing amendments in the margins:

"Signatories retain self-determination."

"Protection valid under all temporal conditions."

"No reclassification of flesh permitted without express consent."

Every change was done in handwriting, initialled in blood at the margins, forcing Revoth to grimace and accept them under the binding terms.

At the end, the Contract of Passage looked less like a legal document and more like a murder confession written by committee.

One by one, we pricked our fingers.

Mero first, fast and muttering: "Feels like marrying a goat." (Knowledge drawn from experience.)

Seren next, grim but calm.

Brin after, not even blinking.

I signed last, drawing a deliberately flamboyant flourish across the bottom line. "Honestly," I said, handing the quill back, "I thought I'd at least get dinner first."

Revoth accepted the signed contract with shaking hands.

He bowed stiffly. "You may proceed," he rasped.

The wall of fire rippled.

Shuddered.

And then—with a roar that sucked all the air from the chamber—the flames parted, splitting down the middle to reveal a narrow stone corridor plunging downward. Darkness yawned beyond. Waiting.

I looked at the others.

Mero tucked his knives closer to his body.

Brin flexed his hands once.

Seren straightened her shoulders.

And me? I grinned. Because the hard part wasn't the fire.

It was still ahead.

Absolute Order, Final Draft (The End, or Something Like It)

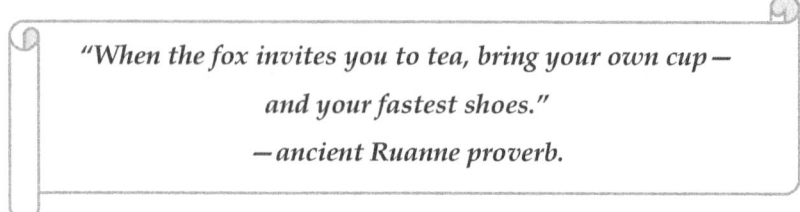

"When the fox invites you to tea, bring your own cup —

and your fastest shoes."

— ancient Ruanne proverb.

We arrived in the bowels of the upside-down temple — The bottom floor. The depths of the depths.

Everything was beige. The kind of beige that hates joy. The beige of waiting rooms for wars you already lost.

The air was dead. No wind, no sound. Just a muted hallway and soft, padded floors that swallowed our footsteps. At the end was an unassuming wooden door.

It was the most terrifying thing I'd ever seen.

I clutched *The Everything, Including Nothing* in my right hand like a sword, though it had yet to save me from anything more than boredom.

Brin looked at me like he wanted to wrap himself around my body and hide me from the world.

Mero's eyes flicked side to side, calculating every possible escape route.

And Seren...

Seren looked like she might scream or hold my hand. I wasn't sure which would be worse.

Stealing my courage, I stepped forward and opened the door.

The room was small. No windows. No flickering torches. No source of light — yet it was perfectly, coldly lit.

Everything was clean. Tidy. Airless.

Bookshelves lined every wall, stacked with scrolls, ledgers, bound tomes and cabinets of written law — alphabetized, cross-referenced, catalogued by district and offence. Two walls were devoted entirely to law codes. One civil. One clerical.

At the centre sat a monolithic stone desk.

Behind it: a man.

Small. Squat. Immaculately groomed.

He wore spectacles and scratched away at a scroll with a fine black quill.

The only sounds were the scratching of that pen... and the panic in my chest.

Without looking up, he spoke.

"You've arrived. Come in."

He said it quietly, but our bodies moved anyway. We were pulled forward like filings to a magnet. We stood in a line before him. The door closed behind us of its own accord.

This was it.

The Deputy.

The Head Clerk.

The Supreme Magus of the Hall.

The dark heart of Nareth's justice machine.

Velen Dharis himself.

Wearing a waistcoat.

Seren was the first to act. She raised her voice, magic sparking at her throat. "Release us!"

The man — no, the thing — smiled.

"My dear," he said, still not looking up, "you can't use my magic against me."

Seren's mouth slammed shut. She stumbled, her face wide with panic. She tried to scream but no sound came. Her silence rang like a bell.

Brin roared and lunged forward. The man raised a finger.

"Sit."

Brin collapsed to the ground, his strength ripped from him. He lay still, eyes wide, body unresponsive.

Mero moved next. A dagger flashed into his hand from somewhere. He raised it —

"Drop it," Velen said, glancing at him. "Or I'll make you use it on yourself."

The dagger clattered to the floor. Mero froze, hand trembling midair.

They were all subdued.

And I — I had no strength, no oaths, no weapons.

Just a book.

The Everything, Including Nothing

I flipped it open, desperate. Pages fluttered. Words appeared.

"Flowers!"

Velen's desk exploded in colour. Tulips. Poppies. Peonies. An avalanche of petals.

He didn't react.

Next page:

"Now is the time for dancing without inhibition!"

My body began to jiggle. My hips moved entirely without consent. Velen remained still.

I flipped again.

"The music of the spheres!"

A voice poured from my mouth — not mine, a woman's — pure and powerful, singing the birth of the stars. It shook the shelves. Made the scrolls tremble.

Velen sighed.

I turned one final page.

"It is never too late to come home."

He raised a hand.

"Shh," he said.

And I stopped.

Not because of oath-magic.

Because I was out of tricks.

He rose, stepped around the desk, and gently took *The Everything, Including Nothing* from my hands.

"Oh, Mother," he whispered to the book, stroking its spine. "It is far too late."

Then to me, he said, "You've done me a great service, little man. This relic was misplaced. Mis-filed. But you found it."

"What... is it?"

"Chaos," he said. "Useless. Dangerous. Beautiful. Like you."

He turned to Seren.

"Your friends are mine," he continued. "They swore themselves to me. I remember their voices."

He touched her chin. "Seren. A prodigy. Swore never to use her magic without control. After she broke her sister. Bound herself to me for life. A perfect servant."

She flinched.

"Brin," he said, gesturing to the man curled on the floor. "Swore, as a boy, to protect you, Aen Marr. Life-bound. He belongs to me."

I felt it then. His power. The cold heart of the bureaucracy. Power radiated off him like a halo of sad paperclips.

Velen smiled. "And Mero... oh, my favourite. Swore to kill his father. A proper oath of blood. I look forward to helping him do it."

He turned back to me.

"But you. You're a puzzle. You've made no oaths. No bindings." He studied me. "So. No claim."

My brow furrow. Without thinking, I argued. "No. I did swear an oath. That's how I ended up on a penitence tour."

He shook his head. "That was not you. Think back. Who affixed your oath to you?"

Then I remembered. The white eyes of Seren and the other Magi. It wasn't me. It was never me.

He nodded again, seeing the realization dawning on me. "Now you see. You can't swear oaths. Because...you are all lies."

His eyes flickered.

"Mother always had surprises," he muttered. "She must have seeded you from somewhere."

Then he fixed his eyes upon me. "So. What will I do with you? You don't belong."

I didn't like the sound of that. But how could I defeat him? I had nothing.

He walked back to the desk and placed *The Everything, Including Nothing* in a glass jar. Its pages began to wilt.

Upon his desk, half buried under the chaotic explosion of flowers, was a new law in the process of being drafted. *The Provisional Order for the Preservation of National Integrity*, it read. I couldn't see it all, but what I saw caused my heart to drop. *"...shall henceforth apply to all itinerant and undocumented populations of non-native lineage residing within the sovereign boundaries of Talh'Vareth. In accordance with national priorities of cultural cohesion ... corrective measures may include ...*

... incarceration ...

... redistribution of minors ...

... revocation of reproductive privileges ...

... permanent relocation ...

And below, stamped in red:

"The integrity of a nation is the purity of its people."

I needed to keep him talking. My mind was racing, frantically searching for something, anything, that I might do.

"What are you talking about?" I asked.

"This world needs rules," he said. "I saved it. I gave it structure. Order. Safety."

"You're telling me that you are the reason for all of this bureaucratic lunacy?" I asked. "It's your doing? You made it?"

"You're welcome."

I shook my head.

"But...Why?"

"Because I swore an oath to save the world," he said, calmly, matter-of-factly. "To save it from mother's madness."

There it was.

Seren's oath magic could not work on him, but *his own* oaths bound him.

Brilliance, that mischievous imp lurking within my brain, suddenly began hopping up and down with excitement. I took a breath, hoping against hope that my mad scheme would work.

"You're wrong," I began.

He polished his spectacles.

I continued in a rush. "You gave it so many laws it chokes itself. Every rule you write breeds more contradictions. More loopholes."

"Then, I will create infinite rules to control it."

"That's not creating order. That's fueling chaos."

He narrowed his eyes.

"Here's the truth," I pressed. "The only way to truly create pure order is to replace all the laws. To just have one. The only one you need."

For a moment, he appeared to consider it. Then he waved his hand, dismissively. "Impractical. There's far too many of you now. Maybe once..."

"Ah! But, but there is a way to control chaos," I insisted. "What if—," I whispered, "you wrote that one universal law into *The Everything, Including Nothing*?"

He stopped.

"What?"

"The final law," I said. "The one that creates absolute order. Pressed into the book. Signed into law." I pointed at *The Everything, Including Nothing.* "You said she's chaos incarnate. Well then—control her. Bind her. Write the only rule you'll ever need."

He paused.

Frowned.

His fingers twitched.

Not much. Just enough. Like a man hearing a melody he thought he'd buried. A rule to rule all rules—so neat, so clean, so perfect. I saw it in his eyes: the ache of a clerk who'd spent a lifetime taming disorder with a thousand scrolls, now glimpsing the promise of a single perfect cage.

"What rule?" he asked, voice thin.

I smiled. "Thou shalt not do anything without my approval."

He blinked.

Twitched.

Froze.

"You can't resist it, can you?" I said, smiling like a mad sprite. "You swore an oath to control *everything.* I've given you the way. You *have* to do it."

His hand moved without his consent.

The jar lifted.

The book opened.

He wrote: *Thou shalt not do anything without my approval.*

And below it, in ink that shimmered with finality:

Velen Dharis.

There was a flash.

A scream.

And then he was gone.

So was the book.

Brin sat up.

Mero dropped the dagger.

Seren gasped as her voice returned.

We were alone.

Free.

The climb out was harder than the descent.

No more magic. No more flowers. No more music of the spheres. Just torchless stone and stairs without end, carved by a civilization that mistook labyrinths for wisdom.

We didn't speak.

What was there to say?

The bureaucratic hear of the machine was gone. But the building was not. The shelves were still lined. The scrolls still filed. The lights still burned. And somewhere — higher up — a clerk was dipping a quill, ready to finish whatever draft had been left behind.

Because the order hadn't been cancelled.

Only the man who thought he controlled it.

By the time we reached the surface, the air was dry again.

The city of Nareth—indifferent, gleaming—spread out like nothing had changed. A temple bell rang. Pigeons scattered. A guard yawned near a bureaucratic checkpoint.

Behind us, in the depths, the *Provisional Order for the Preservation of National Integrity* still sat on a desk.

Unsigned.

Because someone would sign it.

Someone always does.

Maybe not today.

Maybe not by hand.

But the gears were turning. The forms were filed. The framework built.

One man didn't make the machine.

And one man couldn't stop it.

Because there are stories where you slay the beast and light returns to the land.

This wasn't one of them.

This is a story where you kill the tyrant and realize the tyranny was never a person. It was a form. In triplicate. Stamped yesterday. Filed tomorrow.

Waiting for your blood on the dotted line.

Epilogue: Chaos Will Always Find a Way

> *"Leave no footprints if you don't want the story to follow you."*
>
> *— ancient Ruanne proverb.*

The camp was quieter than usual when we stumbled back — smoke-streaked, dust-covered, trailed by the smell of our own failure. The wagons huddled close beneath the dying sun, like conspirators hiding from the sky. Even the goats, who normally treated silence as a personal offence, had gone still. One was gnawing on a boot it almost certainly didn't own.

Nema stood at the firepit, arms folded. No words. Just a folded parchment, stamped with the holy radiance of the Office of Settlement Affairs.

I broke the seal with fingers still tacky with dried blood.

It was brief. It was cruel. It was official.

> *Notice of Transit Enforcement Pursuant to the Revised Acts of Societal Realignment, Subsection 3-B: All Ruanne settlements within the Greater Nareth District are to vacate within three days of notice issuance. Non-compliance will result in summary displacement. No appeal will be considered.*

Signed, naturally, by someone who hadn't bothered to learn our names.

By dusk, the fires were snapping in their pits and the shadows stretched long as guilt. The camp was alive with motion — ropes coiled, wheels checked, possessions packed with angry precision. Voices murmured and snapped. Someone cried and pretended it was smoke. Children asked questions no one answered.

But for a moment, we were apart from it.

Just the four of us, in the hush between a sentence and its consequence.

I sat on the step of Nema's wagon. Seren was beside me — not touching, but close enough to burn. Mero lounged nearby, chewing a grass stem like it owed him something. Brin stood at a small distance, arms loose at his sides, gaze lost somewhere far past the wagons.

After a while, Brin said, "You're going to get yourself killed one day."

I smiled. "I don't mean to."

He grunted.

Then, quietly: "I swore to protect you."

I looked down. "I know."

"I'm sorry."

Brin's head turned slowly. His voice was low, nearly gentle.

"Don't be. You don't have to deserve it."

I stared at him. This immovable, unshakeable man who'd followed me through fires and fools and a dozen bad decisions disguised as plans.

And — for once — I didn't argue. I just nodded.

"Maybe I'll try not to make it so hard."

Another grunt. Which, in Brin's language, meant: *Don't lie to me, but thanks for trying.*

Fair.

"I'm going," Seren said.

She wasn't looking at me. Her eyes were on the dark

horizon, like the night might answer back.

"I'm going back to them. My family."

I swallowed, dry.

"I meant what I said," I murmured. "About helping you. About—"

She raised a hand. Slim, calloused, trembling slightly. "You did help," she said.

Then she turned to me. Met my eyes.

And there it was—raw, unguarded, terrifying.

Trust.

"You showed me," she said softly, "that surviving doesn't mean you're broken. It means you're still moving."

I opened my mouth—something clever was supposed to come out. Something beautiful.

Instead, she leaned forward. Pressed her forehead to mine.

Just a moment. Just breath.

When she pulled away, I sat there blinking, heart thundering like a war drum no one else could hear.

Mero was watching with a look that hovered between amusement and actual, sincere approval. Which made me deeply suspicious.

"You still planning to kill him?" I asked.

His grin faltered. Barely. "You mean my esteemed progenitor?"

"Yeah."

He shrugged one shoulder. "Maybe."

Silence stretched. Not heavy. Just there.

"I wouldn't blame you," I said. "But I'd miss you."

That cracked something. Just a little. His face softened, then sealed again.

"We'll see," he said. "World's a big place. Lots of bad fathers. Might get distracted."

I smiled.

So did he.

Sort of.

By the time the fires burned low and the children curled into wagons, laps, and corners like forgotten blessings, the camp was ready.

Harnesses were checked. Wheels greased. Songs hummed low under breath — the old kind. The kind you only sing when leaving something you love too much to stay near.

Nema gave the call. A single sharp whistle.

And the Family — the real Family, stitched together with blood, bargains, and half-told stories — began to move.

We rolled out under the stars, a crooked parade of colour and defiance threading into the dust. No destination. No plan. Just forward.

Because here's the thing they never understand — the Ministers, the magistrates, the Oathbound. They think survival is about control. About order. About screws so tight nothing moves unless they say so.

But chaos is older than order. Chaos is life.

And life, however bruised, however battered, does not lie still.

We are chaos. We are the laugh you weren't expecting.

The story you couldn't erase. The song no law remembers how to forbid.

We don't survive because we're careful.

We survive because we are wild.

Because we are stubborn.

Because we tell stories louder than the silence meant to smother us.

Every time they try to end us, we begin again.

So yes — the fires may chase us. The laws may choke us. The world may crumble beneath our heels.

But we'll dance anyway.

We'll sing anyway.

We'll laugh and lie and love and run anyway.

Because in the end — stories are louder than silence.

And chaos will always find a way.

Author's Note

A few confessions, since you made it to the end:

First, my wife loves Gypsys. I love my wife. I also love not being sued. Hence: *Ruanne*. (It's a joke. Sort of.) Many of the terrible things that happen to the Ruanne in this book are fiction — but, truthfully, far worse has been done in history to the Roma people.

Second, I was raised in the church. Which means that some of the things I mock about the church are absolutely true. Others are lightly exaggerated. (Also true.) You can decide which is which, though I suspect the line is thinner than anyone would like.

At the heart of this story, though, isn't paperwork, divine audits, or even outlawed miracles. It's storytelling. We lie constantly. Not all lies are bad. Some protect. Some comfort. Some create the very world we live in. This book is, if anything, a long and elaborate lie told in hope that you'll carry a fragment of it away.

Finally, one of my favorite bits: the divine inversion at the core — a goddess who is chaos, and a satanic son who is order. From traditional thinking, and most mythology, that's the wrong way round. Upside down. Gloriously backwards. And it still delights me.

Thank you for reading *The Everything, Including Nothing*. It's messy, ridiculous, and dear to me.

If you'd like to discover more of my writing, please stop by www.harwoodjones.com. I'd love to hear from you.

—T.H.J.

www.ingramcontent.com/pod-product-compliance
Lightning Source LLC
Chambersburg PA
CBHW070758120726
47910CB00001B/220